# INALIENABLE

# ALSO BY THE AUTHOR

## THE STARSTRUCK SAGA

*Starstruck*

*Alienation*

*Traveler*

*Celestial*

*Starbound*

*Earthstuck*

*Inalienable*

## AIX MARKS THE SPOT

## NOVELLAS AND SHORT STORIES

*Miss Planet Earth  (Pew! Pew! - The Quest for More Pew!)*

*The Horrible Habits of Humans  (Pew! Pew! - Bite My Shiny Metal Pew!)*

*Miss Planet Earth and the Amulet of Beb Sha Na*

*Head over Heels (Starstruck Halloween Short)*

*Lasers and Tiaras (Starstruck Short)*

*Study Night at the Museum (Unbound: Stories of Transformation, Love, And Monsters)*

BOOK SEVEN OF THE STARSTRUCK SAGA

# INALIENABLE

## S.E. ANDERSON

BOLIDE

# INALIENABLE

© S.E. Anderson 2021

Cover design by Sarah Anderson

Editorial: Michelle Dunbar, Cayleigh Stickler, Anna Johnstone

First published in 2021 by Bolide Publishing Limited

Bolidepublishing.com

ISBN: 978-1-912996-29-2

FOR MOM AND DAD
NO PUN OR PUNCHLINE
I JUST REALLY LOVE YOU

# ONE

## IF I KNEW WE'D NEED A PRISON BREAK I'D HAVE STARTED A PINTEREST BOARD OF TATTOO ARTISTS I LIKE

**LET ME START BY SAYING I DIDN'T ACTUALLY KILL** anyone.

Not on purpose, anyway.

And not anyone *human*. I should probably specify I have never killed an actual human. I'm not even sure if a person half-controlled by nanobots and bits of wiring could be considered human, but even so, that wasn't murder. The homicide I was currently being held for was for a serial killer in the guise of an FBI agent, but Earth apparently frowns upon alien vigilante justice if said alien looks good in a suit.

Marcy didn't need to know the exact details anyway. Dressed in her heavy winter coat and with big, black circles under her eyes like she hadn't slept in days, she stood on the other side of the metal bars like a burned-out babysitter who'd brought her charge to the zoo and forgot about them—much too tired for inconsequential details about the moral gray areas of taking a life. She slid the coat off her shoulders, revealing a stunning, slinky silk dress better suited for a gala than a jail.

"They can't hold you here for long," she insisted. "They need evidence! And where on earth are they going to get proof that? I mean ... I mean ..."

I gave her a weak smile. "Exactly. We'll be out of here before you know it. Don't worry, okay?"

"My best friend is arrested for *murder*, and you tell me not to worry about it?"

"Marce, I mean it. Don't worry about it."

"Dany has sworn to find you the best damn lawyer that money can buy." She caught my gaze and held it tight. "You'll be out of here before you know it."

She didn't know how literal she was. It would have been so easy to close my eyes, tap my heels, and think of home. I could be back there in the blink of an eye. The only things truly holding me here were the security cameras and the mountain of paperwork that I would be leaving behind.

"I didn't mean to cut your honeymoon short," I said. "I'm sure you and Dany were having an absolutely lovely time in Tibet. You didn't need to come back for me."

"Reality check: You are in *jail*. For *murdering* an FBI agent. In *FLORIDA*. I'm pretty sure that warrants me checking in with you."

Ah, the late Dustin Cross. FBI agent and undercover off-worlder using and abusing his position to snack on women's cerebrospinal fluid. While we'd stopped him and covered our tracks in D.C., the local cops had found his remains—and, apparently, mountains of our DNA, gross—just a few miles from my parent's home. Can you say frame job? Because I want to scream it from the rooftops. They did such a good framing I would hang it on my wall.

But instead of screaming, I said, "It's fine, seriously," and smiled. This was beginning to be a bad habit of mine. "I have friends in the FBI. They'll be able to prove I had nothing to do with killing this man."

"You have—" She took a deep breath, hands on her hips like she were a teapot about to boil over. "Sally, how the hell do you have friends in the FBI?"

"I met her like a year ago."

"And you never told me?"

"Well, it isn't something to mass text about, you know! I barely knew her before the incident in January."

"You mean the hoax?" She pinched the bridge of her nose. "Sally, did you have something to do with the alien hoax?"

"It wasn't a hoax," said Blayde, pulling herself up from the bench as if rising from the dead.

Marcy shrieked, a sound so shrill I almost jumped out of my skin. "Who the hell are you?"

I waved my arm at the alien in the corner. "Marcy, meet Blayde."

"Blade?"

"*Blayde.*"

"Sorry, it just sounds like you're saying 'blade' with a really heavy Australian accent."

Blayde raised a hand as if to wave but dropped it just as quickly. She wasn't too thrilled about the accommodations either, but she was more used to it than I was. At the very least, this cell was much nicer than the one the Atlans had provided us with.

Stars, I needed to stop getting arrested.

"Who on earth is she?" Marcy's voice dropped to a whisper. "She's giving off hella weird vibes."

"My sister has that effect on people," said Zander, reaching through the bars of his own cell. "Does anyone have any food? I'm feeling peckish."

"Zander?" she squawked. "You're … what the hell? You're alive?"

Marcy's eyes grew so fast and wide I thought they might fly out of her skull. Mine would, too, if my very much once-dead friend was standing only a meter away from me. Which had truly happened, and I had later killed him. But it wasn't going to stick, so I didn't count it in my running tally of murders. He was probably still out there somewhere—crap. He couldn't be involved with this arrest, could he?

"Marcy, that's not *Xander*," I said, shaking Nimien out of my thoughts and instead jumping wholeheartedly on the terrible backstory bandwagon. "That's *Zander*. His identical twin brother."

"Hell if he is. I'd recognize him anywhere!" She stomped over to his cell, forcing him back in surprise. "Holy shit, you faked your own death?"

"Sorry." He shook his head, feigning ignorance. "I'm the other Zander. With a Z, not an X. That was my twin."

"Xander and Zander?" She frowned. "This isn't a soap opera!"

"Well, no." Zander came up close to the bars now, putting on a brilliant display of meekness. "His full name was Lysander. Mine actually is Zander. My parents had wanted to call me Alexander, but their friends stole the name and gave it to their child. So, they ended up with Lysander and Zander. Technically, his nickname was Sander, but he hated that and changed it to Xander."

"I think you have your own backstory backwards," muttered Blayde, low enough I'm not even sure I heard her.

"Ho, come on!" Marcy shook her head. "You can't *not* be Xander–Zander–whatever! Also, why would Alexander have the Z name? This is the dumbest crap I've ever heard!"

She turned back to face me. I was dying for a drink at this point. These kinds of conversations were much better held *in* a bar than behind them.

"So," she said, smacking her lips, "I leave you alone for one month—One. *Month*—and you get involved with the FBI and the so-called 'twin' of your dead roommate along with his weird sister, wrapped up in an alien hoax, and get arrested for murder. Am I missing anything?"

"Sally's also dating said twin," said Blayde. I would have strangled her if it served a purpose.

"What?" Marcy rubbed her temples. "This can't be happening. None of this makes any sense. It's like a telenovela written by a drunkard."

When she turned back to look at me, I couldn't read her face, so I plastered on a grin and hoped it would stick.

It did not. Massive fail. A good 3/10. And those points were only for effort.

"So, how was the honeymoon?" I asked through my sheepish smile.

The unreadable face remained illegible. "Ironically, I'm sure you could have Dany arrested for what we were up to. Out of this world, I tell you. But we are in a jail, so I'm going to shut up now."

Blayde let out a bark of a laugh. "Sally, you never told me you Terrans actually had a sense of humor. I would have stuck around longer."

"Again, who is she?" asked Marcy. "Am I supposed to like her?"

"She's my sister," said Zander. "The only family I have. So, you don't have to like her, but you do at least need to put up with her. You put up with Dany, so I know it's possible. Hell, you even married her!"

"There. I knew it. You're Zander! And shut up about these Xs and Zs. There's only one you, and I'd recognize him anywhere."

"Oh, Veesh!" Blayde stormed noisily over to the bars of our cell. "I can't believe you, Zander. You can shatter entire empires just by showing up, you can keep deep covers for months at a time, but one stray word from a friend and you ruin everything! This, all this, is why we don't fraternize. You're an idiot!"

"Hey, you're the one who ruined my cover this time! I was doing fine on my own!"

"No, you weren't. Marcy, was he convincing you with his dashing charms?"

"I knew it!" Marcy said, as if she had just uncovered an ancient secret. "But how did you survive?"

"The truth is"—pause for dramatic sigh—"I'm a ghost! OOooOOooh …"

Marce turned back to me again. "Did his near-death experience snap something in his brain?"

He let out a heavy sigh. "Underneath the plant, there was an abandoned WWII bunker where I found food and shelter as I tried to climb my way back to the surface."

"That's all fine." She waved him off. "I mean, what the hell? At the very least, you could have told me you're alive!"

"You were on your honeymoon!"

"And you survived a semi-nuclear explosion! You could have just left me a voicemail! I know no one listens to those these days but *come on!* I wanted you to be the best man at our wedding. You know, if you had actually been alive for it! Instead, Dany went with Martin from the office, who, believe it or not, hooked up with my sister in the reception hall's bathroom."

# INALIENABLE

"What?" Zander cringed. "Why are you telling me this?"

"I would have rather you two had danced the horizontal cha-cha. At least then I wouldn't have to explain to Mom and Dad why my youngest sibling ran off to Costa Rica with three men and intended to start a llama farm."

"A llama farm?"

"She named her first one Steve," she said. "The llama. Not her polyamorous lover. She just wants our blessing. Speaking of blessings, congrats on getting your not-dead-ex-roomie into your bed!" She gave me the most passive aggressive clap I ever did see. "So, how was it?"

"Marce, he's standing right behind you."

"It's okay. I'll just put my fingers in my ears and make a few funny noises," Zander said, doing just that.

"Well, I'm not." Blayde smirked, readjusting her seat so as to better see me straight on. "So, is my brother good in bed?"

I wanted to slam my head against the wall. "This can't be happening."

"Zander, you can stop that!" Blayde said as she waved at him. "Nothing huge and revealing going on over here after all."

"You do realize we've been so busy babysitting you that we haven't had much activity in the bedroom department, right?" I said.

"Well, sorry that the implosion of my reality has stopped you from *getting it on*. Next time, I'll wait until you've had time to consummate the relationship before I light everything on fire."

"Good god, what is wrong with you people?" Marcy threw her hands up to the sky in a highly dramatic display of frustration. Which, admittedly, the situation certainly deserved.

"Maybe I can explain with an interpretive dance?" With slick arm movements, Zander indicted jail, court, him pleading in said court, and, finally, solitary confinement.

"What?"

"Sally's nervous because she's never been in jail before, Blayde is fine because she's used to it, and I, I could really go for a sandwich right now. Can you find me a sandwich?"

"I'm not your maid," Marcy replied coolly.

"But you're my friend, and we haven't seen each other in two years. Vending machine down the hall? I'll pay you back when I get out."

"My sister. Costa Rica. Three men. Llama named Steve. So, if you want a sandwich, get it yourself."

"I would, but then the government would want to cut me up. And I personally don't want that at the moment."

"Pardon?"

"The CIA really doesn't like me," he said. "They think the old WWII bunker food was so old it gave me superpowers."

"What's that got to do with anything?"

"Just making conversation. Yeah, I've spent the past two years climbing out of a radioactive sinkhole. What about you? It feels like forever since we last talked."

"Yeah, it really does." Marcy's face finally broke into a smile. "It's good to see you, Zander-with-a-Z. You haven't changed a bit." She turned to me now. "Sally, Dany will get you a lawyer; I promise you. But it's up to you if you want him to defend … all three of you."

"Thank you," I said. "I'm so sorry your honeymoon ended like this."

"Hey, what are friends for, if not to pull friends out of tight spots? Really, really tight spots. Honestly, it's better than I had expected with all those rumors. Still, I can't wrap my head around the fact you were arrested in *Florida*."

*Me neither, sister. Me neither.*

"So, that's a no-go on the sandwich then?" asked Zander. "Even vending machine food will be better than what I had to put up with in the pit."

"Sally Webber?" The guard who had processed us stepped into view, practically shoving Marcy to the side. "Your lawyer's here to see you."

"Lawyer?" Marcy blanched. "Oh, no, no, no. There's no way Dany's guy could get here so fast."

The guard was already unlatching the door, giving me no time to process his words. He had me in handcuffs before I even stepped out of the cell. So much for innocent until proven guilty.

"Don't trust anything they say," Marcy hissed, catching my arm as he led me out. "Whoever this person is, they are not on your side. You hear me? *Not on your side.*"

The guard pushed me roughly past Marcy, leading me through the bullpen and into one of the interrogation rooms, which he left and locked without a single word. I had seen enough police procedurals on TV to understand that when you were alone in the interrogation room, it was to make you sweat, so to speak. Isolation did strange things to a person's brain, and half the interrogation took place in total and complete silence, just to make you stew. I knew better than to give in to that anxiety, not when I had powerful new tools at my disposal, such as a perfectly healthy brain and no fear of death.

Even still, those weren't enough to quell my rising anxiety at the thought of Marcy alone with Blayde and Zander. Who knew what kind of crap stories they would feed her.

I was mildly surprised when a short, mousy man slipped into the room before any cop stopped by. He seemed oddly familiar, like a mild recurring character actor or just genetics playing favorites. I forced a smile.

"Ms. Webber," he declared rather than asked as he sat in front of me. This felt like an ill omen somehow. Marcy's words rang in my head. *Not on my side, not on my side.* Any louder, and a pop song would have written itself.

"The one and only," I said, cockier than I wanted to be. He glanced up at the corner of the room directly behind me, and I followed his gaze to the camera there. The little red camera light went dark, and the man pulled out the seat to his right.

"What's going on here?" I asked. It made no difference. He ignored me, placing his briefcase on the table and pulling out sheets of diligently typed paper.

I hadn't been prepared for her arrival. The man could have said something, warned me somehow, but I wouldn't have believed him. A split second later, Foollegg was sitting directly in front of me, arms crossed on the table as if she had been here since before I had walked in.

My skin rose in gooseflesh so quickly I half-expected a brain freeze. Foollegg scanned me up and down like a doll in a store window.

"Hello, Agent Felling. Or should I say Sally Webber? I trust you remember me."

How could I not? An alien higher-up working for the Agency, the Alliance's tourist base on the far side of Earth's moon. A woman who watched over crime perpetrated by non-Terran threats on this tiny planet— and done absolutely nothing about it. So long as it wasn't an Alliance perpetrator, it wasn't their problem. They'd even allowed the almost-incineration of the planet at the hands of the Sky People because there weren't any passports to control. Unbelievable.

"So good to see you, Agent Foollegg." I forced a smile I only hoped would be even half as dashing as Marcy's. "Welcome to Earth, I suppose."

It was surreal to see her here in the flesh. Not that it could have truly been her, no. With her long, spindly neck as strong and supple as a giraffe's, there was no way she could have gotten through the front door of the precinct without being flocked by alien truthers. That's if she was able to fit underneath these short ceilings.

"This is only a projection," said the mousy man, who had still failed to introduce himself. "Agent Foollegg wouldn't set a physical foot on this backwater planet. She is only gracing you with her digital presence because she has an offer that would benefit you both."

Foollegg let out a heavy breath. "I could have told her all that. What are you even good for?"

"Getting you through the door."

"True." Foollegg turned to me, her lips thin and taught like a clothesline. "So, what shall I be calling you today?"

I frowned. "Seeing as how it says 'Webber' on my arrest warrant, well …"

"You can't blame me for that, Sally," she said, revealing far too many teeth. "After all, I am not responsible for the downfall of Agent Cross."

"Exactly," I growled, failing to imitate her stringent tone. "I did your dirty work. It was over. You could have left well enough alone."

"It is not my job to clean up all you Terrans' messes."

"Perhaps. But it's not *our* job to clean up the messes of the off-worlders you allow to enjoy free range across the planet."

# INALIENABLE

She glared at me, those large, brown eyes staring so deep I thought they'd find fossils from the Neolithic era. Instead, they brought up only bubbling frustration.

"We never issued him a visa."

"It doesn't mean he wasn't under your department's jurisdiction. Otherwise, why would you be here, now, with me? I'm starting to believe you're more interested in covering up the fallout of alien crimes than stopping them."

Foollegg pursed her lips. "What exactly do you think I'm doing here?"

"Intimidation, I suppose."

"You don't know me at all, Sally," said Foollegg, shaking her bowling ball head. "I'm here to tell you what's going to happen. It's not a threat if it's a fact."

I said nothing, pressing my sweaty palms together to keep them from shaking.

"You have allied yourself with terrorists," she continued. "Two beings the Alliance has been hunting for centuries. They need to be brought to justice."

"So, you had them arrested by a local PD," I said. "Earth can't be that much of a backwater planet if you trust them to hold the mighty siblings."

"Oh no. It's not Earth that holds them here." Foollegg grinned. Her teeth were each sharpened to a point, a piranha's mouth. "It's you. Why do you think they're still in those holding cells?"

"We could leave any time we want. I was just waiting for a friend."

"If you could have left, you would have. No, you're staying right here for one single reason: You have ties to this planet. A lovely little family. You're staying here for them, and the siblings are staying here for you. You don't have to answer; we know it's true."

I couldn't help but squirm in my chair. "Your threats don't scare me."

*I'm a terrible liar.*

"I told you already these aren't threats, only facts." She leaned back in her chair, phasing through it slightly. A haunting reminder I was being threatened by photons. "You wouldn't risk the truth about you coming out to dear Hal and Laurie. Better they think you're a killer than whatever you are now."

My fear was being replaced by something else— anger. Boil the feeling down, distill it to fury. And she was really putting on the heat.

"What do you want, Foollegg? You already have me in a cell. Stop wasting our time and get to the juicy bits."

"I like you better like this"—she flicked a finger at me—"as opposed to the meek being you were pretending to be when we had first met. You're much more interesting now. Feisty. It's a shame you've chosen the losing side."

This was getting tedious. She seemed to like seeing me squirm.

"We've pulled some strings, rushed your case through the system. The evidence against you is unquestionable. You will not have bail. In a few days, your preliminary hearing will review your case and begin the process of your murder trial. There will be a convenient prison riot a few days after your incarceration, at which time you'll be transferred into Agency hands. The justice of the Alliance will prevail."

Mere *days?* My confidence was draining with every passing microsecond.

*Chanel Blayde. Chanel Blayde.*

"Wow," I said, rolling my eyes. "All this to get us off-planet?"

"Consider it a mercy," she said. "Behave, and your family will think you simply … passed away. Put up a fight, and much worse will happen to them than simply discovering the truth about their daughter and the people she aligned herself with. It might be the last thing they ever learn."

I shivered and blamed it on the out-of-control Florida air conditioning. "You can't possibly say *that's* not a threat."

She swiveled her spindly neck like a twisty straw, her equivalent of a shrug. "There's no reason for us not to be friends. You haven't been with the siblings long; you don't know what they're capable of. What they've done. The lives, the planets they've destroyed. Be reasonable. If your mouth stays shut here on Earth and loose on Pyrina, you do not have to suffer the same fate as them."

"What if I say no?"

She stood as if to leave, all part of the show. "I've told you no threats, only facts, Sally Webber. Think it over. You have a few days to work out the details. Who would you rather be? We're the good guys here. Your friend, the real Felling, has been given a similar ultimatum."

"She's a good agent. She had nothing to do with this."

"We've had our eyes on her for years. She was searching for the siblings—and not covering her tracks very well, I might add—but as I said, we're the good guys. She'll be left alone, so long as you convince your friends to cooperate."

My family. My friends. No one was safe, and all because of the choices I made.

"And what about the Lifeprint?"

This halted her in whatever tracks she had started to take, her hand hovering over the bare table as if to adjust an invisible knob. "You want to know about the bot we recovered? Why?"

"Sue me. I became attached. You said it yourself: attachments are my weakness."

"As was its," she replied. "It was a faulty piece of programming. The bot was wiped."

And with that, her image faded from the interrogation room, leaving me to process how royally screwed I undoubtably was.

# TWO

## ZANDER'S KNOWLEDGE OF DAIRY PRODUCTS IS BOTH IMPRESSIVE AND TASTY

**ORANGE IS NOT MY COLOR, AND IF IT'S YOURS,** more power to you. I've only met one person who can pull of an orange jumpsuit, and she's a slightly peeved extraterrestrial who wasn't too thrilled to be put in handcuffs. Her brother was firmly in the washed-out group of jumpsuit wearers, though it might have been the shackles pulling his mood down. I tried to avoid catching my reflection anywhere—not that I should have been caring about how well I was pulling off the embarrassing outfit. I just wasn't a big fan of the handcuffs.

"This is nothing," said Zander, forcing a smile when I had tried to make conversation with him in the corridor outside of the courtroom. "We're lucky to even have a hearing. Can't tell you how many times I was walked into what I had thought was a courtroom, only to find myself in a gladiatorial ring."

"Speak for yourself," said Blayde. "This orange is worse than the punishment itself. Most planets know how to give their prisoners a sense of style. Why am I not sparkling right now? Much easier to see if I try to make a run for it. What if I tried to run, huh?"

I would have pointed out that orange was just as flashy as actual flashing lights and I was rather glad not to be covered in sequins, but my mouth was dry.

"Stay calm, and don't say anything unless I tell you to," said our lawyer, Hargreaves. A friend of a friend of Dany's, he said when he appeared before us just yesterday. Dany had been true to her word and hired someone who seemed incredibly well put together and much too prominent to pro-bono a lost cause. Her connections made no sense to me, but she never came to visit, so I couldn't ask. Probably didn't want to be seen with the likes of me.

"Just say the word," Blayde whispered as the bailiff lead us into through the large wooden doors, "and we're out of here."

"I'm not blowing up my bridges, and I'm certainly not putting my parents in danger."

This wasn't some kind of surreal conviction on a world light-years away. This was my own planet, my home. Anything that happened here would affect my life, my family, forever. One misstep, and Foollegg would have everyone I know and love destroyed. The Alliance had been hunting for the siblings for a very long time; they weren't going to let them go so easily.

They finally had leverage, and they were going to use it.

I knew what Blayde was thinking: *get it over with*. I only had a few years left with my family anyway; just break the cord and get it over with.

But she didn't say anything. Maybe I was just putting words in her mouth. The mere fact she had let this all play out the way it had meant she didn't want them to die prematurely.

Seeing my parents in the back of the courtroom just made everything a thousand times worse. I had told them over our single phone call that I didn't want them to see me like this, that we were going to throw out the mountain of evidence against us and be home before they knew it. But, still, they came. So had Felling: she sat at the front of the courtroom, right behind us. Marcy sat beside her, though Dany was still absent.

Foollegg must have placed them there: a reminder of what I could lose if I slipped up or lost control of my friends.

I had never been on this side of the courtroom. Or in any courtroom, for that matter. It probably would have been much more exciting if I wasn't on trial for murder.

"We'll find out way out," said Zander. "And I did mention I have a plan, right? We'll be fine."

"You've said that about a hundred times."

"Because it's true." He grinned. "Come on, chin up. Let them get a good first impression."

I straightened my posture. "Better?"

"Just don't let them grin you down."

"Grind you down," I corrected.

"No, grin you down. Smile back and make a statement."

I wasn't a huge fan of this. Grinning worked for him, with his dashing smile. If Blayde and I joined him, we'd look like a pack of cruel, murder-loving hyenas. That or a wannabe-edgy indie band.

The first half hour was all given up to procedure and courtroom business, introducing the judge, the case, the evidence, and so on and so forth. It was hard to follow and too boring to bother committing to memory. Hard to think that I could be bored at my own hearing. Maybe it was all part of the process. Part of me wanted to stand up and shout for them to get this over; it was a sham. After all, what was the point of meticulous procedure?

At least I wouldn't have to sit through the actual trial. No, I'd be fake dead by then.

"Let me just say, Mr. Smith"—our lawyer flipped through his notes—"it's going to be hard to sway the judge to your side, what with your criminal record."

"Criminal record? My record's spotless," he said. Of course it would be. He didn't even exist on this planet. Even his fake persona of Lysander Smith had died in the GrishamCorp cover-up. Whatever criminal past the judge and lawyer were going on was as fabricated as his identity.

"Foollegg again," he said through gritted teeth.

"And probably for me too." Blayde leaned back into her chair, all too jovial for the words coming out of her mouth. "We're gonna get cru-ushed."

I shivered in my chair for the third time that morning, hating every minute of this hearing, knowing that every time we came up with a good argument, a new piece of evidence would conveniently arise to knock us back down again. As soon as they started listing off the evidence, it began to pile and pile and pile. The gun with my fingerprints all over it—another falsehood since Felling had been the one to pull the trigger that had killed her partner—and the security agent who swore he saw us breaking into the abandoned mall, who couldn't have been anywhere near us. The bloodied, bullet-ridden holes in the clothing in the trunk of my car.

"Just a big act. This is just a big act. Oh, I hate this," Blayde snarled, not helping our case. So much for grinning them down. "Foollegg's people really know what they're doing. They didn't have to drag us through the dirt to get what they wanted."

I nodded slowly. "I feel like we're on TV. You know, one of those courtroom shows. It's just too absurd to be real."

"Bullet holes," Zander spat, loud enough for the whole room to hear, "in our clothes. Do we look like Swiss cheese to you?"

"Please, Mr. Smith, you've not been invited to speak," said Hargreaves. He looked about as washed-out as the rest of us, and he wasn't even wearing orange. I was more proud of the fact that Zander remembered local dairy products like a pro.

"Well, I should be!" he said. "I declare, um, I want to go on the stand. Can I be a witness for myself?"

"I highly recommend you don't," said Hargreaves, placing a gentle hand on Zander's arm.

"So, it is possible, then?"

"Kid, the fifth amendment exists for a reason. You have the right to remain silent. It's also a privilege, and right now, I'm seriously asking you to use that privilege and sit back down."

"I'd like to go on the stand. Say my piece."

"I'll allow it," said the judge. "If the defendant has something to say, then he should say it."

"Thank you," said Zander. He marched over to the witness stand with his head high. Once up there, he leaned his head as far as it could go into the microphone. "Do I look like Swiss cheese to you?"

"Your Honor." The prosecutor stood. "The defendant is simply trying to waste our time."

"Hold on, let me show you something." Zander stood straight, reaching for the collar of his jumpsuit, which was difficult seeing as how his hands were bound to his feet. Then, in one smooth move, he tugged.

Loud murmurs rose from the crowd. Felling let out the heaviest sigh I had ever heard, as if our case wasn't hopeless enough.

"Oh lord." Hargreaves dropped his head into his hands.

"Stars above." Blayde snorted. "Why does he always have to take off his shirt to prove a point?"

"Not the first time, I take it."

"You should see his quantum geometry lectures."

"He teaches …?"

She didn't have time to answer before the judge banged his gavel.

Cool. I didn't think I was going to get to see that.

"Who gave the defendant tearaway clothing?" judge Simpson roared.

"He doesn't need tearaway with muscles like that," said Felling, loud enough for us to hear. "Damn. I should have brought popcorn."

"That's my friend. Don't be creepy," said Marcy. "Though he looks incredibly fit for someone who had spent the past two years climbing out of a chasm eating military rations."

"He's my friend too," said Felling. "And I need to get myself some of those rations."

"Mr. Smith," said the judge, too perplexed for anger, "I would kindly ask you to keep your clothing on during the course of this trial or I will hold you in contempt of the court."

"But it's just to prove a point, Your Honor," he said as he exposed his bare torso to the crowd of onlookers. "If what you say is true, then where are the bullet holes?"

He spun around, showing his naked skin to the court. Smooth as a baby's bottom, front to back. I wasn't sure if the gasps were from for the bizarreness of the situation or his Hollywood-quality musculature.

"Your Honor, he's making a mockery of this court," said the prosecutor. The bailiff started toward Zander, who closed his jumpsuit hastily.

"Apparently, there are bullets with my blood on them, but, as you saw, I have no injuries," he said. "So, where are they from, then? Is it possible someone got carried away with their frame job?"

The prosecutor stepped forward. With Zander having thrown procedure in the air, it was hard to tell who was meant to be speaking. I guess the prosecutor was supposed to be questioning the witness. "And the bullet with Ms. Webber's blood on it?"

"Well, just ask her. I'm sure you could tell if she was walking around with gaping bullet holes in her. A wound like that left untreated could have her ripped in half in pain right now, not to mention leave her unable to move properly. You would notice by smell alone right away. And that's for a single wound. According to you, there were three at the scene."

"I, however, would prefer to keep my shirt on," I muttered. How had Foollegg gotten a hold of our blood? My samples—the ones I had been unknowingly giving to the FBI since my accident—had been destroyed by Felling, or so I thought. And Zander wasn't exactly known for giving up his blood all that easily.

"So, Mr. Smith" —the prosecutor was back in his groove now—"can you explain where the blood *did* come from?"

"Well, it's a long story, John. I can call you John, right?"

"No." He flushed red. "That's not even my name."

"Fine, then." Zander crossed his hands over the table, putting on a grave expression. "Judge Simpson, members of the jury—"

"There isn't a jury here, Mr. Smith. This is a preliminary hearing."

He didn't seem to care. "I really don't think there is a case, not without any remains being found."

"There *was* a body found," the prosecutor interjected. "DNA tests prove that it is very much the late Agent Cross's. That's the whole reason you are here, Smith."

"Foollegg again?" I asked Blayde.

"Duh," she replied. "Very convenient. So much for the power of fire."

"Well, then, I owe you all the truth. Of what happened that night."

"Objection." The prosecutor stopped him. "I haven't finished asking the questions."

"Excuse me, I'm at a hearing, right? So, what are you meant to be hearing?" Zander snapped. "Well, it all started when the three of us were called by the FBI because of our special knowledge that would help them with a case. I can't give details because it is classified-"

"Your Honor, he's just going to be a waste of our time," the prosecutor scoffed.

"It's my turn to speak, isn't it? I'm up on the witness stand, so I'm witnessing." He waited for silence. "Now, we hadn't been working on the case for long when we realized that that the culprit was, in fact, the late Dustin Cross. When Cross realized that we knew, he kidnapped Sally and held her hostage. We had to kill him because he was a ruthless extraterrestrial who was trying to take advantage of the women on this planet."

The room erupted into low murmurs. I sighed. This was when it was going to get even more bizarre. Felling's sweet and exaggerated "good heavens" were so much better than my dad almost choking himself to death on the news.

"You killed him …?"

"We had to."

"Because he was—"

"An alien, yes. From Talaga. Looked human enough, of course. You can't go walking around Earth looking like a You can't go walking around Earth looking like a giant land crustacean. "

He put his fingers by his lips, an oversized ant looking for a meal.

The prosecutor liked his dry lips. "And what made you think he was … an extraterrestrial?"

"Because he tried to eat Sally's—sorry, I mean Ms. Webber's—spinal cord. He had a huge second jaw that unlatched from his real one. Ugly bugger." He sighed for emphasis. "And I don't think humans can do that, can they? Please tell me because I haven't been on Earth long enough to know."

"You haven't been on Earth for long?" The judge's jaw dropped ever so slowly. "Please elaborate."

"Oh, because I'm an alien too."

"An alien."

"Do you need me to spell it out for you? A–L–I–E–N. From another planet, not another country. I know you Americans, and I find that quite rude. And not that kind of alien in the movie *Alien*, I mean, who wants the disgusting process of me just bursting out of your stomach? Although, I did once see that happen back at a party near Klipta, and Fiona Grintel—you know, that actress—well, she just had to have another grigri mateol, and you know what those things are made of! No one had expected the fruit to be *pregnant*—"

The judge banged his gavel again, bringing silence crashing down on the room. "Do you think this is funny, boy?"

"No, Your Honor."

"Do you think my courtroom is some kind of theater?"

"No, Your Honor."

"But you claim you're an alien?"

"Yes, sir."

"Where from?"

"Now, that's a long and complicated question. You see, immortality has its drawbacks and—"

"This is the last time I'm doing that woman a favor," Hargreaves spat before flying to his feet. "Your Honor, this man has no idea what he's saying!"

But Zander powered through. "Well, I really do like Earth, though."

The judge was entranced. "Please back up to the moment you said that you are *immortal*."

"Again, let me remind you that I am not currently Swiss cheese." He paused as the murmurs in the courtroom rose higher. "And I must also remind you that you yourself told me to keep my shirt on, or I'd remind everyone here. However, your bailiff is free to shoot me if he wants further proof. Oh, come on. I won't feel it. It just tickles a bit."

Our lawyer dropped his head in his hands, rubbing has scalp raw. Blayde glanced at him quickly, her eyes returning to her brother. A massive smile played on her lips, drawing the light back into her face.

This. This chaos was her element. I could see her bouncing her leg, itching to move. It was taking all her focus to stay grounded.

I didn't want to look back at my parents and see their reactions. It was bad enough I had seen their faces when I was arrested.

"And your friends?" the prosecutor continued. The poor judge had completely frozen.

"My sister's also an immortal, time-jumping alien, but Sally, well, she might be an immortal now, but she's one hundred percent human. Born and raised here on Earth."

"Capa rules!" Blayde shrieked as she jumped up on the table. So much for restraint. "Down with the Alliance! Long live the revolution!"

"But I know you humans," Zander said kindly. "You won't believe me. You guys haven't even made first contact yet. You probably think I'm crazy. Cuckoo for Coco Puffs or whatever."

"Your Honor, it seems my clients have completely lost the plot." Our lawyer let out a heavy sigh. "In light of their revelations, I would like to request a mental health evaluation to determine their state of mind during the actual murder."

"You Honor," Zander pleaded, "I know this sounds crazy, but all you need to do is kill me, and it'll prove to you I'm from another planet!"

The gavel went down. "I think a mental health evaluation is very much in order. All rise."

And four hours later, I was sitting in a bus heading for the Hill Institute for the Criminally Insane. I had never expected anything less than absolute chaos out of Zander's plans. Once again, I wasn't disappointed.

Not the way I was initially planning on spending my Florida vacation, but it was way better than having a fake prison riot waiting for me at the end of the road. Too bad I wouldn't be able to explain this to my parents for a while. Caught between a rock and outer space.

# THREE

## THIS LITTLE INCIDENT WON'T GO IN THE FAMILY CHRISTMAS CARD THIS YEAR

**"I TOLD YOU I HAD A PLAN!"** ZANDER WAS beaming, victory plastered all over his face. He sprawled across his two bus seats, leaving only his forehead in sight. I was far from as comfortable as he was.

"I never said I didn't believe you," I replied, leaning into the turn. Wherever we were driving, it had a lot of winding roads to get there. Rather unsettling for Florida, land of flat, straight lines. "I just want a heads-up next time before I get my name forever listed as criminally insane."

"But it worked, didn't it?" He settled in further as the bus took yet another sharp turn. "No prison riot waiting for us when we get there. Foollegg has an eye on us, just as she wanted, but she can't retrieve us without giving up her hand. All we had to do was tell the truth."

31

# INALIENABLE

He was right about that. My parents weren't going to lose me today, but they did have to put up with the fact that their only remaining child had just been institutionalized. I owed them quite a few apology bouquets.

"But where do we go from here?" I asked. "We can't stay here forever. The Agency will find a way to get their hands on you sooner than later."

"I admit, it's only a temporary solution," he said. "But the Agency didn't plan for this eventuality. That gives us some time to work out our next steps."

"Worst case scenario?" Blayde blurted from across the row. "We just wait it out."

"And let my parents live out the rest of their lives thinking their daughter is a murderer? No thanks. Not to mention someone will realize soon enough that none of us are aging."

"Relax," she said. "We'll figure out a way out long before then. While waiting, we take in the sights, befriend our doctors, and take a nice, relaxing break. Weren't you the one talking that up?"

"Where do you think we're going? Some kind of resort? We're going to a state hospital. For the criminally insane. In Florida. Drugs and barred windows will be the least of our problems. The other inmates could be actual killers."

"You get to know their type over the millennia," said Zander. "Trust me, it'll be fine."

"Though Foollegg might still attempt some kind of extraction, so stay alert," added Blayde.

"Alert for what?" I asked. "How do you expect me to spot a red flag when everything is red alert right now?"

She didn't answer. The bus veered left and flung us against our seats. I grabbed the chair in front of me to steady myself and stop the handcuffs from digging into the skin. Just because it didn't cause me pain didn't mean I liked it.

"Does this vehicle have *any* suspension?" she yelled to the front of the bus, where both our guards and the driver were chatting as if we weren't even here.

"I'm with Sally on this one," said Zander. "This is going to be a nightmare for you. And with everything that happened at the library—"

"I'll deal with it."

"If the great masters of anger management on Julka couldn't help you, I doubt an underfunded hospital on Earth will be any help."

"I've got you, don't I?" she said, softer than I had seen her since our arrest. "Look, am I happy about the way things played out? Of course not. Would I like to nope off this planet right now? Hell yes. But I'm doing this for Sally because you asked me to."

She stood, stretching, and dropped her handcuffs to the floor where they clattered sharply. The bus took another curve far too fast, but she kept walking toward the guards as if she were on solid ground.

"Oh, come on," she said, hammering on the mesh between them. "It's polite to speak to someone when they talk to you, you know. Just because you're driving me to an asylum doesn't make me any less of a person"

"It's regulation, ma'am." The guard nearest her tried to hide his surprise. "How did you get out of your seat?"

"Meh. You mustn't have locked those cuffs on right, but don't worry. If I were going to bite, they would have given me sedatives. First day?"

I pulled at my restraints. I knew I had the strength to break them—I'd done it, proudly, all by myself when Cross had held me captive—but I would probably make things worse for us if I did it now.

"I don't want to have to go back there, Barker," said the other.

"Well, one of us has to," said Barker. "Look, she's right. It's not like they're dangerous. They just think they're aliens."

"They killed an FBI agent."

"Yeah, but it took three of them to do it." Barker turned his focus on Blayde. "You told them you're an alien?"

"Yeah."

"Is it true?"

"Duh. Why else would I tell them that I'm an alien? I personally don't want to spend my valuable time here on Earth stuck in an asylum."

The unnamed guard let out a snicker. "Oh, yes, of course, you're an alien. Invasion of the body snatchers and all that."

"I'm not going out snatching bodies. Veesh. Seriously, though, you arrive on a new planet, tell them in your excitement, 'Hey, guess what? I'm from another planet!' And just because you look like them and not like a reptilian alien, they think you're crazy."

"That and you killed a man."

"The evidence was … circumstantial."

The guards shifted uncomfortably. Blayde turned and strode back to her seat, just as she said, making a big deal of sticking her hands back in cuffs. Locked up nice and tight.

"Can you believe them? They think I'm crazy."

"Blayde, once you get that label, there's no escaping it," I said. "A psych evaluation can ruin your career. There are some serious issues with mental health care on this planet."

"Hey, Zan! Do *you* think I've lost the plot?"

"You're my sister!"

"How is that an answer?"

"How is that a question?"

"Knock it off back there," Barker said, slamming his hand on the mesh.

Zander glanced out the windows. "Man, the weather's not holding up well. You think it's going to rain?"

"Haven't you heard?" the driver said loudly. "Tropical Storm Anthony is coming through here. They say she'll be just wind when she reaches the Hill, but still."

Some days, you just drive clear into a stereotype. You know your expectations are based on myths and hearsay, and then, bam, you're in front of the real thing and you ask yourself how you could have ever expected anything different.

The Hill Institute gave off "Thriller"-quality first impressions. Maybe it was something about the old, ivy-covered stone exterior that made the place generally unwelcoming to the occasional visitor. Or the tall, worn statues of rearing lions—does it always have to be lions?—guarding the huge wooden door that stood as a barrier to the outside world. It was crisscrossed with intricate iron designs depicting ancient leafless trees; the bare, white walls of the hospital could be felt through the windows.

Or maybe it was the thick, green forest that spread far and wide around the building that just screamed "isolation," and not the good kind. More of the no-one-will-hear-you-scream kind of isolation. Which, trust me, I'd seen up close and personal a few times. You don't get more isolated than being thrown out of an airlock.

The heavy, gray clouds that covered the institute physically weighed on us, preparing the way for the oncoming storm. A damp breeze whipped the bare tops of the trees, yet the air itself was stagnant inside the bus, the humidity unbearable.

"Is this it?" Blayde asked as the bus came to a stop in front of the stone stairs. "I expected creepier. You know, screams that can be heard from miles away, the odd messages in ominous red paint written on the institute walls."

"You watch too many horror films," said not-Barker. "This is a hospital."

"Well, thanks for clearing that up. I've seen all of one movie on this planet, and it was about letting go or something."

Barker continued to ignore her, letting himself into our cage. He went for Blayde first, checking her restraints before freeing her from her seat. Not-Barker had finished whatever he was doing at the front of the bus, standing aside before Blayde could get off.

"Well, hello there!" Blayde's voice was sprinkled with fairy dust as she stepped off the bus. "I'm Blayde. With a Y. So very nice to meet you!"

Not-Barker unlatched me and led me off the bus where two women in white coats were waiting. Blayde was beaming so bright she could have lit an entire city block.

"Pleasure to meet you," one woman said, a deadpan reaction to Blayde's performance. "I'm your doctor, Dr. Smith."

"What a coincidence! We're also named Smith," said Blayde. "What a common and unassuming name!"

The doctor was tall and slender, her jet-black hair was supernaturally straight, reaching down below her shoulders. Her beak-like nose was sharp, contrasting with her small brown eyes and her smart, pursed lips. All in all, she gave off the proud air of a bird of prey, roosting on a branch and letting us live another day. She held a clipboard clutched against her chest, her free hand resting upon the plastic, poised to write, but instead twiddling the pen between her index finger and thumb.

"Feel free just to call me doctor"—she forced a smile—"to avoid confusion."

She turned on her heels, leading us through the castle-like doors to the safety of the institute just as the first drops of rain began to fall. Barker and his colleague flanked us, and I couldn't help but wonder who here could be in the Agency's pocket. How would they try to dispose of us, now that a prison riot was out of the question?

The doors slammed shut behind us with a thunderous crash.

"Welcome to the Hill Institute." The doctor had to raise her voice to compensate for the echo of the room. A huge spiral staircase wrapped around the white-washed hall; the only spot of color was a wooden table with a pot of dried flowers pushed up against the stairs. "We are here to help you, so please do not be frightened."

We followed her to a gated-off area attended by a very bored-looking man in staff uniform who buzzed us through without looking up from his crossword puzzle.

"The upstairs floor is off-limits to patients. We're going through administration right now," she explained, as we stopped in a small locked room. "We are going to have to ask you to get changed now. We have a strict dress code in the institute, and while you stay here, you'll need to wear the clothes we provide you."

A nurse arrived with stacks of clothes in different sizes, handing them out to us each individually. We were offered rooms to change in, leaving our jailhouse jumpsuits for what seemed to be a cross between a hospital gown and pajamas. The basic white top and pants were loose-fitting and made out of an uncomfortable, cheap synthetic material that was irritably itchy in the worst of places. I wasn't sure which outfit was worse.

"Now, come this way." A nurse took over, a cheerful smile on her face, as if she were taking kindergarteners on a stroll through the garden. "This is the rec room. You will be free to spend your time here between meetings and curfew. We do have activities planned for each day, so make sure to consult the schedule pinned to that corkboard right over there. Your rooms are down that way. Men have the left wing; women, the right. Any questions so far?"

Blayde's hand shot into the air. "Yeah. Where is everyone?"

"They're at dinner. We eat meals at 8 a.m., 12 p.m., and 6 p.m. You must be in your rooms by 8. Lights out by 9. Got that?"

We nodded. I raised my hand childishly. "And … sessions?"

"Also on the schedule. You meet with the doctors when they have a session scheduled for you, or they may just come and talk to you in the rec room. Now then"—her white teeth shone like polished pearls as she flashed us a sickly-sweet smile of encouragement—"to dinner. And don't worry if you get lost. The staff are very friendly, as they are here to help in your assessment and recovery."

Without another word from her, we were ushered into a massive cafeteria with over a hundred people eating off plastic trays. It would have brought me back to my high school days, if it wasn't for the uniforms.

The sight chilled me. Even wearing the uncomfortable clothes, such as they were, it looked exactly like the library at the heart of the universe, the prison trap Nimien had prepared for us.

And this was supposed to be *good* for my mental health.

"Everyone, listen up!" the white coat who accompanied us called. "Please give a warm welcome to Zander, Blayde, and Sally. I expect each and every one of you to do your part in helping them feel included and safe here. Understood?"

I glanced over at Zander, who, surprisingly, looked rather cheerful, much like his sister. Both waved kindly at the people eating their dinners, like they were the new kids in school.

We lined up to get our food: some overly vibrant mac and cheese, green lettuce, mystery meat, Jell-O, and a glass of water. It was as if Nimien had tried to design my high school but ran out of funding.

Maybe he was involved in this too. I shuddered. I thought all the strings of his time loop had been accounted for. Had he messed around with my future as well as my past?

We were ushered to the few empty seats at the end of a table where most of the people had almost finished with their meals. We tucked right into our food, not having had anything to eat since breakfast. Hospital food still beat jail food.

"Sally, please inform me," said Blayde between chews. "Is this beef or pork? I don't know your world well enough. At first, I was pretty sure it was pork, but now … now, I just think it's really salty beef."

"I like to whisper too!" My neighbor leaned in close. "Whispering is fun!"

I blinked into my food. How had I forgotten the biggest aspect of being locked up was the other people? I had spent so much time trying to think my way out of here that I hadn't planned what I would actually do when I got here.

"What are you three in for?" she asked mysteriously. She brushed her Rapunzel-length black hair behind her ear, grinning.

"That's not polite," her neighbor muttered, eyes on his plate. The young girl kept watching us, expectantly.

"Fine, I'll go first!" She grinned. "I robbed a bank."

"Oh, you did, dear?" said Blayde. She pushed her radioactive pasta around with her fork.

# INALIENABLE

"Don't look like a bank robber, do I?" she asked. "I thought not. But Jeffrey said it had to be done for the good of mankind. So, I walked into the closest bank, waving daddy's rifle, took all the money in the vault, and left."

"And she set the place on fire."

"Shut up, Peter," she said to the young man beside her. "They caught me right after, and I ended up here. So, now, it's your turn." She picked up her cup of water, drinking a long gulp while keeping her unblinking eyes riveted on the three of us.

"We killed a man," Blayde said with a shrug. "He was an alien; he deserved it."

"Oh. Why?"

"He killed four women. Not counting Sally here," she replied. "You know, everyday saving-the-Earth kind of deal. You can thank me later."

"Well, welcome to the Hill," she said, getting up and reaching her arm over the table to shake our hands. "I'm Daisy-May Grant. You?"

"Zander, immortal time traveler from another planet." He smiled. "But don't ask me which one."

"I'm Blayde, immortal time traveler, probably from the same planet he's from." His sister shook the hand extended to her with little to no enthusiasm.

"Sally Webber, also immortal time traveler, but from Earth."

"Cool," Daisy-May said with a grin. "Are you crazy or is it them?"

"Excuse me?"

"Are you three insane or do they just think you are?"

"We're as sane as they come," Zander replied with a shake of the head. "Without going into compartmentalized trauma."

"Then I'm not the only one. They say Jeffrey is a figment of my imagination, but how can he be? He still cares about me. He still visits me, you know, even when I'm in this place."

"How nice of him," I said. This was getting uncomfortable.

"He doesn't really visit," said the boy. "He's dead."

"He's not. He'll be here tomorrow," she said. "Peter here is a pyromaniac. He's not like us."

"How come?" I asked.

She leaned in close, as if she were about to reveal a big, important secret. Her words tickled my ear. "Because he actually is sick. And he knows it. But he's doing amazing."

He seemed like he was only in his mid-teens, the look on his face so young and confused that it made it impossible to guess his age, even though I knew for a fact that this institute was only for legal adults.

"So," I started, wetting my now-dry lips, "what's this place like? The people nice?"

"Oh, it's a real drag," Daisy-May said simply. "Sure, the staff is nice, and the doctors are fine. But the food is rather bland and repetitive. There are a few people here who just can't survive without routine. So, every day of the week is assigned a meal, and it's been like that since I got here."

"How long you been here?"

"About three years, I think." She shrugged. "Give or take. Anyway, it's a bit boring at times. And I do miss Instagram."

"So, I take it you use … Imperial units here, then?" asked Blayde.

"And the movies weren't kidding about the screams," she said, ignoring her. "You get used to them, but it's hard at first to get used to sleeping through the night when people around you have nightmares. Anyway, free period until 8. Bring your trays. Come on!"

I floated through the cafeteria, dropping off my tray with an employee who checked that I had returned all my silverware, the little of it I was given. Then through the rec room, where Daisy-May flung herself at a table, ushering us to join her.

"Is this all you get to do?" Blayde asked. "Draw with crayons?"

"Don't worry, it grows on you. They even have a small library, but you have to ask your doctor first before you check out a book. And there are some games too. Cartoons are on sometimes. And we have movie nights."

"Cool," Zander said, still keeping his grin on. It was hard at this point to distinguish if it was real or fake. "Crayons. Haven't used a crayon in years. So, we just hang out here for another hour?"

"Seems that way." I bit my lip. "This is going to be—"

"Fantastic!" Zander interrupted. "No obligations, no Alliance, and we just get to draw and hang out with colorful characters all day."

"They're criminals," I said. "Actual murderers."

"So are we," he replied. "And you were fine with that."

"You're not murderers. You're heroes," I said. "Remind me how many worlds you'd saved even before I came along."

"Speaking of, we have to figure out our plan, now that we're here," he said, before turning to Daisy-May. "There's more than one doctor in the institute, correct?"

"Yeah!" said Daisy-May. "There's Dr. Smith, and Dr. Shelly, but he thinks his last name is too formal. So, we all call him Drew or Doc Drew. And then, of course, there's Dr. Winfrey. He's an old dear." She paused, looking over her friend's shoulder to check his artwork.

Blayde scrunched up her paper, scowling. "I'm out of practice. Sorry. Wait, why am I sorry? I'm trapped with limited mediums for artistic expression. Someone should be apologizing to me."

"A lot of people here deserve some apologies," Daisy-May said sternly.

I looked down at my half-assed drawing of Galli. Every minute spent in this institution could have been better spent out there, doing. Being. I had to keep reminding myself what I was doing this for, who I was doing this for. If I wanted the Agency to keep their hands off my parents, I would have to behave.

I picked up the brown crayon and scribbled on.

# FOUR

## IT'S NOT AWKWARD UNTIL YOU START QUESTIONING THE PANTS

**HERE'S A FUN ACTIVITY FOR THE WHOLE FAMILY:**
Try your hand at sleep deprivation! There's no more entertaining way to make sure you're not kidnapped in your sleep by your extraterrestrial nemesis. Of course, you're only imagining the rest of your family are with you, due to the fact that you are indeed sleep deprived. My eyes were propped open all night in case Foollegg was waiting for a split second of inattention to snatch me up then tell my parents I was unruly and not available for visits for the next few years until a terrible accident nixes that.

It was a little impressive that I hadn't been assigned a roommate, not that this cell—for lack of a better word—even had the space for one. What a luxury to have privacy, even if it meant I could get old-school abducted by aliens with no one here to be a witness. Not that anyone would have listened to these witnesses, seeing as how me screaming about aliens was how I got locked up in the first place.

Thankfully, I had the wind to keep me awake. Branches whipped and scratched against my small window. A haunting, bone-chilling noise that echoed in my empty room. And my stiff sheets were too starched to let me get comfortable. It felt like crumpling paper when I moved.

Even so, staying awake without Netflix to binge is harder than you might imagine. I made do with trying to remember the entire dialogue of *Avatar*, since it was the longest movie I could think of, and spent the first hour just trying to recall the character names. After a few hours of staring blankly at my door chanting in Navi, a new sound threw itself into the mix: a scream.

I flew to my feet, rushing for the door and pushing the sliding shade away with my sweaty fingers. Two nurses walked down the hallway in quiet tandem. Quick response time, I'd give them that, though their sense of urgency was sorely lacking.

"Hey," I called out. A nurse stopped and turned to face me, seemingly surprised that I was up. "What's happening?"

"Just a nightmare," she said soothingly. "Most of our patients will have a rough night every once and a while."

Without saying anything more, she continued her slow walk down the corridor toward the screams.

This wasn't right. A person didn't scream that loudly for nothing, not this long or this strongly after just a simple nightmare. The stereotype of screaming mental health patients was just that: a stereotype. Amazingly, the screams subsided quickly, which was a relief, though it was worrying that the sound hadn't awoken anyone else. Daisy-May hadn't been kidding.

I shuddered, closing the latch and returning to bed. I wasn't going to be sleeping any more after this, that was for sure.

That scream. Blood-curdling didn't even begin to cover it.

The sound of metal sliding across metal made me jump. So, this was it; the Agency was here. I grabbed for the lamp on the nightstand, only for my hand to slip right off. It was bolted down to the table, which, in turn, was bolted to the floor. I would have to do without a weapon then. Unless the Alliance operatives were somehow allergic to pillows.

In the darkness of my room, I could still make out the source of the noise: the slot in my door had been opened, revealing the fluorescent lighting of the hallway beyond. Were the agents waiting out there, ready to cart me off my homeworld? I braced myself for a fight.

"Hey there!"

I spun on my heels, unleashing the punch I had been winding up. My fist collided with a wall of muscle.

"Ouch! What was that for?" Zander rubbed his sternum as if I'd actually hurt him. He brandished one of his trademark grins.

"Knock it off. It's just me!" he said. "Though I'm sure if Foollegg was here, she would be quite peeved right now."

"Thanks, I guess?" Relief washed over me in a torrent.

Zander was *here*.

I hadn't been alone with him since our minute on the beach, before Foollegg had unleashed the whole fury of the Agency down on us, sending an entire squadron of American cops to bring us in. That had sure killed the mood.

And here he was, tall and beautiful in the moonlight, his sharp cheekbones raised in the dim, a perfect *chiaroscuro*. Despite the straight cut of his institution clothes, he still looked remarkably handsome, as if someone had tried to drape sheets over a Greek statue.

His smile wasn't the only thing he'd brought to my room. His faded yellow blanket was slung over his shoulder, a silver thermos grasped tightly between his fingers.

"What are you doing here?" I asked. "Not that I'm not thrilled to see you."

"I came to see you, silly," he said, inching toward me, though he had run out of hands to reach for me. "I felt bad that we didn't get that date, and I don't want to wait until we're out of here to make my grand romantic gesture. So, I hope you're all right with a medium-sized one."

I melted, my chest filling with warmth, a human jelly donut. I reached for his face, running my hands over his jawline, and he closed his eyes, leaning in. He smelled like minty toothpaste, clean and fresh in the sterile hospital.

# INALIENABLE

"You think I'm that easy?" I chided. "I don't just let anyone in my room. You didn't even knock."

He laughed, kissing my palm. "Even I can't make a room like this romantic. My charms don't reach that far. I have my limits. Come on, we're going out."

My heart fluttered, but the sound of the branches pommeling my window kept me sadly grounded.

He noticed me staring. "Rain won't hit for another hour at least. Coming?"

"Wait, I have nothing to wear!" I laughed. "Of course I'm coming. Let me grab my blanket."

I grabbed the comforter, slinging it over my shoulders and following him to the window. I braced my hand on his bicep, and we jumped lightly to the cold grass outside, the wind blowing against us like we were reeds bending to its mercy.

I found myself laughing. The powerful wind threatened to knock us over, but it gave me an excuse to clutch onto Zander even tighter. And, suddenly, we were on the roof, the wind whipping around our frail bodies, the sky and ground blending into the velvety black dome of sky. We could have been anywhere, everywhere, my only tether to reality being the warmth of Zander's body and the sturdiness of the stonework under my feet.

"You really meant that we were going out," I said, reveling in the wild wind. "As in, outside out!"

"It gets better," he said, though his voice was faint, miles away despite being only inches apart. "Did you see the bell tower on the way in?"

I could barely see anything now, not even the roof in front of me. The clouds were coming in, dimming the faint moonlight we had. But one jump later, and we had pillars around us and what might have been a roof over our head.

Zander took his comforter from his shoulders in one swift move, throwing it down on the edge of the old bell tower. We sat together on the papery warmth of the blanket, wrapping the other one over our heads and shoulders, letting our legs dangle over the ledge.

Nothing below but darkness, nothing ahead but the storm, and nothing between me and Zander but scrubs. I soaked up his warmth knowing I didn't have to share with anyone else.

"Not as impressive as a pyramid," he said, "but I figure you're tired of over-the-top."

"You figured right," I replied, relaxing into him for the first time in days. Oh, how I missed this. "And it was never about the pyramid. I had such a mad crush on you I could barely pay attention to the ground beneath my feet."

"So, no crush this time around?"

"No," I said, shaking his head against his torso, breathing him in. "Whatever this is now is far bigger than a crush."

I tilted my head upward and found his lips waiting for mine and took all that I could get, embracing even the brush of his nose against my cheek. Our hands were too busy keeping our comforter from turning into a sail to have time for anything else.

"Tea?" he asked, when we broke for air. Though now that neither of us actually needed to breathe to stay alive, I'm sure we could have spent the next hour lip-locked.

"You brought tea?"

He unscrewed the top of his thermos and handed it to me. It wasn't anything fancy or flavored, but it was tea, and I guzzled it down.

"Where on earth did you find this?" I asked, stopping myself before I finished the whole thing.

"Nicked it from the kitchen." His words tickled my hair. "They left it open. I didn't think they'd miss warm water and a tea bag anytime soon. I'll have the thermos washed and back in place before the staff arrives in the morning."

"It's perfect," I said, handing it back. "Thank you."

"I was meaning to take you out to dinner and a show. I hope this counts. For two people with all the time in the universe, we really haven't had any time for each other."

"The universe is a big baby."

His eyes turned to the horizon, and with barely a second delay, his face turned to wonder and awe, a grin of satisfaction replacing the frown as he pulled tighter. I let the warmth seep deeper into me.

"I'm really, really, really sorry, Sally," Zander apologized, not for the first time since we were arrested.

"You've got nothing to apologize for. It was the only way forward."

"Of course, I do. If I hadn't insisted that we solve the case for Felling or if I'd gone to the Agency without you …"

"Can it with the what ifs. It's done."

"But all this is because of me."

"You can't take all the credit," I replied. "Do you think I've paid the universe back enough yet for running you over?"

"Years ago." He held me tighter. "When this is all over, we'll find a resort planet and go on an actual date."

"What? This doesn't count as an official date?"

"Too small for what I'm talking about." He shook his head. "As I said, I owe you a grand romantic gesture. No running around the universe until we've at least tried our hand at romance."

"I'd like that," I said. "It would probably be more proper if we had an official date before I asked you to move in with me."

His face went supernova, bursting into light and color. "You mean it?"

"Not that it means much in a wild, infinite universe, but I was only keeping that apartment for you to find me again. And I think Jules is tired of all the different agencies running through the building in the dead of night."

"A reasonable response."

"A new place would do some good, for all of us. A safe place to come to after saving the world. Somewhere Blayde can keep her various wigs, other than my duffle bag."

"I'd like that," he said, beaming. "I've never had a street address before. What's it like paying bills?"

# INALIENABLE

I turned away before he could see the tears in my eyes. A home, with Zander. Even a temporary place that we could call our own would be out of this world. It didn't matter that we'd have to share with Blayde or that we'd be out and away until we found the way back each time. It would be ours. A light at the end of this confusing tunnel.

"The storm is coming," he whispered, shaking with excitement. I turned my gaze up at the sky.

The long, flat horizon glowed white under the filtered moonlight. The lightning lit up the clouds like it were noon, striking the ground miles in every direction, the landscape changing from that of forest and city to that of battle and war. Thunder rumbled and roared, shaking our foundation.

Then came the rain. Like a torrent, it came rolling from the skies, catching my dangling feet in its deluge before I had the time to react.

"Too bad the rain blocked out the lightning," Zander moaned. "It was a good show before that."

I laughed again, relishing in the feeling of hot, heavy raindrops against my legs.

"I want to make a joke about getting a lady wet," I said, "but it seems in poor taste after all the work you put into this."

"Remind me, is that a good or a bad thing for Terrans?"

My stomach did an odd somersault I couldn't exactly decipher. Not a conversation I had expected to have this evening, if at all.

"I never asked, but have you ever, um …" My mouth had gone dry. How were you supposed to phrase these kinds of questions? I had been worried about the sore lack of handbooks on alien roommates that I hadn't even bothered to check Amazon for books on discussing sexual histories with someone who wasn't your species.

"It's been a long time since I've ever been with anyone from Earth," he said, answering what I didn't dare ask. "Not that I even have a clear memory of if I did. But I'm not going to lie and say I've never."

"I just never thought to ask." Was it polite to make some distance during these kinds of talks? I didn't know. "And I've kind of acted under the assumption that you and I were, I don't know, the same."

"Would it bother you? If I wasn't what you were used to."

How do you even answer that? If he were to take off his pants and reveal he had lemurs down there, I would be absolutely terrified. It's not like I had ever thought where I drew the line before.

"I don't know," I said, honestly. "I've dated men, women, a person who was both, a person who was neither. But each time, I knew what I was in for."

A pause. A breath. Silence. His arm still draped over my shoulders, unmoving.

"I shouldn't have said anything," I sputtered. "This shouldn't be something that comes between us, right? Maybe we should have just waited until we were horny and already undressing for this to come up."

"I'm sure that would have traumatized at least one of us," he replied, though I was sure he was saying it for my benefit and he certainly wouldn't care if I had lemurs in my pants. I was relieved there was nothing cold in his tone. I didn't know if I should have been uncomfortable or reassured that he seemed to know how to handle this kind of conversation. "Though neither topic was supposed to come up tonight. I just wanted to watch a storm with you."

"And what a mighty good storm it is."

He laughed, and I forced the confusion from my mind, leaning in for another kiss. The way his lips left me all fluttery inside, there was no way I couldn't love everything about him.

"I do want you," I said, and it was a relief to speak the words. "I want you so badly. I'm sorry we're stuck here because of me."

"It's not your fault," he said, somehow, impossibly, pulling me in tighter. "Truly, we can leave any time. They might not even notice us missing."

"And call this place home in between adventures? No, thank you. I meant what I said. I want us to get someplace real. I'll do whatever I can to get the Alliance to leave us be and get out of here."

"You'd have an easier time taking down the entire Alliance than convincing them of anything when it comes to us."

"Then that's what I'll do."

"What? Convince them?"

"No. Take them down."

If he had a heartbeat, I would have heard it skip. I didn't know if he believed me, but he didn't have to. Nothing had ever been clearer in my mind.

The Alliance had to fall.

They had done so much wrong in the galaxy, least of all their mismanagement of Earth. It wasn't theirs to manage in the first place, but everything I learned about them—from their child-hire program to their propaganda TV hits to their treatment of the Downdwellers on Da-Duhui—every little element came together to reveal corrupt and disgusting leadership, and I wasn't even mentioning their treatment of Zander and Blayde, turning them into rebels just so they had someone to blame for their inevitable catastrophes.

"We should get back," he said, standing. I pulled my legs up from the ledge, trying not to step on his moderately dry comforter. "You need a good night's sleep."

"So do you," I said. "Not that either of us do? I'm still confused on that point. And bone tired. But I can't sleep with the Agency coming."

The rain had become a full cascade, a curtain cutting us off from the rest of the universe. I grabbed his arm.

"We're going to have to run for it," he said, as if it were as simple as walking rather than taking the bus. "Come on. Follow my lead."

With a grin, he flipped the comforter over his head, dashing into the deluge. I followed, afraid of losing him in the curtain of rain, my feet moving faster than I could think.

He ran straight to the ledge, not slowing down, and leapt off, arms outstretched, jumping the last few meters. I did the same, hitting the ground as lightly as a cat, the rain pausing a second above me before hitting me like a blow.

He leapt up on the ledge of my window, extending a hand to help me up. In a second, we were back in my room, the warmth of the institute's radiators making me feel more drenched than I actually was.

"Sorry that your blanket got wet," he said, taking mine form my shoulder and giving it a good shake.

"Hold on. Do you hear that?"

I pointed at the door. There must have been an orderly in the hallway, checking that we were all asleep, though it was far too late for anyone reasonable to be up.

Not that we were in a place with reasonable people.

"What?"

"You didn't hear anything?" I replied, but I was half-convinced I'd imagined it.

Only half.

A sudden scream filled the air, chilling me to the bone even more than the freezing rain had. Zander didn't hesitate, silently dropping everything he had in hand to the floor.

"You coming?" He rushed to the slit on my door.

I gripped his hand, and he jumped out into the corridor again, images of the institute moving around my immobile self. Suddenly, we were somewhere else on the other side of the building, the wails getting lower as every jump brought us closer.

Inside his room, Peter was writhing on the floor in pain, his hands clasping his ears as he shook on the floor. Zander rushed to his side, pinning him down.

Something slithered up the wall behind me.

"Zander, there's something in here," I said.

He nodded, trying to glimpse under Peter's hands. He pried one away, gaping at the gash behind the boy's ear.

"What is it?"

"He's been hurt," Zander stammered. "Something stabbed him. We need to get him out of here."

Peter didn't seem bothered by it, though. He was quiet now, limp in Zander's hands. Even the blood had stopped.

"What could have done that to him?" This couldn't be happening. Maybe the Agency was trying to get us out, threatening the other patients by accident or pure malice; I didn't know.

"How should I know?"

"You've been around a bit longer than me."

Peter was shaking now. He might have been passing out from blood loss. The hole in the side of his head was pink and raw; nothing to be calm about.

A key turned in the lock, the metal jangling against the heavy door. I snapped my head up.

"What do we do?" I hissed.

# INALIENABLE

Zander didn't answer as he let go of Peter and threw himself under the bed. I dove under after him. Squished together, we watched as the orderlies calmly slipped into the room. Light flared as one of them took out a needle, grabbing the boy's arm and delicately injecting fluid into his veins. He sobbed as he gently wrapped his arms around the nurse, his tears muffled by her shirt. Zander tensed against my back.

"Was it your father again?" she asked. He nodded in response, dazed. The nurse shifted, hiding him from view. "It's okay. He's gone now. Here."

She extracted herself from his grasp, handing him a glass of water one of the other orderlies had brought, along with a small, white pill.

"This will help you get back to sleep."

"Thank you," he replied, taking the pill and swallowing it without the help of the water. Calm for a man with a gaping head wound.

"You should drink," the nurse insisted. "You look dehydrated."

He nodded, taking a long gulp and finishing the glass in one draft. She helped him get into bed above us, pulling his sheets over him and tucking him in like a caring mother as he slowly slipped into lower levels of consciousness.

"Who were they?" Peter mumbled.

"Who were who?"

"The man and the woman. The ones who tried to help."

"No one was in here. Don't fret any further."

She left the room, switching off the light as she went, locking the door behind her. I rolled out from under the bed, glancing up at a now motionless Peter, making sure he was asleep.

"What was that?" Zander asked in a hushed whisper.

"Nothing, it appears." Peter's head rested calmly on the pillow, all trace of blood now gone. The wound that had been gaping up at us just seconds ago seemed to have never existed. No wonder the orderlies had been so calm. "Shit. Where did the hole go? You saw it, too, right? It was there."

"What Daisy-May was saying, I thought it was just part of what had brought her here, but do you think when she joked about the screaming—"

"That those aren't just nightmares that make them scream, but *the stuff of*?"

"Yeah. Do you?"

He thought about it for a while. "Let's consider, for a minute, that that's the case. What would be the point?"

"Come on. A monster in a mental institution? A building full of the criminally insane? No one would ever believe the patients."

"But to what end?" He stood, turning away from Peter. "Daisy-May said there was screaming but didn't mention any patients disappearing. Peter seems absolutely fine. If we hadn't seen what we just saw, I wouldn't assume anything is off about this place."

I nodded. Peter's sedatives must have been strong because he wasn't bothered by our ludicrous conversation.

# INALIENABLE

"Do really you think something is feeding—for lack of a better explanation right now—off the patients, like Cross was?"

"I don't know, I don't know." He ran his hands through his thick hair, pulling it back tight. "It would be terribly ironic if that were the case. This is something the Agency should be handling."

"Look what a fine job they did with Cross, though."

"Exactly." He let out a heavy sigh, reaching for my hand. "Out of the star and into the black hole. Isn't that the saying?"

It wasn't, not on Earth, but I knew what he meant. Just when we thought we were safe from Agency interference for at least a while, it turned out we'd probably need their aid.

I needed a good sleep after this. And maybe some wine. Too bad all I had was tea and paper bedsheets.

# FIVE

## CLASSIC SHARED TRAUMA
## OVER A TELEPHONE LINE

**"YOU'RE KIDDING ME, RIGHT?" SAID BLAYDE.** "This is a joke?"

"When have I ever joked about something this serious?" said Zander while shoveling the morning oatmeal into his mouth so fast that his hands blurred. "Something attacked Peter last night."

I picked up my spoon, digging into the oatmeal and raising it in front of my face, the odd texture slopping off the edges and falling back into the dish with a sloshing sound. Besides toast, it was all that was offered. I wasn't a fan in general and wasn't looking forward to it in the slightest.

"You were sneaking about without me?" she hissed. "I was waiting up for a serious conversation on what we were going to do next, and instead, you were running around the halls playing heroes? How come everything exciting always happens to you two?"

"You heard the screams too," I said. "You could have come. Matter of fact, I'm surprised you didn't! There was a whole lot of screaming."

"It was just a nightmare," Blayde snapped, ripping a piece of said toast with a strong tug of her teeth. "Trust me, I was in the room right next to her all night. No one could have gone in or out without me knowing. It was all in her head."

"Her?"

"Josephine," she said. "She screamed rather early in the night, then I had to listen to all the moping crap until sunrise. The other guy, Peter, must have been just the same. You hear one scream in this place, and the rest is just boy crying solar flair. Hum. This is good."

"What now?"

"The oatmeal," she replied. "Tasty little gruel."

"I think it's boy crying lion," said Zander. "Or boy crying bear? One of the terrifying, toothy creatures Terrans seem to hate. Sloth?"

"Shut up, I don't want to hear from you anymore," she said. "Your voice just grinds my eardrums. You know what? You're shunned until further notice. There."

"Come on, Blayde," he started.

"Sally, please inform my brother that the shunning has already begun." She turned to me and dropped her utensils on the tray so that they clattered, making her point for her.

"Fine." I sighed heavily. "Zander, it looks like your sister is going to give you the silent treatment for a while because she's a thousand-year-old child who doesn't want to grow up. Sorry."

"Don't apologize. I'm giving her the cold shoulder too."

"Wait, seriously?" I said. "You're going to shun each other instead of talking it out?"

"Sally, please inform my brother that until he agrees to keep me in the loop, I'm keeping him out of my life." Blayde leaned back in her chair, staring at her brother.

"Please inform Blayde that I'm not giving her another word until she realizes I also have a life."

"Well, I'm not going to be your go-between," I said. "You two grow up and talk it out. It's not up to me to remind you that we have more pressing issues to deal with."

"My wrath?" said Blayde pointedly.

"Blayde, come on. We have a problem. Be professional."

"I *am* being professional. I would have beat you both up right here if I weren't. Also, what even is professional for me? It's not like I'm getting paid to save your planet."

"I thought you were doing it out of the goodness of your heart? Isn't life itself the reward?"

She scowled. "I just don't like you acting like it's my job or anything. Your planet is risking becoming a little entitled."

"Can we get back to the issue at hand?" Zander interjected. "Something is going on in this hospital!"

# INALIENABLE

"I'm sorry, did you hear something? It must have been the wind. Old buildings like this do tend to get drafty."

"Blayde, cut it out," I snapped. "Look, Zander's right. This place isn't right, and the Agency is going to try to extract us sooner or later. They might already be here, and we need to be ready when they act. Ready to fight. And before they do, we need to figure out what happened to Peter last night. That was messed up, and we can't let it go on."

"When did you become so confident?" asked Zander, beaming. "I like it when you take over a case like this."

I turned my gaze into my oatmeal, hiding my blush. I took a hesitant bite, not tasting anything out of the ordinary, though maybe it was a little better than what I was expecting. Before I knew it, the bowl was empty, and I was feeling uncomfortably stuffed.

"It's not a case," Blayde muttered.

"Morning, sunshine!" Daisy-May exclaimed happily as she bounded to my side, slipping into the seat beside me. Peter sat across from her, right beside Blayde, who was kind enough to shift over. "Sunshines, plural, I should say. Sleep well?"

"Yeah," I replied. "I mean, first night and all. Except for the screaming. Did you hear that?"

She shrugged, digging into her oatmeal with relish. "Yeah. There's always at least one. You're lucky if you get one full night of sleep a month. But you learn to sleep through it."

"Ouch," I shivered. "Every night?"

"Everyone gets nightmares, I s'pose. Everyone is haunted by their past in a place like this."

"What about you, Peter?" asked Zander casually.

"Slept fine," he replied, meek as ever.

"Really?" I pushed. "No dreams?"

"Nope," he said, as he reached a hand up to push some of his hair out of his face, curving his fingers around his ear and exposing the skin there for barely a second.

I snorted my orange juice loudly in surprise as I saw the bare patch of skin there with a small, penny-sized, white mark that seemed to fade and blend into the skin, even in the split second that the mark was exposed. Impossible that it had healed so quickly since I had last seen it.

"You sure?" I urged. "Storms can really mess with your head."

"I slept right through it," he said. "Though come to think of it, I did dream of Santa Claus parading around the roof."

"Santa Claus. That's the imp in the red suit, right?" asked Blayde.

"Don't tell her he's fictional," Zander whispered in my ear.

"I thought you weren't supposed to be able to hear her?"

Daisy-May got up, stretched, and ushered for us to follow. According to the schedule, our entire morning was free, so we made our way to the rec room where the girl took out a box of Connect Four, setting it up at the table so that we could take turns playing. I went along with it. To be honest, I wasn't wanting to do anything with crayons, and Connect Four was at least slightly challenging.

Though there were roughly two dozen patients in the room at the moment, it felt oddly empty. The sun had finally come out, rays of actual sunlight flooding in and warming us all. Josephine sat by her window like she had the day before, watching the world evolve and revolve around her as she hugged her knees to her chest. Many of the patients I hadn't had the time to meet yet meandered around the room, chatting amongst themselves, trying to find something interesting to do.

It didn't feel like a mental institution anymore. The people seemed less like criminals and more like people I could relate to. Scary thought. If I had told myself only a year before that I would be traveling the universe with an alien, that I would be immortal, of all things, I would have looked for psychological help as well.

Then again, maybe that was exactly what had happened. I glanced up at Zander, his hair glowing in the early morning sun. It was absurd that I had ever managed to catch his attention, let alone have him fall in love with me as I had with him. Maybe, at some point, my mind snapped and made this whole mess up for me.

I took one look at Blayde, who was drawing literal battle plans with her crayons and tossed that thought away. There was simply no way my mind could conjure up someone like her.

"Phone call for Sally Webber. Sally Webber, can you come over here, please?"

I was jolted back to reality at the sound of my name. I stood robotically before realizing I had no idea what to do about this.

Daisy-May tapped my arm. "Go to the main door, the one with the grate on it," she said, still beaming. I was starting to think she was like a glow stick. That, one day, she had cracked and was just emitting light ever since.

"Thanks!"

I awkwardly waved Zander and Blayde goodbye, getting an encouraging thumbs-up for yours truly. Daisy-May was practically squealing in delight. I got the feeling that phone calls rarely happened in this place.

"I'm Sally," I said as I approached the grate. "There's a call for me?"

The woman on duty nodded. She pushed a button on the control panel in front of her, the grate slid open with a noisy buzz, and it closed behind me as soon as I was through. Another grate in front of me slid aside with yet another loud and grinding buzz.

It had to be my parents calling, unless Foollegg had decided to go old-school and buy minutes. Not that I wanted to talk to either of them. It went without saying that I didn't want to have a cozy chat with the woman who had framed me for murder. As for my parents, you'd be embarrassed, too, if you'd just told the whole world you were an immortal space traveler and aliens had made you kill somebody. Even if every word of it was true.

A nurse was waiting for me on the other side of the grate, politely smiling as if she had no idea what I was in for.

"Sally Webber?" she asked, as if I could be anyone else. I nodded. "You have a phone call."

She spun on her heels, walking forward without another word, expecting me to follow. I glimpsed back at the rec room, the grate blocking most of my view. Out of the corner of my eyes, I could see Blayde, her gray eyes riveted on me, expressionless, one red crayon clutched tightly in her grasp.

I followed the nurse to another room, this one about the size and shape of a broom cupboard. Overly lit, furnished only with a small IKEA table with a lone, old-fashioned rotary phone resting on top. I took my cue, sitting down on the worn chair provided and picking up the phone as the nurse who led me there left me alone, which was actually pretty nice.

I had no delusions about the fact this was probably being taped, though. Not that anyone would believe a word of what came out of my mouth.

"Hello?"

"Sally?" the voice on the other end said.

"Who is this?"

"Oh, sorry. Bad reception. Hold on." Heavy footsteps filled my ears, the line becoming clearer until the fuzziness was completely gone. "Do you hear me now?"

"James?" I felt a smile creep up my cheeks. "Is that you?"

"Yeah, it's me," she said. "Good god. Where do I even start?"

"It's good to hear your voice," I said. "I was so worried about you. When I saw you in the courtroom …"

"Worried about me?" She let out a hearty laugh. "Sally, you really do need that psych eval. You're the one who was arrested on a trumped-up murder charge! I'm the least of your worries."

"I'm not sure you're any safer where you are. The Agency knows who you are, knows you were involved. The only reason they didn't frame you, too, was because they needed leverage against me."

"Wow, your ego needs reduction surgery."

"Felling, I'm not joking about this." I clutched the receiver so hard I felt the plastic begin to give. "Foollegg came to me."

"At the institution?"

"No, in jail, right after we got arrested. She had this whole plan to extract us from prison, so we found a way out of prison."

"That explains your sudden candor," she replied. "I swear I tried to get rid of their files on you. One day, they had barely anything on you. The next, you had a criminal record."

# INALIENABLE

"Barely anything? You mean they had that blood-test thing. Enough for midnight SWAT teams."

"I'm starting to think it wasn't *our* people who ordered them on you that night." Her tone had gone so cold my ear was freezing against the receiver. "Sally, my own partner was an extraterrestrial, and I didn't even know. How am I meant to trust anyone there ever again, knowing what I know now?"

"I wish I had an answer. I really do. Anyone here could be working for them."

"This is so wrong." She was angry now, her icy tone beginning to heat up. That same fury that was rippling through my belly was growing in hers too. "This is *our* planet. They have no right to do with it what they wish."

"The Agency is just the tip of the iceberg," I agreed. "The entire Alliance needs to be put in their place. This is our home. Either they protect it or they get the hell off."

"Get out of that place," she hissed. "And this is coming from a federal agent: Get out of there. Get Zander and Blayde to do whatever they can to get the Agency off Earth. Promise me you'll do that, Sally. No one else can."

"You think we don't want to?" I said, shaking. "Why do you think we're still here? They have my parents, Felling. My mom and dad are going to die if I go anywhere the Agency can't keep an eye on us."

"She threatened your family?"

"Without missing a beat."

"Shit."

For a second, I thought she had ended the call. Neither of us said anything, but her steady breath was a reassuring reminder she was still there.

"We did the right thing," she said. "With Cross. We couldn't stand by and do nothing."

"We did the right thing," I agreed.

"I'm sorry. For everything. He was my partner; I should have seen him for what he was so much earlier. If I had, maybe you wouldn't be in this mess."

"You couldn't have known, James. You couldn't have."

"He was a monster, Sally. A wolf in sheep's clothing, in a puppet body. He solved cases with me! And anyone in my department could be the same. Wearing their human skins and moving pieces in a game I didn't know existed until a week ago."

"I know."

"You told me that you get used to it," she said. "But how? How do you get used to it?"

"You don't, James," I said, and it physically hurt to get the words out. "I was just rolling with the punches. Now, it's like the entire world is made of fists."

She let out a heavy sigh. "Great. Just great. New partner today. Could be an alien and no way of knowing."

"Throw some water on them," I offered. "See if they melt?"

"Very funny. This is serious, Sally."

"You're not listening to serious."

"Right. Roll with the punches. Expect the worst from everyone. Got it. Are they treating you all right, at least?"

"We're fine, all things considered." My fist relaxed a little. If I kept thinking about my hatred of the Alliance, I would corrode from the inside out. "The food is worse than I remember in high school, though everyone is addicted to their oatmeal. Better than being en route to Pyrina in a prison ship."

"And Blayde? I know she's probably not taking being locked up well. How's she holding up?"

"You can't even imagine. I'm glad mom won her over with those brownies or she'd have nothing keeping her from exploding and taking the whole place down with her."

"Great. Tell her I said hi. And Zander too. Do you need me to do anything out here? Seeing as how I can't exactly help with potential break outs."

"Just keep an eye on my parents for me, if you can," I said, breathing a sigh of relief. "The Agency is sure to have people on them. It would be nice to know someone is indeed on their side."

"Of course, count on it."

A knock on the door of the small phone room told me that it was time to wrap it up. I sighed, angry I didn't have more time to myself.

"I've gotta go," I said, frustrated. "Anything you need me to pass on to the siblings?"

"Tell them I said hi, okay? And don't worry, your parents will be fine."

"Thanks for that."

"No problem. I'll call back soon. Please, do ask Zander if there's any way I can tell if my partner's an alien."

"I'll ask."

"See you soon."

"Bye."

The hospital felt like a different world as I was led back through into the rec room. I knew James didn't want me to worry about her, but I did. If I hadn't used her stolen ID when meeting with Foollegg, the Agency might not have known about her involvement with us.

So much for us making a difference. Rather than just helping James solve her case, we also murdered her partner, put her on the Agency's radar, and revealed an actual alien conspiracy to keep Earth ignorant about extraterrestrial life.

A conspiracy we were now a danger to. Anyone here could be an Agency spy; anyone out there could be an Agency spy.

Everyone I knew could be in danger.

And I couldn't do anything from in here.

"How did it go?"

Zander was the only one left at the table, politely waiting for me while Blayde and Daisy-May were who knows where. I sat across from him, letting him see the weight on my shoulders.

"James called," I replied. "She says hi. We've also destroyed her trust in everyone on the planet, so she's not doing the best right now."

"Isn't that a good thing?" he asked. "We shattered her illusions."

"Honestly, I would rather not know about how deep the Agency's roots go, but that's just me."

Zander nodded as he folded over his paper, hiding the golden sunshine he had been doodling there. I was just reaching for my own sheet when Dr. Smith appeared above us, smiling with motherly tenderness that had been all too absent when we'd first met.

"Good morning, Sally," she said. "Did you sleep well?"

"Morning," I replied, slightly put off. Her perfume was on too thick, wafting over me and blocking my sense of smell. "To be honest, the bedsheets feel like paper. Sorry."

She ignored me, placing one hand on the back of my chair, the other on the table, leaning in toward me, her sickly-sweet perfume heavy in the air. I leaned away from her as she loomed over me like a vulture over its dinner. My head conked against Zander's shoulder.

"We're going to get started on our talk this morning," she said. "I'm excited to get to know you."

"Likewise." I gave an awkward smile, and that seemed to be enough.

"Zander, we'll meet this afternoon," she said, though her eyes never left me. "I hope you have a pleasant morning." She marched away just as casually as she arrived, but her perfume lingered.

"I guess I'm off," I said. "Though I feel like I only just sat down."

"At least you won't get bored. I'll start probing for possible Agency plants. Keep an eye on that doctor, just in case."

I swallowed hard. Just a few minutes ago, I'd been talking with James about how anyone could be an off-worlder, and already, I was letting my guard down. I had to be more cautious.

Even Blayde was playing her part. As I followed my doctor through the rec room, I spotted her in the corner with Daisy-May and Peter, completely loose and relaxed. An act, to be sure. Probably pumping them for information, whatever they could give.

She flashed her drawing at me on the way out—a fully fleshed-out, 3D map of the institute with details too small to read. I shouldn't have worried at all.

# SIX

## THERAPY SOUNDED LIKE A GOOD IDEA
## BUT NOW I'VE GOT QUESTIONS

**I FOLLOWED SMITH THROUGH THE MAZE OF THE** institute, away from the common areas and into a hallway segmented with heavy oak doors, the whole while fretting about whether or not I appeared to be fretting enough. I was silently hitting the refresh button on my brain, begging for my anxiety to speak up.

She led me into her office, open and warm with a thick, soft, chocolate brown carpet. A complete change from the sticky, white linoleum floors and artificial lights I had just come from. Floor-to-ceiling bookshelves lined opposite walls on my left and right, while the back wall was curved and entirely made of windows. I had a clear view of the wild, semi-tropical plants on the grounds that made the state so spectacular bending in the wind. How many gators were out there right now, ready to munch on escaping patients?

*Ah, there you are, anxiety. Good to see you again. Can't say I missed you. Ready to help me look like I belong here?*

An oak desk sat before the window, topped with an old-fashioned brass lamp illuminating the two green armchairs and the classic psychiatrist's sofa that stood dead center in the room.

"Sally," she said, closing the door behind us and locking us in, "I'm glad to finally have this time to chat. How are you?"

"I'm fine," I replied quickly, still taken aback by the room. Warm cedar wafted through the air, reaching my nostrils and making me feel safe and relaxed, covering the horrible smell of the woman's perfume.

She waved me over to the patent leather sofa. It was almost straight out of an 80s movie. "Please."

I did as I was bid. The leather creaked under my clothes.

She shook her head. "Please, lie down."

Oh. She was one of those doctors. I said nothing, lifting my legs off the floor, wondering if she gave it a good clean between patients. None of my past therapists had ever asked me to lie down before; I usually sat in their well-worn armchairs.

"Do you know why you're here, Sally?" She took out her clipboard and pen, the click filling the silent room.

I nodded. "We're doing a psych eval."

"A mental health evaluation, yes. But beyond that. Do you understand why the judge sent you to me?"

# INALIENABLE

"So you can tell the courts whether I seriously believe what I'm saying or if I'm making it all up to get away with murder?"

She wrote something down on her notepad, the pen scratching hard against the paper. Or maybe my ears were just getting all that much better. "You have nothing to worry about from me. I just want to hear the truth. I just want to talk. Seeing from your file, this isn't the first time you've met with a psychologist, is it?"

"I met with one regularly after my brother died." Who knew what she already knew. Whether she was working for the U.S. courts or the Agency, she probably had access to more data about my life than I could ever know. "Freak accident. It wasn't pretty. Car lost control and crashed into him, sending him over a cliff. It was horrible. I was diagnosed with clinical depression shortly after that. I'd had depressive episodes off and on before his death, but it was only when his passing allowed me to meet with a psychologist that I got a diagnosis. I'm sure that's in my file."

"I'm sorry for your loss," she said, taking further notes. "I'm worried about your recent treatment history. Though recently your symptoms have been subsiding, you haven't been taking your medication."

My blood went cold. "How do you know that?"

"Your therapist."

"But what about doctor-patient confidentiality?"

"She was court-ordered to give up all pertinent information that could inform this case. She wants to help you, Sally."

I hadn't even realized that my confidentiality would be breached like that. A shiver ran through me. *Of course, it would be, dumbass. You got caught taking the law into your own hands.*

"You stopped going to see her," said Smith. "And, from what I gather, it was quite sudden."

I'd gone on a week-long space adventure where Nimien was sacrificed to the sun and Zander "abandoned" me in my kitchen. I needed time to process, and it wasn't exactly something I could talk about openly with Dr. Lansburgh.

Except.

I could tell all of this to Smith. She was impartial— already thought I had lost the plot or was making all this up. She could be the one to give me the help I need.

Unless she was working for the Agency.

I let out a heavy breath. "I had just seen Zander again. I didn't feel able to talk to her for a little while."

"Understandable. Faces linked with memories of trauma and loss can oftentimes trigger intense emotion. Tell me about your relationship with his brother. He was a work colleague?"

"Oh, they're not brothers," I said. "Zander's immortal. It's the same person."

She scrubbed quickly on her notepad. Any faster and it might have caught fire.

"You told the police he was Lysander Smith's twin brother—Zander and Xander?"

"They wouldn't have believed us," I said. "We needed an excuse for why we didn't have a zombie on our hands."

"Which he is. A zombie, I mean."

"If you adhere to the living-dead definition, sure, but he doesn't eat brains, if that's what you're asking. But don't worry, I kept him out of trouble. Helped him make friends."

"Fascinating." A smile slid up her lips. But I wasn't going to stay here long enough for her to get a book deal out of this. "Tell me about how you two met, then."

"Well, he was my roommate, at first. We ended up getting hired at the power plant together because my at-the-time boyfriend was trying to impress me with his connections."

Which was the least of the truth, but I wasn't going to mention his plan to lock me in a library for the rest of eternity. I was, however, going to start to bring part of the story into the equation. If I wanted to stay here rather than go to prison, that is.

"Funny story," I said without her prompting, "I accidentally ran him over with my car when I was coming back from a party. I wasn't drunk; he just teleported to the wrong place at the wrong time."

She just nodded as if it were the most natural thing in the world for me to say. "And he didn't carry any resentment about that?"

"Didn't faze him in the slightest. It did bother him that it made him lose track of his sister, though. It was the least I could do to invite him to stay in my spare room."

How was she taking this? Did she know this was the truth or believe it was only *my* truth? I tried to gauge her reaction to what I was saying, but she had professional experience in hiding her emotions.

*Dang. Maybe she could teach a class. Definitely a skill I needed.*

"What about his sister? When did you meet her?" she asked, deadpan.

"The first time was right before the plant blew. But she reemerged into my life about a month ago, living Zander in tow."

"Did she give any warning before returning like she did?"

"No. None."

"And what happened after she arrived? Did she ask you for any favors? Money? It was around that time that you had stopped seeing your therapist, if I am correct."

"They were in and out of my life," I said. "To be honest, they were some of the few friends who didn't ask me for money. I'd lost a lot of trust in people after I somehow inherited Grisham's fortune."

"So, what did they want from you?"

Another crossroads: truth or fiction? Not that either would be believable. I decided to go with the truth. It's what she was after, I knew, and if I gave any indication I was lying, it might cost me my safety here.

"They showed up on your doorstep," she stated, leaning forward. "What happened next?"

"Zander promised to take me to another planet, as a thank you for letting him crash at my place."

"And did he?"

"You bet he did. It was amazing. And after a crazy set of events on Da-Duhui—including maggots in pizza and an AI uprising—we accidentally ended up stranded on the wrong side of the galaxy and spent the next week jumping from place to place, trying to find Earth again."

"Um-hum." She nodded to herself, flipping another page over. "Jumping? Is that a figure of speech? How exactly did you three travel?"

"Teleportation. Efficient mode of transportation, though a little temperamental at times. Small price to pay for the universe at your fingertips."

"Who came up with the term?"

"I don't know. It's what they called it long before I even met them."

"And how does it work?" She looked at me with excitement in her eyes, slipping on her reading glasses to either help her keep up with me or to look smarter and instill confidence. Maybe both.

"It's really complicated. I don't even know how to explain it."

"Try."

"Well … you close your eyes, let yourself dissolve into nothing, then hope that when you open your eyes back up that you're someplace safe. It's in us, nothing like a magic watch. No blue box, no phone booth, no huge spinning wheel, no DeLorean. Just us."

She jotted something down quickly. "When did you obtain the ability?"

"I've only had it about … two weeks? Damn. Feels like forever."

"And the immortality?"

"At the same time. It's a package deal."

"How did you learn you had these … gifts?"

"Well, first, I was murdered under a bridge, and then I had jumped over to a mysterious library. In space, of course. It was in our galaxy, though. I haven't even left the Milky Way yet. Either I'm immortal, or I'm dead, even now. Which I doubt because if this is hell, I'm not impressed, and if this is heaven, it's nothing like what the good book says."

"Have you considered that maybe you believe in your own immortality because of your own fear of death? Those around you die in horrible ways, which led you to consider that you yourself cannot die?"

*Oh, yes. Come at me girl. Hit me with these deep correlations.*

I shook my head. "I'm not afraid of death. And the deaths of my brother and Matt may have taken me a long time to get over, but I am not lying to myself."

"Now, Sally, this might be a hard question," she said. "I don't know if you'll be able to answer. But if Zander and his brother are identical in every way, yet one of them died in the GrishamCorp incident, then how can they—and yourself—be immortal?"

She's good at her job, I give her that. I wasn't going to be able to give her any holes to pick. It would have to be the truth, the whole truth, and nothing but the unbelievable truth.

"They're the same person. I did say," I said earnestly. "Zander didn't die. But since his death was already on record, he couldn't very well go telling the cops it was a misunderstanding. Saying he was his own identical twin made more sense at the time."

"This is fascinating, Sally. So, he went underground for two years after faking his own death and then reappeared in your life for a space adventure?"

"That's the gist of it."

"And gave you his superpower."

"Please don't say it like that!" I snapped. "It's my life, not a children's book. But yes."

She put up her hands defensively. "Fine. I'm still trying to fill in the gaps here. What happened after your ... excursion?"

I shrugged. "They left again. In any case, I was too busy with my best friend's wedding to pay much attention to them. But then, the aliens attacked."

"Ah. Yes. The hoax," she said, shaking her head. "Tell me more about that."

"Not much to say there. I realized I was a time traveler when I recognized the ship. I gave Sky People what they wanted—Vasquez—and they left. Simple as that. Then, I rescued Zander and Blayde from a demented ex of mine. It was a really rewarding day."

"I'm going to be honest with you, Sally. Many of the patients I have been seeing lately have had some adverse reactions to the hoax."

"As well they should have," I said. "It wasn't a hoax. They have a right to be traumatized."

She shuffled in her seat. "Let's talk about more pertinent things. Such as your reason for being here. Beyond your reasons for believing these things."

"What do you mean? I don't see why any of this would be what's wrong with me."

"You killed a man, Sally Webber." She shook her head. "I want to know why."

"Look, we told you all this in the hearing. I killed an alien who was trying to suck out my spinal fluid. He'd already gotten four other women that we know of. He—it—had to be stopped."

"He was an officer of the law," she said, "working for the FBI."

"Lady, he kidnapped me and tied me to a chair." I shuffled on the sofa. My sweat was making me stick to the leather. "That's not FBI protocol. When he came at me with a second jaw, I reacted."

"So, you were the one to pull the trigger."

"I was."

Only I wasn't. Not exactly. Felling had done the deed. Then again, Cross had been parading inside my body, using it as his ticket to immortality, whether I had any say in it or not. The memory of the second consciousness laying over mine, reaching in places it had no right to be …

When had I started shaking?

"What were Zander and Blayde doing at the time?" she asked. "Were they in the room where it happened?"

"No," I said, closing my fists. "They were trying to find me. I was alone."

She nodded, a small smile curling the edge of her lips. I knew instantly that I had royally screwed up. In her eyes, I was the true murderer, and they were just covering for me. I could see it now. Practically watched her write the letters on her legal pad.

Agency or Earth, whoever she was working for, it wasn't going to bode well for me.

She reached over to her desk to pull off a small stack of flash cards.

"I'm going to show you some images."

"Oh, the Rorschach test!"

"You know it?"

"Only *of* it," I replied. "I've seen it in on TV. My other therapists never used it as a tool."

She nodded, more for herself than for me. "Do you need me to explain how it works?"

"You show me the blots, and I tell you what I see. Correct?"

She held up the first card. A black blob of bold ink lay sprawled across it, covering the white piece of paper with a strange mix of images.

"Oh! A Downdweller!" I said instantly. My hands flew to cover my mouth. I hadn't planned on being *this* forthcoming.

"What's that?"

"On Da-Duhui, the first planet I ever got to visit. They had been living in the undercity for generations."

"So, an alien?"

"In as many words, yes, I see an alien."

She jotted down some rapid notes on her clipboard, looking up at me every other second to make sure I wasn't running off. Finally done, she handed me another card.

"This is a shark," I replied.

She wrote something down.

Card three: a dragon. Notes. Card four: a cheeseburger. Oh, how I craved a good cheeseburger! More notes. Card five: a very wooly mammoth.

The sound of a ballpoint pen scratching on paper was very audible through each moment of silence.

She handed me the last card, and I felt my face flush. A chill traveled through my skin, raising goosebumps on my arms, the hair on the back of my neck erect. I shivered.

"Are you all right?" the doctor asked with tenderness.

"I'm—" I stopped myself. My automatic response at this point had always been "fine." How was the food? Fine. You enjoy the party? It was fine. I am fine. Fine fine fine. never better. Never worse. I was fine.

But I wasn't.

The doctor did well not to open her mouth. She leaned forward slightly, so as to convey the intimacy of the situation, putting down her stack of inkblot flashcards to give me her full attention. Even her hand had slackened on the constantly scribbling pen.

"I see Cross's teeth," I mumbled. "I see him standing in front of me, his teeth barred—both sets, mind you—ready to kill me."

# INALIENABLE

I was glad that she didn't interrupt. The words were flowing now. No stopping them at this point. Anyone who stood in their way was in danger of losing a body part.

"He tried to kill me. He didn't care that I could have just helped him find what he needed. All he wanted was to live forever. I killed him in self-defense. I know that's supposed to make everything okay, but it really isn't. Because now I'm a murderer."

"If it truly was in self-defense, why didn't you tell the court?" she said quietly.

"That court was built up against me. Literally." I snorted. "And the fact that they had condemned me before hearing me out makes everything even worse."

"Now tell me, why would you kill someone in self-defense if you're immortal?"

Was she actually smirking? My respect for the woman was dropping. Rude.

"Oh, I wasn't worried for myself. I told you, he was a serial killer. I wasn't defending myself but others. And I'm … I'm still afraid."

She wrote a *lot* on her pad after this.

I fell back down heavily on the soft pillow of the sofa, my feet flopping down on the warm leather. I barely noticed. My mind was elsewhere, miles away, months ago, in a dark and abandoned shopping center standing across from a man who wasn't actually a man, the cool metal of the laser saber's grip sending a chill up my spine. The spine that the monster wanted to tap.

"I'm the one who killed him. It wasn't Zander. It wasn't Blayde. It was me. What have I become?"

The doctor said nothing, but the look in her eyes spoke in her place. *You monster,* they seemed to say. *You create these illusions to stop yourself from getting the blame. You feel guilty? You should. You killed that man. He was no alien. And you are no immortal.*

I shook my head, trying to chase out the dark feeling, the dark thoughts. It wasn't as easy as that.

"How do I live with myself now?" I asked the doctor. She didn't reply. "Please, please tell me."

Still no reply.

She was no help. I was in a mental institution with doctors trained to deal with this sort of thing, and still I was a hopeless case. Never mind the rest of it: coming to terms with the fact I was never going to die, dealing with the transgression that was another consciousness taking my body, or something so basic as telling the truth to my parents.

I was entirely a hopeless case.

# SEVEN
## TALK ABOUT A HEAD BANGER

**I TAKE BACK WHAT I SAID ABOUT THE SUCKY** rooms. Sure, they were only a few steps up from prison, but boy was it wonderful to have a place to be alone. At least in here, I didn't have to worry about being observed. I had to be on my toes in case the Agency had finally found the guts to send someone in to take me, sure, but they weren't going to pretend to be friendly first.

So much for 'being myself' being the answer. I'd probably just made everything worse for the people I cared about.

I stretched out, waiting for the nightly screams to return. Focusing on them was a good way to stay awake. Better that than fall asleep and be woken by the sound—or worse. A visit from Zander would be welcome, but his sister had probably gotten to him with her guilt-trip. No adventures outside these four walls tonight.

A thud resonated through my room, echoing slightly across the walls. My heart might have skipped a beat if it had still been beating. Old buildings were always so noisy. The way they creaked, the way they moaned. It was more of a nuisance than creepy, even if they insisted on taking you by surprise.

"Sally," the walls seemed to say, calling me, pulling me in.

No. I couldn't fall sleep. I needed a distraction.

"Sally," the walls moaned feebly, lulling me a little further toward sleep.

Maybe Zander was coming to say hi. I straightened up in bed, trying to peer through the dark, but even my new-and-improved vision wasn't helping.

"Sally."

I heard it much more clearly now. Maybe it wasn't the work of a sleep-addled mind.

"Hello?" I asked. "Who's there?" My hushed whisper revealed nothing; the walls did not respond.

"Help me …"

Okay, so that was most certainly *not* the walls.

I sat up instantly. At first, nothing. I had to be imagining things. Slowly, though, the form of a hunched figure came into shape, hiding in the last dark corner of my cell.

"How did you get …?"

Zander stumbled to the floor at my feet, landing squarely in the small pool of light. It was all I could do not to scream at the sight. The hair that had hung so perfectly in front of his face fell to the side, the dark shadows and hard light revealing a face contorted in pure, mortal agony.

"Zander!" I cried out, falling to his side. My hair stood erect on my arms all the way up the back of my neck. "What happened to you?"

I slid his head into my lap. His breathing was short, raspy. His face covered in a sheen of sweat so dense it looked plastic. His hand was pressed on his stomach, red liquid spilling from the wound he was desperately trying to hide from me.

And he was in pain.

Only once before had I seen him in actual pain, when Nimien had drugged him to exact some kind of sick revenge. The sight was no easier the second time around. Tears were welling in my eyes, my chest tightening so much that I was forgetting how to breathe.

*No. Stop. You have to help him.* I ripped the sheet off my bed, shoving it against the wound at his stomach, hoping beyond hope that it would be enough. Should I call for help? Who even could call for help?

"Foollegg," I hissed, my tears falling freely now. "Was this the Agency? What did they do to you?"

I pressed down on his stomach, hard, but the sheet must have had some kind of hospital starch on it because there wasn't a trace of blood on it. I pushed down harder, trying to stop him from bleeding out.

How he could actually be bleeding out, of all things, was completely beside me.

His hand squeezed around the sheet, pulling it further down in his stomach. I put my own hand on his, shocked to see it free of blood. Even I hadn't managed to do anything. He nodded, his breaths coming out in short, hard rasps.

My impossible man was impossibly dying.

"They said they only wanted me." His lips curled into a smile, warm and bright like a spring morning, before he coughed and send it all to hell. "But they lied, Sally. They are coming for you. They want you and Blayde to burn."

"Who? The Agency?" His words barely registered. His light was dimming, taking my heart with it. "Zander, are you—?"

"Dying?" he interrupted, coughing lightly, the red liquid seeping through his lips. "I think so. This wouldn't be the first time."

"You can't die," I said, incapable of holding tears back any longer. "You can't, Zander. You can do anything, but you can't do this."

"My time is up. I can't protect you anymore, Sally. You have to fight. They're coming."

"You can't die," I repeated, still disbelieving. This could not be happening. It defied the laws of the universe. "We have to fight them together. I can't do this without you; I can't do this alone."

"You have to," he said, or more accurately, exhaled. His voice was so faint now I wasn't sure I was even hearing him speak or was just putting words in his mouth. "You have to fight them. You have to."

"Stay with me, Zander," I pleaded, reaching for his hand. "I'm right here. You don't need to go anywhere. Just wait. Your cells will regenerate. It's just taking some more time, that's all."

His breathing got more strained with every word he attempted to utter. "I'm going."

"Zander, the light in the tunnel is a trap. It's a train. Don't walk into the train."

"I love you."

His eyes fluttered shut, and his breathing stopped. I stifled yet another scream. This was just temporary. Just five minutes of death.

I forced myself to remove my hand from his belly. The sheet hadn't done anything. The blood had only spread out and around the wound but avoided my fingers like it was contaminated.

I watched. I waited.

*Heal.*

*Come on, heal.*

But the cells were frozen. Dead.

Seconds passed. Each tick of the clock on my bedside longer than the last. Seconds turned to minutes. Minutes that felt like an eternity.

Three hundred seconds.

Five minutes had passed.

And Zander was still unconscious.

No.

Zander was dead.

I screamed into the night, my entire being ripping to pieces as I shrieked into the night. Zander could not be dead. He couldn't be. He just couldn't be.

Yet he was.

And the Alliance was coming. The Agency was here, and they knew how to *kill* us. Blayde could already be dead if they'd gone for her next, which they probably had seeing as how Zander had time to speak with me. Which meant I was next.

Zander was dead, and there was nothing between me and the Agency.

Well, maybe Zander's hissing, terrifying corpse as it sprung up, clapping his hands against my ears, sharp stabbing driving deep into my skull. That was enough to make me scream all over again. But I couldn't even hear it. The drilling of metal against bone was filling my ears, ringing through my skull, my head a gong.

I reached up instinctively to cover my ears and found other hands there, not the strong, square hands that Zander had so tenderly wrapped around mine, but long, talon-like fingers that wrapped around the back of my head and forced the drill further inside. The cruel hands held on tighter, and Zander's face distorted in concentration. Only it couldn't have been Zander, not with teeth like that.

Snap. A new ringing filled my head, mixing with my anger and fear. Zander's face, already white, drained of all remaining color in an instant.

# INALIENABLE

Now was my chance. I grabbed the hands firmly and threw my head forward, slamming into Zander's nose.

This time, the scream wasn't mine. I pulled back, the hands falling from my skull, two large, red spikes extending from the palms. The drilling stopped instantly, and all the pressure inside my head was gone.

The ringing only got louder.

"What are you?" spike-handed Zander hissed before melting into a puddle in the floor. A puddle that slid and moved, rushing along and up the wall, escaping through the ventilation grate.

I collapsed, exhausted, pushing myself away from the light with my feet. My hands still gripped my head. The ringing was still there, intensifying, a feedback loop inside my very thoughts. I couldn't make sense of my brain words. I couldn't sense make my brain words. Couldn't words from brain made I.

I clenched my teeth, breathing deep and reaching my fingers behind my ears. I cringed, more out of shock than pain, at the depths of the holes. They were already beginning to close, close around the source of the sound, and I dug in deep, scratching until I pulled out the quarter-sized metal plate behind my ear. It was split in two. Crushed.

My translator sputtered and sparked to death in my hands.

Well, at least the ringing had stopped. But there went the most awesome piece of tech I had ever owned.

I stuffed it under my pillow when my door flew open, letting in two nurses, the same two women we had seen at Peter's side the night before. The taller of the two did a quick double take, her eyes darting from the empty floor to my bed, as if she knew what had been there mere moments before.

"Bad dream, sweetie?" she asked, almost tenderly, reaching for me as her colleague extracted pills from a bottle in her pocket.

"No. No," I said. Since when had I started trembling? "There was a thing here. It looked like Zander. Made me think he was dead. Then it attacked me."

My hand wasn't as steady as I liked when I lifted it to point at the floor. You can't blame me, not after all that. But there was no evidence there. Even my hands were clean, as if I had never held him. As if he hadn't just died in my arms.

"You've had a bad dream, that's all. Don't worry. It's all gone now." Her colleague took my outstretched arm, pressing a needle into the skin. I hardly felt it. I didn't even have the energy to ask her what she was doing to me.

The other nurse handed me a cup and some pills. "Take this."

"But … it wasn't a dream," I said, or at least I think I said. Words were a little slurry at this point. "I wasn't sleeping."

"These will help," she said, pushing them toward me.

"What are these?" I asked.

"Medicine."

"What kind?"

"It helps you sleep."

"Like Nyquil?"

"It's not something off the shelf," she said. "Go ahead, take it. By tomorrow, the dream won't even be a memory." She sat in front of me, staring. I shivered.

"No, thanks. I'll be fine."

"Take it."

"No."

"Doctor's orders."

I shrugged. No harm done. I wasn't even sure if medicine worked the same on me as it once had.

She handed me the pills, and I swallowed them, taking the water next to wash them down. She helped me back into bed, tucking in the sheet around me with a motherly kindness.

"Sleep well." She switched off my light as she walked out of the room.

I stared at the ceiling and quickly knew the answer with a small wave of relief: the pills had no effect on me. Which was for the better because now was most definitely not a time for sleep.

What had just happened? Zander had died. Then he wasn't dead. Then he attacked me. Then he was gone.

My brain pinched.

Wait, what? Pinched?

It suddenly felt too hot in the room. But it was February, wasn't it? Still didn't change the fact that it was too hot to sleep.

I jumped up to my feet. No, it wasn't just the heat. My hands were shaking. Trembling. And my head—the ringing had gone when I had pulled out the broken translator, but now it felt too full, swollen.

My head was spinning. It wasn't supposed to spin.

I tried to stand but slumped to the floor. I couldn't stand anymore. My skin was burning, hot like coals, the linoleum floor freezing cold to my touch. I was on fire. Water dripped off my head—no, rushed like a torrent. Never before had I sweated this much in my life, not even when I had run through a jungle to get away from an alien troll.

Instinct took over. The pressure had to go. The fear too big, the brain bursting. I feebly pushed myself up, dropping my head against the floor. Again. Again. My head banged over and over, repeatedly bashing against the hard floor.

I wasn't in control anymore. My mind was working violently to protect itself and only itself as my brain expanded inside my skull. I reached up to my head, my arm shaking. What was I doing? Why?

My head was about to burst.

*Maybe I should just let it burst? It'll just grow back.*

But it had to go.

I slammed my head on the floor and broke it like a nut.

Some unknown time later, I woke up with blood pooling around my head, but at least my head wasn't exploding anymore.

Anymore? When had it hurt in the first place?

# INALIENABLE

What had I done? Had I done anything?

I must have fallen asleep waiting for the Agency to get me, fallen off the bed and somehow cracked my head open like an egg. Which made no sense. This was a mental institution, a hospital. These places were supposed to be impossible to injure yourself on a normal day, let alone to do it by accident.

There was a dream—a dream of what? It bothered me that I couldn't remember, couldn't quite put my finger on what had bothered me so much.

*Zander.*

*Must check on Zander.*

*Why?*

*Because it's important, stupid.*

*But why is it important?*

*Because.*

Because I was afraid. I knew it. Why? I didn't know. Maybe I just couldn't remember.

I grabbed my balled-up bed sheet, wiping the bloody mess on the floor. My blood, right? I felt my heart in my throat as I realized the blood must have been mine, but what exactly had happened, my mind would not share with me. Panic rose within.

I ran my hand through my hair, feeling the sticky substance there, and it left a red mark on my fingers as I pulled them away. More blood.

*Shit.*

Evidence for all to see.

*The evidence of what, exactly?*

I needed to go see Zander.

I felt oddly nauseous, dizzy on my feet. I didn't think this was supposed to happen to me, not anymore. Not after I'd changed.

I found my eyes staring at the center of the room, dead center of the pool of moonlight. Nothing. Yet I couldn't help but look. I shivered as the ghost of a memory flashed before my eyes, a fleeting instant carrying the sheer terror I had felt before. The instant was so horrifying, so realistic, that I found myself gripping the wall behind me for support. But there was nothing there. The floor was empty, just as it was supposed to be.

I felt a shiver travel from my ears to my toes. Was this what being roofied felt like?

Instinct pulled me through the void between places, and instinct lead me back to him.

"Sally?" Zander asked, as I collapsed on his floor, exhausted and terrified after jumping clear across the institute by feel alone. "What happened?"

My own questions, my own words. I knew I had said the same to him. Only I hadn't. I had said it to the wrong Zander.

"I'm not sure," I stammered before collapsing on his floor, my legs giving out beneath me. Oops. "Can you help me up?"

"What's wrong?"

"Serious *déjà* vu. I think."

He picked me up carefully, placing me on his bed and wrapping his comforter around me. I was shaking now, my teeth chattering. Hell, I was going into shock.

"I heard screaming," he said. "Did you see who it was?"

"I think it was me," I said, through still chattering teeth. "I can't remember. I was sitting on my bed, then I was on the floor. And I think you were there."

He shook his head, sitting on his bed and wrapping a warm arm around me, pulling me close. That seemed to be the cure I needed because my shaking stopped at once.

"Oh, don't cry. It's okay," he said. "You're safe now."

"I don't—I don't know why I'm crying." I wiped the tears away with a finger. "It's like—hold on, Zander, I think you died."

"A nightmare? I guess this place really does induce them."

"But … look."

I pulled away from him only slightly, showing him the side of my head. The wound might have been gone, but the blood that it had left behind was still caught in my hair. He went rigid against me.

"What happened to you?"

"I can't remember, Zan," I replied, shaking my head. "But something tells me it's the same thing that happened to Peter. And maybe to everyone in this damned place."

And as much as I wanted that to be my dramatic ending, as much as I wanted to have that stiff upper-lip and confidence that all this would get better, I broke down crying in his arms and couldn't be coaxed back to my cold, dark room where I would be alone again.

# EIGHT

## BLAYDE GETS FREAKY
## WITH PRESENTATION TOOLS

**"YOU'RE GOING TO HAVE TO START OVER. YOU'RE** not making any sense."

Oatmeal tasted even better than yesterday. I scarfed it down as Blayde watched me from across the table, her eyes peeled. Zander's hand would not let go of mine, probably making it hard for him to eat, but he managed all the same.

"A part of my memory is missing," I said. "Something happened to me last night, and it couldn't have been pretty."

"Okay." She nodded as if this wasn't news to her.

"And my translator was destroyed." I showed her the small metal pieces before shoving them back into my pocket. "Which means I couldn't have imagined it." She nodded again, still saying nothing. "What do I do?"

"The same thing anyone does when they lose something: retrace your steps. Tell me what you do remember. We'll work to recreate the missing images from there."

A shiver I could not control spread through my body. "I'm not sure I want to recreate the images."

"Look, do you want to know why you have a hole in your mind or what?"

"Yup. Yes, I do."

"Fine. So, tell me what you do remember."

"Um …" Easier said than done. Thinking back when you're missing time doesn't exactly have a roadmap. I probed the edges of the memory hole. "I remember— oh, a dream."

"Wow, useful. Dreaming. Don't worry, we'll figure out what happened. And punish those accountable for giving you shit nightmares. Is it the Sandman or the crabapple blanket on Earth? I know it's one or the other."

"Come on, I'm being serious."

"So am I. Bad dreams seem to be rampant in this place. Ask my brother if he's had any."

"Oh, come on, you two are still giving each other the cold shoulder?"

"I'm shunning him. That's different."

"It's still childish." I reached for my toast, disappointed the oatmeal was already gone. "Are you trying to punish him for something?"

She shrugged. "Possibly."

"For what?"

"He's becoming soft." She raised her eyebrows. "And, unfortunately, this isn't the kind of place that looks kindly upon siblings sparring out their differences. Not that we have any swords lying around anyway. Zander needs a bucket of cold water in the face, so to speak. Or a few stabs through the heart."

The memory—vague and misty as it was—came rushing back. Zander: his nose broken and bleeding. His hands: long spikes from his palms. I stared, eyes going dry. Blinked.

*All a dream, right?*

"Oh, come off it." I rolled my eyes. I guess I inherited the ability from her. "We've got too much on our plate to be petty about anything. What is this even about, really? Actually, we might be in an ideal place to get you both some couples counselling."

"We are not a couple," she snapped, "and I don't quite appreciate your tone."

"Family therapy, then. I don't know. I don't care. I've got my own family to look out for, a beast preying on bad dreams and stealing memories, and all this while trying to keep the two of you out of the clutches of your worst enemy. So, excuse me for being snippy."

"They're not our *worst* enemy," she muttered, looking down into her plate. "Just the nearest."

"Attention, can I have all eyes here, please?"

I turned my head for my eyes to rest on the face of Dr. Smith, her eyes bright with excitement. She held in her hand a drinking glass, tapping it ever so slightly with the side of a knife.

"Since the storm two nights ago, a few branches and tree limbs on the grounds are in dire need of clearing up. Anyone who wants to help with the clean-up crew can volunteer for the day, as long as your doctor gives you proper authorization. Just find a nurse and tell them you're interested. It'll probably last most of the day. Did I mention you get an extra helping of jello if you volunteer?"

"Yay, jello," I muttered.

"Yay, jello!" Zander grinned, his enthusiasm shining through. "Anyone fancy some fresh air?"

"What is this jello?" asked Blayde. "Is that the species of meat we've been eating? Anyway, this sounds good. An opportunity for fresh air. And free speech."

"What if it's a trap?" asked Zander. "This is all too convenient. This could be how the Agency gets us— sends us on a clean-up crew, whisks us away, claims we made a run for it to cover it up."

I shuddered. "Good point."

"About the fresh air? I know, right?" said Blayde.

"Do you really expect me to relay everything Zander just said and pretend you didn't hear his entirely fair point?"

She picked up her full glass of orange juice, throwing her head back and chugging the contents in one gulp. She wiped her face with her free hand, placing the glass back down, smiling. "Shall we?"

"Fine. But you two need to work this out. I'm tired of being the adult here."

"I don't know what you're talking about," said Zander but got up nonetheless.

About half an hour later, we found ourselves in brightly colored jumpsuits again and gloves on our hands, braving the February early morning chill just to get some free space. We took a fallen limb over to the east of the main building that was blocking the road, the large pieces already chopped down by one of the institute's caretakers, leaving only the small branches to clear. Our task was simple: Gather every piece we could, fill the bucket, and then carry the bucket to the huge brush pile that was being built a safe distance away from the institute.

Mindless, repetitive work. Good for the mind.

So long as we weren't about to be abducted. I kept an eye on the sky as if they'd just send a ship; I didn't expect them to be subtle.

I picked up a tiny brindle with two fingers, dropping it into the bucket with a dull thump. And I did the same again, just waiting for one of the siblings to speak up.

They were just as alert as I was. They were just being dumb shits about it.

"Do you think we can talk?" I asked, begging for an opening.

"I doubt Barker gives a shit about what we think," said Blayde, pointing to the guard sitting on a downed log a few feet away, looking off into the distance as if we weren't here at all. Not that there was any doubt in my mind that he was just as alert as we were.

"Right. So, is this a trap?"

"It might be," said Zander.

"Great, just great."

"Issues at hand," said Blayde. "First and foremost, impending Agency abduction. Second, terrible hospital service."

"And third, bringing the Alliance down."

"Since when are we destroying the Alliance?" she sputtered. "A bit of a leap there, Sal."

"Blayde, they're so deeply entrenched in my planet that I don't even feel safe here anymore," I said. It was strange how my muscles tensed when I spoke of them, as if my anger were on a leash and had started to pull. "They're meant to protect Terrans from off-world interference, but I don't trust that they do. They don't have our best interests at heart."

"Even so, it doesn't mean we have to *destroy* them," she said. "The Alliance has stood for thousands of years. It's one of the pillars that keeps this galaxy together. We can't go around destroying every interstellar conglomerate we don't like."

"Isn't that exactly what you do?"

"We have our limits, Sally," said Zander. "Blayde, you're unshunned. This is bigger than us."

"Finally!" I said, loud enough that Barker looked up from his mile-long stare. I waved at him awkwardly, and he went right back to it.

"Oh, I'm not un-shunning him back," she said.

"Blayde."

"Fine, fine," she scoffed. "Anyway, Sally, the Alliance has quite a few practices we don't approve of, but they also do a lot of good."

"No, the two of *you* are out doing good, clearing up after them and the carnage they leave behind," I spat. "And then they take credit, blame you, and call you terrorists. Meanwhile, their Agency has free reign on Earth, my home planet, and they act as though they own the place. They did nothing about Cross. They did nothing about the Youpaf! At the very least, we need to bring down the Agency, and then get you out of the Alliance's scopes. It's not like I've forgotten where they get their child-hires from."

"Fine, fine," she said, throwing her hands up in the air, tossing branches all over. "We'll get out of here, and then we're going to take down some of the biggest players in this galaxy. Happy?"

"I can't tell if you're being sarcastic," said Zander, "but that sounds like a good plan."

"Again, this is a goal, not a plan," she said. "You see why you're having problems with following through on your so-called plans?"

"Then let's focus on something closer to home, so to speak. What the hell is going on at this hospital?"

Blayde nodded. "The dreams. You need to remember yours. Start with what you do recall, and we'll go from there."

"Only I don't think they were dreams," I said. "I think … I think Zander *was* in my room last night."

"Oh, lovely." She crossed her arms over her chest. "Please. Spare no detail."

"And, just to set things straight, I *wasn't* in your room last night," Zander added.

I rubbed my temples. Maybe extra blood flow would give me extra clear recall. "The light scared me. I remember when I woke up, on the floor, I kept avoiding the light in my room. But there was nothing there."

"Okay, the dark isn't the scary bit. It's what the light showed you that freaked you out."

"Or what it didn't show me." I shrugged. "Nothing was there."

"So, we can say for certain that something was there at some point." Blayde clapped her hands as I grabbed a handful of the twigs to put on the pile. "Now I need you to picture your room. Just your room. Just the floor in your room. The small spot in the center. The pool of light. You got it?" I nodded. "Now, what's there?"

"Someone's there," I said, faded figments of fiction flickering in front of my eyes. "Someone close. They're bleeding. There's so much blood."

"Go on," she urged. Zander watched from the side, not daring to say a word. "Who is it?"

"They're not supposed to be there. Not supposed to be dying." I felt my eyelids stick together, impossible to pull them open. When had I even shut them? "But he's bleeding. He's dying. Right there, in my arms."

"Who."

"Zander," I replied, without thinking. Yet when the words left my mouth, I felt the shock of the scene once again, as if the name was the key to seeing the truth, the key that unlocked my mind. Images flooded in in a torrent, their painful stories burning at the edges of my mind.

I shrieked, dropping the twigs as I relived the previous night, every instant stretched to last a lifetime, to inflict more pain than the first time. My hands rose unconsciously to my head, holding my ears where a phantom screech of feedback had pained me the night before.

I rubbed the bare patches of skin behind my ear with an index finger, feeling the smoothness that I had not felt in months. My translator had sacrificed itself for me.

"Sally!" Zander rushed to my side as I blinked in confusion.

"Shut her up!" Blayde hushed. "You don't want to alert a nurse, do you?"

Barker glanced over, and I waved, faking a smile. Amazingly, he said nothing. Went back to staring off into the distance. He was either a terrible guard or I was an amazing actress. I highly doubted the latter.

"That's the least of your problems," said Blayde. "But you dragged me out here to talk about the nightmare you had of my brother dying?"

I shook my head. "It wasn't a nightmare, it was—"

"So real? So vivid you could feel it? Yeah. That's called a nightmare, dumbass."

"Blayde," I snapped. "The translator didn't just snap in half for no reason. Zander was dead, then he attacked me. Drilled into my head with his … palm horns."

"So, Zander from, I dunno, the future came back to break your translator. With palm horns. To what end?"

"I can't envision a future where I'd ever want to hurt Sally," Zander snarled.

"I'm still not convinced it is Future You doing all this."

"Neither am I." His face was contorted in confusion. "Try to understand my reasoning. Why I would do something like this. How? It's not possible to control a jump with such precision. And through time! It's like trying to throw a ball into the air and hope that it will land on a grain of sand on the other side of the world. And did I mention? The grain of sand doesn't exist yet. *Not* what anyone would call easy."

"Not easy at all." I nodded. "I also remember feeling this deep dread that everything was falling apart. Like … the Alliance was already here. I think I was supposed to warn Blayde?"

"Future Zander must have wanted to warn us," said Blayde, "and change the past. So, we're supposed to do something about it."

"Why would I ever hurt Sally, though?" asked Zander.

"And why would I forget all these details? I don't think it was Future Zander. I think it was whatever the patients and nurses are calling 'bad dreams.' Only they're not dreams. Something is really happening to the patients here. It's just that they can't remember."

"Maybe you needed to get rid of her translator for some reason that would soon become apparent," said Blayde. "Or just because you wanted to drill through the past version of your girlfriend's brain on a whim and thought a dramatic death could add some color? Euh, needless to say, worst—"

He picked up a branch off the ground, launching it at his sister with amazing accuracy. The limb hit her straight in the face with a loud crack.

"Wha'd'ya do that for?" I asked, watching Blayde's face turn from pale to bruised, then from bruised back to smooth pallor before filling with her usual tan, the blanket of purple on her face spreading out then receding back, like watching ink spill in reverse.

"What do you expect? She deserved it."

She blinked once, sitting back up straight and snapping her neck back into place before getting to her feet.

"I did deserve that, and I apologize." She smiled. Then she turned around, facing the security guard on his log, and dropped her hands to her hips. "And you. You're shit at your job, you know that?"

"I beg your pardon?"

"Except if your job is to watch without interfering," she said. "It's either that, or you see two mentally ill patients beating each other with sticks and you're too lazy to do anything about it."

He disappeared in an instant.

Simultaneously, the siblings leapt forward, bullets from a loaded gun, their legs carrying them forward faster than the eye could track. I watched—jaw to the ground—as they pelted into the forest, their feet barely making a noise as they propelled themselves forward through the trees, disappearing from sight in seconds.

I couldn't just stand there. I took a deep breath, gathered my wits about me, and dashed off after them, following the blur of movement in front of me between the tight trees. There was no slowing down. It was full speed ahead or not at all. The air hit my face, trying to hold me back. Drag is such a drag. But there was no stopping me.

With a loud thump and a yelp of surprise, Zander brought Barker down with a beautiful tackle, the man's face slamming into a pile of leaves. He grabbed his neck, violently jerking him up into a sitting position, crouching in front of him so that they were face to face. Barker snarled at his captors, fierce and animalistic, his eyes losing any impression of humanity. He glared at Zander then at Blade, his eyes finally resting on me, the hatred seeping through and stabbing at me like little daggers. It seemed his shoulder might have gotten dislocated in the tackle by the way it was dangling at his side.

"Cheap skin wrap," Zander concluded. "You know, I thought your people would spend more on disguising their grunts."

# INALIENABLE

The captive spat on the ground. "I'm not telling you anything."

"Oh great. A big damn hero," Blayde growled. She reached up her sleeve, pulling out her laser, and flipped it between her fingers. Ready to destroy a man with office equipment.

He must not have seen Blayde's weapon of choice before and seemed entirely unfazed by the threat. He threw his head back, opening his mouth wide to laugh.

"What?" he asked. "That's all you can muster?"

Blayde walked up close to the man, crouching in front of him so that she could stare right into his eyes.

"Have you ever been to Jakeefa?" she asked, flipping the laser in the air and catching it repeatedly.

The captive shook his head, staring right back into her stormy gray eyes, a snicker forming at the side of his mouth.

"But I'm sure you've heard the stories," Blayde cooed. "Sure of it, even. Come on, admit it. They were the ones that scared you most at night. The ones that kept you up, even when you transitioned out of childhood. The ones that kept you scared of the dark. You must have heard of the warriors of Jakeefa."

"So what if I did?" he snapped, his eyes unblinking.

"I heard the stories too." She grinned. "I mean, it's hard to *not* hear them. And they inspired me. So, do you know what I did?"

Barker shook his head, trembling slightly.

"I went to Jakeefa. I went to their capital, to their master of arms. I asked if she would train me in the art of knife wielding, in the art of the blade. And you know what she said?"

"What?"

"She said no. She would not train me."

He laughed. "Why are you telling me this?"

"Because that's not where the story ends." Blayde sneered. "There's more."

"I'm not interested."

Blayde continued on without his blessing. "So, I walked the length of their planet. I crossed the unnamed sea, I climbed their highest mountain, and I found the man who hated her more than anything else in the world. The one who wanted her to return to the dust that she came from so bad it was killing him. He agreed to train me. And he taught me everything he knew. *Everything.* And as the tradition of their world willed it, I did not train with metal until my first kill. I did not touch an iron blade throughout my training."

"So?"

"So, I climbed down that mountain. I crossed that ocean. I walked the planet back around until I reached their capital. Until I reached their master of arms. The most feared woman in the cosmos, the one who made you check under your bed before you went to sleep for Jakeefian assassins. The woman whose name kept you up nights on end. The one who razed entire armies with nothing but her blade." She paused, waiting for him to interrupt, though he did not. "The Alliance calls me the Iron for a reason. And I prefer to call myself Blayde."

# INALIENABLE

Zander got up, leaving the paralyzed man to deal with his sister, alone. She flipped the pointer once more in her hand, the tip looking more menacing than it had before. The goosebumps that appeared were as real as any. "Now, would you like to know why?"

The man pulled his hand back, but she grabbed it before he could bring his arm out of reach. A shiver passed through his body, and his fingers started to tremble.

Zander put a protective arm in front of me. "Don't."

"I just wanted him to know," she said, baring her teeth, "that the Agency didn't tell him who he was actually dealing with."

"Look, I was just here to make sure you three weren't going anywhere. That's all, I swear! That's all!" Barker stammered.

"And you never assaulted Sally?"

"What? No!" he said rapidly, the fear obvious in his eyes. "Look, I overheard the whole thing, but I had nothing to do with what happened to her. From what the other guards have told me, the nightmares have been going on for years. It's just something that happens at hospitals like this."

"Don't lie to me!" Blayde ordered, pushing the pointer against his throat. "What did you have to do with it?"

"I didn't do anything! No way! I was just here to observe."

She threw him back on the leaves, rising to her feet in an instant and slamming her foot down on his chest before he could even move.

"So, tell me, Agency grunt, how do you report to Foollegg?"

He reached into his jacket, pulling out an ordinary pen. She grabbed it from his grasp.

"Micro transmitter," she muttered, throwing it back to Zander, who caught it one-handed. He gave it to me.

"Look for the antenna," Zander advised. "Transmitter pens are common enough. Where else do you think Earth intelligence agencies got the idea from? There are two main forms. " He twisted the handle up to the sky. "Model one. Great because you can still write with it. Then there's model two, which you just point to the sky and click on. You can't use the actual pen, but it gets rid of the telltale handle hinge."

"Right. How do we get rid of it?"

"Water." Zander chuckled. "A glass of it if you're in a restaurant, but spit works just as well. Or …" He dropped it on the ground, crushing it under the heel of his shoe. He shrugged. "Don't worry. He'll have a panic button somewhere there."

"So, let me get this straight," I said. "Salt. Water. I could get rid of an Alliance spy by simply bringing them to the beach? Why the hell are the off-worlders flocking to Florida, then?"

"Not all of their operatives need skin wraps." Zander pocketed the smashed bits of pen. "Pyrina was established by humans, after all. Distant cousins of yours. Speaking of, we probably need to do something about the old, forgotten legends, right? Seems ironic we keep forgetting."

# INALIENABLE

With a swift movement, Blayde punched Barker, knocking him out cold.

"A hand here?" she asked.

The siblings proceeded to sling the man over their shoulders, leaning forward a little to make it look as if they were struggling under his weight.

"You coming or not?" Blayde yelled back to me.

I had not noticed that I was frozen to the spot until she pointed it out. I was standing, paralyzed, in the same spot I had been for the past quarter of an hour. I shook myself out of my reverie, grinning slightly.

"I'm coming," I replied, keeping up with their pace.

A nurse rushed to our side to help with the unconscious man as soon as we emerged from the thicket of the trees into the clear patch of lawn in front of the institute.

"We found him like this in the woods," Zander said dryly. "A tree limb fell on him. We got worried."

The nurse nodded, and with the help of other institute employees, they managed to drag the man back into the main building. With our guard out of commission, we were brought inside too.

"Do we still get the extra jello?" asked Zander, but he didn't get an answer. Instead, we found ourselves back in the rec room, locked inside for the rest of the day.

"Well, at least we lost our Agency plant for a little while," said Blayde. "But why would Future Zander come back and break your translator? It just doesn't add up."

"It doesn't sound like me." Zander shrugged.

"And what about the blood?" I asked. "Something happened to my brain. I mean, the memories were gone. They're barely here now."

"What's odd is that everyone else at the institute seems to have horrifying nightmares they can't remember. Except if what you're telling me is true, all of them are real."

"We need to see what really happens. But how do we know who's next?"

"Daisy-May?" I suggested.

"Seriously?"

"Jeffrey, remember?" I pointed out. "She seems extra jumpy. He sees her once a month. What if he's legitimately going to come visit her?"

"He's a figment of her imagination." Blayde rolled her eyes. "He's not going to come here!"

"They think we're crazy and don't believe you're aliens. What if it's the same problem with her?"

"So, you're saying she's an off-worlder?" Zander asked.

"With our luck?" I laughed. "Well, for all we know … sorry. Honestly, I highly doubt it. Anyway, if we're telling the truth, she can be too."

"So, you're saying Jeffrey, her imaginary friend that makes her rob banks, is going to come and visit her in an institute for the criminally insane, and he's done this before without anyone noticing?"

"It's a work in progress," I said.

Blayde clapped a hand down on my shoulder. Was I wrong or was this pride? "It's worth checking out."

"Okay then, it's settled." Zander grinned. "Sally and I will—"

"No." Blayde shook her head. "Sally and *I* will go check it out. You, on the other hand, are going to sleep tonight."

"Oh, come on."

"What? It's my turn to do something fun. Just be happy I'm talking to you again."

He sighed heavily as worry knotted in my gut.

"Don't worry, though." Blayde grinned from ear to ear. "Because I have a plan."

# NINE

## A SERIES OF UNFORTUNATE ATTACKS

**"SERIOUSLY?" I HISSED. "THIS IS YOUR PLAN?"**

"If the brilliance of it evades you, I can understand."

"She is literally a foot above our heads."

"So you'd better keep that yapper of yours closed then, hmm?"

Arguing with Blayde seemed like a Sisyphean task, one I was doomed to repeat throughout eternity without ever making any progress. She paid no attention to me, her eyes staring into the darkness of the room, like I should probably have been doing. On the bed above us, Daisy-May shifted slightly, the slats making an irritating squeak.

So far, no dice. Since lights out, we had been waiting for something, anything, but Jeffrey had not come to her room yet, thus we had to stay and keep an eye on things.

# INALIENABLE

Not very pleasant, all in all.

And on the subject of unpleasantness, Blayde had completely stopped speaking to me. Which was fine because I didn't want to say anything to her either. The only reason she had wanted this mission was to get at her brother oh so slightly, and this must have been the least creative way she could have accomplished that. It was definitely the most boring one.

We had been getting so close before the arrest. I had been starting to think of her as one of my closest friends, like the sister I never had. But something was changing, and I didn't know what it was or what to do about it.

Every instant between the second hand's reliable tick seemed like hours, my time gliding away like swans on a lake. Evil swans gliding gracefully over their pond, ready to bite you if you got too close.

Stupid swans. No better than peacocks, with their beady, little eyes of evil.

Oh great. Mind stuck on evil birds. How original.

"I don't think it's going to show," I muttered. "I think Daisy-May's sleeping. She doesn't seem to be waiting for him."

"Oh, she's definitely sleeping," Blayde snapped. "I've been setting my breathing to the rhythm of her snores. Something you should better learn to do in case you're in a stakeout situation like this again."

"This isn't a stakeout. More like … monster watch."

"Still haven't eliminated the evil Future Zander theory yet."

"Girls," came a whisper in the dark, low enough to send a shiver up my spine. Hella creepy vibes.

I glanced in her direction. "What do we do?"

Daisy-May's increasingly loud snoring was the perfect cover. Blayde slid out from under the bed, ushering for me to follow. I pulled myself up, getting to my feet with much less grace than she had. Despite my still improving vision, I couldn't see the man in the dark.

"Jeffrey? Is that you?" Blayde hissed.

Zander's face appeared in the darkness, cold and strangely drenched in sweat. Relief and fear folded over me as one.

"Ah, speak of the devil," said Blayde. "What did I tell you? Future Zander is the one going around terrorizing patients."

"Present Zander, if you please," he said. "Come with me."

He disappeared, probably jumping to the hall since there was nowhere else he could really go. I traded pointed stares with Blayde.

"Do you think it's him?" I asked. After what I remembered from last night, I wasn't sure if I could trust my own senses.

"Whether it is or isn't, it'll tell us something." She pointed at the sleeping girl. "Aren't they so peaceful when they sleep?"

I glanced at Daisy-May's face, her hair wild and disheveled, her nose turned up in her sleep. She snorted slightly.

"Cutest thing ever?" I replied sarcastically. "Wait, what do you mean "they?""

"Earthlings," Blayde smiled, her words both an encouragement and a reproach.

"Are you trying to get a rise out of me?"

"Just testing out the waters of this new you. Snark suits you."

I sighed heavily, making my way to the door and jumping out into the light of the hallway where Zander waited, his body flush with the wall, a look of confusion on his pale face.

"What?" his sister asked, aggravated. "What could possibly bring you to take us off mission? Jeffrey could be in there right now. If we don't—"

"I seriously doubt Jeffrey's anywhere right now."

"And why's that?"

"Because there's a clown in my room."

"A what now?" I stammered.

"A clown. In my room."

Blayde couldn't answer. She was too busy keeping herself from laughing out loud. She bit down on her own finger hard enough to break the skin, snickering from her nose.

Zander glared at her. "I'm not joking. It's an actual clown."

"Is there any other kind?" she sputtered through her bloody lips.

"I mean, red nose"—he mimed, poking his own—"big shoes, animal balloon. Over-the-top makeup. Crazy, synthetic hair. Just … standing in my room."

"Is he still there?" I asked.

"How should I know? I'm here, not over there!"

"Idiot!" Blayde swore under her breath. "We could be missing what's happening in her room right now, all because you think there's a clown in your room?"

"It was making me uncomfortable. I had a right to leave."

She sighed heavily. "Fine. Sally, go check it out. I'll stay here and do some actual investigative work. You see? I don't mind you sharing the air on your own time."

The place where Blayde had been standing now held nothing but air, the image of her fading from my retinas. Her stunned brother shrugged, staring at the spot where she had disappeared.

"My dear little sister," he said, shaking his head slowly. "Always so caring."

"But seriously?" I asked. "A clown?"

"Come and see for yourself," he offered, extending a hand.

My fingers wrapped around his, the warm skin a comfort as the cold of trans-dimensional travel surrounded me, locations flashing before my eyes so quickly I could barely make them out. I held on to the reassuring hand, the calm exerted keeping me from spiraling off into space.

It wasn't supposed to go like this. Zander was anxious; I could feel it, though how, I could not tell. But his nerves were high, as if a simple stakeout was more than just a simple stakeout, as if it were much, much more. He said not a word, not like you could say anything in the in-between place when you were neither here nor there. His silence was heavy, like a weight pulling us both down.

Odd. I thought clowns were meant to make you feel happy.

We stopped jumping in the hallway in front of his room, and I unwillingly let go of his hand. He put a finger to his lips, pointing to the slit in his door. I snapped my mouth closed.

Well, I'll be a monkey's uncle; there was most definitely a clown in his room.

Zander had been right. It was as much of a clown as a clown could be. The face was painted a pale white, a massive red smile plastered childishly over his mouth and eyes, the color slightly too bloody for my taste. His hair was a deep shade of purple, poking from a bright yellow hat and falling shaggily down to his shoulders. A huge pink flower protruded from the outlandish hat, a cheesy, blank smiley face painted on a white heart.

His clothes were classic. His legs were covered in a colorful argyle, oversized pants. He wore a ruffled shirt, each fold alternating in color; hues of blues and reds ran like a torrent from the comedian's neck, like liquid running across his breast. Another flower adorned the disaster, this one bright green and wearing sunglasses. The shoes, the same shade of green as the flowers, were twice as long as any clown's should be in any possible rational thinking, though I was certain that the shoe on the left was slightly shorter than its partner.

It could have been hilarious, but it was just … staring.

"What should we do?" I asked. We were just standing in a corner watching it, not that that was very helpful.

"You?" He thought for a split second. "Go back to Blayde and tell her I wasn't lying. I'll deal with the clown."

"I'm not leaving you alone with that thing."

"It's just a person!" he hissed. "With a balloon!"

"Then why aren't we more worried about it?"

"A clown who just appeared in my room? I don't have a thing against clowns in general, but a man dressed in a clown suit holding a balloon in the middle of the night, not needing any doors—"

"Creepy?"

"Peculiar."

"Fine, be that way, Mr. I'm-scared-of-nothing. Just say hi to the clown. Admit it, it's kind of freaking you out."

"Merely intriguing me."

"As if."

He rolled his eyes. "Stay back, okay? I don't want you to get hurt."

"Remember what we talked about before all this? About me being fine with risks?" I said, giving his hand a tight squeeze. "I can't get hurt."

"I think last night proved quite the opposite."

I opened my mouth, but nothing came out. I had to admit, he was right about that.

"I'll be back in a sec." He popped a quick kiss on my forehead and disappeared. I checked the hallway—it was still clear—and stared so I could have a direct view on Zander through the slot.

"Hi there!" he said with conviction and enthusiasm. "Nice to meet you. I'm Zander, and your name is …?"

"Clyde."

"Hi, Clyde the clown. So nice to have you in my room in the middle of the night. Can I tell you something?"

"Anything!" the clown said cheerfully, grinning wide. The smile literally reached ear to ear, like a slash in the face. "Would you like a little balloon animal? Do you like poodles?"

"The thing is, Clyde, I don't remember inviting you in. Odd, isn't it? And I'm certain you're a kind man, so I hope you don't mind me asking what exactly you are doing here."

"Finishing some business." Clyde snickered, pulling the balloon down to his level and popping it to reveal a long knife impossibly concealed within.

"Okay, wow. That was a quick turn in the conversation!" Zander took a step back. "Way to get to the point, Clyde."

"Let's put a smile on your face!" The clown waved the knife in front of his face, liking his lips.

"Seriously? You're going to kill me with Joker quotes?"

The walking fashion disaster froze. "What, you think you're funny, funny boy?"

"I thought you were supposed to be the funny one. Seriously, what's with the clown getup?"

The clown took a lunge at Zander, who lightly stepped to the side, like a matador, grabbing the outstretched knife arm and twisting it back, forcing the clown to his knees. The weapon dropped from his grasp and fell to the floor before them, where it melted into sand and slid across the floor as if the creepy clown was also a creepy clown magnet.

"Well, that's new," Zander muttered. "So, I take it you're not an Agency assassin here to kill me, are you?"

The clown hissed, a row of huge, sharp teeth protruding from the front of his mouth. I was certain they hadn't been there before. More horrific, monstrous smiles formed on the fronts of the pink and green flowers.

"Oh, you're not human, either? Or even a clown. I mean, not very funny, are you? Not a good career choice for you, if you ask me. You're insulting a centuries old profession."

The clown creature hissed once, staring into Zander's unflinching eyes. It snarled and snapped its teeth like some kind of wild animal.

"So, what are you doing here?" Zander asked, still calm. The monster remained silent. "You're not here to kill me; you would have been much, much more creative. Maybe you would have had a knife in my side at this point. No, you're not trying to kill me, so why the clown act? The teeth? The knife?"

The creature snarled loudly, the row of needle-like teeth glistening in the pale moonlight that fell into the room. Slowly, it started to melt—or crumble, more accurately. It fell apart, like it were made of pixels or millions of grains of sand dissolving into a large puddle of dust. The blob rapidly scurried away.

Zander leapt at the mass, attempting a perfectly executed rugby tackle. It led nowhere as Zander fell through the mass of sand grains, the blob simply climbing over him on its way up the wall and through the corner vent. I jumped into his room. Too late. There was nothing I could do to help, and any evidence of the clown's presence was gone, dust in the wind. In a very literal sense, just sand up a vent.

"Please tell me you saw that," Zander pleaded, pointing at the metal grate in the ceiling. So, a freakish clown threatened my boyfriend with a knife. And teeth.

"Every second," I replied.

"What in the star system is happening here?"

I shrugged. "Well, one thing's for sure."

"What's that?"

"Future You isn't trying to kill us."

And I thought a psychiatric hospital would be calm. Instead, it seemed much more confusing than anything else, and I hadn't even been here a week yet.

We jumped back to Daisy-May's room, the night still young. Blayde was as we left her under the bed, and we scooted in after her, the three of us barely fitting in the tiny space.

"So? No clown?"

"There was, in fact, a clown." I gave her a short summary. She nodded the whole time, grunting only at the end to change it up a bit.

"So, Future Zander is trying to send melting clowns here? What's the point?"

"I don't think it's Future Zander, but the point still stands that we don't know any of the actual mastermind's motives."

"Well, obviously killing isn't the point." Amazingly, Blayde continued to scowl at her brother as she spoke to me. Impressive in the small confines under the bed. The scowl was the only part of her I could see, her white teeth glistening in the pale moonlight.

"Already gathered as much."

"And it wasn't just to break your translator."

"Got that as well. Blayde, I can keep up, you know. You don't have to walk me through everything."

"She's just thinking aloud," said Zander. "Just go with it. She's cranky. And are we even sure it is Future Me? I mean … why would I try and attack Daisy-May? It seems like "Jeffrey" has been visiting her for months. And why the hell would I send myself a *clown?*"

His sister's expression of anger melted into that of confusion. "You may be onto something, here."

"Hang on," I interjected. "How can we be sure Jeffrey himself isn't just a figment of her imagination? Blayde has been here the whole night so far, and nothing showed up."

"Wrong night?" Blayde shrugged.

Something moved in the dark depths of the room, making me jump to attention. It was impossible to see what it was, the darkness of the room as black as ink and twice as thick.

"Blayde," I hissed.

"I know! What are the odds?"

"Did you even expect him to show up?"

She snorted. "No way."

"Honey, I'm home!" the voice rang out, crystal clear in the silence of the room. Zander reached a protective arm in front of me, pressing us all further under the bed.

Instantly, the light on the bedside table switched on, bathing the room in a cold, white glow. In the middle of it, a smartly dressed businessman in a suit and tie stood tall, a briefcase in hand. His jacket lay folded over his right arm, his blue shirt in sharp contrast with his black silk tie, the letters "JG" emblazoned on his shirt pocket. He grinned from ear to ear.

"Jeffrey!" Daisy-May sat upright. "You're back!"

"What's wrong, honey?" he asked, putting down the briefcase on the floor next to him, leaning it against his leg. "You look pale."

She nodded slightly. "I was worried you wouldn't come."

"Oh, what made you think that?" He sat on the bed next to her. The bed creaked with the added weight. The briefcase was nowhere to be seen. "I always come home."

"I haven't seen you for a month."

"I'm sorry. I would have come sooner if I could."

"I missed you."

"I missed you too." He pulled away, getting to his feet and moving to the center of the room, to the pool of light. "Do you mind if I ask a question?"

"What kind of question?" Daisy-May sat erect, her feet dropping inches in front of my face. Neither she nor Jeffrey seemed to see us, thankfully.

"The truthful kind," Jeffrey responded. "Why did you do this to me?"

She froze, paralyzed. Jeffrey extended his hands, both suddenly covered in blood. His head turned to the sky, exposing the fair skin of his neck, the perfection now ruined by a long cut, red liquid pouring out in a torrent. Yet Jeffrey was still standing.

"I didn't!" she shouted. "It wasn't me, it wasn't me …"

"It *was* you. You did this to me." He pointed an accusatory, bloodied finger at the frightened girl. "You killer. You killed me."

"No, no. No, I never." She rocked back and forth on the bed, obviously terrified. "Please, don't … no, please."

The man took a threatening step forward, long spikes sliding out of the palms of his hands. But Daisy-May had her eyes sewn shut in horror, now that she could see the approaching danger.

Suddenly, Jeffrey flew backwards, hit in the chest by a force like that of an oncoming train. Zander. Daisy-May's eyes flew open and so did her mouth.

"Time to move." Blayde disappeared, suddenly behind the terrified girl, her hand tight around Daisy-

May's mouth to muffle the long, siren-like shriek that had started to build.

Zander now had Jeffrey pinned down, but the captive was not completely man anymore. He had started to melt, to morph, his jacket seeming fleshy instead of fabric, though his teeth seemed twice as sharp and just as real as they'd ever been.

Jeffrey's face resembled more monster than man now, with his needle-like teeth poking from what would have once been called a mouth. He writhed on the floor, his hands now weak and spikes entirely missing, as he desperately tried to fight off Zander.

"Where'd the briefcase go?" I asked suddenly, noticing its absence from the room.

And the fact that Jeffery's jacket was still attached to his flailing arms as if by super glue. Every time he waved his arms, the jacket followed without slipping or sliding a centimeter.

That sure wasn't fabric.

"It's a multiform!" Zander exclaimed, keeping his hand over the creature's mouth so it could not interrupt. "A shapeshifter! The briefcase—or any other accessory for that matter—is a part of the design. Look." He grabbed the jacket, giving it a jerk. Jeffrey seemed quite pissed, like Zander had tried to rip his arm off. "You see? One big creature."

"Well, what's it doing in Daisy-May's room?" I asked. "She knew Jeffrey *before* the institute. This doesn't make any sense!"

"No more sense than future dead brother or evil, stabby clowns," Blayde muttered, still clutching Daisy-May, who had fainted or maybe fallen asleep.

"Who are you working for?" Zander asked, grabbing the monster formerly known as Jeffrey and shaking him by the collar. "Tell me!"

The creature dissolved into sand, the floor writhing with little grains, each attached to the main conglomeration like some great ball of fire ants. Like the clown in Zander's room, it started to climb the wall, slowly inching up to the vent in the top of the corner.

"Stop it!" Blayde ordered.

"What do you think I'm doing?" her brother yelled. "It's like trying to catch water!"

"Well, go after it!" she snapped, still gripping her hand over Daisy-May's mouth. Her eyes were fluttering open, taking in a scene that no one should ever have to see.

"The vent's too small for him," I pointed out while slipping off my sweater. "I'll go."

"No."

"Blayde, shut up for one minute and let me help!" Amazingly, it worked. "Laser."

Blayde reached into her pocket, handing me the pointer, which I grabbed before she could change her mind.

"Daisy-May, you're having the wildest dream of your life," I said before I jumped up, extending my legs to balance on the wall, my feet pressed against the sides.

# INALIENABLE

The laser sliced through the vent as if it were butter, the metal grate falling into one of the sibling's waiting hands, though I couldn't see whose. I put the laser between my teeth, pulling myself up into Jeffrey's tube, sliding down on my belly.

The blob of quivering sand was right ahead of me, moving much faster than sand should have a right to move. Much faster than I could keep up. The vents were not very big, leaving almost no space for maneuverability. I threw my hands forward, putting my weight on my forearms and pulling myself a meager inch along. My feet still dangled out the vent.

Someone strong grabbed my feet and gave them a shove into the vent, pushing me along a foot or two.

"Just jump, okay?" Blayde hissed. "Someone's coming, so we're off. Meet you at Zander's."

The vent slammed shut behind me. I took a deep breath, gathering my wits about me. The proximity of the walls bordered on claustrophobic. I dragged myself forward a few more inches. Too slow. I focused slightly, and in half a blink of the eye, I was meters down the silver duct.

I kept myself at a safe distance from the sand creature, silently pausing and jumping, pausing and jumping so as not to make a sound, to not alert it to my presence. The blob seemed to have no idea I was following it, going steadily down the ventilation shaft in front of me, keeping up a brisk pace that would have had me huffing and puffing if I had a need for breathing. It kept going on straight until the main duct split off, then it suddenly went up to the next level.

It was impossible to see over the curve at the top of the junction. I jumped anyway, placing my hands low so as to grab the narrow path and heave myself up manually. Unfortunately, at this point, the blob was gone, and an empty duct lined with vents awaited me. I had somehow traveled upstairs to the off-limits staff floor, and the shapeshifter could be in any of the rooms.

*Oh shit, they were just as vulnerable as the patients.* What was it going to do to them? Were they next on the night's menu?

I slid up close to the nearest vent. Inside the dark room below me, lit only by moonlight, Dr. Smith slept peacefully, her comforter bunched by her side, her hair sprawled in a mess across her pillow. The light lit up the side of her face, her mouth open and drooling on the soft Italian silks that covered the pillows on the cotton sheets that sandwiched her in warmth. She stirred in her sleep, and I cringed. I froze in place, keeping my eyes on her as she threw her arm in the air and flipped onto her other side.

I had no idea she slept at the hospital. I had assumed she had a family waiting for her at home, that she left our world at night.

I waited a few minutes, but she didn't move again. I crawled down the shaft a little way longer, checking the next vent. The room beyond held almost the exact same scene: one of the psychologists, though I couldn't tell which one, sleeping soundly in the comfort of his own bed. No sign of any shape-shifting sand blob, scary clowns, or even Jeffrey, for that matter.

It was a shapeshifter after all. He could be anything, anything at all, any object in that room. Was it a chair now? A desk? An extra pillow? The thing could be anything, anywhere; no way to know where it was or even what is was.

I cursed under my breath. I had lost it. Blayde and Zander had trusted me, and I had let them down.

And worse yet, there was no way for me to turn my head. I was stuck in the shaft.

I closed my eyes focusing on the only beacon I could follow through the void of the universe, a skill even they didn't have, but damn was I thankful I somehow did. Zander was a magnet, and I was drawn to him instantly.

Blink, and I was lying flat on my stomach in the middle of the floor of his room, the tight walls of the duct gone. I breathed a deep sigh of relief.

Seriously, how come I could do this, but the siblings couldn't? It was hella confusing, but at the moment, the real problem at hand was finding the shapeshifter. I turned to the siblings, who were waiting silently by Zander's bed.

"You're all right," he said, relief washing over his words. "Did you see where it went?"

"Upstairs, but I didn't manage to catch it. I lost it after it reached the staff quarters. Must have changed shape once again. I don't know if it had any idea I was after it."

Blayde nodded, leaning back against the wall. Her eyes were drilling into me sharper than the shapeshifter's hand-horns had.

"Now do you believe it's not a future version of me?" Zander asked, turning to her.

"Okay, fine. I admit it wouldn't be like you. But if it isn't time-traveling Zander, what sent it?"

"Can't it be acting on its own?" I asked.

"Could be."

"There are many different species with the power to change shape," said Zander. "Some do it for camouflage, some to feed, some to earn some petty cash by working for a third party. They make for very cheap actors. Some planets don't even need CGI at all. Anyway. Once we find their reasoning, we'll be able to find the species."

"Or vice versa," added Blayde. "Until then, we have no idea what exactly we're dealing with. Someone needs to have a closer look upstairs."

Zander's face lit up like a kid on Christmas. "I'll go!"

Blayde shook her head. "The doc already finds you suspicious. She catches you snooping around upstairs, you're screwed. They'll probably send you to prison or something."

"So, you'll go?" he asked.

"Shut up, I'm hatching a plan," she ordered, sitting back down on his bed and lifting her hands to her head to clear her mind.

"Shouldn't we just go now?" I pointed out. "They're all asleep."

"No," she snapped. "They're asleep, but they can wake up. Better do it during the day when none of them are around." She grinned finally. "I got it."

"A plan?"

"Oh yeah," she snickered.

"Mind sharing?" Zander asked.

"Well, it's rather simple, really." Her smile spread from ear to ear. "Zander, we're going to couple's therapy."

# TEN

## COUPLES COUNSELING AND A HEAPING DOSE OF UNRELIABLE FURNITURE

**I DON'T KNOW ABOUT YOU, BUT I HATE LISTENING** to other people describe their nonsensical dreams. I don't care what your dog turning into a milkshake means. There's probably no symbolism in you eating your roommate's laptop. So, fancy me, sitting at breakfast, trying to poke and prod a girl into giving me all the unabridged details of her night terror.

"I don't know," Blayde said. "I started seeing that other doctor, the older one—Winfrey?—dancing on this very table. Does that mean anything?"

"Probably not," I said, grinning my widest grin. "You know, when people said this place gave you weird dreams, I was ready for the worst. But so far, nothing."

"Didn't I hear *you* scream? Not last night, but the night before?" asked Daisy-May.

"That was different," I said. "There was a spider on my bed."

# INALIENABLE

Not that I actually remembered screaming. Even after the details of the shapeshifter's impersonation of Zander's death started coming back to me, the rest of the night was rather murky. Which probably was for the best.

"You screamed last night," said Blayde, point-blank.

"I did?" she asked. "Huh. I don't remember. I definitely didn't dream. I think … I think Jeffrey was coming to visit. Like every month. You know, normal."

"Normal," I repeated, taking a very long gulp of orange juice. "How does he get in?"

"He climbs in through the window, silly."

"What do you guys talk about? When he visits?" asked Blayde. "You don't see each other that often. I bet he rattles on and on."

"I dunno. Stuff." She bit her cheek, looking down at her empty bowl. "I don't–I don't always remember the details."

"Sounds like me with this guy," Blayde said, nudging her brother playfully in the rib. "Yaps for hours. Never remember a thing he says."

"Hey!" Zander had been silent up until now, brows furrowed in concentration. That or he was just really into his oatmeal today. "Come on. Here?"

She raised her hands defensively. "Hey, I'm just speaking the truth."

"The truth?" he snarled. "The truth is you never listen to me. Do you know how annoying that is?"

"Well, you have Sally to listen to you blab now, so I guess you don't need me around anymore."

"Blayde! She's my *girlfriend*!"

"Yeah, well, you're an idiot!" She rose to her feet. "I'm tired of you pushing me to the side!"

He stood, face red, taller than her by a head. She climbed up on the bench in a childish effort to tower over him. "And I'm tired of you pushing me around!"

"Like this?" she asked, placing both hands on his chest and shoving him away hard.

He stumbled lightly, gasped, and pushed her back. She tumbled off the bench, arms pinwheeling, and fell backward over a table. Trays crashed to the ground as other patients stumbled out of her way.

"Yeah, like that!"

"Bite me!" she snarled, her teeth bared like a wild animal.

"Bring it!"

I was all ready for one of the siblings' famous show of force: lunging and jumping and punching, a scene that would cross the cafeteria, possibly bringing down the entire building around us, so when Zander raised his fists and batted at her, it was more of a letdown than the last season of *Game of Thrones*. Blayde raised her own fists to punch back, and suddenly, they were a poorly animated cartoon, huffing as they spun their fists without ever reaching their target.

"Knock it off, you two!" said a security guard—oh hey, it's not-Barker—as he reached forward to spring them apart.

Blayde scrambled backward with a lack of agility only equated to the increased gravitational well of Mondays.

# INALIENABLE

She grabbed plastic knives as Zander rushed out of not-Barker's reach, and she threw them at him as he ran through the cafeteria, the plastic bouncing off his thick skull.

"Is that all you got, sister of mine?" he taunted, grabbing a tray off the pile of cutlery to be cleaned.

She lunged again, but he sidestepped out of her way a split second before impact, slamming the tray in her face like a baseball bat. Blood gushed down her face.

"You broke my nose?" she stammered. "Holy Santa Claus, I've never seen blood before!"

She threw her hand up to her forehead and collapsed in a heap on the ground, swooning like a dramatic Victorian teen. She wasn't going to be winning any acting awards this century.

The cafeteria erupted into chaos, our fellow patients reacting as any rational people would when two of their own went more bananas than the whole bunch. Dr. Smith was shouting something, but I couldn't hear a word she was saying. Whatever it was either couldn't or wouldn't help the other patients, who ranged from confused to completely terrified.

"Did I say something wrong?" Daisy-May held her face in her hands, peeking through her fingers at the mayhem.

"No, no, they just have a lot of unresolved issues," I said, putting a gentle hand on her shoulder. I, however, wanted to win my acting award. Not that there's some kind of governing body giving them out to weird alien schemes. If there's a higher dimensional being watching right now, please make this my 'for your consideration' reel. "I can't believe them. Oh god, is that real blood?"

"I think she broke her nose," said Peter quietly, the only words I had heard from him all morning.

Zander and Blayde were being ushered away. My distraction was running out. "It's—I need to go."

"Are you all right?" he asked. I nodded. He turned his attention back to Daisy-May, who had covered her face again, taking deep breaths I recognized from my own panic attacks. I desperately wanted to keep my arm around her and help her through this. I remembered my own attacks, clear islands in the sea of murky memories of depressive episodes. But it was either stay and help her for five minutes, or run and save everyone here, forever.

Peter had her. He placed a gentle hand between her shoulder blades, eyes riveted on the face behind her hands.

No one to see me rush off to the bathroom and beyond.

Jumping through the entrance grate was easy. The woman on door duty was watching a YouTube video—a cardio workout she was nodding along to without getting up from her chair—and it wasn't like I needed her to buzz me through when I could just appear in the hall beyond. Thank goodness butterfly kicks were more interesting to watch than security feeds.

It was an odd feeling, being out in the open like this; the ceilings were so high, the windows wider, the massive staircase so dominating. The architecture itself was beautiful and old-fashioned, unlike the sterile feel of the patients' wing. I'd gotten too used to the confines of the hospital too quickly.

I climbed the stairs, bewildered by the ornate carvings in the stone. The only time I had ever seen a staircase so strikingly stunning was when I was on Da-Duhui in the presidential palace, though this one was nowhere near that grand. Even then, I snooped around. Would I never have time to admire staircases?

I reached the landing and found myself in the last place I had expected to be. I went from sepia Kansas to the mystical, technicolor land of Oz. The floor was carpeted, and expensively so. The walls were now a white marble, the doors of hard oak, the light fixtures of gold and brass in intricate designs. I half expected to see a yellow brick road winding down the corridor.

I cursed that I didn't have time to admire my surroundings. I tiptoed down the hallway, taking the first door at random, and using the sight through the keyhole to get me inside. Inside the room I had seen when I had followed the sand blob the night before: Smith's bedroom. Did all the doctors live here? I walked in, looking for anything out of the ordinary, something that was missing from the night before or anything that had since arrived.

The room was proof that the doctor had perfect taste. Like her office, the warm autumn tones were present in everything, from the oak furniture to the reds and golds in the Italian silk sheets. I sat on the bed, awestruck. Wow, the mattress was comfortable. Amazingly so.

I fell back on the bed, floating on the cloud of comfort the soft duvet offered. It was amazing. This was coming from the girl who hadn't slept in a comfortable bed in weeks. You know: Jail. Mental institution. At this point, I couldn't tell if her bed was the norm that I had once had or an outstanding exception.

I wasn't going to pull a Goldilocks. No time to rest now. They would notice soon enough that I had disappeared, and I didn't want to be caught this far from the patients' quarters when they did. *Back to work, Sally Webber.*

Nothing seemed unusual in the room, that was sure. It seemed perfect, not an item out of place, not a cobweb or a fly. I rose to my feet, fluffing the bed behind me to make sure I left no trace of my visit. I opened the closet quickly, checking for a sand conglomeration that could be hidden inside. Nothing. Good. I didn't know if I should feel happy or annoyed.

The hallway was still as silent and empty when I exited the room as it had been when I had first arrived. I crossed it, pushing open the door right across from Smith's. This one was just as ornate, if not more so, bordering on over the top. The poor man's idea of a rich man's luxury. But who cares when the golden quilt that covered the bed was inviting. So warm, so cozy.

# INALIENABLE

With a muffled _fwomp_, I landed on the bed, relishing in the softness of it. I was on a cloud. It was perfect.

An ugly squelch filled the room. I opened an eye tentatively, staring at the ceiling. My hand flew to my mouth to muffle a yelp of shock and horror.

The blob. It was there, latched to the plaster ceiling right above me. I rose to my feet, edging away as slowly as I could. Would it even see me? Hear me?

I answered that question quickly enough. In my hesitant walk backwards, my shoulder hit a lamp, sending it crashing to the ground. I guess they weren't bolted down like in the patients' rooms. The nightstand wobbled, hitting the wall, sending a tremor up to the ceiling, and a ripple spread through the sandy mass.

The blob stiffened, the silent squelching stopping instantly. Eww, what had it been doing? It froze, and even though it had no eyes, I could feel it staring straight through me.

With a sound like a suction cup detaching, the sandy blob dropped from the ceiling, falling onto the bed and shooting off into the hallway like a strange liquid bullet.

Great, just great. I rushed after it, pulling the laser pointer from my pocket. I was out of the room in an instant, glancing up and down the hallway, but it was already gone.

_Shit._

No time to panic. I took a deep breath, allowing my eyes to focus. No, it wasn't gone. Something was sliding under the door two rooms up the hallway, glimmering slightly in the sunlight that spilled through the windows on the end of the corridor. I sprinted down to the door, lunging for the blob, failing to grab even a single grain.

The door flew open. I turned to glance up at the confused face of the oldest doctor on staff.

Shit. What was his name?

"Ms. Weaver?" He asked, confused. "What are you …? How?"

"It's Webber, Doctor," I replied. Damn. I could have said literally anything else. I took his hand, allowing myself to be pulled up to my feet. "You've gotta get out of here now!"

"Why?" He glanced up and down the hallway. "Is everything all right, Ms. Webber?"

"Not really!" I brushed myself off and tried to push past him. He stood in the way. "There's a shapeshifting alien blob loose in the institute, and I can't seem to catch it."

"You're not meant to be up here," he said. Then, squinting, added, "Have you spoken to Dr. Smith?"

"I don't have time for this!" I didn't even know the guy. I've seen him, what, once? It's not like we had any real orientation. Anyway, not my doctor, not my problem. "You know what? I'm going to show you something. Don't freak out. "

I flipped the laser pointer on, pointing it to my arm and slicing down with quick precision. The doctor cringed.

"Ms. Webber, stop," he ordered, grabbing my hand, but it was too late.

"Just look," I said, feeling dramatic AF. "It'll prove that everything I'm telling you is true."

He watched, eyes going wide as saucers—the UFO kind, not the dinner plates—as the puckered, red skin healed over. I would never get tired of the sight myself. His grip on my wrist slackened.

"Well, I'll be the uncle of a monkey," he muttered, readjusting his glasses.

"Now do you believe me?"

He nodded slightly.

"Come in. We must talk." He gestured to the room behind him. I glanced over his shoulder, scanning floor and ceiling for the conglomerate. Pleased with its absence, I made my way in.

"It attacked me and my friends last night," I said. "And we're sure it's been around for a while, terrorizing other patients at the institute."

"If it's been around for so long, why hasn't anyone said anything?"

"The patients here scream every night, and no one cares. Even you sleep right through it. Maybe they have said something, but they're crazy so nobody believes them? For some reason, though, not many people remember being attacked in the first place."

"That's unfortunate." He shook his head. "It's just your word against theirs."

"But I'm the immortal space traveler."

"Touché. In any case, perhaps the forgetting is a blessing to them. Most patients here—if not all—have too much trauma to begin with. The whole point is to unburden them of it, to help them find the tools they need to prosper; not to load them up with more pain. Yes, perhaps it's better they don't remember."

"You believe me, right?"

"Yes, I do." The doctor nodded. He has this kind solemnity to him, like making eye contact was some kind of promise. The relief that washed over me was as thick and warm as tomato soup.

"Good. Now, it's *our* word against theirs. They'll believe their doctor."

"What's you plan?"

"Um, I guess we find the creature first?"

"You said it could change forms. How do we find it?"

"I don't know. But it seems to be engineered to scare us: the clown with a murderous vendetta, the dying boyfriend, the accusatory imaginary friend—"

"Maybe there's a connection between the form and its victim? The clown, who did he attack?"

"Zander."

"And the imaginary friend?"

"Daisy-May."

"Ah, Jeffrey?"

"Yuuuuup."

"This is worse than trying to scare their victims." The doctor shook his head. "They're trying to *traumatize* them. This is malicious."

"How so?"

"Daisy-May … is not right in her head."

"She can't be *that* bad. She has an imaginary friend ... who makes her go heisting. So?"

"Jeffrey's not imaginary." He bit his lower lip. "Jeffrey Grant, Daisy-May Grant's husband. Though I should say *late* husband."

"She ...?"

"She murdered him, and she robbed a bank. In that order. She's so torn up about it she's convinced he's always been nothing more than a friend. Imaginary."

"That's horrible," I said. I had no idea she'd been through that. I cast a glance to the vent, dragging my mind away from the horrible truth of a terrified girl. The paint under the wall there was dull as I ran my fingers over it, as if sanded down or worn down from years of use. "Are you meant to be telling me any of this? I thought there was doctor patient confidentiality."

"Hum," doc muttered.

"How does it know its victim's fears, though? It has to be close to the patients. I don't know. Maybe he's one of them; I mean us. And he's hiding right among us."

"Hum," he repeated.

"That would explain a lot," I continued. "It gets close to someone then uses that knowledge of them to scare them, but to what end? And why does it stab them behind the ears?" I paused, but the doctor said nothing. "Is it to feed? The fears thing seems to connect us all, but why would it think Zander was afraid of clowns?"

"Sally!"

I spun on my heels, and—what the hell—Zander was panting in the doorway, sweat dripping down his brow. "That's not the real Winfrey! He's getting away and probably going to call security on you!"

Ah! That was his name!

Winfrey, the blob. It all made sense! Unless the blob wasn't always Winfrey and was just pretending because I'd gotten close. Was the real Winfrey at breakfast this morning?

But there were even weirder questions to answer. Zander wasn't supposed to be here. "How did you get up here?" I asked.

"Same way you did! Come on, we need to go now!"

"I thought you were in couple's therapy?"

He laughed. "Yeah, as if that was going to work out."

I waited for him to add something, yet he still stood, finger pointing in expectation, face twisted with worry.

"Come on, we don't have much time!"

"Teach me the basics of quantum geometry!" I ordered.

"What?"

"Seriously. Lightning fast, just the basics of it." I gave him my most seductive smile, which was unpracticed and probably looked more like I was gassy. "Please?"

"Sally, we gotta go—"

I swung my arm, punching him square across the jaw, something which would have been nothing more than a mosquito bite to Zander, yet he crumpled on the floor like a dropped sock puppet.

# INALIENABLE

*Wow, that was a freebie.*

Whether it was the real Winfrey or not, it was still the blob I had been hunting. I ripped a sheet off his bed, spreading it out on the floor, rolling the unconscious alien life form onto it. I tied the ends as tight as I could, bending over to hoist the heavy weight of the shapeshifter onto my shoulder.

A single blow to the head was enough to bring the shapeshifter down, it seemed. Easier than I had expected. What wasn't so easier was hoisting the mass over my shoulder, which, let's face it, I really was in no shape to do.

Thank goodness for inter-dimensional travel.

*Focus now. I have to do this right.*

I closed my eyes, holding tightly to the sheet. Same planet, same building, one floor down: Zander was a light in the darkness, a lighthouse to lead my ship through the void. I dissolved into nothing, whizzing through the in-between space, weightless, senseless. All too soon, the sensation of pure freedom and exhilaration was gone; my eyes flew open to the warm office of Dr. Smith.

The Tibetan singing bowl was still singing when I interrupted their meditative circle, dropping the unconscious mass of Winfrey onto the oil diffuser.

Zander flew to his feet, untangling his meditative legs in mid-air, grabbing the puddle off my shoulder before I fully materialized. Smith flew backwards into her desk, a silent yelp passing her lips.

"Are you okay?" he asked, helping me lower the sheet to the floor.

My face was red hot, beaming with pride. "I'm fine. For real, this time. I caught it!"

Now it was his turn to light up that smile. "Really?"

"It was imitating you. *Again*"

"I dare to think what gave it away," he said, pointing at the sheet.

I finally turned my attention to Smith, who was standing with her hands grasping the edges of her desk. It looked like she was halfway between calling security and passing out.

"How did you—?" She tried to stand, but she fell back against the desk again, catching herself before she toppled to the floor. Blayde took a step toward her, but Smith waved her away.

"I didn't lie to you. I'm an immortal space traveler," I said, then found myself giggling. Just pure anxious giggles. "It really does sound stupid when I say that, doesn't it? I thought it would be way more badass."

"Well, you can probably see why I didn't believe you," she muttered. Her hands were shaking, and she clutched the desk tighter.

"Yeah. But, hey, I'm not holding it against you."

"Somebody help me!" came the feeble voice of a young girl muffled by the sheets. Instantly, the doctor rushed to our side, crouching down to work at the knots that held my captive.

"Don't do that!" I shouted. "It's a trap!"

# INALIENABLE

She took no heed of my words, ripping open the sheet with quiet determination. Daisy-May gave a frightened look around the office, her face bloodied and bruised.

"Where am I?" she asked, bewildered and shaken. An extra-long sniffle graced her button nose. "What happened?"

"You're in my office. You're safe." The doctor ran a soothing hand through Daisy-May's hair.

"She … she hit me over the head. I—" Then she burst into sobs, leaning her head against Smith's chest. All other eyes in the room were riveted at me with varying degrees of shock.

"Look, I swear it was *Zander* when I first knotted the bag," I said defensively. "And it was Winfrey before that. Shapeshifter!"

"How could you?" Smith spat. "You …"

"That is not the real Daisy-May!" I shouted. "This is Winfrey! Or, at least, it looked like Winfrey. Shapeshifters! I just freaking appeared out of thin air in your office. Would I be lying about this too?"

Blayde took a step toward me, frowning. "Are you certain?"

"Positively, without a doubt. This is *not* Daisy-May."

"I believe you," said Blayde.

"So do I," Zander added.

"You three are sick. Immortal space travelers, sure. Maybe. Still trying to process that bit. But just because that's true doesn't mean that you aren't still sick."

"Hand the shapeshifter over, Doctor," Blayde ordered.

Smith hugged the girl closer. "I am not letting this patient into your hands! You've done enough already!"

"Hand her over, Smith, or I'll have to take her by force."

"Are you … threatening me?"

"I guess I am," Blayde said sternly, placing a hand on her hip. "So, hand her over."

"No."

"I warned you."

"And I'm warning you. You need help."

Blayde stepped forward, grabbing the doppelganger by the crook of her arm and gently trying to drag her away from the doctor. Fake Daisy-May shrieked like a banshee. Even stone cold Blayde saw her resolve falter, a frown flickering on her stony features.

"It's not her," Zander repeated, taking a step back and locking his arms around the handles of the large wooden door. "It's a shapeshifter, Blayde."

Blayde shoved the doctor back heavily to the floor, grabbing the shapeshifter around the waist as the fake Daisy-May kicked and screamed. The shapeshifter balled her fists and hit Blayde across the chest, her legs falling behind her. Blayde dropped her down on a sofa, keeping a tight grip on the tiny woman's wrist.

"Shut up!" she spat. "We have questions!"

Daisy-May stopped her fighting suddenly, leaning back on the chair with a look of smug satisfaction on her face. She chuckled slightly, her form morphing back to Dr. Winfrey.

"'Figures," Blayde sneered. "The doctor is the monster."

"Too bad I can't think of any Frankenstein jokes right now," I muttered. Shit, not the right time. Thankfully, I was the least interesting person in the room right now.

"You really *are* the real Dr. Winfrey, aren't you?" Blayde continued. "You seem to have better control of this form. More detail. Your version of Daisy-May was sloppy. You didn't even make her hairs individually; it looked absolutely horrendous while Dr. Smith hugged her."

"Spur of the moment," he replied sharply. "You caught me off guard. I was stressed, and stressors can infringe on our ability to perform even our most basic tasks. Which you would know, if you listened to me at all during our session."

"So, you're the one who's been sneaking into the rooms? Scaring the patients?"

He chuckled. "Sharp as a tack, this one."

Blayde was frustratingly bored. "May I ask … why?"

"You can ask as much as you want, I don't have to tell you. I know my rights."

"Rights?" Blayde laughed. "What, you think you get to call on the protection of Terran law?"

"Vigilante?" he asked. He didn't seem to know who we were. Either he was a poor actor from the Agency or he really was just an off-worlder acting alone.

"In a way." She took a step back, giving me a curt nod. I came to her side, an extra set of hands if she needed one. "Okay, answer me this: Where are you from?"

He shook his head. "My lips are sealed."

"Then tell me who you pray to," she snarled, "because you're going to meet him soon enough."

He sighed heavily. "You think you have control over me? You think because you can speak big, act big, threaten me and my staff that you can push me around?" He threw his head back, laughing with every muscle in his abdomen.

"Guess again."

In an instant, the form of the former Dr. Winfrey lost its shape, crumbling to the floor, the glob of sand rushing across the floor. It climbed the wall in an instant, disappearing through the vent faster than dirt up a vacuum cleaner.

Blayde swore loudly, tossing a handful of inert sand on the ground. "It's gone. Again!" She turned to me. "Well, congrats on finding the doc. But now he's loose. Any ideas?"

"I'm not the one who lost him this time!" I snapped. "You did! You figure this one out. You're meant to be the expert."

"Dang, I take back what I said about Sally's snark. I'm getting pretty tired of it. Grow up." She turned to Smith, licking her lips. "You. You hugged Daisy-May-slash-Winfrey. Caressed her hair. How could you not notice that the hair was fake? It wasn't even in individual strands!"

"I was scared!" she shouted. "That's one of my patients you were accusing of being a shapeshifter. I didn't know what to think."

"It said 'our ability,' so you know what that makes me think? It makes me think there are other shapeshifters here."

"You didn't bat an eyelid when your patient turned into your colleague, so you know something." Zander added, turning to us. "We have to hurry. He's probably already told the others. We don't know how many of them are in on it."

"We can't rush the process!" Blayde snapped. She took Smith roughly by the scruff of her neck. The woman shivered. Blayde's fist froze above her face, the hand opening to grab a single hair. Tug. The jet-black hair crumbled to dust before it hit the floor.

"What's the point of all this?" She gave Smith a sharp shake. "Why scare your own patients? Is it to keep them here longer? Why? Gods, please don't tell me this is a ploy for more funding. I'm tired of that."

"Help!" Smith's skin turned red, cuts blossoming on her cheeks. The skin around her eyes turned a deep purple, so deep it was almost black.

"We'll tell them everything," Blayde snarled.

"Who will they believe?" Smith's hair fell out in patches, big, bloody clumps clinging to her scalp. Her lip split itself in two. "Me, a doctor and their boss, or you, a bunch of loonies?"

"That's no way to talk to your patients!" Blayde dropped her, and she hit the ground with a soft thump. "We have to get outta here."

"Window!" I yelled.

Blayde turned to look at me. "Shut up, Sally. No need to tell the world!"

She reached down, pulling her arm back and swinging it full force at Smith's face. The shapeshifter's eyes shut, her body going limp. Unconscious or faking like Winfrey? It didn't matter. Either way, we had to go—now.

Blayde was suddenly on the other side of the wall of windows, arms akimbo, face sullen. Zander grabbed my hand, and we jumped out after her.

"So, outside, anyway?" I asked.

"No open or broken windows. They'll be confused but probably won't check the grounds for a while. Not with the way they have the outside locked off from anyone and everyone. Come on, they'll be after us already."

"Two shapeshifters in one day." Zander grinned; I could even detect a hint of excitement. "Finally, this place is getting interesting!"

"What, so mysterious, scary figures in patients' rooms weren't enough?"

"Sure. But now's the point where we find out what we're up against, yet we have the thrill of coming up with a plan that may or may not work. Best part! That and hand-to-hand combat. I've been dying without physical activity."

"Hate to break it to you, brother of mine, but we have no idea what we're up against," said Blayde. "They're shapeshifters, but why are they here? We don't know what they want. We don't even know how they work."

"So, what do we do now?" I asked, eyeing down the two experts. "No weapons. Up against two shapeshifters—"

"Or more," Zander said morosely.

"With no idea of means or motivation, believed crazy by the rest of the people who could actually help."

"Well, not every person who could actually help," Blayde said, grimacing.

My heart, as it was, fell sharply. "Oh no."

"It is their prerogative," said Zander. He let out a heavy sigh. "Look. Shapeshifters abusing mental patients? This is literally everything the Agency claims to stand against. Maybe alerting them will get us into the Agency's good graces."

"But they've never done anything!" I hissed.

"That you know of," he said. "In any case, it's worth a try. We even have a way of contacting them. Barker should be around here somewhere."

"But what if *he* doesn't believe us?" I asked.

"Oh, he'll believe us. What other option does he have?"

# ELEVEN

## THIS ISN'T SHUTTER ISLAND, BUT WE'VE GOT A STORM AND SOME SHUTTERS SO IT MIGHT DO THE TRICK

"HELLO, ALLIANCE BOY," SAID BLAYDE AS she plopped herself down at the foot of his bed. "Did ya miss me?"

The infirmary was practically empty. We had planned to distract the nurse with a booboo, but there was no need as there was nobody here. Was the nurse another shapeshifter possibly? Or just some random Terran caught up in the hunt for us?

Barker was propped up on his cot, eyes going wide at the sight of Blayde as he dropped a battered copy of Marie Claire on his lap. His arm sat in a sling, still recovering from our quick jaunt in the woods from the day before. He seemed as pleased to see us as a lobster to see a pot.

"Oh, no," he sputtered. "No, no, no. I already told you everything I know. Please don't touch me."

"Don't worry, I'm not here to get anything out of you," she said, flipping her hair back. "Why does everyone always think that? Actually, we have info *for* you."

"You have info … for me?" he repeated. He didn't seem all that convinced either.

"Yes." She grinned. "Info! For the Alliance."

"Stop." Barker lifted his free hand in front of him. "Don't come any closer."

"Seriously?" Blayde plucked up the magazine he had dropped, flicking through the pages with her thumb and forefinger, dropping it on the floor when she was sufficiently disappointed. She held up a hair—a single, wispy hair—and tossed it to me. I let it fall to the floor, her point made: Barker wasn't a shapeshifter. "Kid, if I wanted to come closer, trust me, I would come closer. But obviously, that's not what I'm here for."

"What are you here for?"

"As I said, I have info that's vital for the Alliance."

"I'm not in any position to make a trade," he spat.

"Trade?" Blayde laughed a ridiculously high-pitched laugh of a girl who's getting exactly what she wants. "I don't want anything. Well, maybe just one thing."

"What's that?"

"I want immunity," she said, suddenly serious, rising back to her feet. "Just six months off the radar. That's it."

His brow furrowed. "You can do a lot of harm in six months."

"Oh, but you're going to like my intel."

"It's not like I can grant you anything. Who do you think I am? And should I mention … screw you, asswipe! You broke my arm!"

"Fine, then." She shrugged. "The Alliance will never know what went down here. Oh, and you'll probably never get your father's respect."

"Dad?" He frowned impossibly deeper. "What do you know of my father?"

She shrugged once more. "Oh, I know a lot. It's all on your face. You're an open book."

"What do you mean?"

"I've seen your kind before," she said smugly. "Rich families. Your father's embarrassed by what you've become. A slob, a brat, someone's flunky; there's always something. There's an unspoken rule that the more you have, the more you want. And he wanted you to be so much more. Isn't that it?"

He said nothing. I was starting to think I needed to be anywhere but here. There was something strangely intimate in the encounter, like she was somehow reading his mind by the way he squirmed under her gaze.

"So, you join the army, but you're rich, not much use, too skinny or too doughy, your pockets brimming with bribe money. They put you on some forgotten world out on the rim of the Alliance where you won't get in anyone's way. Beyond the rim, in this case. Eager to prove you are your father's son and much more than he expects, eager to make him proud, you sign up for the first seemingly dangerous mission that comes your way, only to be sadly disappointed when you realize it will never live up to your father's expectations. But today's your lucky day. You give them this info, you'll get that danger you wanted. The excitement," she cooed, circling him, her smile brimming ear to ear. "All you have to do is relay a transmission, and you'll be able to go home a better man. A man proud to be who he is."

The boy struggled to keep a straight face. It was obvious he was contemplating Blayde's offer and seemingly eager to accept.

"Come on. We know you didn't report your blown cover or the Agency would have acted already. You don't want them to know about the incident in the woods, and neither do we. What we want is a clear channel of communication between us. We want to help, Barker. And we can start by helping you."

"I can't promise anything," he said halfheartedly. "I don't think they'll listen to me."

"Maybe you should hear us out before you write it off." Zander took a step forward. Blayde spun around, glaring at him.

Zander continued anyway. "Let's just say that there's a danger here no one has seen for decades. A danger that, if eradicated, would make you the savior of over a hundred Terran civilians. Enough to earn you a medal for aid to an underdeveloped world."

Now that definitely got his attention. "What kind of danger?"

"Off-worlders taking advantage of underdeveloped species for personal gain," Zander asserted. "Which goes against protocol 113—"

"131," corrected Blayde.

"Yes, 131 of the Laws of Treatment of Non-Contact Planets Inside of Alliance Control," Zander continued.

A protocol no one seemed to have told me about before. The acid in my stomach rolled over again. So, they *did* have a prerogative to protect and defend us. They were just choosing to ignore it.

Also, who had the right to call us *underdeveloped*?

"I'm sorry, but what on Earth are you four going on about?" asked the last doctor I hadn't met yet—the one they called Drew, if I remembered correctly—as he emerged from the shadows, a copy of *Encyclopedia Britannica Volume 10* in his hand, his finger serving a bookmark for the moment. He scanned us each over, large bugs under a microscopic microscope.

"Oh, Dr. Drew!" I exclaimed, jumping between him and the siblings. "How are you? Doing well? I don't think we've met yet, I'm—"

"Sally Webber, yes, I know who you are," he said. "You're not supposed to be in here."

"Well, we got worried not seeing our favorite guard out today," I insisted. "We were the ones who found Barker after he got injured yesterday. We just wanted to be sure he's all right."

"That doesn't explain how you got here. Who let you through?"

"I take it you haven't talked to your colleagues for a little while, have you?"

"Me?" He smiled. "No, I've been here all morning. Engrossed in this book, actually. Did you know the— hold on, why? Did something happen?"

"You'll want to sit down," said Zander.

"I'd rather stand."

"I'd rather you sit," Zander said so sternly that the man felt compelled to follow his instructions, plopping down on the empty cot behind him without looking.

"Now," said Blayde, "I'll run you through the basics. Dr. Smith and Dr. Winfrey are shapeshifters who have been feeding off the patients of this institute."

"That's it?" Barker scoffed.

"What?" Drew scoffed as well, though with much more panache, his mustache bristling.

"They've been doing something with their minds," Blayde continued. "Faking scenes to induce terror then stabbing their victims through their skulls."

"You're telling me off-worlders have infiltrated the highest ranks of this institution, and the Agency had no prior knowledge of this? *Ha*. They probably have a permit."

"The hell?" I stammered, pushing myself forward. "You can get a permit to abuse Terrans?"

"Sally," said Zander, extending his hand forward to keep me from strangling Barker. I hadn't even realized my hands were at his throat before Zander pulled me back.

# S. E. ANDERSON

"Please tell me that it's not true," I stammered. "Look, I knew the Agency was shit at protecting Terrans from off-worlders, but goings so far as to give out permits?"

"He's an idiot," Zander said. "That's not how the permits work."

"You knew about this?" I spat. "Shit. You should have told me. I had a right to know that."

"Shut it! This is not the time nor the place," Blayde shouted, before turning to Barker. "Kiddo, if these off-worlders had Agency permit for doing so much as breathing, you would have been told about it when they placed you here. Were you briefed on anything like that?"

He shook his head. "No."

"Then it just goes to tell you these off-worlders are doing something frashing illegal, am I right?"

"Will you please calm down?" Dr. Drew was back on his feet now, forehead aglow with sweat. "This is all absolute hogwash. I will not enable this shared delusion. I've been working with my colleagues for years now. They never took advantage of their patients. They're some of my closest friends. They could never."

"And yet we've seen them," Blayde insisted, coolly. "They're shapeshifters. We haven't identified their homeworld, yet, but we don't have time for the small details. We just have to stop them."

"Do you hear yourself?" Drew put his hands to his skull, pressing in. "Just … stay here. I'll be right back."

With that, he rushed from the infirmary, clutching his book tight to his chest. No doubt to gather some backup.

"Right. We don't have much time," said Blayde. "The shapeshifters know that we've flagged them. We're counting on the fact they haven't pegged you for an Agency plant yet. You need to get your people down here now or this place might very well explode."

"With what evidence?" Barker stammered. "It's your word against … everything. All this. For all I know, for all anyone knows, you're just trying a creative ploy to slip out of our grasp. Let me tell you this now: There is no escape. They have you."

"Ah! So, the Agency *is* planning on an extraction?" said Zander. "Well then, they're going to have to hurry up because we're running. Barker, you have done a terrible job, your charge is on its way out. Peace."

Which would have made for a badass exit, if it wasn't for my terrible timing.

"Is it getting dark?" I asked.

Indeed, it was.

*Chuck. Chuck. Chuck.*

Hurricane shutters were sliding down the windows, squeezing all sunlight out of the room until there wasn't one drop left. Barker seemed as confused as we were.

"What's happening?" Blayde pointed at the window with a sharp jut of her chin.

"Hurricane shutters," I said.

"Is there a hurricane coming?"

"Unless you've heard of one that I haven't," I replied marching forward to try the handle of the window. It was latched shut. "Also, February in Florida. A little early for hurricanes."

Zander rushed past me, grabbing for the infirmary door. Locked.

"I mean, just our luck. Drew is probably one of them too," he said. "Just who here isn't a shapeshifter?"

"All mono-morphs here," she said. "Zander, get us out of here."

"Gladly," he said, kicking the lock. The door swung open.

The hallway beyond was just as dark as the infirmary. The shutters must have come down on the entire building, effectively trapping all of us in.

The fluorescent lights flickered on one by one.

"Well, this is just dandy," said Blayde. "Believe us now, soldier boy?"

"Believe what?" he stammered.

"Look, you either believe what we're saying about the shapeshifters abusing the patients and trying to kill us, or you think that we're trying to escape. Either way, shouldn't you get your Agency buddies on the line?"

He muttered something under his breath I couldn't make out. I wasn't sure it was meant to be anything at all. But he swung his feet over the edge of the bed and ripped his sling from his arm, stretching out the joint.

"I don't quite know what I believe," he said, "but I have orders not to let you out of my sight. "

# INALIENABLE

"That's not worth much, seeing as how you spent the past day hiding out here," said Blayde, before turning on her heels and taking off down the hallway.

Screw it. More running.

Barker followed us back to the rec room where nurses and patients alike sat around on the sofas and tables, watching the barred windows as if it was their own personal show. Calm, thankfully.

"Oh, you three!" Daisy-May exclaimed, rushing forward from her perch on the arm of the old Lazy Boy. "Where were you? Did you see what happened?"

"Doctors Drew, Smith, and Winfrey are in some kind of a conspiracy together," I said. "So, that's been a little time consuming."

"A conspiracy?" she asked, wide eyed. "What kind of conspiracy? I love conspiracies!"

*Not this kind*, I wanted to say. How many times had she been met with a doctor pretending to be Jeffrey, only to be roofied into ignorance? "We found out a secret about them. Now they want us dead."

Half of the room had been listening in, so half of the room gasped. Most of the staff simply rolled their eyes. The rest of them were finding it hard to keep a straight face.

"No need to worry." A burly lumberjack-built man rose to his feet, his hand raised in dismissal and head shaking in a reassuring refusal of our theory. "Just an unexpected hurricane. Everything's just in place for when the storm hits."

"Then why have we all been brought in here?" Peter muttered. He slid off the table, turning to face the crowd with a sudden courage I had never seen in him. "Why aren't we going back to our activities? Don't lie to us; something's going on, isn't it? Why doesn't the rest of the staff know about the storm so they could reassure us? Isn't that the point, keeping us from panicking?"

His speech gave rise to many nods of approval from the crowd.

"How many of you hear screams in the night?" Zander asked, climbing up on the table behind Peter. Almost all hands rose, some less eagerly than others. "Yet how many of you are actively doing the screaming?"

This time, no hands reached in the air. Of course not. These should have been the questions we were asking from day one.

"The truth is every single one of you screams. Yet not one of you remembers doing it. A few of you have vague memories. Faint images, places you don't want to linger. Maybe you all do. Something terrifying hiding at the edge of your mind. Something you push back like the good doctors tell you to do."

"Think!" Blayde shouted, making me practically leap out of my skin. "Use that brilliant brain of yours!"

"Um, sis, I am," said Zander.

"Shut it. I'm not talking to you." She shook her head back, rubbing her temples with her fingertips. "Come on. Shapeshifters. Terrorize victims. Stabby, stabby brain thing. Think."

"Stabby what now?" Peter sputtered.

"It's okay, bro," said Zander. "Sometimes she's like that."

"Bro?"

"Pachoolee!" Blayde shouted.

"Yahtzee!" came a cry from the crowd.

"We're playing Yahtzee?" asked someone else.

"I got it." Blayde spun on her heels, snapping her fingers. "The shapeshifters? They're from Pachoolee!"

Zander nodded in agreement. "Can't believe I didn't see it before."

I stared blankly. "Does that help us?"

"It just might," said Zander. "What do you know about vampires?"

"Oh, please don't tell me vampires are real."

"They're not," he said, but my relief was short-lived. "But they're based on a grain of truth. You see, the inhabitants of Pachoolee feed off *Toxoplasma gondii*, a parasite that runs rampant on Earth. The parasites take up residence in the amygdala, the part of the brain that controls fear. The Pachooleeans have been living on Earth for centuries, clever enough to stay out of the limelight. Unfortunately, they got a bad reputation in the mid-1700s when they developed a terrible addiction to the chemicals excreted from the amygdala when the victim was terrified—thank you, plague victims! Replaced toxoplasma with chomping on the whole human amygdala. They took up the guise of vampires, seductive beings who could learn their victims' fears before replicating them and feeding on the result. Bats and rats? Meant much more back then when the plague was still heavy on the collective consciousness. Terrifying. Trust me, I was there."

"There are generations of them here," added Blayde, "which explains why they don't seem to know who we are. And why they have so much practice flying under the Agency's radar."

"So, now they're here," I spat, "where people are court-ordered to tell them their deepest, darkest secrets—and, more importantly, their fears. And no one would believe the victims if they suddenly decided to tell anyone what was happening. They're creating trauma in order to feed off of it. *They're farming it.*"

Zander nodded, glancing around the rest of the room with a sweep of his eyes, realizing that all their faces were intent on his, watching his every move with anxiety and confusion. He gave them a reassuring smile, but their stares did not break away. And no amount of reassuring smiles was going to dispel the disgust growing in my gut.

"So" —he turned to Barker—"now would be a good time to call your bosses."

"I've been trying!" He replied, obviously distressed. "I'm not getting a response!"

He repeatedly banged furiously on a small metal button, his face twisted with fear. He knew what we were facing. At least now he believed us too.

"Hold on. Hold on," I said. "I'm no neuroscientist, but if they take the whole amygdala, wouldn't we not be able to fear them anymore? Not to mention the patients here would probably notice if part of their brains just up and vanished one day. There would be side effects to say the least."

Blayde snapped her fingers. "They must be able to grow it back. That explains a lot, mostly why none of their victims bear any marks of their attack. They drug them, and the cells regenerate—like us, but less awesome and in a much less concentrated dose. That's what happened to you. Your natural replicating cells were battling with the chemically-induced cell regeneration."

"And the victims don't remember anything before they roofie us on top of everything else," I said. "I bet you anything the night nurses are just another form of theirs. This is a whole operation. Who knows how long this had been going on."

"What are you three talking about?" a nurse asked, staring at us with wide eyes. "This ain't no alien conspiracy. It's a *hurricane*. Please, get off the table. We don't want anyone to get hurt now."

"What is everyone doing in here?" Blayde asked. "Shouldn't someone be trying to get these shutters up? Or at least try to figure out what's happening with the building?"

The nurse whipped out her electronic pager. A small message scrolled across it: "Assemble everyone in the rec room. Assemble everyone in the rec room." Over and over again.

"We've gotta get out of here," Blayde snapped, turning to the rest of the patients and nurses grouped in the small common room. "This is a trap."

"No, it isn't," the nurse said comfortingly, placing her hands on Blayde. I could see the gears turning in her head as she fought the instinct to shake her off. "There is absolutely no need to worry."

"Listen, health specialist." She sidestepped her way out of the woman's grasp. "I know you're just doing your job. I know you think I'm crazy. But I'm done playing your games. We need to get all the patients out of this institute before it turns into a little house of horrors."

"Please, calm down. We don't want to frighten the other patients."

"Frighten them?" Blayde laughed. "Frighten? If they're scared now, they'll be no match for what's to come. They've got the worst fears coming at them to feed off their minds; they need to be warned. They need the truth."

"I got a signal!" Barker shouted. Almost instantly, the image of him fizzled into nothing, a loud electrical hum filled the room, making our ears ring as we watched him disappear into thin air.

This was definitely an alien conspiracy.

# TWELVE
## A PSA ON THE DANGERS OF PDA

**RIOTS ARE A LITTLE OVERWHELMING FOR** everyone, so make sure you pack snacks. And I seriously don't recommend you have one in a mental institution. They can be draining for everyone involved. Self-care, people. Self-care.

I was just as shocked as the patients were to see Barker disappear into thin air. Okay, maybe a little less; I'd seen people pull it off before—but never an Agency operative who I thought was as dull as a dishpan.

"The Alliance has teleportation tech?" I asked over the throng of casual screams.

"Call-backs! They're called call-backs!" Zander shouted, which only made the patients cry out louder. He seemed more frustrated that Barker disappeared than anything else, practically sulking. His arms were crossed over his chest, and I swear I saw him micro-frown. "The device sends an electrical pulse through one's body and sends the atoms to a home plate. Only works one way."

"This is good, right?" I asked. "He's bringing the Agency down here. They'll arrest those Patch-whatever people for their secret human fear farm, right?"

"Pachoolee. And not if they find us first," said Blayde. "Come on, we have to get out of here."

She hopped off the table, rushing for the staff door. I dove down after her.

"Is that Elvis?" Zander shouted above the throng. The screams of the crowd changed into something much more confused. A little bit better than panic.

"And leave all these people in the hands of the shapeshifters?" I stammered, as we pressed through the throng of people.

"The Agency will have no choice but to do something," she said. She was a snowplow through the crowd, but they were too distracted to mind. "Same as they'll have no choice but to arrest us, either."

"But what if the Agency doesn't send its people? Or what if they arrive too late?"

"Would you rather we all end up on an Alliance prison ship?" she spat. "You do you, but I'm getting out of this place before some shapeshifter who thinks they know me turns into my worst fear and tries to suck my brain dry. And if we find a way out, nothing's stopping the others from following us to freedom."

"I'm not leaving them in here," I said. "Who knows what the doctors will do to the patients once they're backed into a corner."

Blayde reached the metal door at the back of the room, the one now covering the grated exit to the outdoor world. She grabbed the handle, giving it a sharp twist.

The door, unsurprisingly, did not budge.

"Wonderful," she muttered, glancing in the crack between the door and the frame. "Not a glimmer of light." She flipped the laser from her pocket, aiming it at the lock. It barely made a mark. "Shit. This place has been re-enforced with arctronian steel."

"Let me guess, impenetrable stuff?" I asked. "What about the windows?"

She took few steps to her right, viciously attacking the handle of the nearest window. It didn't move an inch. She pulled her arm back as far as it could go, bringing it forward full force to the glass. A deafening crack resonated in the room, making my spine tense. She shook her hand back into place.

Exasperated, she stared at the unyielding pane of glass. A snarl drew itself on her face, a snarl so vicious I was glad I was not the window that stood in her way. She dragged her laser against the transparent surface.

Not a scratch.

"That's why they gathered everyone here," she said, dropping her hands from the window and smoothing the fabric of her pants, calm as can be. "It's expensive to reinforce an entire hospital. Probably saved a ton by focusing on just one room. Doors open in but don't let out. They have to get rid of the evidence. They can't let a single patient get away."

"Well, shit, do something!" I sputtered. "Come on. You're Blayde! The Iron or whatever! You of all people can think of a way out of here!"

"Don't you think I'm trying?" she hissed. "What do you think I'm doing, watering flowers here? Veesh, Sally."

I scanned the room for Zander, suddenly aware of his absence. In the din, I could hear him, his words wafting over the now quasi-silent room. While we had been running and slamming on things, he had stayed on the table trying to calm the patients. No one was paying attention to the two of us at all.

"Now, you've seen a lot in the past few minutes," he said, his voice steady and warm. My heart fluttered with pride. That was my guy up there. That was my guy that everyone was focused on, who was calming down a sea of terrified, trapped people. "A guard disappeared into thin air right there. And, for some reason, we're all rounded up in this tiny room. You probably want to know why. Right?"

Mutters of agreement rose from the crowd. He nodded along with them. If he were in a suit rather than hospital scrubs, I would have thought him quite presidential.

"This is the truth, the whole truth, nothing but the truth, and the only way you're going to survive today is by following me without argument. Now, first things first, let's get this over with. Your doctors—Smith, Winfrey and Drew—they're shapeshifting aliens."

"Aren't *you* a shapeshifting alien?" Daisy-May pointed out, inspiring the crowd's collective gasp.

"Nope, time-traveling and immortal are what I am. Shapeshifting? Thank the stars above that I am not."

"That's so cool," she muttered.

"Now, these doctors have been using you for their own gain. Giving you the terrible dreams you only barely remember and feeding off your fear. But we all know the screams. They managed to heal your wounds and stitch you back up, not disrupting your everyday lives in the slightest, though maybe giving you a strange addiction to oatmeal. But they're not playing it safe anymore. The mere fact that they've trapped us in here shows that they are afraid. They are trapped, and the Agency knows they are here. And very soon, this nightmare—and all of our nightmares—will be over."

"We can't test them all," I whispered, and Blayde nodded. "A shapeshifter could be in here. With us."

I grabbed an entranced nurse, pulling a hair off his head. He yipped, but the strand was still solid in my hands.

"We're all still breathing," I said.

"That's a good thing, isn't it?" he asked, rubbing his scalp. "If this is a coping mechanism, I would prefer you respect my bodily autonomy, thank you very much."

"How do the vents work in the rec room?" I asked him, gripping his arm tighter than I should have. "How does the air still get in?"

"How should I know?"

"Does your building have blueprints?"

"Seriously, where in my job description is it written that I should know the building's blueprints?"

"It's a yes-or-no question."

"Yes, they probably have blueprints. No, I have no idea where they are." He paused. "But if you think that I'm gonna let claustrophobic patients clamber through vents—"

"They can put up with a lot and face many a fear when their life's in actual danger," said Blayde. "Adrenaline is a helluva drug."

"Are you threatening them?"

"Me?" she asked. "No, I'm not. Weren't you listening at all to anything that's been going on?"

"I got lost at the part about the aliens."

"Well, that's pretty much the gist of it," Blayde said with a shrug.

"But we can't let our guard down," Zander continued. "The–um–Space Police might not come at all. All we have is each other. And you know what happens when someone is trapped; they lash out. I'm not going to sugarcoat it: *They. Want. To. Kill. You.* Each and every one of you. They will turn into whatever you fear most."

"Like boggarts!" someone cried.

# INALIENABLE

"Good analogy." Zander nodded. "But since none of us are wizards—"

"I'm a wizard!" said someone.

"Since not all of us are wizards, we need to stick together. I want you all to pluck a hair off the head of the person to your right. Then we do the left. If that hair does not remain a hair after leaving their scalp, just shout."

"Zander's got a handle on this here," said Blayde, turning to me with a grin. So much for taking things seriously. "You and me, we'll look for the building's blueprints. But I have a stop I want to make first."

· · · · · · ● · · · · · · · · ·

**SNEAKING THROUGH VENTS. JUMPING THROUGH** grates to find the administrative wing. Blayde picked the locks with a keen precision that could only have been earned from years upon years of itchy fingers. The door swung inward, a row of shiny metal lockers covering the wall in front of us from the floor to the ceiling.

"Zapping the door would have gained us some time," I said.

She rolled her eyes. "I don't always have to do everything rough. Can't I just pick a lock now and then without being nagged with all these questions?"

"Well, *sor-ry*. What are we looking for exactly?"

"This," she said smugly, punching a small spot on the bottom left of the metal locker. It popped open with a resounding whack. "Wait. No. The next one."

Blayde repeated this on the locker on the right and reached inside. Out came her red leather jacket, her arms slipping smoothly into the sleeves, the veteran of ancient battles draped over her shoulders once again. Her journal went straight to her inside pocket, a smidge of weight off her shoulders.

She paused for a second, then ripped off the jacket and placed it on the bench in the corner. Without any modesty whatsoever, she started stripping off her hospital clothes and stuffing them back into the locker, pulling her own clothes back on. Her skinny jeans replaced the white unisex pants; the black tank top the white long-sleeved T-shirt; the creamy white cardigan; her raw red jacket. Off went the white Keds. On went the black lace-up boots.

"Much better," she said. "Thanks for watching."

"You never opened my locker!"

"Ah. True."

She whipped out her laser and shot a beam at the locker in front of me. The door creaked open. "All yours. Have at it."

"You're gonna have to teach me how to do that."

"Well, first, you take your clothes off, then you put the new ones on."

I bottled up my frustration and kicked off my papery shoes. Despite the old ones being still sandy from the beach where I had been arrested, they were mine, dammit, and they made everything better. The rest of my clothes made me feel fully human again.

# INALIENABLE

Blayde ransacked Zander's locker next, pulling out his coat and clothes. I slipped the jacket on, though it was much too big and slid off my shoulders. There. Comfortably warm. It even smelled of him, all ash and stardust.

I didn't dare look through the pockets. I could feel them stuffed with mysteries, but they were his mysteries, secrets the universe wasn't ready to provide. I tied his jeans and tee together, flinging them over my chest like a sash. He'd be happy to have them when this was all over.

"Right. Now for those blueprints."

The administrative offices were just next door, so we pushed our way through the unlocked entrance. Cabinets covered most of the walls: patient information, medical and criminal records. Patients, patients … patience.

No blueprints.

"Did you find anything?" I asked.

"Yeah, I just didn't say anything because I like watching you struggle," she said. "No. Of course not. The last cabinet I haven't checked is that one, but it's locked."

I opened the file on security. "Hold that. I think I found what we're looking for."

"What?"

"Evacuation plans!"

"Shouldn't they be on the walls?"

"Not very nice of them. Think we should call in a tip, say they're not up to code?"

I placed the small black-and-white maps on the desk, smoothing them out. Blayde grabbed a highlighter from the pencil pot.

"Here." She scribbled on the paper. "Too big to be a chimney, not the right place to be a bathroom."

"That looks like the old bell tower," I said, taping my finger on the spot. "Zander and I found it on our first night here. Well, he did."

"Do you think we can get the patients out through it?" she asked.

"It's wide enough, sure," I replied. I couldn't help but feel the excitement rising inside me. It was impossible to hold back a grin. "If one of us can get up there, we can open it and jump the patients to safety. First, we have to get them through the vents out of the rec room, though, since we can't jump it blind. Not all of them are going to be onboard with that."

"Let's go save some lives," she said. "Heroes!"

She took a step toward the exit, leaning her head out the door and glancing back and forth to see if the coast was clear.

A hand clamped my mouth before I could follow her. It held in my scream, another arm grabbing my waist and restraining me entirely. Crap!

"Don't make a sound," a voice whispered, the breath tickling my ear.

The old cabinet we hadn't had the time to check out? Well, that was freaking gone. The shapeshifter had been here the whole time, waiting, watching.

Seeing everything.

"Sally?" Blayde called back, hissing. "Come on. Hero time."

"Over here!" a voice called from up the hallway. My voice. Footsteps getting louder, coming this way.

I watched as another me breezed past, stopping in front of the office door.

It was surreal seeing myself through my own eyes. Seeing Zander's big leather coat, much too large for me, bulking up my shoulders. Was that really how the back of my hair looked? When was the last time I'd had a haircut?

"Sorry, jumped ahead," the other me said with a grin. But my face was all wrong. It was mine, but the shapeshifter wasn't using it right. The smile was off. That or I just didn't recognize my own teeth. I fought against the arm restraining me, but it wasn't a human arm. It had wrapped fully around me, fused with the body on both ends. It just went from waist to waist like a tight seat belt.

And biting was a no go, unless I actually wanted a mouthful of sand.

"Stick with me, okay? Zander would get in such a fit if he let me get a scratch on you."

"Yeah, I would." Zander appeared from around the corner, placing his arm over my shoulders. Far too much swagger for the real Zander. Not when people were counting on him to save their lives.

I tried to press my tongue through my captor's fingers, but the fingers were gone. The palm tasted like sawdust and grime. Its grip tightened.

"Zan?" Blayde asked sternly. "I thought you were staying with the patients."

"Well, we thought it would be important for both of us to break the news to you, together," he said, pulling the faux-Sally closer to him.

*Fally?*

No, wait, she didn't deserve a name; she shouldn't exist. She didn't exist. It was my body; she had no right to parade around wearing it like that.

"What kind of news?" Blayde asked, a small tremor entering into her voice.

"Big news!" other me announced with a broad grin. She flashed her the beautiful diamond the size of a pigeon's egg resting on her ring finger, her left hand dipping heavy with its weight.

"Sally and I are getting married!" Faux-Zander said excitedly. Other me laughed with excitement, leaning up to kiss him.

"What?" Blayde's confidence shattered so loudly I was certain that chunks of it could be found lodged deep in the institute's walls.

"We want you be maid of honor at the wedding!" other me said with girlish glee.

"We're thinking June!"

"We've already started looking at dress designs and cakes and such. Oh, and a house. We need a safe place for Zander Junior to grow up …"

Faux-Zander placed a hand on the fake Sally's belly. "We didn't want to tell you until we knew the gender!"

"I'm pregnant!"

"We've known for some time yet, but you're the only person we've told so far."

They kissed once again, yet with a little more fire now. Well, if you could call it fire. I'd seen more chemistry in a Hallmark special.

Ugh, gross. His hand was pulling her leg up around his hip and she was leaning back, somehow eating his face in the process. That couldn't have been how we really looked; if so, then I honestly did owe Blayde an apology.

The only thing up with my stomach was its hunger for actual food. No buns in this oven. Oh great, now I'm craving buns. Seriously, they could have gone a little out of their way to feed us something other than oatmeal and toast for breakfast.

Screw it, I was getting distracted. I tried to shake the creature off me again, but it gripped tighter, following my every move and pulling me back. I was sinking into it like vertical quicksand.

So, this was her greatest fear. Doctor Smith had ripped the dying Zander scene straight from my eval. She may have been a monster, but she was a damn good psychiatrist—or psychologist? —knowing exactly what knife was most likely to make me bleed. Blayde couldn't truly see us like this, could she? If Zander and my relationship was what was most likely to scare her, then she wasn't being cold to me this past week; she was being *civil*.

"We're afraid what teleporting could do to the baby, so we're not going to go anywhere for a while," Faux-Zander added, coming up for air. He didn't drop fake Sally's leg. She kept licking his stubble. "And then we have to stay here a little. You know, we're not going to expose an innocent babe to the dangers of space travel."

"You're going to be an aunt!"

"You're free to stay with us on Earth!" Zander grinned broadly. "You could go into teaching, if you want to!"

"You're attractive. I'm sure there's a guy here for you!" other me added. "Humans are good in bed."

"We sleep together!" Faux-Zander chirped.

"Auntie Blayde. Would you rather be called Baba or Dede? Baba's easier for a baby."

Suddenly, the fake couple started to kiss again, somehow, impossibly, more enthusiastically than before. Blayde's face was as white and empty as this page was when I had writer's block.

"Baba!" Fake-Zander said as he broke away from the kiss.

"Let's move to Toronto!" other me exclaimed.

"Blayde has a lot of money saved away. We could buy a very expensive house!"

"I like to make you spend money on me! I'm frivolous!"

"And very hot!" he exclaimed.

"Aunt Blayde!" she added.

# INALIENABLE

Blayde was frozen there, watching their increasingly surreal entangling of limbs. It was like something out of hentai. No wonder she blanched.

I swung my elbow back into the creature holding me, but it met nothing but shifting sand, its suction pulling me in fast.

I closed my eyes to the disgusting sight just as other Sally stuck her foot down Zander's waistband. *Deep breath. All you have to do is jump a meter, a single meter. Well, more if you can manage it. Just out of the creature's clutches. You can't bring a single grain with you.*

My eyes flew open, and I flung myself into the hallway, leaving the beast behind, landing squarely around other Sally. She screamed as I tackled her, dropping to the ground like a wet sandy mass. I mean, it wasn't a stable structure to begin with.

Did I have any qualms about punching my own face? Why, yes, indeed I had a few. But all I had to do was look at those purple hickeys on her neck before having my rage meter refill to the brim.

"That's my face, you douchecanoe!" I sputtered. "Give it back!"

Other Zander was trying to pull me off, his strong arm wrapping around my neck, tight enough to cut off the air. But screw it. I didn't need air like I used to. I was going to pass out at some point, but not before I made this face-stealing sand bitch stop impersonating me.

I was starting to see stars, and not the cool gas kinds. Still pretty and sparkly, though. Other Zander ripped me straight up and flung me to the ground, throwing himself on top of me with his fingers still on my throat.

Zander's face stared down at me with pure hatred in his eyes. He pushed me back further into the ground, slamming my head into the linoleum-covered floor. As the stars flickered more freely, it was hard to see the wrong in his features. It was, unmistakably, Zander.

Killing me.

He screamed, falling to the side. Blayde stood over him, laser pointer in hand, shooting another beam of ripping red light into his core. He screamed again, dissolving into a puddle of grains, rolling up the wall and into the nearest vent. Other me was nowhere to be seen.

"You good?" Blayde asked.

Already, my throat was knitting itself back into order. I exhaled heavily. "I'm good."

I sat up, brushing sand from my eyes. The creature had lost some cohesion when she had hit him, it seemed. I coughed up the particles that had made up my fake fiancé.

"What's this?" I asked, picking up a brown bullet from the ground. "Did you … where did you get a gun?"

"I didn't," she replied, coolly. "That's not a bullet. The Pachoolean left it behind."

I dropped it instantly. "Did the thing … crap itself?"

"Hot sand clump," she said, bending over to examine it herself. "It formed when my laser shot through it, like when lightning strikes the beach. I suppose Pachooleeans are silicon-based life forms."

"So, you had absolutely no idea what was going to happen when you shot the thing?"

"No, but isn't it neat?" she said, grinning. "Inert. Silicon released from thought. Need a hand?"

She helped me to my feet. Her face had filled with color, as if none of this had ever happened.

"Are you good?" I asked her.

"Of course. Why wouldn't I be?"

"Well, with the whole facing your worst fear and all …"

Blayde's face fell before she exploded with laughter. She collapsed to the floor, eyes bursting with tears, slapping her knee as she spun around on the linoleum.

"Facing my worst fear," she howled. "That's a good one!"

"Hey, you're making a scene," I said, but my voice was drowned out by her guffaws.

"Smoochy smoochy. I'm so scared!" she managed to blurt out in between laughs. "That's beautiful, Sally."

"But, look, Blayde, I saw your face," I said. Maybe I shouldn't have insisted. But I was her friend, dammit. Whether she liked it or not. "You were terrified."

"I wasn't scared. I was offended!" She pushed herself up to her feet, clutching her abs. "I'm pissed because *that's* what she thought my greatest fear was. When, obviously, *I'm* the one who hates clowns."

"So, if I told you I was marrying Zander and/or pregnant with your brother's child, you wouldn't shoot me with your laser?"

"I knew she wasn't you," Blayde snapped. "Why? Are you?"

"What? Marrying your brother or pregnant?"

She shrugged.

"No. But if I was, I would tell you, you know that right? I would make sure all weapons are out of reach first, though."

She snickered. "Zander doesn't need to hear about this."

"No, he doesn't," I agreed.

"In any case, at least now we know how to get these damn things," she said sternly.

"We zap them with lasers? How big can your laser pointer shoot?"

"It's a laser." Blayde rolled her eyes. "The light doesn't diverge. It's one single beam."

"So?" I asked. "Poke them in a lot of places. They'll be as good as dead."

"If it has to come to that. Worst case scenario, they just get smaller and smaller until nothing's left. But our first priority is to get everyone out safely."

"I'm right behind you."

No obstacles lay in our way as we made our way down the corridors of the institute. Blayde read the map, instructing me to turn here, there, and so on, until we reached a very long and surprisingly empty stretch of hallway.

"Sally?" Smith's voice called, echoing through some distant stretch of corridor. "Come out, Sally. You need to calm down. Rid your mind of such delusions; there is nothing wrong here. Your head is playing tricks on you!"

"Are you a delusion?" I asked Blayde.

She punched me in the shoulder. "Did you feel that?"

"I dunno, it could have been my mind playing tricks on me."

She chuckled. "Come on, just ignore her."

We turned our attention to the wall on the end of the corridor where the bell tower's base had once been. Unfortunately, a lone metal door stood in our way, cruelly laughing at us the way cold metal doors do.

"Blocked off," I muttered, sliding my hand across the frustrating thing. "Are you sure it's here?"

"I can read maps in at least five different galaxies— that I know of. Do you seriously think a 2D Terran map is going to best me?"

"We're gonna need much more than a laser pointer to cut a way through this. You realize this, don't you?"

"Shut up. I'm thinking."

Amazingly, her big brain power time seemed to be working. Sparks shot forward, bursting through the door, landing on my clothes before I patted them out, awestruck.

"Blayde, are you doing this?" I asked, having to raise my voice over the deafening sound of grinding metal. "With your mind?" I added for good measure. "Man, I'm sorry I interrupted your thinking. This is amazing."

"Sally, I have never had—and do not and probably never will in the foreseeable future—have telekinesis."

"Then what exactly is happening right now?"

"Frash. It's the Agency."

"What?"

"You heard me. Agency! Run!"

I spun on my heels, my feet hitting the ground so fast that my poor sneakers were hot with the friction. But running was no use. The instant the metal door fell on the floor behind me, the sound chasing me down the hallway, someone put two bullets into my back.

And I died, which was fine since it hadn't happened in a while. I just didn't want to make a habit of it.

# THIRTEEN

## SUPPORT COMES IN MANY FORMS BUT
## THIS ONE'S NOT RIGHT FOR ME

**IT'S A RELIEF WHEN THE BULLETS FINALLY ROLL** out of your skin. Even better when the wounds close shut, the brain releasing a rush of endorphins to say that everything is a-ok. Ah. Thanks, brain. Why weren't you doing this back when I needed you in high school?

"Shut up," Blayde hissed.

"But I haven't said anything." I rolled over on my back. There was neither a sky nor a ceiling up there, but there was fabric for some reason. Very handsome fabric. Very green.

"I never said you did. I just told you to shut up."

Always looking out for me. What a sweetie. I sat up, which was tough with my hands zip tied together. I was on a plastic mat on the floor—no, ground. Grass was all around us. Somehow, I had been brought outside.

It was a mild relief to know there definitely was a way out of the hospital. The sucky part was knowing the Agency was controlling it.

"Why are we in a tent?" I asked. The makeshift building was large enough for a state fair pie-eating contest. Probably not what we were actually here for.

"Zip!" said Blayde.

"Why didn't we just jump instead of run? Seriously. It's like you *want* to be caught."

"Quora quora quora, reep quoeh quo fubo folo?"

Even without the words making a lick of sense, the voice that uttered them chilled me to the bone. Foollegg burst through the door flap, her lips a line so thin she had possibly painted them on with liner. Her eyes shot between me and Blayde, her hand resting passively on the butt of her weapon. The dark black Agency body armor that climbed her lanky frame made her look like an elongated ant, flimsy but well protected.

"Geh coo no?" she asked, a smile playing on her lips. Blayde flashed her most devious smile.

"We're not pulling any tricks, Foollegg," she said. "We'd already be gone if this were some kind of trap."

"Hold on," I stammered. "Why are you speaking English when she's speaking … whatever?"

"Oh, right. Foollegg, do you not have a translator?"

"I can speak English, thank you very much," she said in a convincing Texan accent, but still she reached into her pocket to retrieve a little gray box, which she hung around her neck. "Anywho, the Iron and the …

tagalong? I'm sorry, we haven't come up with a better name for you yet."

"You could probably be a little more creative than a Girl Scout cookie," I said. "But I won't blame you. Could your annual budget not cover a better translator? Has the Agency been hit with some tough times?"

"Nickname pending, then," Foollegg shrugged as she unfurled a collapsible stool and took a seat in front of us, rubbing her pale white hands together. "To rehash: this is the best escape you could come up with? It has to be the most convoluted thing I've ever seen."

"At which point I told her we would have already left if that were the case," said Blayde. "Right, Sally's up to speed. Can we hurry this up, please?"

"You lock down a mental institution, block every way in and out of the place, and trapped a hundred people inside. News vans are surrounding the front of the complex. And you know humans. You can never keep their greedy little hands off a little bit of gossip. What's this all for?"

"I told you it's not us," Blayde insisted. "There are at least three Pachooleeans loose in there, and they're ravenously hungry."

"Oh, and I'm just supposed to believe the" —she checked her notes—"2734rd time offender?"

"If you don't believe her"—I hopped to my feet, oddly proud of the stupid move—"believe the first-time offender instead. Except I haven't committed any crimes."

"You broke into the Agency literally a week ago," she said. "And you killed—"

"Apart from that." I shrugged. "But seriously, why would I lie?"

"Hello? I have your parents' accidental gas leak on speed dial."

Shit. I forced myself to stand tall, to not shake under her words. "Okay, maybe for that. But I'm not. Where's Barker? He'll tell you everything!"

"Barker?" Foollegg blinked, slowly.

"The kid you sent to spy on us," I said. "Wait, who am I calling kid? He's older than me."

"Oh—Junior!" Foollegg slapped her leg, giddy.

"Your son?"

"Not mine. Snooke's," she replied, moderately gleefully. "The man *insisted* his son was the only person for the job. Instead, he damages his wrap and rushes back to us sobbing about sand monsters."

"That explains why he had a stick up his ass," said Blayde. "Cramming a neck like that into a human skin wrap? The compression field must have been enormous! No wonder your Agency can't afford to give you proper translators, Foollegg."

Foollegg's lips dropped back into a straight line. "Where's your brother?"

"Protecting the hundred patients inside from the ravenous Pachooleeans," she spat. "Thanks for asking. Where's yours?"

# INALIENABLE

"Leading the Alliance to a victory on the other side of the galaxy." She crossed her arms across her chest, her face turning blue. Maybe she was blushing; maybe she was having a stroke.

"Oh, are you at war again?" asked Blayde. "Seems like you have much bigger stars to seize than little old me."

"It's amazing you've eluded our capture for so long when you're so … clueless. Astounding, even."

"I try my best. So, what are you going to do? Arrest us? Fake our deaths in this riot? Let the newscasters spread the tale of our insane taking-over of the mental institution we were incarcerated in on false pretenses and faked-up evidence, while dragging us back by the hair to your lords and masters on Pyrina, so you can stand on a podium and receive your medal and early retirement, eternal fame, and riches? Makes for a great story."

"And the threat you pose to the Alliance would be eradicated."

"Wait, what about me?" I asked. "Don't I have rights? This is my home planet. Doesn't that count for anything?"

"You lost your rights the instant you threw your lot in with these two."

"It's not I like a signed a form or anything," I muttered.

The tent flaps flew open, and a human ball of flame burst through. Her skin glowing like literal polished gold, standing in bright red stilettos, she dwarfed Foollegg in sheer star power alone. Her thin arms were deceptively strong as she dragged in a heavy protest sign large enough for me to sleep on that had writing in an alphabet I couldn't read. A long face with a round chin, a small nose, narrow lips, set off by electric blue eyes that clashed with the short, curly, dark orange hair styled with a military cut.

"Woah," I couldn't help but say. She was followed shortly behind by two Agency soldiers, who she swatted away with the sign.

"What are *you* doing here?" Foollegg spat.

"La so ray teela mee latee," said the stranger, huffing as she heaved the sign down, hard, on one of the guards. The other one raised his baton, but she lifted her sign again, and he froze, obviously terrified.

"Will you please not resort to violence?" said Foollegg defeatedly. "This is a rescue mission."

"Ozusgri. Yu'n folo geh nupo calo cho gollumc ulo glougoja cho umja lockosg choi jocolbo."

"What the hell is going on?" I hissed to Blayde. "And why am I only getting half the convo?"

"Oh, she doesn't have a translator either," she replied. "Shit, I forgot how useless communication was without one."

"But I understand Foollegg when she's speaking to her."

"Yeah, because she has a translator." She must have noticed I wasn't following at all because she sighed and launched into a long-winded explanation as the two aliens continued to argue on their own.

"So, translators take brainwaves in so they can modulate the response to match," she explained. "You're not actually hearing words; your brain is just interpreting the *content* as words. One person with a translator can speak to anyone surrounding them and understand while being understood. Which is why you can follow Foollegg's side of this mess. Meanwhile, the angry orange lady doesn't have one, so you won't understand a lick of what she says."

"I was hoping for an explanation about their argument," I said. "It seems intense."

"Oh!" the stranger said, eyes going wide as she saw me. She raced to my side. "Did they hurt you? Don't worry, I'm going to get you out of here!"

"And she speaks English," said Blayde. "That makes things easier."

The stranger turned to Foollegg, glowering. "I demand you release this Earthling! You have no right to detain her! This isn't your planet, and they aren't your people!"

"Who are you calling Earthling?" I sputtered. "Wait, hold on, what did you just say?"

"Don't say a word, sweet thing." The woman turned back and ruffled my hair. "Skydancer Willowcrest, defender of Terran rights, is here to save the day."

Foollegg's eyes managed to roll despite being all pupil and nothing else. "She's not in danger, Willowcrest.

She's a criminal. Haven't you been watching the news? I know how much you enjoy consuming Terran media."

"Yet another Earthling you've got your sights on," Willowcrest snarled. "The Agency doesn't know when to stop, does it?"

"That's what I've been saying!" I sputtered. "Foollegg, save the world or leave it alone. Don't stick around pretending you care while using bureaucracy as an excuse to cover up what a terrible job you've been doing actually keeping off-worlders under wraps."

"Are you kidding me?" Foollegg rubbed one of her pale white hands over her clear scalp. "What do you think I'm trying to do here? Your *friends* are off-worlders. They are a threat to your world. Let me do my job!"

"They rescued the planet," I spat. "I was there! And will you listen to us? Right now, three ravenous shapeshifters are hunting the patients of this institute. You want me to let you do your job? *Go and do it!*"

"And lose you in the process? No, thank you."

"She's not yours to begin with!" said Willowcrest, dropping to a knee by my side, reaching for my hair. I let her pet it, awkwardly, still trying to figure out where she stood. She smelled of lilacs. Not half bad.

"Will you get out of our way, Willowcrest?" Foollegg croaked. "Your people are making a mess of this operation!"

"No, that's what *you're* doing," she replied. "IHOP demands you treat the locals of this planet with the dignity and respect that they deserve. If your operation goes against this, then we will fight it with our last breaths."

"Wait, why is IHOP involved with this?" I asked. "Don't tell me that the International House of Pancakes is some kind of alien front. I'm tired of having my mind blown."

"No, we're for the Protection of Earthlings and Terran Autonomy." Willowcrest beamed. "We're aware the acronym is less catchy in English than in Pyrinian, but the intention is there."

"It's also already taken. And doesn't spell IHOP."

"Right, I'm getting tired of this," said Blayde, snapping her zip ties in one swift move and standing up. "I'd say it was nice to meet you, Willowcrest, but I will not remember you when the day is over, so I'd rather not die. Sally?"

"Hold it right there," Foollegg said, raising her phone high. "Remember what I said, Sally. One more step, and your"—she took one look at Willowcrest and blanched more than she already was—"and your credit score is going to tank."

"And you're threatening her!" Willowcrest gasped. "This is exactly what I'm talking about! You have no right to threaten the locals. They were here first!"

"I would remind you you're not a local to this planet either," said Foollegg, raising a brow.

"But I have chosen to live in peace and harmony with all the inhabitants of this world," Willowcrest said airily.

"And as a result, they have welcomed me with open arms."

"They have welcomed the Terran version of you. How many of these earthlings would accept you if they knew where you were from? This is why we are here. We protect off-worlders like you. We defend your way of life. We make it so that you don't have to fear your neighbors."

"And as a result, they have a reason to fear theirs," she spat. "Retaliation. Cover-ups. Where does it end?"

"Will you both shut up already?" Blayde shouted. The two guards seemed relieved to hear her say anything. Both were still slightly dazed from their encounter with the protest sign, and it didn't seem they were big fans of Willowcrest.

"Look," Blayde continued, "we don't have much time. It's going to be a PR nightmare if these patients die at the hands of off-worlders. I, for one, am not going to stand for the loss of innocent life. Come on, Sally, we have work to do while they're faffing around."

"You don't have to tell me twice," I replied. "Willowcrest, It's great meeting you. I'm completely for your cause. Though you might want to remove Earthling from the name. It's slightly offensive."

"We mean it as a term of endearment, dear," she said.

"Yeah, well, I'm not feeling all that endeared," I replied.

"We didn't ask you."

"Sally," Foollegg insisted, "you walk out that door—if you even make it that far—and there will be consequences."

"I trust Willowcrest will disagree." I reached for Blayde's hand. "And why the hell would I use the door?"

I pulled Blayde into a jump before she could do it herself, flinging us away from the tent. I rose to my feet the second I touched solid ground, letting my eyes adjust to the sudden gloomy atmosphere of Smith's office. Blayde moaned.

"Here? Why here?" she asked, grabbing my wrists and ripping them apart, freeing me from the pesky zip ties.

"A little thank you would be nice," I said. " This was the last place I jumped to. I seemed to remember the way back. I didn't want to jump straight to Zander, freak the patients out any more."

"Have I ever asked for thanks?"

"Nearly every time. Come on, we need to find Zander the old-fashioned way," I said, making for the door. "We can slip back through the vents and—"

"Then where do we go?" She pushed her way out into the hallway, skipping down the length. "I heard Maka Naka Seven is amazing this time of year. Though I'm not sure what time that is exactly."

"Blayde, come on."

"I mean it! So long, desert planets! So long, war-ridden scum! So long, Alliance! We would be free. Shh!" she ordered.

The last bit had nothing to do with our conversation. I obeyed instantly.

She jutted her chin around the corner of the door. The rec room door was wide open, Agency soldiers with human faces helping the captive patients and staff … fill out paperwork? So far, no one had left, though each had a clipboard in hand and was scribbling their credentials on it, some with nurses by their sides to help them out.

Blayde took a few steps away from the door. "He's not in there."

"Do you think they have him captured somewhere?"

She shook her head. "He's probably hiding out. We need to find him."

"Blayde, is this you just saying everything that goes through your head?"

"No way. Now, we must think where he's hiding."

"You are, aren't you? My best guess is he went back to the infirmary. It was the last non-rec room place we'd all been together."

She nodded, sighing heavily. "Fine. Let's go."

She marched down the hallway toward the infirmary, not even waiting for me. This was getting exasperating. She reached down her throat, grabbing the laser pointer she had stashed there, pulling it out and wiping it off on a corner of her tank top. She sliced open the lock.

Zander rushed at us with two sharpened chair legs in hand. Blayde put her hands up defensively.

"Banana cream pie is the best kind of pie," she announced.

"I disagree." Zander held the chair leg out.

"So do I."

He turned to me, glaring. I racked my brain for something, anything I could say. "Uh, neither of us is the Miranda?"

His shoulders slumped with relief. "You found my jacket!"

"We got your clothes, too," I said, removing the bizarre clothing sash. His hand brushed mine for a second, the reassuring warmth spreading through me.

"Okay, touching reunion. Such chemistry! We've gotta get out," Blayde announced, stepping between us.

"What about the Pachooleeans?" I asked.

"And risk getting caught by the Agency? Let's not distract them from actually doing their job for once."

"They wouldn't figure out that we're innocent even if one of the higher dimensional unicorns stopped partying for a split second so they could descend rapturously from the sky and hand them a stone tablet telling the truth. They'd probably have the tablet processed, decide that the apparition was a hallucination from the high oxygen levels of Earth, and the scorch marks in the ceiling were from an exploding fax machine," said Zander.

I rolled my eyes. "And I'm not letting my parents die."

"The Alliance doesn't use fax machines," Blayde muttered. "And gods hate putting things in writing."

"Come on, can we just keep these creeps off the streets of my planet? Please?" I begged.

Blayde sighed, staring at Zander. "Fine, but then we go, okay?"

"Fine." I agreed. "So, what's the plan?"

"Well, all we need to do is put the shapeshifters on display. Foollegg will have to act then."

"But we need to track them down first," I said.

"Or bait them."

"Or wait for them to tear down on their snacks," Zander pointed out. "The patients aren't being moved quickly enough. The shapeshifters are probably waiting for them, so they can snatch a few up on their way out."

"We check the hallways," said Blayde, snapping her fingers.

"The vents," I added.

"Perfect place to lie in wait," said Zander. "Girls, we're ducting out."

"Seriously?" I asked, plucking a hair from his head. "You're going with *ducting out*? I was kinda hoping this hair was fake because that was the worst pun I've ever heard from you. Ever."

He rolled his eyes. "Taking to the vents?"

I shook my head. "Still no."

# FOURTEEN

## PLEASE ALLOW ME THIS OPPORTUNITY
## TO VENT ABOUT PUNS

**THOSE WHO THINK THAT PUNS ARE THE LOWEST** form of humor certainly haven't had to deal with a non-terrestrial making terrible ones while the two of you fling yourselves into danger. I'm not saying they're good or that this single situation redeems them, oh no. You just haven't felt the true extent of how terrible they can really be.

"I've got it! At least we'll have an opportunity to vent!"

It was a good thing he was behind me, so he couldn't see me roll my eyes all the way to the back of my head. He'd gone through half a dozen vent jokes in just as many minutes, and the longer we'd crawl through them without finding evidence of the shapeshifter, the more he would inevitably torment us with.

"How about … this vent will be the end of me?" he asked, and Blayde snickered from the rear of the pack.

"That … wasn't even a pun," I said.

"It was in whatever language I'm hearing," she said. "And believe it or not, it was actually a good one."

I groaned. It was hard enough to ramp army style through the cold vents but doing so while followed by terrible humor wasn't making it any easier.

"I could comment on the view," said Zander, and I heard the distance sound of skin against flesh—Blayde slapping him the way I could not.

"Oh, come on, what's with you?"

"It's that or the vent jokes," he said.

"Or you could combine the two?" Blayde chortled.

"You can't be serious! Blayde, I thought you were with me on this?"

"I wasn't going to pass up that golden opportunity," she said.

"And shouldn't we, I don't know, shut up? The Pachooleeans could be listening to us!"

"Please. If they haven't given themselves ears, they can't hear a thing. And I doubt they've gone to the trouble."

"Good, because we sound like a bus load of teenagers on a field trip," I said.

"Except we're not in a field," said Blayde.

"I don't know if that was intentionally lazy humor or not, but please. It's usually not up to me to beg everyone to focus."

That shut them up, thankfully. If this were a school field trip, then I was the frazzled class mom who signed up without knowing what she was in for.

**PLEASE**

# INALIENABLE

For defenders of the universe, they sure needed a lot of wrangling.

"Okay, I can see it," I said, stopping in my tracks when the vent branched off and revealed a puke-colored clog. It was massive, though—three times as large as the first blob I had encountered. Smith, Winfrey, and Drew all combined together, waiting silently for the danger to pass.

"Okay, what now?" I hissed.

Zander handed me the laser, passing it forward from Blayde, who said simply, "Turn them into poop bullets."

"This is disturbing."

"Hey, it's your planet you're protecting!"

"That's not the disturbing part," I shuddered.

Right. Planet saving. I could do this. All I had to do was channel that anger I was feeling: the knowledge that this clump of sand had impersonated doctors, people we were meant to trust, only to abuse their patients by terrorizing them and farming their fear. It was easy to be angry about that.

But even so, accepting that it was my turn to kill a living being? They might have been monsters, but they were alive, sentient. I was already a murderer, but I couldn't let that define me. Just because I'd killed once in self-defense didn't mean I was ready to kill again.

"Do you need me to do it?" asked Zander, but before I could say anything, Blade was already telling him off.

"Her planet, her turn," said Blayde. "Sally, you know what the right thing to do is here. You can't run around calling for justice if you can't carry out the sentence yourself."

She was right, though I didn't have the guts to say it. I took a deep breath, raising the laser high. I pictured Daisy-May in my mind, her forced to relive Jeffrey's taunts over and over again, never being free of this institute. She deserved justice. She deserved help from real doctors. I flicked the switch, sending a beam of light at the sand pile. The silicon glowed red for a few second before taking on a strange bubbly form.

"Guys, I think it's working!" I yelled back. But as I spoke, the bubbles took on a shape. The sand began to form limbs, legs, a face with sharp cheekbones, a worn leather coat.

I was staring into the face of Zander, and I was killing him.

"Sally ... please," he begged, raising a boiling hand toward me, so close we could almost touch.

I wanted to scream. Zander was melting, torn in agony. I knew, logically, that this wasn't him, wasn't *my* Zander, just a poor facsimile of him. But it was still his beautiful face, his pain. I could see him in the library, so clearly, Nimien gleeful in his torture.

I was trembling like a leaf, but I couldn't let go of the laser. If I had to do anything, just one thing, it was to squeeze that button down as if my life depended on it. Even if it meant watching Zander boil alive.

His face twisted. The pain was gone in an instant, replaced by frown lines and tight lips.

"You disgust me," he spat. All attempts for petty pity points disappeared in the blink of an eye. "You and your whole family. And that little dog thing too! *Yap yap yap* all day long. And I'm not just talking about the dog."

"Is that what I sound like?" Zander's hand clutched my ankle—not tightly, just enough to show that he was there, grounding me in the moment, tying me to his warmth.

"You talk so big about wanting to see the stars then complain the whole time," said the Zander before me. Even as we spoke, part of him turned brown, dead pixels on a screen glitching out one by one. "Well, guess what, Sally? I'm through with you. Done. You can stay here and do whatever you want for the rest of your miserable eternal life."

He wasn't going for my pity now; he was going for my heart. And it was working. My trembling had intensified. It wasn't Zander telling me things, but now I would always have this memory engraved in my brain of his mouth forming those scathing words.

Because they came from somewhere. The creature only knew what we had told it, back when we thought it was someone we could trust.

"Sally, I'm right here. That guy in front of you is an imposter. Does my hair really look that bad today?"

"Plus, I could have any woman I want," fake Zander sneered. "You were hot, but I'm already bored. You're nothing to me now. Nothing."

"Sally, I'm right behind you."

"You think you're the first?" He chuckled. "I've left hundreds of girls just like you across hundreds of galaxies, and I probably will keep on doing it when I'm done with you too. That's just who I am. You were nothing but a number to me. You were nothing."

"You're everything to me."

"I hate you, Sally Webber."

"Sally, it's not me," my Zander said, anchoring me to reality with his hand tight on my ankle. "Don't listen to what he says."

"You know why he's saying that, right?" said fake Zander, somehow, impossibly, smiling. "He doesn't want you to know the things he told me in our session. He's afraid you won't like what you'll hear. Won't you, Zander?"

"Ever hear of doctor-patient confidentiality?" I stammered, clutching the laser even tighter in my fist.

"That's my girl!" Zander said. "I'd come over there and beat you myself, but she's got you all on her own."

"What the hell is going on up there?" asked Blayde from way behind us. "Did Zander short-circuit?"

"I loathe you, Sally Webber," said the Zander before me. "You're nothing to me."

"Sally, I love you."

I turned my head around to stare at the real Zander behind me. His lips were a tight line, his brow furrowed in concentration as if he himself were holding the laser. My frustration was his own.

Zander loved me. *He loved me.*

"You do?" I stammered in response.

"With all my heart, I love you."

Despite it all, I found myself grinning so wide I couldn't feel my cheeks. "I love you more."

"I do not want to be a part of this," Blayde muttered. "Is anyone dealing with the Pachoolee problem?"

She seemed to have caught a glance of the real problem over my shoulder now because her tone changed quickly.

"Dang, that's a bad hair job," she said. "Okay, you two, break it up. Angry sand Zander still needs to be dealt with."

I returned my gaze to the sneering creature in front of me. I sneered back at him.

"I do not fear you," I announced. "You are nothing but a nightmare. Get off this planet."

The form started to change.

Zander was gone. In his place, some green chick with wavy blond hair jeered at me, her teeth long and pointed, the long wings on her back fighting the constraining space of the tiny ventilation shaft. Her pointed pixie face was red with hatred, which was a feat indeed, since the rest of her skin was an eye-popping forest green. Her tiny frame quaked with fury.

"Okay, start backing up!" I called, turning my attention down the line. "They're now a tiny, winged green chick who doesn't seem to like us butting in on her space. The laser's not working fast enough!"

Zander leaned over for a closer look, and I could see as his confidence draining from his face.

"FAIRIES!" he cried in terror.

The girl had very sharp nails when she grabbed at my arm. I sliced off the whole hand with a quick swing of the laser, and I backed up, Zander pulling my ankle, but we weren't fast enough. She slashed and bit at my face, ripping out clumps of hair as she screeched an ear-splitting siren.

"Out here!" Blayde ordered, backing out of the vent and pulling Zander out behind her. He grabbed my waist to pull me down after him and slammed the grate down in front of the fairy.

"Run!" he ordered, taking his own command to heart and rushing down the corridor with actual fear propelling him forward.

The fairy burst from the vent and flew at Zander, still screeching. She was not alone; two other green ladies followed her out of the air duct, shrieking like a pack of banshees, smaller than they'd been.

"Fairies? That's your real fear?" I asked as we pelted down the staff corridor.

"Have you seen them?" he asked. "Now you understand why I don't get Shakespeare!"

"Bill was sweet," said Blayde, pumping her arms at her side.

"I never said he wasn't! I just don't like his obsession with—this!"

I didn't have time to think over the implication that fairies were real because at that moment, we rounded a corner and crashed into the last person I expected to block our path: the one and only Foollegg.

We collided at full force, sprawling to the ground in a scene worthy of an anime meet-cute. Though there was nothing cute about me fully body-tackling the head of the Agency's security in her full-body gear.

"Get off me, Terran!" she ordered, before her eyes had time to catch what had been chasing us this whole time. I didn't think they could get any larger than they already were, but I was proved wrong. She gasped as the three angry green fairies came veering around the corner, trying to dive bomb us.

I didn't think. I pulled the two of us through the fabric between dimensions, tossing us down the hallway in order to gain precious seconds on the arriving bunch. Zander's arm reached out of nowhere and pulled me into an empty room by the scruff of my neck, Blayde shoving in Foollegg before slamming the door shut behind us.

"What the void was that?" Foollegg stammered, pushing herself to her feet. Zander was already pulling off his shirt—of course—and using it to stuff the bottom of the door in case the not-really-fairies tried to get in that way. It wasn't enough fabric to go all the way around; they would get in eventually.

"Need I remind you what we've been trying to tell you?" Blayde spat.

"You saved me," Foollegg mumbled, rubbing her stomach where I had tackled her. "You just saved my life. I was going to arrest you, and you saved me."

"Don't mention it," I said.

"Hate fairies," said Zander, shuddering.

"You?" Foollegg asked.

"Seriously, did anyone actually see them? All those teeth and nails? Or am I just talking gibberish?"

"They're freaky," I agreed. "Also … real?"

Blayde flicked a switch. I hadn't realized that we were standing around in the dark until then. "Sally, is that a human escape pod?"

I turned where she was pointing. "That's a boiler."

"Then we're celestially screwed."

"Got a plan anyone?" I asked.

Foollegg let out a heavy breath. "I've lost contact with my team. The building seems reinforced against all outgoing transmissions."

"Barker should have told you as much," said Zander. "Didn't you listen to any of his warnings?"

"And let Snooke get all the platinum? Not hardly."

"So, no help from the Agency, then?" asked Blayde.

"Well, you have me."

"So, no help from the Agency, then," she repeated. "Okay, good. We can do this."

"This isn't good," Zander muttered, peeking through the keyhole. "But it's better than fairies. It's not targeting me anymore. Now it's just some … bogey-monster."

"What do you mean?"

"You know"—he mimed—"big shoulders, brown leathery skin, looks like crap."

"Bad design?"

"No, it legitimately looks like human excrement."

"Any idea how we can stop it?" Blayde turned to Foollegg. "My laser is too slow. If they get out, we may never catch them. They'll start over in another city, another continent."

"I know the stakes, all right?" she spat. "What do you want me to say? That I believe you now?"

"No, it's too late for that. I need you to fix this. You're meant to be in charge. Tell us what we need to do."

She scratched her dry skull with her pale hand. "I've never dealt with their kind before. I have a Terran gun— can't bring anything else Earthside, lest our weapons fall into Terran hands—but that's no use against a silicon-based life form."

"Then what good are you?" I couldn't keep my rage from bubbling up inside. Screw the consequences; she couldn't blow my parents up from in here, anyway. "What is the point of having you, the Agency, at all? You never do anything! It shouldn't be up to me to fight off every threat that makes its way to Earth!"

I turned to Zander and Blayde, fuming. Literally, my face was so hot I'm sure my hair was starting to singe. "Look. We need to burn this sucker. We're in the boiler room. There has to be something we can do."

Blayde snapped her fingers. "Lightning through sand. Electric current!"

I tossed her the laser, and she cut a slice straight into the boiler's belly. Hot water spilled out into the floor, scalding to the touch. The four of us scuttled out of its way, jumping on shelves, gripping onto pipes.

"We need a charge," said Blayde. Zander's hand rested on the door handle, ready to spring it open. "A battery. Anything. Anyone. Quickly."

Full credit to her, Foollegg instantly pulled the translator from her neck. Half wrapped around one of the shelves, she pulled the guts out of the small device, saying nothing. Must have been some kind of tiny power generator, not tech I was used to. A curt nod to Zander, and he ripped the door open.

The bogey monster was even worse in person, just a steaming pile of brown goo grinding toward us, somehow, impossibly, grinning as it saw Zander in the doorway. It started to transform, a fairy head opening on his shoulder, another on his stomach, pulling away from the brown conglomeration, ready to reach, to attack.

Foollegg shorted the translator, tossing it into the water and crushing it under foot. The thing about an electrical current is that you don't know it's there until it finds an obstacle, and that it most definitely did. All we needed was a single spark, a powerful burst. It sprung and traveled through the water, through the soaked sole of the sand conglomeration, up and through and—

The creature screamed, each of its three mouths arching in horror, the three fairies trying to drag themselves into the air, failing and flaying.

The screams died down to silence, leaving nothing but a terrible statue in its wake.

# FIFTEEN

## DEUS EX-TRATERRESTRIAL

**ZANDER SWUNG FROM THE DOORFRAME HE** had been clutching, landing lightly into the water below, a tiny splash breaking our silence. We were all breathing heavily, as if from running a marathon. The threat had come, and we had conquered. But the award for most dangerous in the room went to the next highest-ranking player, and she was stepping off her shelf with the grace of a gazelle.

"He just couldn't get past the language barrier." Zander shook his head apologetically, placing a hand on the glass monstrosity. It didn't budge. Victory was ours.

"That doesn't work." Blayde snorted. "Seriously, Stop."

"Fine. Foollegg, you all right?"

"Chug quuc." She paused, breathing heavily, and launched into a long and possibly beautiful speech. I didn't know; I couldn't understand a lick of it now that her translator had sacrificed itself for us. She turned to me, her eyes going wide. "I'm fine. Though my reality is shifting slightly, so I need a minute. The patients … you could have run from us, but you stayed to save them."

"Well, we got to know most of them pretty well. Daisy-May was particularly sweet." Blayde grinned as she admired the statue. The creature was frozen mid-shapeshift, three winged creatures pulling away from a thick central mass, their faces twisted in expressions of horror and hatred. Ugly as a turd. She turned to Foollegg, her face suddenly serious. "You probably want to arrest us now."

Shit, did we have to fight? I poised myself, eyeing the distance between me and Zander, gauging if we had time to escape. But the thought hit me like a train. Foollegg still had my parents. I couldn't go. None of this had saved me from her.

"I would love to." She took step forward, checking the strange and hauntingly beautiful glass sculpture that had been trying to kill us mere moments ago. "But I can't."

But Foollegg sounded calm, even sweet with her next words. Not that one could easily deduce expressions from another species you knew nothing about. I stared at Blayde instead, and she seemed cool and collected.

"How so?" asked Blayde.

"You saved my life," Foollegg replied, flicking her forked tongue the way I would flick my hair. "I've seen something the Alliance has been hiding from us for years, centuries. And I would hate to put it behind bars."

"And what's that?" Blayde asked.

"Hope. Truth. To be honest, I'm not sure. But arresting you now seems unwise. Now, run before the adrenaline runs out and I realize what a terrible mistake I'm making. Enjoy the off-grid of Earth."

"What makes you think we're staying planet-side?" Zander asked.

"Does it matter what I think? Goodbye, Iron and the Sand. And Sally Webber."

"No nickname?" I asked.

"I haven't found one that fits yet. But trust me, it will be catchy when I do. I hope I'll see you again on better terms."

"When you're not holding an anvil over my parents' house?"

She flicked her tongue again. "Just don't cause any more trouble. Now, go!"

With that, she spun on her heels, bounding out of the boiler room and leaping down the expanse of hallway, slipping for a split second in a patch of water. Zander shrugged, placing a hand on my shoulder.

"You look puzzled," he said. "Are you all right?"

"We have to go," said Blayde. "Come on, before she gets back."

"What just happened?"

Blayde was already grabbing my hand and reaching for Zander's. I ripped mine away, flying backwards down the corridor a good jump away out of her grasp.

"We can't just leave," I spat.

"She only gave us a small window here," said Blayde. "We have to run."

"My parents!"

"You heard her. They'll be fine!" She dashed for me, and I sidestepped, rushing down the hallway.

Oh shit. I couldn't outrun Blayde. Why was I even running away? She jumped, as I knew she would, and I did the same, landing just a foot to the right and rushing back the way we came.

"Just–stand–still!" Blayde hissed.

"We can't leave!" I stammered. "We could end up anywhere! What's the point of that?"

"Being chased by someone is our default these days," said Blayde. "So long as they don't get in our way, who gives a crap? Will you stop with the running?"

"I do. I give a crap," I said. "I've had it up to here with the Alliance. I know you said they're necessary but come on. I'm not just talking about the way they manhandle my planet. I'm talking about Da-Duhui, the mess with the *Traveler*, the hidden histories, and, oh yeah, the freaking abandoned Youpaf who were left spiraling around my solar system for, like, a million years."

Blayde stopped running, but I wasn't convinced. At least she wouldn't try to jump us anywhere without Zander on board. I stood still at the end of the hallway, my back to the stairs.

"In the very least, it's terrible mismanagement," said Zander. "Sally, the Alliance spans hundreds of star systems. Thousands of planets. You can't possibly expect us to do anything about that. Even when we try to help them, we're labeled terrorists. What do you think they'll do when we really do come after them?"

"No, not us," I spat. "If you won't want anything to do with this, fine. I'll do it myself. Just me."

Blayde took a step toward me, and I retreated. "You know, I thought I liked this new Sally snark, but it sounds like you need to go right back upstairs and lock yourself in with those patients."

"I'm not crazy."

"Going up against the *entire Alliance* just because you're pissed at them sure sounds crazy."

"You don't sound like yourself," said Zander. "Why don't you sit down?"

"I don't sound like myself?" I laughed. "What about you? You're supposed to be the thorn in the Alliance's side, and right now you seem to have forgotten how to stab."

"Sally, listen to me." Blayde frowned. "We don't care what the Alliance thinks of us. If we happen to help someone in trouble, cool. We've been doing that as long as we can remember, and we're not stopping now. But we're not bona-fide revolutionaries. You *do* understand that, right? We're not the terrorists they have been warning their people we are."

"You can't possibly not care about that."

"That's not the point. We help. We don't destroy institutions that do more good than harm."

"But you admit they do harm," I said. "Please. Maybe you don't have a homeworld to call your own, but look at it from my point of view. My people—it feels weird calling them that, but that's what they are—are being abused by the very people the Alliance is supposed to be protecting us from. Again and again and again, they let the wrong people through their nets, and they do nothing about it while remaining fixated on catching you two. Zander said it himself, at the very least, it's terrible mismanagement, but there are real deaths linked to their mistakes. And that's just on my planet."

Zander put a gentle hand on my shoulder. I forced myself not to give in, not to lean into his warmth.

"We have to be able to do something about it," I said, slipping away. "I'm not suggesting we blow up the Agency or anything. But we have to do something to the upper leadership. I meant what I said. If you won't help me, I'll do it myself."

"Sally, you can't," said Zander. "You're just one person."

"I saved my planet before. Twice now."

"Both times by *dying*."

"I have unlimited deaths stocked up, so why not use them to mean something?" I spun to face him. "Zander, you of all people should care. It's one of the things I love the most about you: just how much you're willing to do for perfect strangers. I'm just one person, but the two of you have done the impossible time and time again. Hell, you used to brag about toppling civilizations with chocolate bars or dance-offs. Are you afraid you're rusty?"

"Well, what do you want us to say?" Blayde flung her hands up in the air. "Sure, Sally, we're going to take on the Alliance all by our lonesome and save your planet and so many others from their corrupted clutches?"

"That would be great, actually," I said. "Can you please say that?"

"What's gotten into you, Sally?" Zander's hand slid down my arm, taking my hand. "Where did all this fire come from? Should we be worried?"

"Maybe?" I shrugged. "I guess when the rest of my brain screams louder than my anxiety, I have a lot more to say."

"A coup is hard to plan," he said. "Especially in a system that sprawls over hundreds of planets in dozens of solar systems where the populace is brainwashed into believing they have free will. We can't issue a takedown of the Alliance; it's impossible."

"Impossible?" I snorted. "You know, I think that the first time I ever heard you say that."

"We're not all-powerful, Sally," said Blayde. "We can't just snap our fingers and change the universe."

"Plus, we've probably tried at least five times before," said Zander. "Every time we tear down the emperor, king, vapor entity … they always pop back up with the same stuff they've always had."

"Well, it does give us something to do," said Blayde. "I haven't toppled a civilization in a long time."

"Great! Blayde's on board! Zander?"

"I'm only doing this to keep the two of you safe," he muttered, but his hand squeezed mine tighter, and I knew I had his full support. "I can't have you both running off saving Earth without me."

My arms flew around his neck before I could stop them. He hugged me back just as tight.

"Great," said Blayde. "Foollegg will be back any minute, and we can't jump anywhere without a plan. How do we get out of this place, then?"

"I have an idea," I said, letting go of Zander but taking his hand instead. "I'll give IHOP something to protect."

· · · · · · · ● · · · · · · · · ·

**TERRANS ARE FRIENDS, NOT FOOD! THAT WAS THE** first sign I saw as I broke through the chimney and out into the light. *Your trash is a human's downfall*, said the second. *Earth is for Earthlings* was the third and arguably the catchiest despite being oddly offensive at the same time. I wasn't sure if they were protesting the Agency or the Pachooleeans, but either way, I was all for their cause.

I slid down the tiles and jumped to a tree, hiding behind the safety of its widest branches, Zander close behind, his face smudged with dust. The chimney had been boarded up for years, but it was a large enough conduit to get us to the outside without running into the

Agency men in FBI uniforms leading patients out of the now-smashed front door, a firetruck waiting for them there. The same agents were also trying to corral the news reporters away from the off-world protestors, and the latter were trying to vie for as much screen time as possible. By the way the agents moved, it was obvious this wasn't the first time they'd played this song and dance.

"Do you think they'll be okay?" I asked, waiting for Blayde to appear. Zander pulled me into his arms, kissing me lightly on the forehead, his touch drawing the anxiety from my body.

"The Agency might suck at tracking off-worlders, but they're the masters of bureaucracy. The patients will be rehomed right away."

"You make that sound like they're pets being removed from an abusive owner."

"Do you expect the Agency to treat them any better than that?"

"Cuddle on your own time," said Blayde. "We have to hurry."

We dropped out of the tree and rushed toward the protestors. Willowcrest was leading the pack, shouting slogans that only rhymed in her own head. The second she saw me, her eyes went wide.

"You!" she stammered, dropping the megaphone.

"I'm Terran," I said. I didn't need more of an introduction. I had this whole speech prepared about how much the Agency sucked and how much I supported IHOP's cause, but they didn't need to hear it.

We were whisked away to the back of a van, hidden from Agency sight and ferried to safety by a sweet teenager in a wooly cap and fingerless gloves who introduced themselves as Willowcrest's child, Evanuel. Ev to their friends, which we immediately were.

"My mother married a genderless being from another dimension," they explained as they drove us down the institute driveway to sweet, sweet freedom. In the back of the van, under some thick fleece blankets for good measure, we made friendly conversation. "Literally just a ball of floating thought and a little thistle. I call it Om. They couldn't conceive naturally, naturally. So, they adopted me. You wouldn't believe how common it is for Terrans to be raised by extraterrestrials. At least in my circles. Most of my friends have at least one off-world parent."

I would have been much more interested if I were fully awake. One thing my brain didn't seem to have found the solution to just yet was the whole issue of burn-out. In less than two weeks, I'd been arrested and brought to the institute. In less than two days, I'd found and fought three alien threats. I needed a stiff drink and a good night's sleep.

"Do you think Foollegg will keep her word?" I asked Zander tentatively as I nodded off, rocked by the gentle sway of the van on the flat Florida roads.

"She let us go, didn't she?" he replied. "She'll probably still be chasing us, but it sounds like your family will be safe for the time being."

"We need a plan," I said. The van swerved off the highway; it had been a short drive.

"So, this new Sally has all the snark, none of the spark, huh?" asked Blayde. "Too bad you didn't somehow acquire brilliant planning skills along with the rest of the bloody side effects."

"Well, it's not like I know the inner workings of the Alliance. Just the end result."

"You can get up now," said Ev. "We're here!"

*Here* turned out to be a motel off the highway, and Ev lead us into their room, which was stocked full of markers and posterboard. Some abandoned slogans sat propped up against the wall, proclaiming that *Earth = not mine, not yours, too many chores*; and *if you really belonged here, why are you water intolerant?*

"Too much of a mouthful," said Ev as they motioned toward the signs, tossing their car keys on the table. The keychain was promptly swallowed up by markers and a pile of spilled glitter. "I keep telling them half their slogans don't work in English, but do they trust the actual American? Nope."

I said nothing, collapsing on their bed, staring up at the ceiling. I was out. My parents were off the hook, for the time being. Why couldn't I feel good about any of it?

"Thank you for helping us, Ev," said Zander. "We owe you and your mother big time."

"You need a shirt," they said suddenly. "You can't go very far without a shirt."

I propped myself up on the bed as Ev tossed Zander a shirt from their suitcase. "How did you get here so fast?"

"Mother listens in to all Agency wavelengths," they said, shrugging. "We've got a decrypter. Anyway, we got word yesterday there was something going on here and drove down. A good thing, too, because we were right here when the emergency signal went out. Can you believe that shit? The Agency, sitting idly by, while off-worlders take advantage of—well, of course you can; you were there."

"We're taking them down," I said, falling back onto the bed. "Some way or another, we're taking them down."

· · · · · · ● ● ● · · · · · · · ·

**I HAD APPARENTLY FALLEN ASLEEP BECAUSE WHEN** I opened my eyes again there was Chinese takeout on the table. Willowcrest was occupying one of the seats at the table, practically glowing, her child at her side and Zander and Blayde shoveling food down their gullets across from them.

"You didn't wake me for food?" I muttered, rolling up to a seat.

"You evidently needed to catch up on your sleep," Zander said, waving me over. I lazily plopped myself on his lap, treating myself to a massive heap of fried rice. It tasted like heaven in a little takeout box.

"We were just filling them in on the details," said Blayde. "Brainstorming some plans for getting the Alliance to intervene, which is your job, need I remind you."

"I'm trying," I said. "How much have you told them?"

"They're the Iron and the Sand, bane of the Alliance's existence, and you're trying to get the Agency to leave your planet alone," said Willowcrest. "That about covers it, right?"

"Sounds about right," I replied. "Did I miss anything else?"

"Director Foollegg has released a press junket detailing your escape," she announced. "Conveniently leaving out your involvement saving their asses."

"Their engagement was based on your attempt to escape," added Ev, "which has apparently traumatized the patients."

"So, we're still wanted 'criminals,'" I said. "Any results from the brainstorming?"

"Ev suggests we go for the top," said Blayde. "Good kid. Doesn't know much about the Alliance. Never left their planet, but has the right idea."

Ev looked up from their wontons. "Thanks? I guess?"

"So, kill their president-emperor person?" I asked. "I'm still not clear on what he is."

"No one is," Willowcrest muttered.

"Barge into the heart of the Alliance and murder their leader? You think that's going to solve anything? Come on, be realistic, Sally!" Blayde snapped.

"Realistic?" I laughed. "I'm on the run with the two most wanted, misunderstood criminals in the universe! You can't tell me to be realistic. Look at where I'm standing!"

Zander chortled, either at my retort or at his sister's stern face.

"You can't tear one man down and expect change to follow," she said. "You either get chaos or a new leader worse than the first."

"We need to somehow be redeemed in their eyes," said Zander. "I mean, maybe then we can have some say on how they deal with things."

Blayde scoffed. "I seriously doubt there's a way to go from terrorists to heroes overnight. It's not like they've given us credit for the amazing shit we've already done for them. I mean Da-Duhui alone should have given us some brownie points. Or our brave rescue of the *Traveler*. Instead, they had to wipe that footage, lest their people see how much they've been lied to. And that was on camera."

"Then we have to settle for something more symbolic," said Zander. "Something heroic and public. That's it."

"That's it?" I asked. "Like, save a famous baby or an ambassador's daughter?"

"No, someone far more important. The president himself."

"Ah, so he is a president."

"Officially, yes. But that's just a fancy way of saying 'you elected my n-teenth great-grandfather to office, and my family's been here ever since.'"

"Right," said Blayde. "So, we stalk the most influential guy this side of the galaxy and then save his life as publicly as possible so they can't doubt that the Iron and Sand are on their side. Boom, pardoned, and they'll just forget about the other thousand things we supposedly did?"

"Should work," said Zander. "It's a start, at least."

"Perfect," I replied. "Instead of killing the president, we save his life. By ... pretending to kill him."

"You're absolutely sure they weren't just patients?" Ev whispered to their mom under their breath.

"Even if they are," said Willowcrest, "they'll look great on our posters."

"I was being sarcastic," said Blayde, most likely pretending to ignore them, "but it's a start. At the very least, they'll have to stop chasing us. Then we can start working on details, like having them live up to their responsibilities here on earth. Now for logistics: reaching the president of the Alliance. Or getting off-planet and inside their seat of government without being caught."

"We could ask Meedian for help," I said. "He probably has a ship or knows someone with access to a ship."

"We can't bring the Agency to his doorstep," said Blayde. "It's too risky. He's meant to be our friend. I know we only just met him, but how many decades of friendship would we be ruining if we did that?"

"Random jumping is out of the question," Zander agreed. "Or we might lose Earth, and that's a big no-no since coming back is the whole point."

"I could do it."

Their eyes landed on me, though I was used to their shock by now. It wasn't like I was saying anything more ridiculous than I already had been. Willowcrest and Ev looked much more confused than shocked, but that was understandable.

"I seem to always be able to find you, Zander," I said. "It's the only way I seem to know to jump at all: finding you. But I've never tried looking for … another you. I mean, if you're my beacon to the now, couldn't every Zander at any point in time and space act as a beacon too?"

They said nothing, awestruck. I wanted to blush, shy away. But, hey, for once I was the one who could do something they couldn't.

"All I have to do is find my way to the Zander you were on the *Traveler*," I said. "If I can jump to him, we can ride the ship back into Alliance territory."

"All the way back to Pyrina," Blayde breathed. "Sally, if you can pull it off, then …"

"I didn't want to believe—I just … is this happening?" said Zander. "Are we going to plunge into Alliance territory and get our freedom back?"

"If we play our cards right," I said, "we can even save my world in the process."

"Well, then, I'm not waiting a minute longer," said Blayde. "Let's go stalk the president."

"This," said Ev, turning to their mother, "is by far the best birthday present you've ever gotten me."

# SIXTEEN

## REMEMBER THOSE BROOM CLOSETS I LIKED SO MUCH? WELL, THEY'RE BACK!

**THERE'S ONLY SO MANY THINGS YOU NEED** to bring along with you on an interstellar mission to 'save' the president of the galaxy, and, thankfully, for the broke space traveler, you can gather most of them last minute at the local dollar store.

First of all, a solar-powered phone charger because an interstellar plug adaptor is useless to anyone who doesn't have over a hundred pairs of hands and room for an extra three suitcases.

Secondly, a Bic pen–*for women*. You always need a pen in the vast emptiness of space, but they will always, inevitably, go missing. Sacrificing one to the universe ensures your loose change wasn't going to go missing instead. Various rubber bands and binder clips are also acceptable. Does it have to be gender specific? Not really, but they were out of gender-free products at this point, so it was all we were left with.

Thirdly, stress balls. No one knows stress like Terrans, and our balls are renown for being the sturdiest across a dozen solar systems. No puns intended. The squishy ones are also highly toxic to most races, and they make for a good projectile in a pinch.

And finally, a dollar store bag of Starburst in case you need to bribe your way through enemy territory. Because apparently sugary Earth treats are a highly prized commodity out there.

"That or you just have a sweet tooth," said Blayde, rolling her eyes over-dramatically at her brother.

"I admit to nothing. But I'm taking two bags just in case."

And to carry all this? With my duffel bag stuffed somewhere at my parent's place—safe, I hoped—we needed a new one. The Dollar Store didn't exactly promise high-quality goods, and the sturdiest backpack we could find doubled as a stuffed dog for anxious kindergartener.

Blayde was delighted, not that she'd admit it out loud. But she insisted it was hers.

Named it Surly Bop.

Everything was set. I had scheduled snail mail to my parents and Marcy, explaining that I was safe but would be on the run and thus incommunicado for a little while. Hopefully, Felling would stay true to her word and keep an eye on them. I didn't have a physical address for her, but I sent it to my parents for them to keep if or when she touched base.

To my parents, I did the typical teen thing where I said, quite clearly, that I was just going *out*. I was sure I could mooch that point for a few more years.

"Try to get us as close to the moment we left as you can," said Zander, as we circled up in our motel room, grasping each other's hands like we were about to summon something dark and unholy. "We don't want to mess with our timelines."

Willowcrest and Ev were watching intently, enjoying the rest of their Starburst and the show. Their moderately omniscient gaseous parent had appeared momentarily just to catch an autograph from their two favorite rogues.

"Make it out to Om," they had said, though the last part was less of a name and more the sound a gong makes when someone throws a chicken at it. "I just can't believe my offspring got to save you, and I wasn't around to witness it!"

Now, they too, were watching, and I was starting to get a little stage fright. There's nothing like trying to jump yourself and your closest friends halfway across the galaxy, trying to find an exact time and date out of the infinity of the universe, but to do so with an audience was reckless, let alone a little egotistical.

"I'll do the best I can," I said, trying to put them out of my mind. "Do you think … do you think Nimien knew about all this?"

"Don't think about him," said Zander, squeezing my hand. "Just get us there."

"And try to find us a nice, warm broom closet," Blayde added. "A crowded room would ruin everything."

"I can't make any promises," I said. "If you think you can do better, you drive us yourself."

She had nothing else to say about that.

"Right, deep breath. Here we go." I closed my eyes, letting myself break down into my infinitesimal parts. That was the easiest bit of the whole process, the merging with the universe, like stepping into a warm bath. Nothing like traveling with the siblings, all cold void and infinite nothings.

Driving was so much better.

Eternity stretched out before me—no, through me, my cells one with the universe, no longer anything between me and infinity. If I had lungs, I would catch my breath. If I had eyes, they would be crying.

Up close and personal, the universe was even more beautiful than I could ever have imagined. It was like it was standing before me, nude and vulnerable. I could see every nook and cranny, and it was so much bigger and deeper than any of us could possibly have known.

There were infinite Zanders in the infinite universe. If I had a way of writing them down, I would have finished Meedian's map in the blink of an eye. It was going to be impossible to find the *Traveler* in all this mess.

# INALIENABLE

But I could. I knew exactly where it was, and it wasn't thanks to Zander from the past. I didn't need to know why, I just *knew*. I could follow the thread through the void, bringing us into the heart of the ship that had caused us so much grief.

We came into existence in a small, empty hallway. Blayde's hand was the first to break free, her spritely body spinning around to immediately recon the space.

"Well, I'll be darned," she said, scratching her head. "This really is the *Traveler*."

"Didn't I tell you this girl is amazing?" said Zander, giving my hand an extra tight squeeze before letting go and examining the small space himself. "How close to target are we?"

"Tee so' tee meemeetee laso meela, teedoh tee teemeetee tee mee soso," came a familiar voice. I spun around, but it wasn't as close as it sounded, just a voice bouncing off a wall.

"I remember this conversation," said the Zander beside me. "Couldn't have been more than a few minutes before we left."

"Awesome," I said, hardly believing it myself.

"Yeah, yeah, you rule," said Blayde, tiptoeing past us, pressing herself against the wall of the corridor and peering through the open doorway. She nodded to herself, turning back to us. "Transfer deck, behind the bridge. You're going to have to show me how you do this, Sally."

I said nothing. I wasn't sure I could teach anyone anything at this point. It had been, dare I say, *easy*. With a little extra courage, I was sure I could find the place again without Zander to guide the way. The siblings had made it very clear that control was not something they had with jumping. Maybe there was something wrong with me that allowed me to do what they could not. Maybe when Cross had been in my head, he unlocked something that was meant to stay locked away.

The other Zander was making a point or something because he wouldn't stop talking. It was the same warm tone he always had when he explained some intergalactic nonsense to me, but with all the clicks and nasal splits, I couldn't make heads or tails of it.

"Why can't I understand you?" I asked. "It all made sense when I was, well, *her*."

"We're out of range," said Zander. "We need to get you a new translator."

Another voice response, quick and quippy, a little annoyed by the sounds of it. And with a jolt, I realized it was me.

"Marcoli's lucky to have gotten out," I was saying, "but Nim's not in the system yet. We can still help him. There's still time."

Ouch. Here I was, advocating for the boy who would one day grow up to manipulate this whole stupid day into action. I cringed internally. I didn't want to be reminded of this mistake.

"We're talking about the child-hire program?" I clenched my fist. "Right. Let's also put that on our agenda for radical change."

"Righty-o," said Zander. "We should probably have picked up a notepad at the Dollar-Store-where-nothing-is-actually-a-dollar."

Blayde's eyebrows flew up her forehead as a third person joined the throng. Other Blayde spoke rapidly in the same chirpy language as her brother. Was that their language, spoken on whatever world they had come from? Or just what they were speaking when they got their translators?

"Hard to believe this is the moment that tipped everything," Blayde said, turning to face me. "Just say the word, Sally. We can step in, tell them to leave Nimien to his own fate, and neither of us will have to deal with the library shit."

"Oh no," I said. "I made this decision once before. I'm not making it again. I don't want to mess with time, not when I don't know what I'm doing."

"You do that simply by existing," she said, turning back to the conversation before us. The sound of spitting filled the room. Past Blayde and I were sealing the pact. Current Blayde shuddered.

"This time travel thing is some messed up shit," she grumbled. "We could fix so much."

"Sally's right," said Zander coolly. "Let's not mess with the timestream until we know what we're doing, okay?"

"Frash. We need to go," said Blayde, disappearing. Zander and I followed suit and jumped down the hallway, just in time for past Blayde to march through, Jurrah's hand in hers.

Only for Jurrah to press her up against the bulkhead, lips entangling, past Blayde falling into the embrace.

"Ah. She did say she was going to say goodbye," muttered Zander.

"That seems like a really, really sweet goodbye," I whispered.

Neither of them had any sense of their surroundings. Like lightning, their passionate kiss was fast and hot, a ferocious end to their short-lived reunion.

Current Blayde appeared before us, glaring. Her hands clamped down on our shoulders, and she whisked us away.

"I found us a janitor's closet," she said. "We can wait out the return to Pyrina in here."

"You think that's a good idea?" I said. "We have no idea if the ship's even going to Pyrina after this. I was planning on stealing one of the shuttles or something."

"We can wait it out," said Blayde, pushing open the broom closet door. It looked oddly familiar. For all I knew, it could have been the same one we had landed in. That or the ship's architects copied and pasted their designs on every floor.

"You're kidding me, right?"

My blood chilled in my veins. Now, that was a voice I had never expected to hear ever again. I turned around, slowly, trying to see the scene from his point of view. The three felons who had just saved his life, who claimed they were jumping away, caught red-handed—or foot-bucketed, in Blayde's case—getting right back into the broom closet they had first been found stowing away in.

"Hey, Kork," I said, giving him the most awkward of waves. "Long time no see."

He was just the same as I had left him after our short and sparky goodbye. Even now, I could feel the ghost of his kiss on my lips. It had ranked number one on my list of top ten most epic kisses until Zander came along and filled the entire docket.

All that beautiful captain posture was thrown to the proverbial wind when he saw us. His eyes went wide, rivaling Foollegg's, and with one mighty crash he toppled over.

"Oh shit," said Blayde, ripping her foot from the bucket she had casually stepped in. The bucket whirred upwards, shouting utter nonsense that made me glad my translator was gone. She kicked it down the hallway. "The captain just passed out."

"Isn't it my job to state the obvious?" I stammered, sprinting to his side. He was slowly waking up, dazed, his eyes fluttering open and shut. "We have to get him out of here. He wasn't supposed to see us."

"How did you …? Are you out of uniform?" he muttered. "How did you change?"

"It's okay, Kork," I stammered in reply. "Call it a transporter malfunction, all right?"

"Get him to his quarters," said Blayde. "Sally, I take it you remember where they are?"

"Don't go there." I hoisted the captain on my shoulder, Zander slipping under his other arm to keep him balanced. I knew this had to be awkward for him, but unlike his sister, he didn't say a word.

Now, a lot has happened since we'd last been on the *Traveler,* but there was no way I was forgetting the most confusing almost-hookup I'd ever had. When the sexy starship captain who'd stolen Captain Kirk's identity to make a name for himself in the Alliance did so to cover his real name, which happened to be my ex's. Which I knew now was part of said ex's ploy to mess with my head, which was all truly confusing and more than a little creepy.

But none of it was Kork's fault. So, I'd let Nimien win without me knowing it, throwing away a perfectly good evening that could have been amazing. Which I couldn't bring up now because my current boyfriend was helping me carry the passed-out Kirk-pretending space captain/failed one night stand to the room where it had almost happened.

Smooth move, Sally Webber. You are a master of seduction and romance. Keeping it real.

His quarters were still the most amazing space room I'd ever seen. We used his handprint to let us in, leaving the fluorescents of the crew hallways and entering a sanctuary of wood paneling and a carpeted floor. Gentle, warm light that didn't interfere with the massive window that looked out into the sea of stars beyond, a void thousands of light years from home.

Zander dropped him gently on his couch.

"Dang, it's—" Blayde finished her sentence off with the sound a grape makes when flung against corrugated iron. "I haven't had this shit in forever. Zander, hand me a glass."

"Blayde," he snapped, "we're not here to drink the captain's secret stash. Now, help me convince him he passed out from natural causes."

"It's too late for that," I said. "I think he's awake."

"Of course I'm awake," he said, pushing himself up on his couch. "Get away from my bar. It's taken me a decade to get it stocked how I like."

"We just rescued your sorry ass," she muttered. "And all we got were Crandle's leftovers."

"Sorry, Kork," I said, as calmly as I could. "It's a long and complicated story."

"Let me guess. You have a mop fetish."

"What? No!"

"It would explain why you gravitate toward janitors' closets," he insisted. "That, or Alliance intel is incorrect, and rumors of your spontaneous travel are greatly exaggerated. Is this like a Narnia thing? Where you can only travel through closets?"

"This has nothing to do with the closet," said Zander. "Forget the closet."

"Matthew," I said, hoping that using his real name would mean something to him, still unready to utter the moniker Matt. "This is going to sound terribly strange, but we're future versions of the people who just left your ship."

He said nothing. I had expecting him to sputter and complain, but this was a man raised on *Star Trek*. He could handle a bit of time travel.

"Right," I said. "It's a long story. It's been about a month, maybe two, since I left the observation deck of the *Traveler*. Since then, we've figured out how to time travel, and we had to come back here for a free trip to Pyrina. Okay, turns out, not a very long story after all."

"You … what? Time travel?" he stammered. "What about the kid? At least tell me he ended up out of your bullshit."

"Well, not great news on that front," said Zander. "We managed to find Earth, but Nim got killed by some jerks from Atlantis, turned immortal, and it turns out he's the reason you were abducted from Earth in the first place. He manipulated a series of events to trick Sally into becoming like us. That's an even longer story."

"He *what?*"

"It's been a long two months," I said.

"Sally saved Earth," said Zander.

"Twice," I added. "Three times if you count the mental hospital. Literal nightmare monsters."

"Hey, the first time was the whole planet. The next two, you killed off some assholes," said Blayde. "And you had help with those, don't forget."

And with that, Kork fainted again.

"Do you think he's in shock?" she asked, sipping the purple juice. "Or did we just fry his brain?"

"Probably a bit of both," said Zander, rising to his feet. "Come on. Maybe he has a nice closet we can hide in."

"What is it with you two and closets?" I asked. "The entire ship is just set design. I bet you we can find empty crew quarters easier than an unused closet any day."

"Not on my watch," Kork muttered. The man could regain consciousness hella fast.

"Great, what are going to do with him?" asked Blayde. "This is probably the worst plan we have ever come up with."

"Hey, to break a civilization, you have to break a few eggs," said Zander.

"Break a ..." Kork pushed himself back up in the couch cushions. "Please don't tell me you're planning a coup."

"I wouldn't go that far," said Blayde, swirling her drink.

"I told you not to drink my stuff," he said, glaring at her. "It's expensive. Not to mention almost impossible to get."

"You're Captain-frashing-Kork," she said. "You can get whatever the hell you want. Hell, you almost even had Sally here."

"Do you have to keep bringing that up?" I snapped. "Sorry, Captain. We're just trying to hitch a ride to Pyrina. We might not have been stowaways the first time we landed on your ship, but we are now."

"Now," he growled. "Now, just when we're regrouping with the rest of the Alliance fleet. Now, when we have to tell our superiors everything that happened on board. Now when we have to pretend we had no idea who you were the whole time you were helping us?"

"But we *were* helping you," said Zander. I could see his mental anguish keeping him from pointing finger guns. "Think you can throw us a bone here?"

"I thought the whole letting-you-sneak-away-without-any-attention was the bone?"

"We won't be any trouble," I insisted. "Pretend you saw us get back. We'll find some place to lay low until you dock again."

"Not another freaking broom cupboard," said Kork.

We did better. We hid in his closet.

# SEVENTEEN

## NOT TO KINK-SHAME, BUT MY FEET REALLY HURT

**"I SAID YOU COULD HIDE IN MY QUARTERS,** not my apartment!"

A well-cooked frittata was not enough to cheer up the starship captain under house arrest. Blayde frowned as she put down the pan, letting it land on the pristine counter with a loud *thtonk*.

Despite the ornate decor of Kork's apartment, I just couldn't keep from staring out the window at the city below. It was nothing short of majestic: metal and glass structures that spanned every inch of the planet's surface, except for the single sea in the distance, which I was told harbored the administrative core of the Alliance somewhere far beyond. Like Da-Duhui, but crisper, more modern in every way. No stonework in anything I could see—at least not in this quadrant of the city-planet. Just spires of materials our world had no words for as of yet.

The sky was a perfect fuchsia as the sun set behind the tallest space-scrapers, casting rose light over the white of the apartment. The clouds glittered a stunning deep gold. In an attempt to harness the smog, swarms of nanobots had been unleashed over the city but had evolved beyond their programming and now were quite territorial. They still did their job—I had been told as much by the cloyingly cheerful tourist welcome video I watched on Kork's data pad while crammed between his shoe shelf and sock drawer—but their swarm clouds were now thicker than the smog they had been created to destroy.

The air always smelled like slightly toasted bed sheets as a result. Clean sheets, but again, slightly toasted.

I glanced at the digits above Kork's fridge: 25:35. It was still odd, seeing all those extra numbers on the clock. The planet had a thirty-hour rotation—much longer than an Earth hour, since their time was decimal-based—so quite literally a long day all in all. It would be hours until the sun rose again over our neighborhood.

Despite being at the very heart of the civilization I wanted nothing more than to tear down, I couldn't help but enjoy the thrill of being on an alien world once again. And a glorious one at that.

"You're going to have to find somewhere else to stay," said Kork. "And I mean this in the nicest way possible. There's just not enough room in this place for the four of us."

# INALIENABLE

"Not enough room?" Blayde stammered. "Have you seen this place? You could probably build two extra floors without the ceiling even having a clue."

It was true that his apartment was lavish. If I hadn't snuck out of the *Traveler* myself while we docked in lower orbit, I could easily believe I'd never left at all. All gleaming curved walls and white furniture. It was like he lived on set.

"You will have to be careful what you say," he continued. "If you say anything—"

"Oh, don't worry. I debugged the place before you even made it up here," she said.

"You did what? Frash! They're going to know if—"

"I took down the audio grid of the entire building. Veesh, calm down, will you? It's like you want them spying on your every word."

"I'm on house arrest for having worked with you," he insisted. "If they find you here, that's going to be the least of my worries."

"Oh, relax," Zander said calmly from the white leather couch, a cup of pink noodles in hand, the sickly-sweet smell of roses filling the apartment. Surly-Bop sat on the uncomfortable-looking armchair across from him, his dead button eyes gazing into our very souls. "You're their biggest star. They can't hurt you."

"They already have to recast half the bridge!" he sputtered. "They can easily write me out at the same time."

"I highly doubt that."

"You don't know them like I do."

Zander choked on his noodles, sending pink flying over the couch. A little robot appeared instantly to clean up the mess, singing a cute jingle as it did.

"Kork, I hate to break it to you, but the Alliance has been chasing us for centuries longer than you've been alive," he said, brushing his arm across his mouth.

"All the more reason for you to move out."

"When exactly did we move in?"

"Doesn't anyone want real food?" asked Blayde, slamming the skillet onto the table. "I worked hard on making you all something fresh, and now you're all acting like children."

"I just wanted beef bites," Kork muttered. We moved to the dining table without arguing further. Who knew what Blade would do to anyone who disrespected her cooking. "And speaking of food, if my food consumption increases dramatically, they'll know something's up."

"We'll be gone by the morning," said Zander. He waved a hand to Blayde, who handed him a plate of food anyway.

"I told you not to ruin your dinner with junk food," she spat. "Rose noodles are a bane to the galaxy."

The frittata was heavenly and not an actual frittata by any sense of the word, but until I got my hands on a new translator it would do just fine. The hard part was trying to eat it with a prong, which seemed to be the only cutlery available in the entire kitchen.

Kork, as tense as he was, seemed to relax a little with every bite. I'd be tense, too, if the most powerful governing force in the galaxy put me on house arrest.

"So," he said, finally, "where will you go? Wait, wrong question. What will you do? Should I be worried? Do I need to find a pirate ship?"

"We promised, no coup," I said.

"Hear us out," said Blayde. "The only way we're going to get a pardon is by doing a service to the Alliance."

Kork furrowed his brows. "You want to clean the streets or something?"

"No, the Alliance would probably claim we were weaponizing hygiene." She let out a heavy sigh. "Then they would still be going strong *and* probably recommend everyone throw trash out their window to scare us away. No, we need to do something bigger. Something so huge and public the Alliance has no choice but pardon us."

"Pardon you?" Kork stammered. "You think there's a way for them to pardon you? You saved our asses on the *Traveler*, and they still thought it was some kind of act of rebellion. What could you possibly do to gain a pardon?"

"Easy," said Zander. "We save the emperor's life."

"You mean president."

"I'm sorry. Slip of the tongue."

"And let me go back to the part where you're saving his life? What from?"

"Well, unless we can find actual danger to save us from, it'll have to be from one of us," said Blayde. "Preferably Sally since she's a nobody."

"Woohoo, I mean nothing," I said.

Zander reached for my hand, giving it a soft squeeze. Kork's eyes went wide. "You were gone for two minutes, and now you're an item?"

"That's what I said!" interjected Blayde.

"It's been two months!" I said. "And that's not the issue here! Blayde, you want me to, what? Try my darnedest to kill the president?"

"My head is spinning," said Kork.

"Well, you shoot at him, one of us takes the bullet for him, and bam, we're glorious heroes," Blayde continued. "It's so easy I can't believe I didn't think about it decades ago."

"That's going to be enough to reverse centuries of you being public enemy number one?"

"If it's public enough a performance, sure," she said with a shrug.

This plan was so dumb it would have voted *me* president if it had hands. "And you're sure it'll work?"

"Well, my second idea was to lead the revolt against the Alliance and then become heroes of the revolution. But my shortest estimation sets us at about fifty-three years' worth of grueling effort."

"Time I can't spend away from my family," I replied. "Fine. I'll do it."

"That was heavily implied."

"I'd much rather bring the entire Alliance down, personally," I said, "but I suppose this is a good first step."

"The thing is, it's damn hard to topple a civilization such as the Alliance," said Blayde. "While each planet is practically self-governing, there's too much reliance on the core to sustain each world independently. To keep order on this scale, the president's law must be absolute, so he rules by decree. We could kill him, but then what? Sure, we've taken down tyrants before, but they tend to be poorly organized and already have a rebellion to oppose them. The anti-Alliance groups are sparse. Killing the president just means his son becomes president after him."

"Except his son has been … missing," said Kork. "It must be seven years now? Lots of theories about *that*, let me tell you."

"Rules by decree, child takes throne—yeah, sounds like an emperor to me," I said. "So, instead of killing him, you want us to fake kill him, so we can fake save him and get a real pardon so we can make real change."

"You got it," said Zander. "It's going to work!"

"Are you speaking from experience or just agreeing with her because she's your sister?"

He shrugged. "Isn't that the same thing?"

Kork shook his head once again. "This is the dumbest plan I've ever heard."

"Well, can you think of anything better?"

"I said it was dumb, not that I don't think it will work."

"So, you'll help us?" asked Zander.

"You deserve a pardon for what you did for us," said Kork, putting down his prong on his empty plate. "And for all the other times we probably don't know about. I even know how I can get you into the birthday ball."

"Is that what I think it is?" I asked.

"A ball for the president's birthday?" said Blayde. "Is there going to be cake?"

"Is there going to be—of course there's going to be cake! It's a birthday!"

"That would be a golden opportunity," said Zander, turning to Kork. "If you could get us in, that would be incredible."

"Well, I'm only allowed a single plus one," he said. "I would gladly bring Sally as my date."

I blushed. I don't know why; it wasn't as if I still had feelings for him. But the whole idea of going to an interstellar ball with a starship captain at my side sounded incredibly glorious.

"So long as *you* don't mind?" he asked Zander. I wasn't sure where the inflection was coming from. Was it friendly or was his real question, *Will you rip off my face if I do?* "Is it even proper for me to ask?"

"It's our safest bet," he said, no face ripping today. "Considering that I'm going to have to charm someone into taking me, I have nothing to say."

"Two questions," said Blayde. "One, when is this thing? And two, will you even be allowed to go?"

"I'm Captain James T. Kork," he said. "If I don't show my face at the biggest event of the season, the populace will know something is up. It's the whole reason the *Traveler* was brought back to Pyrina in the first place rather than rerouting somewhere quiet where we could clean up the mess we made. Besides, if they decide to dump my character, it would be in a much more dramatic way than have me, I don't know, die in my sleep or get diarrheic space parasites. And to answer your first question, it's sometime next week. I haven't looked at a calendar since I got back because the three of you have been taking up every waking moment."

"We're not that hands-on, you know," I said. "It's not like we're Alvin and the Chipmunks."

"Right, so we've got a week to plan to infiltrate this ball," said Blayde. "That's a week to craft new identities, find two extra invitations and disguises, craft a weapon that'll make it through security undetected, and find Sally a translator."

"Oh, Sally," said Kork.

"What, *oh, Sally*?" I asked. "Please don't tell me I have to shave my head or something. Does my hair grow back or am I like a Barbie doll?"

"She doesn't know the Lithero, does she?"

I shook my head. "Is that like the VP or something?"

"Frash." Blayde ran her hands through her hair. "We're going to have to teach Sally the Lithero."

"She can handle it," said Zander.

"I'm not a child. Stop talking about me as if I'm not here," I snapped. "What do I have to learn?"

"It's a dance," he said. "You're going to have to master it. With your charm, more than one young suitor will ask to dance with you, and you're no Alliance somebody if you can't dance the Lithero."

My heart fell into my stomach, plunged through, then ripped a hole in my gut. *Ker-splat.* "There'll be dancing involved?"

"It's a ball. What do you expect?" said Blayde, standing. She tossed the skillet into the sink and returned to the table, looking slightly less stressed.

"Finding the buffet?" I frowned. "Wait, no, scratch that. I've had some disagreements with Alliance gala food before."

Zander snorted. "Understatement of the century."

"You may not understand this, coming from your time and place and all, but dancing is probably the most important lie detector test in the universe." Blayde was awfully close to my face now, one hand on the table, her other on the back of my chair. I'd never seen her like this. This wasn't anger, not exactly. This was fear. Actual fear from the most fearless woman in the universe. Was she genuinely—hold your shock and awe—afraid *for* me? "You can only dance when you are completely honest with yourself and others around you. Your feet will always give you away. In a single week, you are a human of noble Alliance upbringing, not an unemployed Terran from one of their backwater annexes. And your feet will have to believe it, too, or you're as vulnerable as if you walked in there naked with one of Willowcrest's signs."

"Wow," said Kork. "You are *really* into dancing."

Blayde was already storming off to his room before he could even get out of his chair. By the sounds of it, she was ripping it to shreds.

"Don't you have any dress shoes?" she shouted. Kork was already there and said something that quickly disappeared into a marble of alien words as they left my range of translatability.

I turned to Zander. "She can't be serious about this dancing thing."

"Trust me, she is," he replied. He stood, starting to clear the table but barely had time to stack the plates before Kork and Blade emerged, holding up what I could only assume were BDSM manacles for claws. A long, black leather tube, closed at one end, with a sharp blade jutting almost parallel. Covered in ribbons, I should add.

"Put these on," she said, tossing them to me.

"Sorry, not my kink," I replied, tossing them back.

"Fine, do I have to do everything myself?"

She dropped onto the sofa, slipping her feet into the tube, and it hit me in that instant that these were shoes, shoes so tall and thin that they were unrecognizable, high heels so high the foot was on points. She laced the ribbons up all the way to her knees and stood, pushing the coffee table away. She was a whole head taller now, eye to eye with Zander and Kork.

"Don't scratch the floor!" Kork stammered. "I'll never get the deposit back on this place!"

"I need a partner," she said. Kork and Zander exchanged cautious glances. "Come on! I'm the only one in the shoes. This shouldn't be hard for any of you."

"Wait, everyone is wearing these?" I asked. I still hadn't moved from my seat at the table, so overwhelmingly confused I couldn't find the controls for my feet.

"Well, it used to be just the men," said Zander with a shrug. "But then people argued that most species don't even have a concept of male, and most species either don't have feet or they have too many feet, and it's so time consuming to put them on that they never take them off in the first place. And the smell. But I'm getting off point. The real point is that they're very *in* right now, and everybody who is anybody wears them."

"They make the booty pop in dress uniforms," said Kork. "I think that's part of the reason they invite us captains in the first place."

"Right. Kork, give us some music, please?"

"Computer—oh, right, you killed my AI." He pulled out a phone-shaped device, and an instant later an ethereal sound filled the room, a soft wind instrument with an electronic beat in the background.

She ushered her brother over with a movement of her hand, taking her stance in front of him in the open space of the living room with the rigid severity of a strict tutor. They both stared into each other's eyes with stern faces, chins out, hands behind their backs with index fingers interlocked. Zander had ditched his shoes and was standing on the very tips of his toes, as effortlessly as if he were suspended.

"Watch," she said, shooting me one of those telling looks. "Because you have a week to master it."

A basic, almost primitive beat pulsed into the room, the siblings clapping on the first and third beat as they circled each other, eyes still locked, heads still high, legs stiff as they rose to bend at the knee, then stomped back down on the last beat. *Clap, clap, stomp clap* and repeat until more instruments were added.

I sat on the sofa as what sounded like a base—an elephant hyped on caffeine and a theremin—joined in the music, the dance as the sibling joined hands moving across the floor with grace as their arms dipped, their feet kicking away to the side as they relied on their partner's strength to keep their balance. They separated and moved away from each other, seeming to dance with invisible partners for what had to be the moment of the dance when everyone danced with each other, their hands returning to their backs, index fingers crossed like little daggers, their feet leaping like in a strange form of Riverdance.

And, suddenly, they were back together, kicking and twirling and clapping to the odd beat in a complex pattern of perfection, both partners relying on each other's moves to finish the dance, their parts like a puzzle coming together over the course of the song.

The music ended, and they returned to their initial position, bowing deeply to finish to their piece. I felt like they had just completed a work of art, the colors fading from my memory with every single one of my blinks. Blayde turned to me, her arms akimbo.

"So, you get the picture?"

"I'm never going to be able to do that. You realize that, don't you?" I replied honestly.

"You haven't even tried yet," said Zander. "I swear it's fun!"

"Oh, trust me, I've tried it. In my head. Where it belongs. Even in there, I've already tripped at least three times."

"Come on, you're going to have to give it a go eventually," he said encouragingly. "That or we have to get Kork to take a shot at the man, and that'll kill his very convincing military film career."

"Did you intend to sound patronizing?" said Kork. "Because that sounded patronizing. And need I remind you that very convincing military film career is what's getting you in the door?"

"She'll have to do more than give it a go. She'll have to perfect it." Blayde tossed me the sad excuse for shoes, turning to the kitchen to drink from the tap as I struggled with the fit.

Zander came over to my side, silently lacing up the other shoe as reference for the one I was struggling with. I replicated the knots as closely as I could, his voice guiding me whenever I messed up. Blayde watched from the kitchen island, her legs crossed, a glass of water in her hand, her eyes stern as they locked on me. Kork sat beside her, a little dazed.

I got to my feet, struggling to keep my balance. Flashbacks of those ballet classes I had fought so hard for only to despise so much flooded my periphery vision. The shoes tried to relieve a bit of the difficulty by shifting the weight off the tip of the toes to the heel of the foot, but that meant you had to teach yourself how to walk again by using only one pressure point on the shoe instead of walking heel to toe.

At this point, a new song had started, the rhythmic interlude only at its beginning. I stood to face Zander in the small space of the apartment, wobbling slightly in my new shoes. He gave me a reassuring smile as we started to circle, while Blayde coached loudly from the kitchen.

"Knee, clap, knee, clap, knee, stomp, clap, and again."

And again and again, until, as predicted, my feet slipped out from under me, and I fell face first into the floor, a loud crack resounding from the collision.

"Are you all right?" Zander asked, helping me back up.

"Yeah, I'm fine. Hold on," I replied before pushing my nose back into its rightful place. He wiped the blood off my lip.

Kork gaped. "What the hell happened in those two-month-minutes?"

"Well, maybe you can cram a lifetime's worth of dance classes into next week," said Blayde. "Because you're going to have to do better than that. I don't think I have time to make a new plan, anyway. So, dance like your life depends on it."

"Give her a break, Blayde. It's not like she's going to get it right on her first try. Most people spend their whole lives perfecting it."

"All the more reason for her to step it up a notch," she snapped. "Sally, I'm not sugarcoating this. Appearance is everything here. Any power we want to reclaim from the Alliance starts now, and it starts here. Dance for your parents' lives. Dance for Felling's life. Dance for Marcy's life. Because in a way, their lives all depend on it."

I nodded, following his instructions as we attempted the dance once again. I lasted twice as long this time before tripping over my own toes and tumbling over again, my nose remaining intact this attempt. Again, Zander helped me up, instructed me on what I did wrong, and as soon as a new song started up, we were at it again.

By the end of the evening, I seriously wished my parents could see me now.

# EIGHTEEN
## MY LOVE LANGUAGE IS CEREAL

**TRUE TO OUR WORD, WE DIDN'T OVERSTAY OUR** welcome—any longer than we already had. We jumped out of the apartment before Kork was even awake. It was easy enough waking early when you didn't have a cozy bed to sleep in and the couch was more decorative than actually meant to be sat on, let alone slept on. When this was all over, that's what I needed most: sleep. I never thought I'd miss a motel before.

Despite the city spanning the entire planet, Zander and Blayde insisted we couldn't take the metro. This had nothing to do with their fear of being recognized, though, admittedly, it was a possibility since some entrances were covered by LifePrints. Instead it had everything to do with an ancient feud between city planning AIs, which despised each other or something. Which is how we found ourselves on the ground level of the infinite city, strolling down a market street in the rumbling hours of the early morning.

It was nothing like Da-Duhui. Here, sunlight reached even the lowest tier, thanks to a complicated set of mirrors that focused the light no matter what time of day it was. The street we were on was packed tightly with people from every corner of the galaxy: humans side by side with furry monsters and gaseous globs. Market stalls lined the road as far as the eye could see, which wasn't particularly far due to the aforementioned crowd.

It was a world of color and sound and, above all else, smell. Spices from every plant from every planet were sold in drifting spheres of stock. Vendors shouted their wares, bright holographic lights sprawling in lieu of banners. A beautiful day if I ever did see one.

"You see?" said Blayde, flinging her arms wide, much to the frowns—and other unrecognizable expressions of those around her. "This is what a real market looks like. Not like that rinky-dink place you took us to in Washington."

"I didn't take you there. Felling had been kidnapped," I said. "But I get your point. This is a beautiful market."

"Pyrina is one of the most beautiful cities I've ever been to," said Zander. "And it doesn't matter where you visit; it's always gorgeous. Clean. Sunny where it needs to be and shady everywhere else."

"Speaking of," muttered Blayde, before dashing off to a side alley, Surly-Bop bouncing on her back.

# INALIENABLE

"Should we go after her?" I asked, as she disappeared into the shadows.

"Nah. Less conspicuous this way. Have you seen the monkeys?"

He gripped my hand and led me across the road to a small stall covered with what most definitely were not monkeys. Something I might perhaps call a land squid: eight fleshy appendages connected to a small head with massive eyes; the critters were about the size of a Yorkie and oddly cute. Zander was stroking a blue one sitting on a little swing, and I couldn't tell which one was cooing at the other.

"Are they … pets?" I asked, afraid to pet one myself. They didn't look soft, a bit like a hairless cat, and that just made my skin crawl.

"Yeah. For those who can't afford robots, these little beasties are the next best thing. More like service animals, if you will."

The person running the stall looked like the creature they were selling, except larger than me. They got up, taking a monkey down from the perch, babbling so quickly I could not catch what she was saying even if I did have a working translator. Zander must have gotten the gist of it, taking the animal she offered him and placing it on my shoulder before I could retort. Instantly, it clambered up my hair, sitting itself on the top of my scalp.

"Zander," I sputtered, "what's it doing?"

"Just showing off," he said as he reached for my phone, and I heard the unmistakable sound of the shutter snapping shut.

"Oy, pics? Really?"

"Come on, a monkey is sitting on your head, braiding your hair. A moment to remember, right? From what I learned about Instagram, this is prime material."

"It's not a monkey," I said. "And I'm pretty sure the Agency would literally kill me if I put this online. Also, it's braiding my hair?"

"And it's amazing at it." He reached his arm up, the little creature scampering up it to his shoulder, where its eight legs immediately got to work on him. "Cute, right?"

He fished in his pocket for the right currency, tipping the stall owner as the critter returned to its perch. Zander's gravity-defying hair now had long French braids up the sides, following the curve of his scalp and giving him a sort of faux-hawk in the middle.

"You have to tip them well," he said, turning back to me. "Cosmetology school is expensive. Trust me."

I slipped back into my comfortable confusion. It was the only way to enjoy this foreign place without having my brain explode. Take everything surprising as it came, without asking any questions I didn't have the brainpower to store the answers to.

Such as, why were there butterflies on chains over there? They might not have been actual butterflies, come to think of it, and were they pets or food? I saw one guy petting them and another chomping on them. Another bought a dozen and strung them up to his grocer bags, which promptly flew away. And all this in the matter of minutes I was watching.

"Pyrina to Sally?" asked Zander, reaching for my hand again. "You okay?"

"I need to upgrade my brain's processing power," I said. "There's just so much here."

"Let's get some breakfast," he said. "Sit down for a bit."

We grabbed seat at a hole-in-the-wall cafe, and I let Zander order for me, seeing as how I couldn't translate what I didn't even know. The result was a pink drink about the consistency of a latte and a sweet-smelling bun covered in herbs.

"You didn't get me any?" asked Blayde, sliding in between us before I could take a sip or a bite or even pick which I wanted to start with.

Zander signaled the waiter. "Didn't know how long it would take. How'd it go?"

She grinned one of her very proudest smiles, dropping three black grains onto the table. "New identities. ID chips, brand new, stolen from a hospital before they were put into circulation. I'll load them up when we reach the apartment. It's a bit of a slum, but I spent the last of the stress balls to get it, so it's the best we can afford if we don't want to show up to the ball nude."

"You got us a roof?"

"And a few leads on ways into the ball. Eat, and we'll track down our new digs. Oh, and Sally, I grabbed you these on the way."

She handed me a square bag, and I didn't even have to take it to know what it was. "Not those torturous dress shoes!"

"You have to learn to dance in them," she insisted. "Your training starts today."

"I thought it had started last night?"

"That was just the warm-up. Now put them on and drink your bilk. That'll fortify you, and you're going to need to be heavily fortified."

Zander sighed for me as I endured his sister's pushing. We ate, paid, and were back on the street, though this time I was now a whole foot taller and flopping around like the wacky inflatable balloon man.

"Is this really necessary?" asked Zander, following behind me like I was learning to ride a bike without capsizing for the first time. Blayde was entirely against any handholding, though I wasn't sure that was part of her so-called training.

"She's the one who wanted this," she replied. "If she finds *this* difficult, how could she handle tearing down years of systematic oppression over her own people?"

She had a point there. I sucked in my gut and powered on, flailing, yes, but with determination.

••••••••●••••••••

# INALIENABLE

**AFTER A LONG WALK AND A CONFUSING**
encounter where I almost crushed the entire micro-organism district, we finally found our new home. The second the door closed behind me, I knew very well I wouldn't have to worry about losing the address because I wasn't going to be leaving anytime soon.

"You call this a slum?" I said as Blayde brushed past me.

"Yeah, have you seen it?" She threw her arms wide.

"It's nicer than my place!"

"Why do you think I hated your apartment so much?"

Cleaning nanos were literally dirt cheap in this city—the hives of smog nanos frequently rained them down—and every surface of the apartment was spotless. White and clean like Kork's place, the only difference was that there no windows, though a large television on the wall pulled off the illusion rather well.

So, not only had we found a clean apartment with a TV and I don't know how many bedrooms, but all it had cost was a few stress balls too.

"Right," said Blayde, "I'll craft the new identities. Zander, you start building an organic gun that'll make it through the weapons detectors at the ball. And, Sally, you work on your footwork."

"Isn't there something more, I don't know, useful I could be doing?"

"Not really," said Blayde. "By the way, I like the hair."

And with that, she locked herself in a room, leaving the two of us alone with the TV, cool braids, and a whole lot of confusion.

"Well, you heard her," said Zander. "I guess we get to work."

So, I clapped until my hands were raw. I stomped until my heels and my shoes had become one with each other, not just by feeling but by flesh as well. I stomped as I watched the TV advertise pictures of Earth as a travel destination I didn't have the translator for, and I stomped as I drank carton after carton of milk.

The shoes stayed on every waking minute in the apartment. They stayed on as Blayde came and went, each time her hands full of new wonders: yards and yards of exotic silks one time, buckets of bones the next, fifteen cartons of cereal nearing the end of our first day.

"I'm going to need your help on this," she said, dropping the boxes on the kitchen island.

"Shh, I'm practicing," I said.

"Don't be facetious. Come and help, or do you want to spend the ball pretending you took a vow of silence?"

I sat down at the bar, my feet tingling from ten straight hours of dancing, and followed her lead, ripping into the cartons and shaking the baggies of cereal around.

"What are we looking for?" I asked.

"A translator, dummy," she said. "The cereal brand has got this goody thing at the moment. Not every box has one, but the odds are good. Plus, it'll keep us fed all week. Ah!"

She ripped open her bag, pulling out a small box. Inside, the washer-shaped device that held my salvation: access to all languages in existence.

"Hold on," I said. "If the Agency can't afford a decent translator for Foollegg, how can cereal brands afford to give them away?"

"Corporate branding," she said with a shrug. "They're not the best quality, but it's the best we can do right now. Need help putting it in?"

I knew the drill by now. She was kind enough to lend me her laser, and all it took was a small cut behind my ear to insert the translator.

I blinked at the cereal boxes before me, once covered in gibberish, and saw their letters rearrange themselves into English. *Alphabet Breakfast*, they said, bright yellow letters on red. *Put the eating back in reading.*

"So?" asked Blayde. "Does it work?"

"Oh my gosh," I stammered, and for an instant, it felt like I was on solid ground again, even with my feet dangling from the chair in their strappy shoes. Without language, I had no voice. Now, speech was all mine again.

"I take that as a yes. Ah, Zander, you're done?"

Zander stepped out of the bathroom, brandishing the ugliest weapon I'd ever seen in my life. It looked like those catapults you make out of pens and rubber bands in primary school, except this one had a second job as the skeleton of a yet unknown animal.

"That's disgusting," I said, and Zander nodded.

"But it won't register as a weapon," he replied, putting it on the table amidst the piles of cereal. Not very sanitary.

"Will it even fire bullets?" I asked.

"Not bullets," said Blayde, leaning her head back and pointing at her mouth. My face lost all color as I put two and two together.

"No, no way. Absolutely no way. No way."

"Fine." She shrugged, throwing her head back further and reaching her hand into her mouth. Her bloody fingers clutched a molar. "Coward."

"It's gross!"

"Who cares? Unlimited ammo!" She grinned, and I sank into my chair. It wasn't too late to call this whole thing off. Throw ourselves a traditional little revolution instead of this whole mess. "How in the universe are you still sane and stable right now?"

"Well, you're the one who broke me out of a mental institution. I guess that says a lot more about you than it does about me."

"No, it doesn't! And if you want the power of fresh, clean teeth, but you're also craving pudding, you know you should always turn to *Chummy Chews* first! Now available at any local pharmacy. Races from the gamma sector may experience a slight tingling in their tenth extremities."

I clapped my hands over my mouth. At first, I thought the stares were bad, but those were made worse when the siblings burst out laughing.

"Stop!" I begged. "I don't know what just happened!"

"Blayde," said Zander, forcing himself to frown, though I could see his laughter was still going strong in his gut. "You couldn't find her anything better than a corporate-sponsored gimmick?"

"I was out of Starburst," she said. "They've decreased in value since the last time we were here, and you ate half our stash!"

"Get it out of me!" I screamed. "I'm not a walking billboard!"

"Hold on, we can fix this," said Zander. "For the time being, just stay calm. It's going to be fine, okay?"

I nodded. I didn't want to speak any more than I had to, lest I discover the other sponsors programmed into my head.

"It's the only translator we have," said Blayde. "She'll have to get used to it."

"You created new identities out of nothing. You can probably fix the thing, can't you?"

"Maybe. But that's not a priority right now."

"Not a … hello? She can't go to a ball and start telling everyone to buy pharmacy-grade gum! They'll know right away she's not supposed to be there!"

"Well, I guess she'll just have to keep her mouth shut, then," she said, huffing in frustration. "But at least she'll know what's going on. Look, you two, I have a meeting with a contact in just a few minutes about getting the rest of our presidential invites. We'll talk about this when I get back. Until then, practice talking with your feet instead of your mouth. All right? All right. And leave some cereal for me."

I'm pretty sure she jumped instead of walking the last few feet to the door because she disappeared faster than I could say anything, leaving Zander and me alone at the table. He looked as shocked as I felt.

"She seems a little overwhelmed," I said. "Did I say something?"

"She always gets like this when planning heists," he replied, letting out a heavy sigh. Slowly, he started stuffing the cereal bags into their boxes, opening the empty cupboards and jamming them in. "She's a perfectionist. Doesn't leave any opportunity for error."

"And we're clear opportunities for error."

"Exactly."

I got back on my feet—or my toes, I should say—and used my phone to select some music, easing into the tempo and clapping to the beat. Blayde faded from my mind; Zander faded from my mind; everything faded away until it was just me and the music, my body moving in time with a song that meant nothing to my Terran ears.

I was going to get this dance. I was going to fool the entire ball and then save my friends from the Alliance. All I had to do was dance my part.

And not fall flat on my ass, like I'd just done.

"Sally," said Zander, rushing to my side, "are you … never mind."

# INALIENABLE

I flashed him a smile, letting him help me up, nonetheless. Of course, I was fine. Nothing hurt but my pride.

"Do you need a partner?" he asked, his hand still on mine.

"Only if you can keep up."

He let out a small chuckle, making signals at the TV until it switched to a music channel, pictures of forests in lieu of a music video. The same channel Kork must have tuned into the night before. If someone wanted to dance the Lithero 24/7—or 30/10 as time went on Pyrina—they need look no further.

Together, apart. Clapping, stomping around and around the room. The moves were easier with Zander at my side: part partner, part guide. I could play off his moves for balance and direction.

And that smile, that blinding smile! I pushed myself harder just to see more of his teeth. Now that my feet were far beyond the stage of feeling numb and slipping into what could almost be called muscle memory, I was actually enjoying myself. There was something about being able to twirl around the room to rousing music with the man you loved that made everything else seem totally insignificant.

Which, of course, was the exact moment of inattention it took for my feet to slip out from under me once again, causing me to collapse on the floor, dragging down Zander with me.

Unintentional, I swear. Also unintentional were my lips on his, my hands cautiously on his chest.

Unintentional was his response, though his arms wrapping around my waist felt like a promise, and his lips on mine like a vow.

Absolutely intentional were my hands reaching under his shirt and his own pulling off my top.

After what could have been hours, though it couldn't have been more than minutes, we broke away for air we didn't need, his hands warm against my back.

"You deserve much better than a floor," he whispered.

"I don't care," I replied, lowering my lips to his, though my hair reached his face first, making him laugh. His eyes sparkled with joy as he brushed the strand, docking it behind my ear. "This is the first time we've been alone—truly alone!—in what might possibly have been forever. I'm not risking it."

He sat up, one arm keeping me to him, and suddenly he was standing, my legs wrapped tightly around his torso to keep me from slipping down. My lips were latched onto his—for a secondary degree of protection, you see—as he marched us through the apartment, across the floor I had trampled so hard, and through the door to a room I hadn't even had the chance to explore.

Okay, I admit, he was right. A bed underneath my back was heaven right now. And with how much I was missing beds, I could have sunk into a sleepy stupor right then and there.

Though maybe I was just drowsy from lack of oxygen.

# INALIENABLE

"You see?" said Zander, peeling away slightly. "No time wasted, nothing risked."

"No time wasted," I agreed.

Time was wasted, however, as we struggled to get off the shoes I had been strapped into for almost an entire day. My feet had swollen to an abysmal size, meaning the poor footwear had to be pried off, and the second my feet were free, they each released a sigh of relief so strong it winded us both for a few seconds. But then we were laughing again, and the rest of our clothes put up less of a fight, and time wasn't wasted any more.

"Zander," I said, his name rolling off my tongue like a prayer. The desire that had been building within me, denied and shoved down for so long, was bursting through every pore in my body, so strong and so fast that my head was spinning. I parted my lips once more, but my tongue began to act on its own accord, words spilling from a leaky bucket. "Have you ever wanted to know what it feels like to be another species? Head on down to *Hal's Hall of Mirrors*, where you can see for yourself! Open ten days a week, even on holidays. Must be under five units tall to access the building."

I guess he wanted me as much as I did him because the Hall of Mirrors was met with our laughter. Our bodies spoke a language that didn't need a translator.

# NINETEEN

## THE INVISIBLE HAND OF THE ECONOMY IS AN IMPRESSIVELY GOOD DANCER

**BY THE TIME YOU GET AROUND TO YOUR SECOND** alien gala, you get a little blasé about things. Especially about the limo. No one wants to drive around in a giant hovering car when you have to deal with the traffic of the most populated planets in the galaxy. And that wasn't even counting the flashbacks of falling.

"We're not going to be late," said Zander, but it sounded like he was only trying to convince himself. I felt like a huffy debutante, my bright pink ball gown taking up the entire back seat, a good ten feet behind Zander, who was looking quite trim in his chauffeur uniform. Why the hell he splurged on something like that when it was literally for a two-minute drop-off was beyond me. If I could toot my own horn, I would say it was because he was fond of more than just costume changes.

# INALIENABLE

"You'd think people as advanced as the great Alliance would have solved something as trivial as traffic by now," I muttered. "They have flying cars, for goodness sake. Why the hell are we stationary?"

He said something I couldn't hear over the din of the cars outside. That and the empty distance between us.

"What?" I asked.

"A few streets are shut off for the parade," he repeated. "There's a giraffe!"

I pulled a teenage prom move and opened the sunroof of the limo, standing straight so I could peek over. That wasn't a giraffe flying by; it was mountain: black flesh ripped from the night sky wafting down the main street as gracefully as if it we were all suddenly underwater. Why a living giraffe grown of pure darkness was smiling down Main Street was anybody's guess.

I gawked at the sight, then promptly coughed at the fumes.

"Why is there a giraffe parade?" I asked, shutting the sunroof. "Also, space giraffes?"

"What? Giraffes can't live in space?"

"I always thought that was just superstition," I replied. My gown was stiff, and sitting back down was a chore. My feet were numb in their pointed shoes. "Or wasn't it whales? Also, yeah, nothing is meant to actually live in space. It's an endless void."

"Giraffes are explorers. Why do you think they have such long necks?"

"None of that makes any sense," I said. "Is my translator acting up again?"

"Seeing as how I don't suddenly crave gum, I think you're fine."

The giraffe passed, traffic resumed, and Zander wove us through until joining the line of limos full of other attendees.

"You look amazing," he said, and I caught his gaze in the rear-view mirror. "So much for being inconspicuous. All eyes will be on you."

I felt a blush coming on. "Says the face of the latest hot chauffeur calendar."

"Is that a thing?"

"You would be every month. And they would be wishing for an Earth calendar just for the extra two spreads."

He beamed, bringing us forward a few more meters. Through the windshield, up ahead as it was, I could barely make out the hint of the building we would be crashing, the gorgeous stone structure that stood by itself in the middle of the crowded city.

"Agreement Hall," said Zander. "Though I'm sure it sounds fancier in Old Pyrinian. This is where the Alliance came into being. The very spot it was signed into existence."

"Great place for a dance party," I muttered.

"Always. Remembering the sacrifice of our ancestors through joy and celebration. Well, it would be fitting if it weren't for the abuse of power and all. But, hey, free cake!"

"Free cake," I agreed.

"You're nervous."

"Of course I am. I'm about to take a shot at the president. It's not a fun prospect."

"Sure it is. Blayde's going to stop it, sure, but isn't it going to be cathartic?"

"Let's hope so," I replied. "I'll see you in there."

The limo came to park in front of the grand hall, and Zander let himself out, slipping into character. As my door opened, I was looking at a stranger, a man I probably knew as well as a gardener or a maid. Because I was no longer Sally Webber either. I was Lady Glosilda of the Bluest Isle. And I was definitely not here to commit murder.

Despite the dark sky above, it was like stepping out into the midday sun. The spotlights filled the world with pink fire and rose-scented air. It was hour twenty-four, and the party of the century was just getting started.

It's not every day the president turned one hundred.

Suddenly, I was on the red carpet, blinded by the huge spotlights, waving at the crowd who cheered for me without even knowing who I was. I smiled, trying to ignore the knot in my stomach that kept twisting and turning as my anxiety rose, leaving Zander to pull the limo out of the way to make his own separate entrance.

I lifted the hem of my dress and ascended the stairs, passing by the silver android who announced my name to an enraptured audience. I had thought the party on Da-Duhui was extravagant, but this ball redefined the word. Opulence overflowed from the balconies down into the hall, oozing silk and silver, and hundreds of races crammed into a single room, bold and beautiful and drop-dead gorgeous.

I caught my breath, but only once. This was meant to be my world, after all. I wasn't supposed to be surprised by races that had been my neighbors all my life.

"Is this absolutely necessary?" I asked the android as it ran a wand over the front and back of my dress. For a second, I feared the wand would detect the gun, somehow, despite all the work Zander had put into making it as un-gun-like as possible, but it remained silent.

"Safety is my number one concern, ma'am," he said. "Thank you."

My date waited for me in the atrium, and he was right: He did look even more dashing in his dress uniform. Captain James T. Kork was a miracle of human achievement, all muscle and poise, black uniform tight around his figure and heavy with the medals of his many accomplishments. While most of them were fictional, the medals themselves definitely were not. We bowed to each other in Alliance fashion, then I latched myself to his arm, happy for a friendly face to lead me through.

"You look sublime," he said. "I couldn't possibly guess your planet of origin."

"I could say the same of you," I replied. "I can't thank you enough for inviting me."

# INALIENABLE

"Oh please," he said, shrugging off his coat. We reached the top of the Lithorn-wood stairs—the silver swirls in between the rungs so effectively polished that they forced you to look up instead—that led into the main hall, and he slipped in between two pillars to hand the coat to the attendant there, a woman whose eyes stared right through me. She smiled and gave Kork a dazzling wink. Blayde.

"I thought she would come as a guest," said Kork, turning away from her. Familiarity would not do.

"It was easier to just get her hired as staff," I said. "She's got references like you wouldn't believe. I don't know if there really is a coat-check university, but apparently she's their valedictorian."

We stepped through the arches and into the main hall. It was almost impossible not to gasp at this room. This hall was even larger and grander than anything I had ever seen in my entire life, the ceiling tall and arched and inlaid with a mosaic of precious stones from all four corners of the Alliance rather than painted. It depicted scenes from their mythology, which somehow involved winged sea slugs and unicorn-headed men fighting against purple flowers, which occasionally showered the crowd with sparkles. And yet, it was so perfectly done I couldn't for the life of me find a reason to laugh.

The end of the hall held a raised dais with a podium at its center. The orchestra itself was floating around the hall, drifting on the currents of their own music, somehow playing together even when one drifted so far that his seat almost rammed into the champagne tower.

I call it champagne, but, you know, it certainly wasn't.

And there, covering the entire wall behind the podium, was a face I recognized from our hours of practicing my aim. A man I hated with every fiber of my being, who had absolutely no idea that I even existed.

The President of the Alliance himself, Phellied Straiddies, his stern face glaring down at us, covered in the broad colors of the Alliance: bright red and sunshine yellow framed with silver. Even in this picture that was supposed to show the best side of him, he looked as if he had just been gifted a fruit bouquet and was not going to accept it lying down.

Huge columns the width of trailers surrounded the entire dance floor, but there was a surprisingly small turnout of people, or so it seemed, shrunken in relation with the immensity of the hall. Where the atrium had been crowded, this hall lost all sense of scale and dwarfed the attendees. On the dance floor, the gowns of the rich and famous of the Alliance twirled in unison, each of the beings so graceful on their torturous shoes, the rainbow of satin colors draping every species that graced these halls.

I looked up, eyesight flickering with spots of color, finding the thin catwalk the Alliance military were diligently patrolling. They were tiny against the unicorns in the sky. Even so, I could still make out their weapons:

rather large guns for such an event. The scale of it all was making me dizzy.

Kork and I made our way across the hall, avoiding the spinning dancers as they twirled, smiling, following the difficult steps to perfection. Wasn't going there right away. I scanned the hors d'oeuvres, wary from my past experiences with the food on Da-Duhui. But with a now-iron stomach and being slightly used to the food on this planet, maybe I could take a step in the right direction.

Okay, purple octopus tentacles, I'll give you a try.

That was a mistake.

It was not octopus.

It wasn't completely dead, either.

With a swipe of my hand, I grabbed a napkin, pretending to gently dab at my face while actually spitting out the wiggling remains into the paper that hid my mouth. I glanced over at Kork, afraid he might have seen, but he appeared to be doing the same thing. His eyes went wide like I had caught him with his hand in the cookie jar.

"So, uh, you and Zander?"

He just had to go *there*? And I, who was trying to avoid giving my translator an opportunity to speak for me, here I had to go answering things.

"Long two months," I said.

"Did I say something wrong?" he asked. "You seem to be avoiding conversation."

"Oh, it's not you," I said, tapping the spot behind my ear. "We found me a replacement translator, but it's not very reliable and keeps trying to sell people gimmicks. I'd rather someone else do all the talking."

"You *can't* be here," came a voice, aghast. I didn't turn, hoping to be forgotten, as I dropped the napkin into the trash, obscuring the action with the ruffles of my dress. But who would know me here? Here, of all places? Kork seemed more confused than I was.

Someone tapped me on the shoulder, a hint of laughter in their voice. "Sally Webber, is that you?"

I spun on my heels and practically fell over in shock. What were the odds? Another gala. Another planet. Another time. And yet Sekai was standing in front of me yet again, more medals on her chest, more pride in her smile, brilliant and healthy green as I'd ever seen her.

"Impossible," I stammered. "The odds are quite literally astronomical."

The Killian high commander smiled. "Fancy seeing you here! My date didn't tell me you were going to be here. Sir Red of Naz? I know you've heard of him."

I turned back to Kork, who was trying very hard not to look confused. "Captain James T. Kork, may I present to you Sekai No-Oji, ambassador of the Killian homeworld."

She clicked her heels together. "I've heard tales of your exploits, Captain. Let me rephrase that. I watch those tales *religiously*."

"It's always a pleasure to meet a fan," he said, meeting her bow. "How do you two know each other?"

"Oh, Zander blew up my workplace to save her crashed spaceship from capitalism," I said. No big deal.

"He knows?" she hissed. "Captain *Kork* knows the truth about the siblings?"

"Who doesn't?" he muttered into his drink.

That would be a conversation for later, with fewer prying eyes. "What happened since the Da-Duhui gala? The robots—"

"I left shortly after I spoke to you. Missed them completely. But is it true? Was it really Zander and Blayde who caused the destruction?"

"Right to the point, aren't you?" I said. "No, *hey, Sally, how did you escape the terrible mind-controlled zombie people?*"

"Well, I assumed the two points were related somehow," she said, winking. "So, you did manage to find them again?"

"And we even saved the planet in the process," I said, a little too smugly. "Not that you'd hear that in the news."

"Ah, well, it's too bad we didn't get to see each other in action." She took a large swig of something purple. "It's good to see you alive and well, Sally Webber." Her voice dropped to a whisper. "And I'm glad I can help you all in your small way. Let's not spoil the evening with criminal conversations. So very nice to meet you, Captain Kork." She extended an arm to me. "Would you care to dance?"

I glanced up at Kork, who pointed his thumb at the buffet; he'd catch up with me later.

"Gladly." I smiled, taking the Killian's velveted arm to be whisked away on the dance floor. It was such a relief to see a friendly face here tonight. And this time, it hadn't been arranged by my psycho time-space-stalker ex.

I was glad to have the steps engrained in my muscle memory, so I only had to focus on looking my upper-class best. I smiled at my partner whenever the opportunity arose, glad to see her smiling back. I had been wondering what had happened to her since our last meeting, sincerely worried that she had gotten caught up with the murderous, possessed robot people. But this was Sekai No-Oji, who had survived thousands of years under my planet's surface, regained her life after a madman had abused her for literal power, rose through the ranks and became an ambassador—to the civilization I had vowed to tear down. Oops.

Maybe Earth and Kili would make their own Alliance.

Sekai was an incredible dancer. While I simply flowed through the steps, she lived them, every motion expressive; a story shouted from each muscle. Her race had softer bones than mine, making her less rigid, but that didn't explain sheer talent. Dancing with her like holding your own in a tornado.

The song ended, and we clapped, but before I could ask her anything further, I was whisked away by another partner. Staying silent was harder than it seemed, especially since this being wanted to talk about a new bill that was being passed while dancing, something about limiting planetary intervention from high-dimensional life forms. Instead, I focused on the Lithero, concentrating on not losing my balance on the insanely vertical shoes as he ranted about taxes, rim planets, and the constant threat of literal gods taking over the economy.

"The great hand of the economy might be invisible," he insisted. Well, one of his three heads insisted. "But it doesn't mean it's not corporeal."

A bow, a thank you, then another dance partner, this one moderately human but even more intent on talking.

"Nice party, isn't it?" he asked politely.

"Wonderful," I replied, suddenly finding it easy to dance with this man. Maybe I had learned a thing or two about dancing after all. That or my numb feet had Stockholm syndrome.

"Is this your first presidential event?"

"Yes, as a matter of fact. You?"

"I've lost count." He smiled, dipping me quickly and pulling me back up before he could drop me on the floor. Like a seamstress dropping a bolt of silk and catching it before it unraveled.

"How does this one compare?"

"The best, by far." He smiled. "The dancers are better, the women much more beautiful."

I felt heat in my face as the dance split to the group part, the smallest partner on one side, their hands clapping in unison, the taller stomping theirs every five or eight, I couldn't keep track, and then regrouped into the proper couples.

"I must say, you are sublime," he said, and I blushed, though the intensity of his stare was a little much. Royal galas were a lot. "Are you enjoying the party?"

"I've never had an opportunity to dance the Lithero so many times in one night, that's for certain."

"I wouldn't have guessed that. You move so gracefully," he said politely. "I didn't catch your name?"

"Lady Glosilda. And if you currently have sore feet, try Captain Dauntless's foot pomade. Hand-crafted out of the horns of smeelzibess–donated, not harvested, 100% cruelty free! Makes any foot a baby foot."

It was bound to happen. I tried on my most apologetic smile for size.

"Sir Red of Naz, pleasure." He didn't let go of my hands, even though the dance—and my product placement—had ended.

I stared up at the face, and recognition hit me like the octopus returning from the dead to threaten me for not enjoying his severed limb.

"Oh, you almost had me," I said. "Red of Naz is much classier than Derzan."

"Drats, I thought I did."

Zander's eyes were still his eyes, but the rest of his face was utterly alien to me. He had applied prosthetics so effectively I wouldn't have given him a second glance in a crowd. Well, except I probably would have since the prosthetics did nothing to diminish his rugged handsomeness.

"You thought I wouldn't recognize you?"

"I wondered."

"Well, I did." I glanced over the foreign face. "The eyebrows are so … *villainous*."

"Do you like them?" he asked, raising his chin up to look more menacing. The goatee was a little over the top. "With Blayde, too much is not enough."

"No, they're an attractive touch. Though slightly creepy."

A new song began, and Kork was here. We danced together in a swirl of silks, and I was laughing, actually laughing, having what one might call an actual ball.

My next partner was hard to pinpoint because the only part of him I could see was a fluttering red cape. I was half certain this was the so-called invisible hand of the economy, but I wasn't going to let my translator ruin this wonderful night.

No. Only what I did next could do that.

The music changed suddenly to a strange heroic tune, a pleasant upbeat fanfare. Three men rose from their places in the floating orchestra, their six arms playing the complex instruments that had no comparison to back on Earth, though each sounded like full brass bands. They wobbled as their drifting platforms arranged themselves behind the podium. The dancers froze, all eyes turned to the stage, where a lone man stood with his arms crossed behind his back, leaning into the podium as if he were afraid he would not get picked up by the microphone.

"Milords, ladies, gentleman, women, argroueth, and granouns," he said, excitement filling the room from all the dancers. "Please welcome President Straiddies!"

Applause rose through the hall as the man of the hour walked onto the stage to his podium, waving absentmindedly. His wrinkles were prominent on his face, like a crumpled rag, but it wasn't his looks that earned him the applause; it was his power, the power he seemed to radiate from every angle. Shadows played across his face as the stage lights turned on him, darkness falling on the audience who stared at him, intent on his every word.

I opened my purse, my eyes still on the president, fiddling for the gun, ripping the lining as quietly as humanly possible. All eyes were on him now, so intent on his hypnotic voice that I was almost invisible, all my sounds muted. I released the safety, cocked it, and aimed it at the man's heart, waiting for the signal to come, for the man of the century to welcome us to his party.

I breathed deeply, trying to keep my nerves under control, for the moment to come.

The bullet sliced through his chest as silence fell in the hall.

The man staggered, clawing at the place where the blood tried to escape his body, losing his balance in the process. His face looked at the audience, mouth forming a small O of surprise. He fell without a word, his body flopping like a forgotten rag doll, his feet the only part his audience could see.

Finally, a scream erupted from the hall, a lone scream that resonated though the building, soon to be joined by countless others who had just lost their grip on reality.

# INALIENABLE

Blayde turned from the front row to stare at me as I stuffed the weapon back into my purse, her eyes huge, accusing, and confused all the same.

"Way to literally jump the gun," she spat. "Now, we've lost our only chance at your stupid plan."

"That wasn't me!" I sputtered. "Someone else was trying to kill him!"

"Correction: Someone else *has* killed him," she said.

"Not me!"

It didn't matter anyway. The president had just been assassinated.

That was when the shooting started.

One by one, they fell like flies: men, women, argroueths and granouns, lords and ladies. The quick ones darted for cover, hiding behind the columns instead of running around the hall like idiots, while others fell, shot in the back by an unknown killer, the hall suddenly full of corpses and many different colors of blood.

I searched for the siblings, but they were nowhere in sight. Without any clue into what to do in this type of situation, I covered my ears, closing my eyes as I dove behind the bar.

# TWENTY

## IF EVERYONE WANTS TO ATTACK YOU ON YOUR BIRTHDAY, THAT'S PROBABLY NOT A GOOD SIGN

**IF EVERYONE WANTS TO ATTACK YOU ON YOUR** birthday, that's probably not a good sign

The trick to staying calm in any situation is to assess, calculate, and react, no matter how much screaming you want to do. While you can always scream in terror after the fact, any planning and action done too late will be utterly useless. So, you're better off promising yourself a good ol' screamfest for when you make it through this.

Because you are going to make it through this.

*This* being armed gunmen surrounding the hall on all sides. The soldiers are down for the count on the security catwalk, replaced by armed gunmen in red spandex suits. *This* being the fact that there is a man dying next to you in a pool of his own blood, and everyone else behind the bar with you is already dead too. *This* being that you can't find your friends and—

selfishly, you admit—you resent that you still haven't gotten your pardon, and even if you were to save the situation now, which you're not sure you can, it's not going to get them anywhere because the president you wanted dead actually *is* dead now, and that's made everything worse.

But no. It won't be for nothing. You're the only one who doesn't have to worry about stupid risks getting you killed. You can save them.

And then you realize you're dissociating, and that's terrible way of solving a crisis, so I got a handle on myself and took a few deep breaths.

I wasn't supposed to have panic attacks, but muscle memory was a powerful thing. My chest was heaving, breaths coming in and out in short, useless gasps, not enough ever reaching my lungs. I clutched my hands into fists. *Shut up, panic. Shut up, anxiety. You get your turn later.*

I turned to the man beside me, the one slowly wheezing to death. I didn't have to be a nurse to tell he wasn't going to make it through the night. Something akin to a plasma beam had sliced a hole right through his stomach, revealing the blue guts within. He was well dressed—then again, so was everyone at this party—but he had pins on his lapel, not military like Kork but something worthy of Alliance recognition.

He looked up at me—mostly human, not entirely— and laughed. "Oh, that went well."

"Great party, right?" I replied.

"It wasn't meant to end like this."

For a second, I was going to agree with him, add to the sarcasm. But then it struck me. He didn't mean the party. He meant whatever *this* was. The *this* that had him dying in front of me and me fighting off a panic attack I was no longer meant to be having.

"What did you do?" I asked, my voice no higher than a whisper.

He rolled his head back and forth on the floor. "They told me they would liberate everyone. All I had to do was give them information."

"Information to what?"

"This was going to be the night that everything changes." He sobbed. "But I didn't want this. I didn't want … this."

"It's okay; it's going to be okay." Wait, why was I saying that? This man was somehow responsible for this massacre. I shouldn't be comforting him at all.

"Are they here?"

"Who?"

"*Them.*" With a trembling hand, he reached up to pull a small book from his jacket pocket. It was too feeble to pull it out entirely, so I reached over, gently prying it free from his fingers.

It was a small book, wrapped in plastic like most library books are, embossed with silver letters. *A Tale of Two Siblings.*

*Oh, shit.*

"You wanted them here," I said, rifling through the pages. A children's book, full of children's illustrations,

Zander and Blayde fighting monsters and negotiating with kings. It looked like a lost book in the *Chronicles of Narnia.*

"They'll stop this, right?" the man—the murderer, the instigator, the whatever who made this happen—coughed in pain. Blue blood squirted from his insides.

"Yes."

"Promise?"

"I promise."

"Good. I don't want to go out like this, you know. I never thought it would end like this." He paused. "I only wanted to change the world."

"Well, you sure did that," I said coolly. He had other people's blood on his hands far before his own. "What did you do?"

"Don't let it end like this. Tell them I said something meaningful!"

And with that, the man just … *died.*

In all that time, I hadn't noticed the shooting had finally stopped, and with his death, the hall was suddenly silent, except for strange, broken sobs that rose and burst like bubbles in a lake. My own breathing was calm now, even, but so, so loud.

The stranger, an upper echelon of the Alliance, knew about the siblings. Wanted them here. Was he connected to the men in the red spandex suits? Rebels without a cause or terrorists with unsavory motivations? Was he somehow responsible for them being here?

Well, none of it mattered now. He was dead. So, whatever he wanted didn't hold much weight.

I focused on my breathing again, taking the storybook and slipping it into the bodice of my dress. The purse was gone, but I still had my gun. Unlimited ammo, Blayde had said, so long as I was courageous enough to rip out my own teeth.

I risked a glance over the bar, peeking up above the now-soiled wood out into the ballroom beyond. Chaos dotted the horizon. Bodies—dead or playing dead, who could say—lay crumpled on the floor, a rainbow of blood staining the tiles. I could feel nausea building in my gut, threatening to release. Good thing I had experience in the traumatic puke department. I forced down the bile, collapsing back in the puddle of booze, trying instead to find an exit to build a plan.

Fact: It wasn't going to be hard to jump clear of the devastation. If I wanted to go, I could. But I wasn't going anywhere without Zander and Blayde. We needed to regroup and come up with another strategy to win over the Alliance's pardon.

Possibility: If Zander and Blayde were seen—heck, probably even if they weren't—this whole disaster would be pinned on them. *Per usual.* Maybe that's why my now-dead neighbor wanted them here? So that his rebels could have scapegoats or something.

Seeing the dead bodies sprawled on the ground made it all suddenly, coolly clear. This is what the siblings had been blamed for for centuries. So much death.

# INALIENABLE

Whenever the Alliance had a problem, who was it easier to blame? Was it better to admit they were fractured and their dissidents came from within, or pin it all on beings who had risen to a mythical status? One thing was certain: Our plan to save the president probably would not have been enough to turn back any of that.

Conclusion: I had to save Zander and Blayde.

Sidebar: They probably could have left if it wasn't for me.

I swore under my breath. Of course, I was going to screw this up for them. The longer I screwed around not knowing where they were, the worse this would be.

Prospect: They were probably saving the day as we speak. I was just a selfish jerk. We had a party to save.

With a sudden crash, glasses fell around me, spilling into the tile floor and spraying me with booze. Two pairs of boots landed in front of me, heavily splashing in a puddle. I had no time to think—play the damsel in distress or bring them down? —before they sat down beside me, back to the bar, pushing the dead man aside and sandwiching me in.

And with a silent laugh of relief, I found myself between my two favorite captains, James T. Kork and Sekai No-Oji.

"Took you two long enough," I said. Which made no sense but sounded badass, so I couldn't help myself. Sekai handed me a gun, which, thankfully, wasn't loaded with teeth.

"You're all right?" asked Kork, casting a glance to the bodies surrounding us. "Not injured?"

Oh right. "Shit, no one told you guys?"

"What?" Sekai scooted forward, still crouched, using her overly large eyes to scan more of the room than I could ever hope to see. "Please do not tell me you are with child. That makes protecting you all the more … delicate."

I could have laughed it was so absurd. "Um, no. I just … I can't get hurt anymore. You didn't need to come back for me; I should have been coming for you."

"Oh, lah-dee-dah," said Kork, eyes going almost as wide was Sekai's. "I thought you were dead! What the hell happened in those two months?"

"Congratulations on your mutation," said Sekai. "Can we not linger here? We need to find an exit."

"You two get out of here," I replied. "I'm going to try and stop whatever this is."

"You can't expect us to leave all the fun to you," said Kork. "It's my frashing job to defend the Alliance, and defend it I shall."

"I will not stand for the killing of innocents," said Sekai, brandishing what appeared to be a long tuning fork, only for the pronged end to erupt in a burst of electricity. Where had that been when we'd crystalized the doctors in the basement of the Hill? "And I will not crouch in terror either."

I couldn't believe my luck, two seasoned military veterans landing practically in my lap. Granted, one was mostly a TV actor these days, and the other had spent millennia underground, so they might be a little rusty.

# INALIENABLE

But with them, I could think of more than of just escape; I could think of an actual plan to take down literal terrorists.

"Do we know what we're up against?" I asked, while casually examining the weapon Sekai had handed me. I'd never seen it before in my life, but it was gun-shaped and had a trigger, so I assumed it was a point-and-boom type thingamajig.

"I've counted twenty-four hostiles," said Sekai. "All on the upper catwalk. The doors to the atrium have been secured from the outside, as well as service entrances and exits. We suppose they'll trickle down to the ground floor once they think they've picked everyone off from above."

"Any idea what they want?" I asked. "Do they just want to kill for the sake of killing? And if they want to kill germs, they should be using a refreshing blast from *Neodine* Eterna-Gel! This multipurpose cream will kill any bacteria from any surface. Find it in your local bodega. Now available in space scent. Do you want your home to smell like an unending void? Use new space-scented *Neodine*! *Neodine*: It keeps you clean!"

"What. The. Frash." Sekai turned to Kork, and I wondered if I'd ever seen her slacken her posture before; it was almost imperceptible, but enough to make me jolt.

"She has a faulty translator," he mumbled.

"I'll say. And, no, I don't know what the rebels want. They haven't made any demands in here. I suppose they just want us all dead."

"And then what? Have they taken hostages? Do they have a way out?"

"We don't know," said Kork, his eyes peeled on the dance floor. "And if this is a suicide mission, then they came here to die. Our retribution would only give them what they want."

"So, we need to capture them," said Sekai, "and contain them until leadership arrives."

"Don't you get it? Leadership is already here and littering the ballroom floor." Kork ran his hands over his bald scalp, trailing sweat over what I sincerely hoped was just mud. "Not everyone who matters to the Alliance is here tonight, but almost. And now, there's barely anyone left."

"Saints," said Sekai, breathing in sharply. "Then what is the point in us doing anything? We've already lost. The Alliance is untethered."

"I wouldn't go that far," said Kork. "There are redundancies. Planetary mayors. Ministers who didn't make it here. Backups after backups. The Alliance will recover; it always does. But the mere fact this could happen … well, we've seen the impossible."

"Good thing I know two impossible people here tonight," I said. "They'll do something. They'll make this right."

"I don't think they can," said Kork.

"Then what can we do?" asked Sekai. "I'm not going to die at the hands of some chaos-loving rebels. Retribution, my left nostril. We take down every one of these children of pond scum and feed them to their mothers."

Kork's eyes lit up with a fire I had never seen before. "Why do I suddenly want to grab a sword, hop on a horse, and ride into battle behind you?"

"I do not know what a horse is, but I would be honored to have you in battle beside me."

"So, that's it?" I stammered, hating to interrupt such a cinematic moment. "We're just going to revenge-kill the rebels without finding out who they are and what they want?"

"Do you have a better idea?" asked Kork.

"I'd rather neither of you die today," I said. "So maybe we can tone it down with retribution, go instead for the surgical strike?"

"What do you suggest?"

"Firstly, we need to connect with Zander and Blayde," I said, and he rolled his eyes. "Oh, come on, you know as well as I they're probably ten steps ahead of us. I don't want us to fly in, guns a'blazing, and ruin whatever they're planning. I'd rather be with them than in their way, you know?"

"It sounds to me like you're waiting for them to somehow save the day when day-saving is literally anyone's game."

"Well, they do have millennia of experience."

"Fair point. But—"

"But nothing. They have millennia of experience. This is probably not their first foray with terrorists, considering the Alliance thinks that's what they are in the first place. Hell, it's not even my first time being on the wrong end of a ball gone bad. Even Sekai was there for that!"

She nodded. "It is true. They avoided a planet-wide massacre on Da-Duhui."

"If you three are done talking," said a gruff voice, "we'd like the pleasure of your company."

I looked straight up into the arm of a man in a bright red Spandex suit.

"Ah, ah, ah," he said and pressed something hard into the top of my head. "One false move, and the lady gets her brain liquified."

I rolled my eyes. I mean, what else do you do when you realize the situation is stupid? I winked at Kork then Sekai. Then Kork again. I must have looked like I was having a stroke. But it worked because the two of them drew their weapons and splattered the rebel to kingdom come. His weapon fell in my lap.

"Beautiful," I said. It was easier to say the words then to believe them. I was shaking like a leaf, my mind replaying the sound of the man's last small gasp as he was killed above me. I staggered forward, away from his body that was now flung on the bar.

And, above him, three rebels in red tight suits rushed at us, the source of the only noise in the entire hall.

"Right," said Kork, "I suppose this is where we make our stand."

"Three against three," said Sekai. "I do like those odds."

# INALIENABLE

I raised my weapon, pictured the president there, and I fired.

My gun released a burst of concentrated plasma, hitting the first rebel square in the chest. He staggered but drew himself up like a zombie, advancing again. I pictured the sand monstrosity in the vent and fired again.

I hit him square in the head.

There's an uncomfortable disconnect that comes from doing the wrong thing for all the right reasons. Killing a man because he was about to kill you. Killing a man because he'd already killed countless people and would undoubtably kill others, including you. You have all the right reasons to pull the trigger, and yet when you see him collapse on the floor, lifeless, a visceral scream leaves your lips, like you've broken a law so intrinsic and primitive, you know the universe will demand retribution.

Except today, you are the retribution.

And I really need to stop dissociating.

A burst of plasma erupted near my ear, shattering one of the remaining bottles and sending glass showering over us. That had been too close, close enough to almost touch Sekai, and I couldn't let anything happen to her. Oh no, not on my watch. I flung myself forward, leaping over the bar and raising my weapon once more. I was off balance as I fired, bursts of heat tearing from my gun and ripping into the men in red suits.

Screaming from behind me—a war cry from planet Kili, mingling with a scream from Earth—Sekai and Kork burst out after me with their weapons drawn. We spun out, points of a deadly triangle, landing in a formation that was as natural as breathing, defending each other's backs as we swept the room for more killers.

Four down, countless more to go.

So, of course, the stained windows behind the presidential podium chose that minute to explode, raining glass down upon us all.

A cold wind blew through the blood-soaked hall, bringing with it the crisp scent of car fumes and distant sea. Smell wasn't all it brought. Beings dressed head to toe in black, soaring through the air, jet packs on their feet and bug-like masks covering their faces. They swarmed the hall like flies buzzing around the jeweled ceiling, some landing on the catwalk and punching out the rebels in red.

"The cavalry has arrived," I stammered. "Shit, they're going to think we—"

"No, those are not Alliance soldiers," said Kork, struggling to get the words out. "Their uniforms. That's not Alliance-issued body armor."

"Who are they?" hissed Sekai. "Do I shoot?"

"Lower your weapons," said one of the bug-eyed men, holding his position three meters up and away from us. "You are now hostages of the *First Pact*."

"The who?" I stammered.

"Trash," spat Sekai. "You let your men turn this place into a death pond. For what?"

"Oh, them?" He pointed up at the catwalk where a raging fight was taking place between red and black. Not allies, after all. "They call themselves rebels, but they're just scum. We're the real threat, and we've come here with—"

"Can't you see it's already over?" I asked, stepping forward. I was a nobody to the Alliance, but Kork, he was their literal poster boy. I couldn't let him fall into their hands. "Those rebels you call scum have already killed everyone here. There's nothing left for you. No point left to be made."

"The mere fact that people are left alive means we have what those idiots could never understand," he said. "Leverage."

"Leverage this, douche canoe. Run!"

I shouted as I leapt into the air, grabbing one of the badass jet-boots firmly and letting gravity do the rest. It slipped off the foot, and the second-wave rebel swore as he tumbled forward, giving Kork and Sekai the split-second distraction they needed to get out of the man's way.

The boot kept flying, soaring through the empty ballroom like a child on fairy dust, taking me with it. Admittedly, I could have just let go, but this was a flying boot, and I'd be damned if I just let it fly away without me.

I stuffed my hand deep into it, hoping to Iron Man this thing, but I ended up gagging at the sweaty foot smell and feel, retracting my now sopping wet hand so fast that the boot spun on its side, dropping me squarely on my ass. I pulled out my pistol and whipped it around, trying to find the man who had taunted us, but he was nowhere to be seen.

I screamed as I was ripped upward, betrayed by my own elegantly-knotted hair, more out of shock than actual pain. I was flying, soaring upward, dragged by my follicles onto the catwalk where a battle raged.

Well, we started on the bottom, and now we are here.

And here just plain sucks.

# TWENTY-ONE
## THE BUFFET, AND OTHER THINGS I SHOULD HAVE BEEN PAYING ATTENTION TO

### *Zander*

**IT'S NOT FUN WHEN YOU DO SOMEONE'S JOB FOR** them then they take all the credit, especially when you just saved the world. Trust me, I'm the guy who apparently ruined half the planets I had actually saved, letting the guy who literally just got himself killed get lifted up on all the praise I was well owed.

Those victory statues are rather unflattering when they have someone else squashing your face under their boot. I've got at least five of those that I know of, and did I want a single one? No, thank you.

I'm not sour. Well, not entirely. A little bitter maybe. A grape that's just beginning to turn.

"Do you have a visual?" I asked, trying to push all thoughts of grapes out of my head. You never want to go up against rebels on an empty stomach, and I had avoided the hors d'oeuvres like an idiot, thinking I would need to look lean and trim while saving the president. You never know what kind of reaction you'll have to alien food; the bloat is real, people.

Blayde had been smart. She'd tackled a mini puff tray on her way to safety. Her pockets—because, of course, her uniform would have pockets; how did her dress have pockets but my tuniclad didn't? —brimmed with snacks, but she wasn't sharing. She pushed herself flush with the wall, one hand clasping her laser pointer, the other furiously shoving assorted green balls into her mouth as if her life depended on it. She let only the barest sliver of her eye out over into the bottleneck, then turned back, seemingly relieved, trotting to our hiding place in the secondary coat check with the rest of our small pocket of survivors.

"I've counted just four on this side of the hall," she said between mouthfuls. "These are really good. My compliments to the chef. They haven't moved downstairs yet. They've infiltrated the upper levels, including the security catwalk, and seem to be waiting for us to do something stupid so they can gun us down."

"So, they should all be fine sitting it out down here," I said, turning my head away from the others as I slid the metal cheekbone from out under my skin. Stars above, it felt so much better not having it poke into my nose.

"Until the rebels come down for their final sweep," said Blayde. "I don't know yet if they're taking hostages. It doesn't look like they left anyone out there alive."

# INALIENABLE

I pulled the other false cheekbone out, tossing it to the floor. "Any sign of Sally?"

"No, but if she knows what's best for herself, she'd be lying low," Blayde replied. She reached into her pocket, and, finding it empty, heaved a heavy sigh. "We don't know how long this mess will last."

"You!" The old man in the corner jumped to his feet with the agility of a much younger man. He was, of course, pointing at me. Because why fit in even for a second?

"What, you?" You get good at faking confusion after lifetimes of practice. "You mean me?"

"You're" —the man dropped his trembling finger— "the Sand. Which means … "

"The Sand is a terrible moniker. Yeah, I know, right?"

Now that had gotten the attention of the others. At least they had already finished their screaming in the earlier throng. I hear sore throats made it hard to express terror.

"You! You did this!" shouted the older man in a jittery warble. "You brought the rebels down upon us! They're with you!"

"Believe it or not, we're on your side," said Blayde. She had striped her prosthetics out so quickly that I hadn't even seen her do it. "We didn't know anything about this attack."

"Trust me," I added, hand out to show I was no threat, "I want to get out alive as much as any of you."

The man could barely refrain himself from laughing.

"What the frash do you mean?" he spat. "Get out alive? *You can't die!*"

"Language," muttered one of the young girls in the corner.

"Just trust me, okay?" said Zander. "None of us want to be here right now."

"In this coat check?" asked the girl. "We must stay calm. Coats get scared, too, you know. If we make too much noise, who knows what they'll do."

"Oh lordy," Blayde muttered. "A coat enthusiast."

"Or out of this situation," I said, talking over her. I think she just had a momentary mental snap because she froze, staring at the girl with all the confusion I wanted to share. "And we're going to get out of here. There are—"

"Seven of them," said Blayde. "Against two of us. So, hey! You see? Clear majority. Safe and sound."

"I meant there are nine of us and who knows how many rebels out there." At what point would she shut up and let me do all the talking? "We need to stick together if we have any hope of getting out of this. Of the coat check and the situation."

"And why should we trust you?" asked the senior. "You're criminals with nothing to lose. All we have is your word that you're not involved with the others. What are the odds of having two separate bands of rebels at the same event at the same time?"

"He's got you there, Zan," said Blayde. "The odds are absolutely, hilariously low. Is it more likely—gasp!—that maybe we're not terrorists at all?"

"Right. Do we need the civies to take down the rebels?" I asked her.

"Negatory."

"Where's the president?"

"Dead."

"Oh, that's just great. You're sure?"

"Yes, brother-of-mine, I'm pretty sure no pulse and no breathing in his case means dead. He's as dead as a doornail."

Some whispering rose from the girls who were huddled in the back corner. None of the four seemed in the least bit scared. Their tone was gossipy rather than frightened. They all seemed the same age, probably in their late teens, each with their hair done in up in fashionable curls and wearing vibrant-colored dresses. I caught the gaze of the girl who swore the coats would attack, and she went a sapphire blue.

"Weapons?" I asked Blayde, peeling my gaze from them. Were they planning something? Hard to tell.

"I've got my laser. Do you have a gun?"

"And my bag of teeth."

"Perfect. Anybody else?"

They all shook their heads. The old man raised his hand.

"I've got an antique Falerian revolver," he said.

"You any good with it?"

"I can defend myself."

"Okay, good." Blayde rubbed her hands together. "Zander, plans?"

"None yet. And you *hate* my plans. Why don't you ever come up with something?"

She rose to her feet, taking off the torturous shoes, wiggling her toes to help her concentration. She looked over the strange assembly of guests who only wanted a way out. There were the four girls in their own corner, talking rather loudly about what to do if the coats came alive. It was hard to tell if they would be useful: all children of the rich and powerful, so some of their parents had prepared them for life in political office, while others for a life defending estates on the rim. Their hands—those who had hands, one had long, green tentacles—were manicured. Perfect, but that told me nothing about the technology they could afford. A callous could be hidden easier than a mole these days. While ages of maturity varied on their different worlds, they seemed to be on the cusp of adulthood. Probably strong in a fight if they had to be, but a real loss to the Alliance if they were to fall.

I shook the thought from my head. I wasn't putting anyone in harm's way. Everyone in my care was getting out of here alive.

A young human woman stared intently at all the happenings, her eyes locked on me. They were wide, trying to capture everything that was going on, her blinks infrequent and slow, a strange thing to notice but impossible to ignore once you did. Her gown was not a perfect fit, the makeup done in haste, and although her clothes were expensive, she didn't seem the rich type. She wasn't meant to be here any more than I was.

The last man with them was probably the most terrified. A young man in his twenties, wearing an old-fashioned apron, making him, without a doubt, a member of the staff since bedazzled aprons had been out at least three seasons now. His eyes darted left and right, his body quivering, teeth chattering—the whole set.

The old man near the door, however, was still a mystery. He wore a perfectly tailored suit, old-fashioned yet not outdated. His wrinkled face conveyed age, yet the spotless skin showed just how much money could add more years to one's life. He glanced back and forth, jumpy, which was predictable, as for any man in a near-death situation. A sash marking him as part of the presidential entourage hung limply from his shoulder.

"As much as you talk of helping us"—he pointed a scrawny finger at us—"it doesn't change the fact that you're criminals. You blew up the library, for Pyro's sake."

"Oh, you heard about that?" asked Blayde. "I thought all that happened outside of time. No matter. We had our reasons for doing that."

"Um … which were?" I whispered. "I was cool with overthrowing Nimien, but burning it was … weird."

"We're all going to die; we're all going to die," chanted the waiter.

Blayde turned to the senior. "Did you meet the head abbot? Turns out, he was a psychopath who built the library as a dumb trap to torture us and enslave a friend of ours and then take over the universe. Wasn't worth keeping open."

"You blew up the *Berbabsywell* Library too? Damn you! That bastion was holding the universe together!"

"What library were you talking about?"

"Pyrinian Central!"

"Oh. We didn't do that. Did we?"

"I doubt it," said Blayde. "I don't have anything against libraries in general. Just those run by egomaniacs with an evil, non-literacy-related agenda."

"And the Earth Agency?"

"Oh, well, that was a massive misunderstanding," I said. "That wasn't an attack. We were playing video games at an arcade, and it escalated. We didn't do anything wrong!"

"And we're supposed to take your word for it?"

Blayde rolled her eyes, returning to me. She was right. This wasn't an argument we could win with words.

"We could jump them out to safety?" I whispered.

"And take them where? They could end up in a time period before the Alliance even formed. No, thanks."

"If any of you have any call-backs or panic buttons, please use them now," Blayde ordered our pack of survivors.

"I pressed my alarm when we first came in," said the old man. "They know we're here; they probably can't get in."

"The presidential security sucks," she snarled. "They can't get past a few insurgents?"

"From what I gather, it's more than just a *few* insurgents. They took down security in less than a minute. They're organized. They have people on the inside."

"But it was a dumb attack," said Blayde. "They got the president, but the vice president didn't even come tonight. Most of the people killed were just minor nobles and others who have nothing to do with the government. Assassinating the people in charge of the problem is rebellion. Killing innocents is an act of terrorism."

"Rebellion *is* terrorism if you get caught doing it," the woman pointed out, calm and composed. Who was she?

"They haven't even tried to take over any of the smaller planets yet," the older man said, angry and annoyed. "They wanted to start big, it's obvious, but they can't take down the government in one badly put-together coup."

"You've got to admit they managed to get this far. It's not so badly put-together," I said.

"But from here, what happens? The Alliance cannot fall in a day; it's too widespread. It's more than one person. As we speak, there are ministers, vice presidents, senators, congressmen, a whole strong government that can survive if their figurehead is taken down; they have before." The old man shrugged. "Unless ... maybe they struck the rest of the Alliance's houses of power at once, and we simply don't know about it yet."

"Hello! Hello, one and all!"

All heads turned in the direction of the door. Blayde scooted over to get a good vantage point, her body flush with the wall once more, her entire being one with the shadows. She stared over the coat check desk, looking for the voice's source. She didn't have to look far. On the catwalk, over the stage, straight on the over end of the hall from them, a man in a standard bulletproof vest and the basic sea-black uniform of a reassigned child-hire stood with a megaphone in one hand and a rifle in the other. To his left, three or four women from the party were lined up, most on the verge of or in tears.

"Who is it?" I hissed.

"Left-handed reassigned child-hire, 1.8 meters I would guess, brown hair, no other distinguishing marks. Accent places him from Regis. Any guesses?"

"No. You have any idea?" I asked our group. Nothing but shrugs.

"He's dressed in black. Frash, they're all in black. Zander, there's been a coup within the coup. Another group has taken charge."

"Frash indeed."

"As you may all have guessed by now, the situation is not good. We have the doors booby trapped, so don't even try to get out if you value your continued existence. You even stare at the doors sideways, you blow up. Boom, that's it, and you'll take out anyone near you. Wait too long to give yourself up, and boom, you take out everyone. So, all I can say, is this: Surrender to us, and your lives have a chance of being spared. All we want is hostages, and those, we keep alive. That is a promise. You have one hour, then we blow the entire building."

Blayde swore under her breath. "Way to crash a party. Or crash the party crashers. Who is this?" She scanned the hall while she had the chance, searching for any signs of life. Someone from the line-up caught her eye. "Zan, they've got Sally."

I felt as if I has just been dropped off the top of a spacescraper, and no one was willing to scrape me off the pavement.

*The rebels have Sally.*

"Frash," I swore.

"Language," said the girl afraid of coats.

"How come she always gets caught? Always!" I stammered. "I thought this would end with Nimien. But no, she's been marked by the stars for bad luck or something."

"And ironically, she's ended up with you," said Blayde. I swiped at her. "And this is fantastic! Now, *we* have someone on the inside. Think about it. We distract the leader, she steals a gun, and gets rid of him. It's easy."

"Blayde, how is she meant to know that's what we want?"

She shrugged. "It was just an idea." She glanced over at the door down the hallway, well concealed from the rebels who were now patrolling the raised pathway. "I'm going to check on the booby traps. Stay here, okay? Make sure everyone stays quiet."

She jumped.

I returned to the coat room, where the small group of people huddled in silence. I rubbed my hands together, trying to rub out the jitters. Sally was in the hands of a murderer, and while she had the experience, I wasn't thrilled about the situation in the slightest.

"All right, we need a plan. Anyone? Any idea how we can all get out of here in one piece, probably freeing the hostages along the way?"

"We're all going to die; we're all going to die," chanted the waiter.

"Are you really immortal?" one of the girls asked.

"Gen, stop!" Another one giggled.

"No, really!" the one named Gen said with an over-exaggerated smile, her eyes pinned on me. Dammit, I didn't have time for this. "Is it true what they say on TV?"

"Uh, yeah, yes, I am. So, plans, anyone?"

"That's hot," she said with a giggle.

"REALLY hot," said another.

I rolled my eyes. I wasn't a teen heartthrob. At least, not today. "Let's continue. Shall we get back on track? We all want to survive, so we all need to work together."

"Are you two married?"

"What?" I sputtered. "No, we're siblings. She's my sister!"

"So, you're single?"

"I don't know why I would tell you this, but no. No, I'm seeing someone."

"Oh, that's too bad." Another girl gave me a mischievous smile. "Because, you know, I *am* about to die and—"

"Are you mad, child?" the old man spat. "Do you have a death wish? Throwing yourself at this murderer—"

"Woah, don't throw out words like murderer!" I sputtered.

"You fangirls continue to confuse me," he said. "Obsessing over a dangerous man. I don't get the appeal. He could literally kill you in an instant. No regrets, no questions asked."

"A lot of regrets and a lot of questions, but none when it comes to you," Blayde said, a little too harshly, waltzing back into the room. "If no one has anything else to say, then, well, it's my turn to speak."

"What did you find?"

"The doors are all wired to a mainframe, probably where the leader is positioned. They will blow individually if you try to open the door or all at the same time if he flicks the switch, taking the whole building down. It's wired in such a way that I can't split the signal from the command box to the explosives. If the wire is snapped, it blows. So, disarming it, for the moment, is out of the question. We need to get to the main control box, disarm it there. Or we could try negotiations. Any ideas?"

"I have one," I said, trying to break free from the young women's gaze. "We could do the royal hostage trick. It's worked before."

"We could try," she said, pulling her hair up into a ponytail. She ripped a fur collar from one of the coats, making the girl called Gen squeak. The fur made for a convincing wig. "Anyone know if the president currently had a consort? Anyone?"

"He did," replied the old man.

"Ooooh, definitely," Gen said, beaming. "She was in last Tressuary's issue of *Pyrina Royal.*"

"Is she here tonight?"

"No, she stayed back at her estate," said the senior.

"You sure about this?"

"Yes, positive, I work—well, worked—very close with the president."

"We're all going to die; we're all going to die," chanted the waiter.

"What does she look like?"

"Oh, she's ghastly." The girl in red silk robes sighed heavily, brushing the debris off her skirt. "Stuck up type, you know."

"Okay, good." I rose to my feet, grabbing my gun and heading out to the hall. I paused at the coat clerk's desk. "If all goes to plan, you'll be able to get out in a few minutes."

"Can't we come with you?" Gen begged, becoming increasingly more pestilent by the minute. My poor nerves couldn't take much more.

# INALIENABLE

"Not if you want to stay alive." I turned to my sister, aiming the gun at her chest. She feigned terror. "Come on, Mrs. Straiddies. We've got a party to save."

# TWENTY-TWO

## A CAT, AN AMOEBA, AND TWO HUMANS
## WALK INTO A BALL

*Sally*

**THIS DID NOT LOOK GOOD, BUT THEN AGAIN,** nothing really had of late.

Three other beings were crammed with me in the small guard room, the smell of sweat and foundation powder heavy in the air. A few members of the rebel group meandered in and out of the space, sometimes with a few strong words like, "Don't you leave here or we shoot" or "When this is over tonight, we're going to have a fun time."

Gross and not at all creative.

Of course, they didn't mean it. Intimidation was just their way of boosting their confidence or feeling powerful. I guess mirror affirmations weren't enough for them. No way to feel scared when everyone is more terrified of you than you are of them. But the other hostages had no way of knowing this, and it rendered them completely useless; they shivered in fear and terror, on the verge of breaking down into tears.

This was not my first hostage situation, but it was the first one where other people were stuck with me. And since none of them were lucky enough to have regenerative cells, it was up to me to find a way out for all of them.

Not an easy feat.

Last time, however, I had been taken hostage by two complete dolts. At least I had that going for me. Put a bit of a damper on my time in Da-Duhui, let me tell you that. I could attempt to jump the others out, but I hadn't jumped anyone but me before. At least, if you didn't count jumping the siblings, and I'm convinced they give me a hand. On top of that, I didn't want to give up my identity yet if I didn't have to. No, I would have to think of another way to get everyone out.

What if Zander and Blayde distracted the rebels, and I stole one of their weapons? That could work, couldn't it? It wasn't like the siblings would know what I was going for; they wouldn't have my back. Plus, there were too many other people with guns. Someone other than me could get hurt.

I looked around me at the scared faces of the three other hostages. The only thing that they had in common was their gowns: large, ornate, works of art, impossible to run in. One looked human like me, though with gravity-defying hair that was still the rage since the mayoral gala on Da-Duhui. She could have been my mother, if Mom had splurged for diamond skin implants. Another, an oversized single-celled organism, mildly opaque green, and soft at the edges like an amoeba. How and why she had shoes attached to her body was beyond me. Last but not least, a pink cat with its hair spiked into ridges. Our ragtag team of riches.

I cleared my throat. "Ahem."

They looked up at me in confusion. One stepped up from terrified cowering, so that's a start.

"What if I told you that help was on the way?" I asked.

They said nothing. I reached my fingers into the doorjamb, pressing it open slightly to look out into the room beyond. The catwalk was made of a fine grating so that security could look all the way down at the dancers, and I felt my stomach flip when I saw, once again, how high up we were.

What was the point of giving up mortality when losing my fear of heights wasn't part of the deal?

The two guards who were meant to be watching us were leaning over the catwalk rail, smoking up a storm and chatting loudly enough that I didn't have to worry about being overheard. I pushed the door slowly shut.

"Have any of you heard of the Iron and the Sand?" I asked.

Wrong question. The amoeba turned a violent shade of pink, possibly trying to camouflage herself into the cat person. A cat person whose entire hair just went straight as they hissed.

"They're the rebels?" stammered the cat. "But there are so many of them!"

"No, they're—"

"I should have known they were behind this!" The human clenched her fists. "Just like them to ruin an event of this scale! They've always had it out for this administration!"

"Actually, they're our rescue party," I replied. "Will you please calm down?"

"Calm down?" she spat. "They're ruthless killing machines!"

"No, they're not," I replied. "They're—it's a long story."

"Oh, come on, it's obvious! It's just like them to do something like this!" she sputtered. "They're enemies of the Alliance; all they want to do it tear it down!"

I could feel bile rise in my throat, and I forced it down. Just in time to hold myself back from rolling my eyes as well. Damn, my whole body was annoyed. "They're not behind this."

"How can we trust you?" the girl asked. "You could be in cahoots with them!"

I threw my hands up in the air. "I'm literally being held hostage right now. Just like all of you."

"This could be a trap!"

"How, in any way, would me being held a hostage be a trap?" I asked.

"You could be a plant to mislead us!" she said, jumping lightly to her feet. "They could be tricking us, so we reveal Alliance secrets! I'm not going to be tricked!"

"I'm not trying to trick you!" I sighed heavily. "I want us all to get out alive, so we should probably work together to achieve that."

"And what of the siblings?" she snarled, "They're lying, thieving, murderous criminals. And you just want us to believe that just by them being around we'll get out of here in one piece?"

"Well, technically? Yes."

"She's insane." The woman rolled her eyes, rubbing the back of her hand across her forehead. "We're all going to go insane."

"I think she's telling the truth." The cat person shrugged. They brushed their paws through their hair, straightening it.

"What are you, senile?"

"When I was just your age, I met the siblings." The cat person bristled. "I was out in the forest on Rhiti and was attacked by the Moss Monster." I had no idea what they were talking about, but I had more good sense in me than to try and interrupt the story. "They fought it off and helped me back home. But when I told my parents, they said I wasn't to speak of them. The Alliance said they were terrorists, so by associating with them, I must be one too. *What?* I thought to myself. They just couldn't be." They turned to me, forcing a smile despite the circumstances. "I believe you."

"Well, I don't," the human scoffed.

"I do," the amoeba said. "It's not that I believe her, not entirely, but it's better than sitting here doing nothing. Unless your whole plan is to wait for them to rescue us, in which case that's exactly what we're supposed to do?"

"You have got to be kidding me," said the human. "You are seriously going along with this? These are the Iron and the Sand we're talking about. You think the rebels out there are bad? These two have been murdering throughout history!"

"I don't think they usually hire goons with guns, do you?" asked the cat. "The stories always have them working alone."

"Working. What you call working, I call murder."

"Can we please stop arguing?" asked the amoeba. "It makes my—"

Whatever they said next, my translator was too crappy to interpret, but they flailed their skin, and the two others cringed. Probably awful.

"We're with you," said the cat. "Do you have a plan?"

"Well, I'm working on one. And if work is getting too stressful, you need to sit back and relax with a delicious bowl of *chachachaaaa* stress parasites. Your stress melts away while you do your treaty-contracted diligence of feeding the parasites and protecting the star system in the process. A real win-win!"

"She has nothing." They fell back down onto the small table, lying flat as their hair practically deflated.

"Hello, up there!"

A voice came from down in the hall, followed by the unmistakable sound of an assault rifle firing, quite literally cutting me off mid-sentence. Well, that was exciting. I slipped my fingers through the crack of the door and edged it open.

"I've got a deal that will be of great benefit for the both of us, so come out, come out, wherever you are!"

Out on the raised path, people started to rush by, confused, panicked. Predictably, one of the rebels came in, leading us hostages out in single file to the side of their leader, right above the stage where we had stood mere minutes before to pronounce the evening's threats.

Ah. There he was.

Zander stood in the middle of the hall, rifle pointed straight at the ceiling, the other hand balanced lightly on his hip, a smirk plastered on his face as he looked up at the rebel's leader with what seemed to be a child's glee.

"Hi," he said politely, his voice carrying in the emptiness of the hall. "Guess who?"

"Frash," said the other woman hostage. "You weren't kidding. The Sand is frashing here."

Whatever the amoeba had been worried about must have happened because they lost all cohesion and became a puddle on the floor. Well, can't say she didn't warn us.

Man, it was good to see *him* in one piece.

"I'm guessing you probably know who I am. I mean, my mugshot's been plastered across every billboard and television screen off and on for the past, oh, hundred years? Or are we going on two centuries now? Honestly, not the best photo of me there is, but back to business!"

The leader leaned against the rail, eyes wide. Of course, he knew who the man below him was. Every single person in the Alliance knew by now. He probably wasn't expecting him to be one of the party's attendants. Oops.

Unless he was one of the men who the storybook-man had helped plan this evening?

"You want us dead. Now, I can live with that. I've been dead before, but there are some people here who have done nothing wrong, and you have no right to detain them. So, all I'm asking is that you let them all go. That's it. Nobody gets hurt."

"That's not going to happen," the leader replied, taking the megaphone that was handed to him, moderately nervous as he spoke up to the most feared criminal this end of the cosmos. Infamy had its perks.

"Would it help if I said please?" Zander grinned cheerfully, his confidence radiating from his entire being. He looked, for all intents and purposes, as if he was going to take off dancing, if it wasn't for the dead bodies strewn about the floor.

"Not in the slightest," the rebel replied, gaining confidence as he spoke. "Sorry," he added, more like an afterthought.

"But what is it all for?" Zander asked, his face suddenly turning serious. "I mean, blowing up the party of the century is not something someone does for any old reason."

"That was just a pleasant coincidence," the leader cried, his followers raising their weapons high, cheering and chanting. "They killed the president—or should I say, the emperor—but we're the ones who'll ensure the Alliance will fall!"

The rebels shrieked in celebration, firing their weapons at the ceiling, huge chunks of the painted ceiling fresco falling to the ground around Zander.

"It won't!" Zander exclaimed, as a stern woman came to join him in the middle of the hall. "Because of her! Guess who?"

He waited, but no one replied. He shrugged, taking the woman's hand.

"Or are you tired of guessing games? The president's wife is here! Or should I say, the president's widow? That's right, you just murdered the love of this woman's life!"

His words didn't seem to have the effect on them that he had anticipated. The rebels stared at him blankly, not registering what he was saying. He continued.

"Yes, the president's wife was in attendance today! I can bet my life's savings that you didn't expect that, huh?"

"What, you think we care?" the rebel commander asked.

"And, as you know, proclamation 67943 of the Alliance treaties states that when the president is assassinated, his wife automatically takes on the role of leading the people unless their child is of age. That's right, Madame President is standing right here!"

# INALIENABLE

"You're making that up," the leader hissed.

"Look it up! Law 67943 states that when the president dies, his wife and his heir take on the role of leading the Allied planets."

"I've worked in the Alliance Archives on Pyrina on the suspended islands. I've read the articles of the Alliance, and they do say that the president is replaced with his heir, but the wife is never mentioned." He grinned, as if to say "checkmate."

Zander shrugged, obviously not fazed by this argument.

"Well, yes, it was a clever lie. But guess what? She's not the only innocent one here today! No, and are you ready for the bombshell? The president's consort is pregnant! That's right. She's preggers, everyone!"

This time, he got no immediate response. All assembled stared at him with their jaws hanging on the floor.

"Isn't anyone going to congratulate her? The president has an heir! The heir is—" he struggled for words at this point, randomly pointing at the woman's belly—"can I say floating in amniotic fluid?"

The consort slapped him clear across the face, not that it ever bothered him.

"Well, technically, he's right" —he waved his hands around—"right here. The president's heir is alive, and he has done you no wrong. Are you going to tell me that you're going to kill him as well? How would the people you are rebelling *for* react?"

The rebels looked at each other in disbelief. None seemed to know how to react to the sequence of events that had just presented themselves before them. Finally, after what seemed like eternity, the leader spoke up, his voice low and shaken.

"And how do we know this is not another one of your lies?"

"Just look at her!" he proclaimed. "Isn't that a beautiful baby belly?"

The woman by his side snarled at him quickly but returned to smiling at the rebels, grinning broadly as she blushed, rubbing both hands over her belly in a peculiar, loving way.

"Now, you don't want to go assassinating a woman and her unborn child. No, that would tarnish your good name as liberators of the citizens. Imagine the scandal. The horror. How much credibility would you have? You'd be written down as rebels on the spot. So, what to do? What to do?" He paused, waving his arms to show the enormity of the situation. He grinned, and I could almost imagine the raised eyebrows his sister had put on him still there, a villainous look on his otherwise charming face.

"I'll tell you what to do. I've been speaking to the recent widow, and she has decided to give herself up in the name of justice, if you let us all go free. And when I say all of us, I mean all of us: me, my sister in the back, the survivors, your hostages. You can hold her hostage, whatever you want, if you let everyone else go free right now. Use her to control the government. Marry her and rule the Alliance before her child comes of age. You can make a lot of changes when you're in charge. Good deal, right?" He didn't wait for an answer. "You have thirty minutes. Take it or I take you down. Oh, and Lady Glosilda, how goes the day?"

"All is well, sir!" I replied, curtseying.

"Oh, she knows him!" The amoeba—having somehow regained cohesion—behind me slapped me on the back, their voice high-pitched and scared.

"You think it's that easy, do you?" the leader asked, aiming his gun at my head. "Because I don't give a reptilian's tail for her. We're here for complete takeover. You take it or leave it. You go back and tell any of those little survivors you rounded up that the only option here is to hand themselves over or what happens to Lady Glosilda—"

I didn't hear the rest; the bullet slicing through my brain made it a bit difficult to follow. I felt my brain splatter out from behind me as I fell to the floor, losing consciousness on the way down.

Ah, dead again. It felt like I had gone on a vacation, and now was back to work: get taken hostage, die a few times in the process; it's all part of saving a few people. Or maybe an entire planetary Alliance. Oh well.

I regained consciousness quickly, keeping myself in the corpse position—only yoga pose I was any good at—as the men prodded me with their boots, walking over me as they left the catwalk, laughing at a joke I never heard. I stayed on the floor, counting the seconds and calculated the amount of rose-flavored pasta cups I had eaten in the past week. I was not proud of the end result. Finally, I was certain they were gone. I got to my feet, struggling a little on the horrible shoes. Just to make things easier on myself, I should take them off. Easier said than done. The insane knots in the ribbons had only gotten tighter with time, making it harder for me to free my feet.

How impolite, leaving a lady's corpse in the middle of the walkway.

I finally got to my feet, wiping the blood from my head with the back of my hand. The hall was empty, and all the hostages had gone back to the guard room, the watch keeping their eyes and guns on the main dance floor and Zander having left with Blayde by his side. The catwalk itself was empty at the moment, which was very lucky for me.

*Beep.*

A quiet, almost unmistakable bleep echoed through the hall. I turned my head around in a flash, trying to find where it came from.

*Beep.*

There it was again.

*Beep.*

*BOOM.*

Rubble, debris, and what I was certain were bodily organs came flying out from one of the archways on the other side of the hall.

# INALIENABLE

Someone had tried to escape through one of the doors, and, as promised, it had blown.

What an idiot, I thought to myself. That person could have survived. And yet there was another name to add to the victim list, probably a John Doe with his body in itty-bitty, blown-up pieces.

Maybe–maybe it was a nameless hero. Sacrificing himself, so as to blow a wall open for others to escape through.

Maybe something I could do if I weren't stuck up here. Not that I was exactly stuck up here. There was only so much I *could* do.

Rifle shots resonated through the hall, and I realized, my gut dropping, that the rebels had expected this. A sentry was watching now, guarding the new exit if there even was one.

No one could escape.

# TWENTY-THREE

## THE BUFFET, AND OTHER THINGS I SHOULD HAVE BEEN PAYING ATTENTION TO

### *Zander*

**"DOES ANYONE HAVE A SHIRT THAT IS NOT** covered in blood or belonging to the recently departed?"

Blayde groaned as I stepped back into the coat check. In her eyes, this was just another excuse for me to rip off my shirt. But I hadn't *ripped* it off. It'd blown to smithereens while I was testing the bombs. Spoiler alert: The rebels weren't kidding.

"Does anyone mind me stealing a coat? I promise I'll give it back to the original owner when I'm done, if they're still alive." With too many wide eyes and dropped jaws, there wasn't much help to be had, so I reached up for a coat instead.

A small hand rose among the crowd. "I do!"

"Shut up, Gen!" the red-dressed girl hushed.

"Oh, Bells, come on."

# INALIENABLE

"You four, if you don't have anything useful to add to the situation, then keep those yappers zipped, okay?" Blayde's commanding voice was not one to argue with, so they obeyed. Even I hesitated before pulling out the green coat I had found that appeared to be my size. It was as if someone had shot and skinned an exotic plant and wore it as a trophy. Except that the plant was somehow still breathing. I put it back on the rack.

"Do not disturb the sleeping coats," said Gen. "I'm not kidding. Most Uppers are tired of the populace even touching their coats, so they've bred them to be fiercely loyal. You would know that if you were actually from high society."

"I do know that," I replied. "Which is why I haven't been bitten yet. Now will you excuse me? I do have an image to uphold."

I pulled a purple coat off the rack, and despite it being inert and my size, it was terribly outdated. I cringed and put it back on the shelf. It wasn't doing its real owner any favors.

"We're trying to stay alive, not win a fashion award," Blayde hissed.

"It's still a gala."

She got up, ripped a red and gold doohickey off the shelf, and tossed it at me. The coat hissed, but it must have been old and moderately senile because it let me put it on. I did up the shiny buttons and smoothed the collar around my neck. That would do.

"Now. Are you going to put on pants?" asked Blayde.

"They're fine, aren't they? I'm covered in all the areas that bother people."

"Knees are totally out this season," said Gen.

"Could someone tell me what's going on?" said the human woman. "Why is the Sand not wearing a shirt, and why are his pants ripped or singed or whatever?"

"Can you please stop with that name?" I said. "I went to check up on the doors. The rebels weren't bluffing. It totally blew."

"You … " She blinked repeatedly.

"Touched the doorknob, and the door blew up. Clothes don't repair themselves, but I do."

"So, you blew up along with it?"

"Um, yeah." I paused, running my tongue over my fresh set of teeth. Worst part about exploding was that everything in the newly regrown mouth both felt and tasted like gasoline that was told it would be a cocktail when it grows up. "I just hate new teeth. If I sound funny, it's just because I'm wearing them in. You got that?"

Our small group of survivors nodded in unison.

"So, you literally blew up?" asked the woman.

"Yup."

"And then grew back from scratch?"

"Don't worry too much about it. It happens," said Blayde, running her hands through her hair. She was still dressed in her terrible facsimile of the royal consort, baby bump and all. Could not have been comfortable. "So, does this give us an exit or not?"

I shook my head. "Unfortunately not. The bombs are rigged to blow up anyone attempting to leave, not the actual door holding us in. We're trapped."

She glanced down the hallway. "The rebels have a clear vantage point on the outside. They must be keeping the security away. I heard some shots earlier. I can assume it came from over there."

"This is impossible," the older man said, obviously shaken. "Alliance security is comprised of the highest trained men in the known universe. How can they be overpowered so easily?"

"Because they've never actually had to deal with a real uprising," I said. "Not so close to home. They assume that rebels don't want to harm innocents. But these rebels don't care, and they are not taking any chances when it comes to getting their way, whatever that is. Motivations are unclear at this point. All this to say, even the Alliance's best can't go up against them because they haven't been trained to deal with real threats. These rebels literally care for a cause more than their own lives; your men have never made that commitment. To them, guarding the Alliance is all standing around looking smart." I hate having all these empty looks. These speeches were wasted on shell-shocked survivors in a cupboard. "Sorry. We'll get you out of here; we promise. Every single one of you. We still have about 30 minutes before they blow the place. That's twenty minutes of sensible action, and ten minutes for a last-minute panic, if it comes to that. All you have to do is stay here and do what we tell you to. We're going to need you to trust us. Can you do that?"

"Do it for the baby?" asked Blayde, warbling her voice.

I would have punched her if it weren't for the baby. "But seriously, can you?"

The old man nodded. "It's the best chance we have."

"I'm all for it," the human woman agreed.

"We're already dead," said the waiter.

"I'll do anything you like." Gen smirked, with a wink.

The others just nodded. I liked them the best.

"Now, what are you good at? What are your jobs on the outside?" Zander asked.

"Journalist," said the woman.

"Minister of transport," the senior muttered.

"Really?" Zander's eyes widened. "Ouch. I'm so sorry about the Pyrinian AI kerfuffle. I swear I'm not behind it."

"We'll have time for that later," the minister said, rising to his feet. "I can shoot, but my eyesight isn't what it once was. My operation is scheduled for next week. Ironic, isn't it? If I stay alive, I get better eyesight. If I die because of my horrible eyes, I'll never be able to get them fixed."

"Maybe more apropos than ironic." Blayde turned to the four teens, a stern look on her face. "And you? Too young to be working age. What do your parents do?"

"Daddy's in charge of the marines." Gen waved her face with her hand, still looking at me. This eye contact was drying out my pores.

"Navy."

"Army."

"Fleet."

"Do any of you know how to use a gun?"

They shook their heads.

Blayde sighed. "Don't think we have much chance."

"Of course, we do. We still have Sally, don't we?"

"Your friend, Lady Glosilda?" the minister asked. "But isn't she … dead?"

"Not for long." I smiled. "She doesn't die that easily."

"She's like you?" he asked. "There are more of you?"

"It's complicated. Plus, it's not like I can just tell everything to a minister of the Alliance. You guys really have it out for me."

"That we do." The minister shrugged. "But it's not like you make it easy for us to like you, either."

"We do our best to save the people. We don't have to go apologizing for that. We don't have to run around explaining everything we do and why we do it. We have had to come up against rather nasty things in our lives, things that would rip into your skull and haunt you forever in your nightmares, things that would chill your bones and never let them thaw. We've had to save entire planets from destruction, save civilizations from pulling themselves apart. The things we've seen would make you want to tear your eyes out. And yet we can't. So, don't tell me to apologize for what I've done."

"The Alliance doesn't need your help!"

"Tell that to the people who died tonight. To the people who are sitting in this room and just want to get out alive." I was starting to get vertigo from standing on my soapbox. "Plus, we've had to step in more times than you know to fix Alliance cock-ups. Remember that accident at the food processing plant, pff, must be about three decades years ago?"

"How could we forget?"

"Well, aren't you glad your entire government didn't fall prey to a deadly outbreak of that flesh-eating bacteria?"

"They never—"

"Exactly. We notified the head of production and the head of inspection, but they just shrugged it off. Ignored us."

"That's what happens when you place a *reptilian* child-hire on your food production line," Blayde added. "They carry some diseases that you just aren't prepared to deal with."

"Nobody died that day. All the bad food just … went down the wrong shoot and was incinerated. Maybe you were a little behind on your quota. And maybe the inspector never let you see the proof of the disaster we averted to keep his own butt out of the fire. So, you and the Alliance blame us for the entire thing and the death of at least thirty other workers who had nothing to do with the situation. Just to make us look like the bad guys instead of them."

"*I* never did that!" The minister shook his head in disgust, then caught himself. "I'm in charge of the transport systems. I had no hand in that."

"We never said you did," said Blayde. "But the Alliance has never been kind to us."

"So, why help us at all? What possible reason do you have for going to all this trouble and enduring the ridicule?"

Blayde scoffed, rubbing her baby bump. "You think this is ridicule?"

I only shrugged. "Well, once you've done everything and anything there is to do in the universe, there really isn't much else left, is there? Maybe making the universe a little bit better for the people who live in it is the only thing worth doing if you have an eternity at hand."

"That or take it over," said the minister.

"Maybe we'll do that next," said Blayde. "Look, I know we need this guy, but can I hand him over to the coats? You two are getting too chatty, and we have a party to save."

"The coats!" I said, smacking my freshly minted head.

"What, the coats?" asked Blayde.

"Have you seen how many there are?"

Blayde glanced up, down, around. "Yes. There are a lot. Good on you for counting."

"Gen," I said, turning to the girl, who lit up as I spoke to her. "How much do you know about coats?"

"Everything." She beamed.

"Not just the fashion, right? Their breeding and defenses?"

Blayde let out a sound like a bark masquerading as a laugh. "You can't be serious."

"Here's the plan," I said, rubbing my hands together. Derzan, it felt good to have a plan. "That door I just tried to blow, it's no longer got explosives—I took care of that—so it's probably heavily guarded. I'll take care of those guards while Blayde leads you out of here. I'm sure she can laser her way out of here."

"Laser is not a verb," she said. "And the coats …"

"They're the distraction. Or I should say, we're the distraction."

I took off my shoes, which were surprisingly still intact; long heels were sturdier than one might imagine from their flimsy shape. I tossed one in my hand gently, gauging its weight.

"Gen," I said, dropping my voice, "which of the coats will be the most territorial?"

"The most expensive put up the biggest fight," she said, scanning the racks. "Probably last year's *Harbena*, spring collection, the eight-arm-plus model. That one there."

She pointed at one a few rows up, almost near the ceiling. Easy peasy.

"Everyone, lie flat on the floor. Keep your hands behind your heads, and don't move an inch until Blayde says the word. You got that?"

I stood up taller as they all slid onto the floor, groggily filling up the few square meters of floorspace. I had to back up and sit on the desk for there to be enough space.

"Now don't. Move. An inch."

# INALIENABLE

The shoe sailed through the air, my aim true, smacking the *Harbena* square in the thorax pocket. The coat reared, swinging on its hanger, freeing itself from its binds and plummeting toward the floor. The eight sleeves whipped through the air as it fell, dragging the others down with it.

Quite literally kicking and screaming.

I had severely underestimated the numbers of coats on the racks. Suddenly, a flock of angry, territorial coats with nothing to lose were soaring toward me, hundreds strong. Simultaneously the exact thing I was hoping to accomplish and the most terrifying sight my eyes had seen … at least in the past hour, I think. So, I did what I did best: I spun around and took off running.

I sprinted down the hallway toward the door I had attempted to blow, a thunder of coats behind me, furiously flapping their sleeves and pressing antigravity units as they rushed me. I pushed myself harder, bare feet pounding on the marble, trying not to slip in the mess of abandoned fluids that coated the tile and stone.

It would have all gone down smoothly if I hadn't collided face-first with Kork before I even reached the door.

"Frash!" he shouted, as we tumbled down together, a tangle of weapons and limbs. None of his were broken from what I could tell. Hells, he looked pristine in his uniform, like he always did on the screen.

I jumped to my feet before touching the floor, leaving him to finish collapsing on his own, only to find wide-eyed Sekai by my side. Note that she does have enormous eyes, but now she was more wide-eyed than usual, and with a stampede of coats following me, I had no choice but to slam into her, too, knocking her to the floor in a flurry of confused grunts.

The coats flew over us, low-dragging sleeves running over our tangle of limbs, brushing by and spinning down the hallway, ready to decimate anything in their path. I rolled off Sekai, again jumping to my feet once the flock had passed, staring down the chandeliered corridor in hopes the beasties reached their goal.

Only they didn't.

Movement in the main ballroom must have drawn their attention because they left the corridor suddenly, hundreds if not thousands of coats spilling into the massive hall at once. By the sounds of the screams, they were wreaking quite the havoc of their own.

"Zander?" asked Kork, panting heavily. "What are you doing here?"

"Same old, same old," I replied, reaching out a hand to help drag him up to his feet.

"Saving the day?"

"Hardly."

"What were those?" asked Sekai. "Please don't tell me you've ruined my coat. I had mine grown in my mother's lake; it's priceless."

Blayde came to a stop behind me, a line of exhausted survivors behind her. More than I had left her with, believe it or not. There had to be a dozen of us in the hallway now.

"So much for a distraction," she snapped. "Now we're sitting ducks."

"I hate to say this."

"Then don't say it."

"You agree?"

"It has to be done, doesn't it? Time is of the essence, and we're just blabbing." She pulled out her laser, taking a heavy breath. "Let's end this."

I turned to Kork. "You protect them, all right? Try to keep them looking at the coats. Don't let them see."

I turned off my mind and ran.

The act of killing is not art, no matter what many of the teachers I've had over my many lifetimes have said over and over again. Art creates beauty, meaning. Killing is destruction and death. Just because it has to be done for the greater good doesn't mean there's any pride to be had in the act itself.

Saving a life is heroic. Taking one is always a loss for the universe.

So, when I jumped behind the guard, snapped his neck, and took his rifle, it didn't bring me relief.

When I aimed the rifle and shot off another rebel in the stomach, I didn't count it as a victory.

Blayde and I moved in synch, our many lifetimes of training and experience taking over our bodies as we flowed through the motions of bringing death to those who revel in killing. The men kept coming, bullets ripping through me as I jumped and took them down. It was disgustingly easy.

An arm wrapped around my neck, attempting to twist, but I flung him over my shoulder, launching him as far as I could. Jump, and I was the one behind him. We had rejected restraint. We didn't need to give these men a fighting chance, not when we knew what they would do with it. Punches land harder when you don't hold yourself back. Necks break and bones snap when lives are on the line. We did the job in front of us, but there was no glory in it for anyone.

We flowed down the corridor, each jump bringing us closer to freeing the survivors of this carnage. The door was clear now, but we couldn't stop, not until we knew the threat was gone, not when there were still rebels on the loose.

"Zander," came a voice, soft and distant.

The voice brought me back into myself. I looked up, away from the carnage at my feet, but the voice was too low to be coming from the corridor. Could I have imagined it? Absolutely.

"Hey, Zander! You up for negotiations?"

I definitely hadn't imagined that. Blayde looked up at me, eyes wide. She wiped the spray from her face.

"It could be a trap," she said, as she sliced the life from the guard at her feet.

"You always say that," I replied. "You know what to do if it is."

And with that, I turned toward the grand hall, carving a path of death toward the voice of my beloved.

# TWENTY-FOUR

## NEXT TIME I'M IN A REBELLION I'LL READ UP MORE ON THE SUBJECT BEFOREHAND

*Sally*

**PEOPLE ARE BOUND TO NOTICE A ZOMBIE** creeping around a catwalk in her massive bloody gown. There wasn't exactly a lot of places to hide. I'm proud I lasted a few minutes before getting caught, but I won't tell you exactly how many because it's still embarrassing.

"Look who we found sneaking around the sentry walk."

The rebel led me into the small temporary office, pushing me with the butt of his gun. I kept my hands in the air, but having just returned from the dead didn't give the opposition any confidence. My makeshift knife was tied to my ankle with the extra ribbon from the shoe, still undetected. So far, I didn't need it.

"What the three suns?" their leader stammered, pushing himself up to stand in shock as I was led in. "She was dead! You all saw that, right? I shot her!"

"Obviously not well enough since she's alive," my captor pointed out. A man who could talk back, suggested he was somewhat high up in whatever organization this was.

"Unless I'm her twin?" These conversations over my death had become tiresome and boring to me at this point.

He relaxed a little. "True. She must have had a twin."

"Psych! No, I'm the girl you shot, but I'm still trying to wrap my head around the fact you immediately jumped to me rising from the dead before making any other guesses first. It's a little weird."

"I saw her brains, you know." The man behind the leader stared at me, wide eyed. He poked his fingers under his chin, reenacting my death, using a hand to indicate my brain splattering out behind on the wall.

"Can you do that as an interpretive dance? It could do with a little more pizzazz." I shook my head. "Come on, grow up. There's a lot in the universe you don't know about."

"It could be a robot!" someone pointed out.

"Um, my preferred pronoun is *she*, not *it*. You could have had the decency to ask," I snapped.

"I checked her pulse; she was dead. Maybe an Alliance plant? Check her again!" the rebel leader ordered.

"Why does everyone think I'm some kind of plant?" I asked. "Not even the other hostages trust me. This is getting a little frustrating."

# INALIENABLE

One of the men grabbed my arm, holding it in place as he felt around my wrist. "No pulse," he muttered. Then he stabbed a knife through it.

"Hey! What's your problem?" I ripped my hand back. "Of course, I'm alive. I'm living and breathing, aren't I?"

"It's all blood and bones and muscles. She's alive," he pointed out. "But with no pulse."

"Of course I don't have a pulse, not with people constantly getting slicey with my arms!"

"But how?" Realization crept across the leader's face. "Ah, you're like them."

He didn't need to continue. We all knew what he meant. I nodded.

"Who are you?" I asked.

"Barshook. Leader of the Anti-Alliance Alliance."

"Seriously?" I laughed, sitting on the chair in front of his desk, pulling the knife out of its hiding place. They moved to take it from me, but I stared them down until they backed off.

"Guys, you'll never get taken seriously with a name like that. Try something like *The New Order* or something along those lines next time you stage an attack." I shrugged. "You've really got to have the name down before you try and take over the government, or no one will ever side with you. It's all in the name, remember that. It's all about the branding. Please tell me you did market research before all this?"

They looked surprised. I didn't blame them. Confusion was exactly what I was going for. The secret out of any situation, I had learned from Zander, was to keep talking until you knocked them out of their element.

"And whose side are you on, exactly?" asked Barshook, sitting across from me on his side of the desk.

"Yours." I grinned. "Well, technically, I'm all for taking down the Alliance, but this is a mess. All you'll have managed to do here tonight is prick the side of a mighty lion. And slaughter a lot of innocent people. You're not going to get away with that."

"What of the Iron and the Sand?" he asked.

"Oh, I think they agree with me. They hate the Alliance like I do—possibly even more; lifetimes worth of fury, you see—but they've always been about helping those the Alliance hurts, whereas you've just proven you don't care for lives. All they're trying to do is get everyone out of here alive, and too bad for you that you're standing in their way, because … well, you know what happens when someone gets in their way." I gave him a sly smile. "Oh, don't look so surprised. What did you expect when you came tonight? A pat on the back for massacring innocents?"

"Innocents? The oligarchs of a crumbling, decadent society?" Barshook trembled with fury. "We're trying to make the Planetary Alliance what it once was: a democracy, free of terror and totalitarianism."

"By bringing your own terror? I know what you're trying to do, and I agree with your ideals, but I need to say this again because you're not listening to me: You're not doing it right. Do you suffer from dry tentacles? Try *Oli Oli Oil!* It's soft and cruelty-free, as our goo is harvested only from the gentlest retchings of the Great Way beast of Namura. When your tentacles begin to dry and peel, reach for *Oli Oli Oil!*"

"What. The. Frash?" asked Barshook.

"I'm sorry. I got my translator from a cereal box."

"That's okay," said the miming man. "We do what we can. I got mine in a social media giveaway."

"Shut up, Shizel," Barshook hissed. He turned back to me. "So, Oli Oli Oil, what do you suggest we should have done differently?"

"Back the Alliance leadership into a corner. The people, all the impoverished, all the suppressed, they are already on your side. All you need to do is lead the charge, and you can't do that with a thoughtless slaughter. Start with the outer planets, those farther away. Those are the easiest to take back since they are out of reach from the Alliance's immediate response teams. After that, you can easily choke them out and work your way in toward the center. Wait. It's not up to me to tell you how to lead a rebellion! What the hell? Anyway, the spark to light the flame will come from people standing up for their rights, not killing a bunch of busboys and waitstaff who were just doing their jobs at an expensive gala."

"A lecture. From a hostage. This is the day I'm having." The man pinched the bridge of his nose between his fingers. "Why are you telling me this?"

"Because I want justice as much as any of you. Hell, that's why I'm here tonight! I just don't want anyone else to die here."

"We gave them a chance," said Barshook with a shrug, leaning back into his chair. "We cleaned up the other rebel group, the ones doing the actual senseless killing. We warned them about the bomb. They still have a chance to give themselves up. They don't have to die."

"And by 'they,' you mean whoever is left alive. How do you know anyone is even down there?"

They looked at each other quickly, and I leaned back against the chair to wait for their response. Time was ticking; I had to do *something*.

All I could do was keep talking.

"Tell you what, how about negotiations? With Zander and Blayde, of course. One, the other, or both. And believe me, the offer does not stand for a long time. Eventually, those holding them captive …" This time I showed my teeth with my grin. The universal sign of 'don't screw with me.'

One of the men in black rushed in, his mask hanging around his neck, and slammed the door shut behind him. "The coats! The coats!"

Or maybe I didn't have to do anything. Maybe, just this once, I could sit back and let this all play out.

"What the frash?" stammered Barshook, but before he could finish his thought, the door was practically thrown off its hinges by strong and repeated punches.

# INALIENABLE

"The coats!" said the out-of-breath rebel. "They're loose! And they're *pissed*!"

"You fool! You led them right to us!"

The door blasted open, a massive blue cape flying inside and wrapping itself around the man's neck, squeezing his life out until his face was the same color as the fabric. Before anyone could react, a yellow overcoat and a random assortment of light beige jackets rushed in after the cape, dive-bombing the men closest to the door.

"The Sand!" screamed Barshook. "The Sand is behind this, isn't he?"

Outside the door, madness flew through the hall. The coats were attacking any movement on the catwalks with impunity, choking men with their many sleeves and tossing them off the catwalk to break on the ground far below. It was hard to tell what exactly was driving the coats to kill, but they seemed to be fueled entirely by bloodlust.

A big blue coat with innumerable arms drifted to the middle of the room and let out a bloodcurdling screech. In an instant, all the coats flocked to it, and in the next, they were rushing out of the shattered windows, hundreds if not thousands of coats rushing outside in one cloud of furious textiles.

It had been only a few seconds, but the damage was done: the rebel's numbers had halved. A small voice in the back of my mind rang clear. I could take them alone, couldn't I?

Could I seriously end the lives of a dozen or more angry rebels?

Maybe, but not in twenty minutes.

Oh god, was this really my thought process now?

It was only when Barshook grabbed my arm that I realized I hadn't moved since the coats first barged into his makeshift base of operations.

"Fine." Barshook nodded—actually nodded! "Give me Zander, and we'll discuss this."

They let me stand. They let me walk. I strode out of the office and back onto the catwalk, making no mistake that I was in no way clear just yet. I clutched the railing with both hands and leaned over.

The scene at my feet was of utter devastation. Two bands of rebels piled on top of the corpses of the ball guests, a colorful strata of carnage. No sign of Kork and Sekai, thank goodness.

"Zander!" I shouted before I turned my head and smacked myself with a megaphone. "Oh, thanks."

"You know, I told them about our branding being off. We're not appealing to our target demographic. Especially not with all the—"Shizel mimed shooting down below as I took the megaphone from his hands.

"Killing?" He nodded.

"Yeah. The other rebels, the *First Pact* group? Suns, I hate them. Now everyone will think we're all about shooting when all in all we're about blowing people up. Well, the ones who deserve to be blown up."

"Well, thanks, Shizel. Do you have any idea what that coat thing was about?"

"They get territorial," he said with a shrug. "When we're in charge, we'll outlaw the breading of exotic coats. They're an abomination. Your friends must have riled them up somehow."

I held the megaphone up. "Hey, Zander! You up for any negotiations?"

This was not the Zander I knew.

He strode out from the shadows, rifle in hand, a gaudy coat replacing his once-immaculate silks. His face glowed resplendent under a layer of terrifying gore. My heart stopped for a second, and I realized it was the first time I had ever felt revulsion seeing him.

This was the Zander Foollegg had warned me I would find. This was the Zander that struck fear in the heart of the Alliance, the one man who terrified the terrorists.

"I agree to negotiations," he said, his voice carrying through the now-silent hall. "So long as you agree to a ceasefire for the duration of the talks. Deal?"

"Deal," yelled Barshook. I handed him the megaphone. "Deal!"

"Good," said Zander and, in an instant, he was standing on the catwalk with us. His coat was ripped through with bullet holes, and his own blood mixed with the fibers, body matter dripping from his face.

It's hard to describe the feeling of disgust and relief welling up side-by-side inside my chest. My man, the scourge of the galaxy. This was how the Alliance saw him. Not in the glory of victory but an omen of death.

How he must hate this.

He stared Barshook in the eyes. "Then let us discuss the terms of this—wait, is this your surrender or something else?"

"Leave your rifle at the door."

"Fine," Zander acquiesced. "Only if you put yours down as well."

Barshook stood still, frozen. Zander shrugged, keeping his rifle as he entered the office and sat across the desk from the rebel leader in the chair I had been sitting in only mere minutes before He crossed his legs, leaning back casually.

"I'll start," he said, not waiting for anyone else to speak. "We want out of here. All of us, in one piece. But you already know that."

"And we want the Alliance to fall."

Zander frowned. "That's a tall order. You killed the president and quite a lot of the ministers."

"That was … unfortunate," said Barshook. "Our predecessors were less delicate than we intended. Our intention was to take him hostage."

"That doesn't matter in the eyes of those waiting outside to see if their loved ones survived this massacre. Their deaths won't make the Alliance fall. It's much too big for that. This is a terrorist act, not a full-blown rebellion. It's not going to be easy to get out of this on top."

"Whose side are you on?"

"Anti-Alliance, but I'll work tooth and nail to get everyone out alive."

"Hey! That's our name! Brand recognition!" said Shizel.

"Then join us," Barshook offered. "With you on our side, t he Alliance would fall in a day."

"I'm sorry, I can't do that," he paused, but no one pushed him. "What were you, before you became a terrorist?"

"*Rebel*. And I was a guard. Alliance Library. Before that, child-hire."

"And now you're here, murdering the guilty and the innocent at the same time, with no attempt to differentiate between them. Deciding who lives and who dies based on what? From where I'm sitting, I can't see much difference between you and the Alliance, and it seems like you don't have much of a plan for after your big take-over, either. How will you manage and maintain a thousand different worlds and their subsidiaries? How far will you fall before you realize that you can't do it like this?" Zander paused, waiting for the man to say something. Anything to redeem his name. Instead, the man bared his fangs. Boy, they were sharp. "Now, our earlier offer still stands. For you to take the president's wife in exchange for our lives. What do you say?"

The leader shook his head. "Never. We do not need her. Trading her for everything we have in our power is a tall order, one which we shall not take. "

"So, you surrender?"

"We will not surrender. We will not withdraw. The bomb stays active. You still have seventeen minutes."

"And your initial threat still stands?"

"Yes." Barshook nodded. "The presidential hall will blow, and all those who have not surrendered will die in it."

"And you realize the consequences of this?"

"I do. Sixteen minutes now."

"Fine, then. These negotiations are over, and so is the ceasefire." He gave the man a mischievous smile. "If you ever want to agree to our terms, then all you have to do is shout."

# TWENTY-FIVE
## DEFUSING BOMBS AND OTHER TENSE SITUATIONS

**THE BIGGEST LIE THAT PHYSICISTS HAVE EVER TOLD** is that the relativity of time only affects things that are in motion.

I don't know about you, but I was perfectly immobile when time stood still. I didn't have to move when Zander flung himself onto the catwalk, Blayde appearing by his side, their weapons drawn. I didn't have time to even attempt to move when they began to fire.

The rebels hadn't moved either.

What scientists have failed to study, too, is when time has stopped for long enough that it has to snap back into place, moving extra fast to make up for having forgotten to move forward at all. In an instant, the world was in motion once more. Zander and Blade were gone, and I was alone in the abandoned office, my jaw practically to the floor.

First things first, pick that jaw back up, Sally Webber. You need it to keep the screaming inside.

Second step, take all those feelings, every confusing reaction, every panicked curse, and shove them deep, deep inside. Calculate and react, no matter how much screaming you want to do. I promised myself I could scream later.

Third step, do something. Because I was still in this office, and time was ticking down to the explosion that would end us all.

I pelted out onto the sentry walk, leaping at the first guard I saw, knocking him out with a well-practiced punch—my only move, but a damn good one—grabbing his gun and dropping the heel of my dress shoe for a much better replacement.

Now finally armed, I ran, best as one can with broken sky-high heels, down the catwalk, glad not to encounter any security since they were caught up with Blayde and Zander somewhere on the other side of the building judging from the ruckus.

I reached the small hostage room in less than a minute, taking a shot to the elbow in exchange for giving a badass kick to the face. He screamed as I apologized.

I threw open the door to a sea of red.

"Shit, wrong hostages," I stammered, before accidentally unleashing the first wave of rebels back into the fray. Don't blame me. It's not like I had much time to memorize my surroundings here. They slammed into me, knocking me down as they rushed out onto the catwalk, screaming war cries. I didn't have time to get trampled. I rolled off to the side, only to roll entirely off the catwalk itself.

Luckily the ground was a long way off. I felt myself fall—once my greatest fear, now a mild inconvenience—and jumped back to a safer place just before hitting the ground, the coolest moment of my life so far.

*Don't think about the massacre; don't think about the massacre.*

The men in red spandex suits were now fighting the remaining guards, which at least was an adequate distraction, leaving me able to move around almost entirely freely. If it wasn't for the flying plasma beams, I wouldn't have been able to stroll around avoiding the conflict entirely.

The next door I found just happened to be the right one, so kudos for me this time. I barged into the room of hostages and felt a wave of relief wash over me when I saw they were unharmed.

"Alive!" The amoeba became a puddle once more. I sure hoped she was quick about becoming solid this time.

"This is part of the trap, right?" asked the human woman, flinging herself away from the cat person. "The Alliance is seriously testing our faith in the president!"

"Shut the void up, Karen!" screamed the cat.

"Are you kidding me?" I stammered, slinging my weapon over my back. "I'm going to get you out of here alive, but if you don't come with me, you have a very high chance of dying, okay? Now, hands, quickly! And don't look so angry. If the wind changes, your face will stay that way forever."

The cat and the human grabbed onto each other in an instant, though it seemed they had been rather entangled a moment before. A lump rose from the puddle of goo and wrapped itself around my leg.

*Right.*

I grabbed as much goo as I could carry, casting a glance over the edge of the catwalk and jumping them to the ground. The rebels were too busy dealing with the siblings and each other to keep an eye on us, and we ran—or, in the case of the amoeba, squelched—toward the young woman in the shadows who waved at us.

"This way!" she called. "Coat check!"

"Go, go over there!" I ordered, as Sekai barged into the hall, waving her arms wider and more excitedly than her human counterpart. I could only hope Kork had made it there too.

"What about you?" the cat person asked, her furry paw still clutched in mine.

"I have stuff I need to do. No, don't worry about me! Just go!"

I ran down an avenue of columns, relieved to see more people were alive and trying their best to remain hidden in the shadows. Some of the people I had thought were dead on the dance floor were pushing themselves up on shaky feet and rushing for the coat check, either living-dead or formerly playing dead. A wave of water trickled out of a giant hamster ball that rushed toward the stairs, letting out little moans of disgust.

"They're too busy to shoot down here!" I told everyone I encountered, as I tripped over the bodies of the already deceased. "Just run! You're getting out of here!"

Maybe Sekai and Kork had found a way out; there was no way to be sure. All I knew was that this building was going to blow in who knew how many minutes, and Zander and Blayde were too busy fighting the onslaught of rebels to find and diffuse a bomb.

Did I know how to diffuse a bomb?

Hell no.

I took a breath and jumped back to the catwalk. How could the fighting still be going on with so many already dead? There couldn't possibly still be rebels up here, but they were fighting tooth and nail.

"Oh, come on, be reasonable!" shouted Zander over the fray. "You've lost. Just give up already!"

Obviously, they took no heed of his advice. Most continued to try to shoot at the siblings from various vantage points around them, but it proved as unsuccessful as trying to ask the chicken why he actually crossed the road. The men in the red spandex suits— the First Pact?—seemed to think the siblings were on their side since they were so obviously fighting the other rebels in black, so there was a lot of cheering despite the confusing mess.

*The bomb, the bomb, where was the bomb?*

I turned around and ran back toward the office, not having a clear line of sight to jump there directly. I did eventually get there, leaning back against the wall as I listened for the sound of anyone inside. The din of gunshots made it impossible to hear anything, so I just had to go for it, gathering my courage and holding my rifle up and steady.

The office was empty, luckily for me. I breathed a sigh of relief. Even Barshook had run off, probably to hide away from any actual fighting. He seemed the type to run; he had the flying boots.

Damn, I wanted flying boots. Why didn't I steal a pair from the catwalk?

*Not the time, Sally. There's a bomb somewhere here.*

Near the wall, a lunch box-sized gadget lay on its side, cables running from it into the wall. I picked it up, certain it had some importance. I was not wrong. Each of the cable inputs were marked, each with the name of a door.

The detonator.

*Wow, that was easy.*

I looked from left to right, making sure I wasn't missing anything. Nope, this was the only detonator-looking thingy anywhere in the room. On the top, a big, flashy countdown was on 1:56.

Now to defuse a bomb. I pulled my phone from my bra. A minute and a half to go.

"Come on, come on," I begged my phone. Screw the data costs; I needed access to the internet, and I needed it now.

It wasn't connected.

"Siri!" I begged. "How do I diffuse a bomb?"

*"I'm sorry,"* said my phone. *"I do not speak panicked screaming. Do you need me to call emergency services?"*

I grabbed the megaphone off the desk, checking the settings and boosting the megaphone to maximum power. I could probably distract them with some horrible, off-key signing, but what use would that be?

"Does anyone know how to diffuse a bomb?" I shouted. "We only have a minute!"

"Turn that thing off, please."

I turned. Behind me was literally the last person I expected to see.

Myself.

She ripped out wires with expert precision, fingers flying over the device. So much faster than my own. She was dressed comfortably in jeans and a plain, brand-free t-shirt, like she'd just come from an inoffensive event where she'd won a contest for not standing out.

Except she was so much more muscular than I was now. I reached up, feeling my flabby excuse for arms, wondering when my biceps would finally show. Because other than that, she looked just like me.

"You're … me?" I stammered.

"Shush, I'm working here," she replied.

Nothing exploded. Not that I had expected anything to. It was just nice that I wasn't responsible for the entire building blowing up. Either one of me. She took the detonator device and handed it to me, her hand brushing mine for a second.

"Shit," I swore. "Doesn't that make this a paradox?"

"I don't see why it would," the other me replied. "It's not like the universe has rules against this."

"Doesn't it? I mean it shouldn't be possible that two of me exist in the same space and time."

"First of all," she said, and I wondered at what point I was allowed to feel like I was treating myself unfairly, "we are not the same person. I've grown since I was you. I've died more times than I can count since I was you. The only thing we have in common is that I was you. Once. A long time ago."

I squinted. "How long ago?"

"You'll figure that out when you are me. A little something to look forward to." She winked.

"Hold on a minute," I said, taking a massive step back. "How do I even know you're me? Not that I'm not grateful and all, but I saw the Pachooleeans pull this same trick just last week."

"Oh right." She reached up, pulling a hair from her head, letting it fall to the floor. It remained intact. "And you shouldn't do that time-wasting thing where you ask me a dumb question and I impress you by answering with amazing swagger you haven't gotten yet."

So, I asked her a question, one so private I won't even put into writing. And she answered with swagger I could only imagine having some day.

# INALIENABLE

"Will today ever make sense?" I asked. "Like, who are all these people? What's going on?"

"Oh, it's been a while," she said, scratching her head. "Right. So, the First Pact—the rebels in red—wanted to make a whole big statement by massacring everyone and getting away scot-free. Just create chaos and throw the Alliance in shambles, especially since the prince is missing. You will not believe who that is when they resurface, by the way. But the Anti-Alliance Alliance also had a coup scheduled for the same night, planning on taking the president hostage and forcing action. Most of them are former child-hires, so they really do have an axe to grind. They get here, see the place already in shambles, decide, 'frash that, let's do this anyway,' and issued demands—but most legislators are dead, so fat chance they'll go through. And you're probably wondering why the biggest event of the year was so easily turned into a nightmare. Well, your bomb problem was a freebie. I have something I'd like to trade you."

With my head still reeling and my confusion seeping out of my face thick enough to leave pimples, she reached into the pocket of her jeans, retrieving what looked like a ring box. Before I opened my mouth to say anything about how absurd it was that she could propose to me, especially considering we hardly knew each other and had only just met, she popped it open to reveal a tiny washer-shaped piece of metal.

"A translator?" I gasped.

"Top of the line," she explained. "This bad boy even freaking translates *facial expressions*. No more nodding and hoping it'll get by!"

I reached for it, and she snapped the box shut on my fingers. "Oy! Not cool!"

"I need the book first."

"What book?"

"Don't play dumb. The one sticking out of your bustier," she said, reaching out her free hand. "The one Minister Jubin handed you behind the bar as he died."

I pulled out the storybook. I had already forgotten that I'd picked it up. Now all I wanted to do was read it cover to cover. "Why? What is this about? Who was he?"

"He was Jorgi Jubin, Minister of the Defense and the reason there was a gap in security tonight. You see, he's recently become obsessed with the fictional representations of the siblings in Alliance history and wanted to capture them himself in order to find out the truth. He allied himself with the Anti-Alliance Alliance, expecting the siblings to show up and reveal their true colors, either as saviors or enemies. They had an agreement where Bar Stool—that's his name, right? Again, it's been ages—would go easy on him. But the First Pact showed up first, and Bob's your uncle. Now, give it up. It's not like you're going to use it."

"It doesn't explain why he was carrying a children's book around," I grumbled, handing it over. "Or what you need it in the first place."

# INALIENABLE

"You'll get it back when you're me," she said. "Look, Sally, life is going to really change for you when you get back, and you don't need this book for when you do. But you see me right here, right now? You've always got your own back. Whatever happens, know that it's going to be okay. You're one of the few people in the entire universe who can make it through this day with absolute certainty."

I frowned. "This isn't helping me trust you, you know."

"So, don't come back!" she said, laughing. "When you're me, don't come back to the past and help yourself out. Make that pledge right this very minute. People always act like they need to go backwards in time to change the future, but you are altering it with every decision you make today. So, go on. Change it. If I'm still here, it's because Future You knows what I'm doing is right."

So, I stood there and promised myself I wouldn't come back. Three guesses who never left the room.

"Take the deal. It'll make sense soon. Trust me. I'll even swap out your translator myself."

Her fingers were delicate when she peeled out the cereal gimmick. The new translator slipped gently behind my ear, a bright sunbeam in this terrifying day. She gently took the storybook from my hands and clutched it against her chest.

"Security will be coming through as soon as you give the all-clear," she said. "Stay true to yourself, okay?"

And with that, she jumped away, leaving me holding the defused detonator in silence.

I staggered out onto the catwalk, brandishing the detonator high above my head. I didn't need a megaphone to scream this time.

"It's over!" My throat struggled under the strain of my cry. "The doors are disarmed!"

I expected security to flood the place immediately, but I was met only with silence. Whatever fights were still ongoing on the catwalk, they were the dregs of the attack, factions exhausted and ripping themselves to shreds. A battle arena devoid of players.

Except, of course, for Barshook.

What does one do when all hope is lost? What on earth is so sexy about becoming a martyr? The rebel drifted in the empty air at the very center of the hall, holding enough explosives to detonate a small moon.

"Barshook," said Zander, suddenly incredibly still on the catwalk, "put that down right now."

I jumped to his side, the detonator still in my hands. The man must have ripped the last of the explosives from the doors around the hall, but if he had, where was security? Why hadn't anyone barged into the hall to take the place by force?

There was something fishy here. And it wasn't the tank of belly-up amphibian ball guests.

"Is that really what you want?" said Barshook. "Because if I put this down now, then goodbye to Agreement Hall."

"I hate it when they do that," said Blayde, before turning to the hovering man. "It's over, Barshook. No one else has to die tonight."

"If I'm going down, I'm taking everyone here down with me," he spat. "I'm not going to die in an Alliance prison."

"Screw it," said Blayde. "I can probably tackle him from here."

"And do what?" Zander hissed. "Without him as the face of this failed rebellion, guess who's going to become scapegoats *again*? This is not how I wanted this night to go."

"It's not like we have much of a choice," said Blayde. "We either all blow up and then reconstitute in an Alliance prison, or we take Barshook away with us and try again for a pardon when this all blows over."

"Another century should do," said Zander. He reached for my hand. "Let's go, then."

"A century?" I stammered. "No!"

Future Me was right. It was up to me to define how I wanted to spent my eternity, and not being able to see my family and friends again for fear of Alliance and Agency retaliation was not going to stand.

I was going to define my future, and I was going to do it now.

The body at my feet was one of the black-clad rebels, Barshook's men, which meant anti-gravity boots like the ones Barshook was wearing. I slipped them from his feet, trying to ignore the fact that the body was dead, killed by Zander's own hand.

What was Barstook waiting for? Some excuse to drop the explosives and go? The courage to end it all? So long as he wasn't moving, we were fine; we had some time.

I didn't know how to defuse a mechanical detonator back there. But a human one? Maybe.

"Sally," Blayde hissed, "we can buy shoes another time."

"Give me five minutes," I said. "And then, if I screw up, you can take us all away from here. We'll try again in a century. But I'm going to fight for my family."

Zander's hand was soft on my shoulder as I laced up the boots. "I know of a million reasons you shouldn't go up there."

"I know of at least one why I absolutely should," I said. "And that's that no one else is going to die tonight."

The boots shuddered to life around my toes, and I drifted steadily into the air, rising up, up, and straight to the ceiling. Damn. But Barshook still wasn't moving, so I had time.

I used my free hand to push myself along the jewel-encrusted ceiling, a good twenty or so meters above Barshook's location. The boots kept wanting to push me up. Soon, I was practically swimming. My back pressed against the mosaic and my fingers the only things keeping me moving forward.

I crinkled my toes, and the boots descended lightly, just a few meters, but enough that using them was starting to make sense. I crinkled more, lowered further.

Soon, I was level enough with Barshook, a good distance away but close enough to speak.

"He's right, you know," I said, as gently as possible. "It is over."

"I know," he replied. "I know."

"I know how you feel about the Alliance," I continued, forcing my eyes to meet his. Too much death at my feet. "They have my home planet under their proverbial thumb. They don't give a crap about it."

"They don't give a crap about a lot of things," he said, and, in that instant, I saw that he was as young as I was. Maybe younger, even. A frustrated kid who wanted to make a difference in the world. Who was tricked by a minister to enact this foolish plan.

A man with a handful of explosives who'd already killed the president of the galaxy.

"Do you really want to end the night with more death?" I asked, reaching my hand forward. I drifted maybe an inch in his direction, and he flinched. Not enough to drop the explosives, thankfully, but enough that I knew I couldn't go anywhere.

"I would much rather die for my cause, thank you."

"Then go ahead and die for it," I said. "I wouldn't want to go to an Alliance prison any more than you do. But you don't get take anyone else out with you. There's no more point to be made here tonight."

"Aren't you supposed to be arguing that I should live?" he said.

"Is that what you want me to say? Because I'm not a therapist. Hell, I had to deal with my own suicidal ideation for quite a long time, but I never tried to blow up the government or hurt anyone else. I'm out of my depth here."

"Then why are you even here?"

"I don't know, man. I just thought I could help, so I tried to help. It's literally the only thing I can do."

"Then I'm sorry," he said and opened his arms.

I didn't think. I threw myself forward, not sure if I was moving with the boots or jumping through space, but I grabbed that bundle of explosives as it fell toward the ground and breathed them somewhere new.

Somewhere empty.

Somewhere without people or places or things.

I felt the cold before I opened my eyes. Were they pried shut? I hadn't noticed. I was hanging in the void of space, somewhere in the in-between, interstellar distances insignificant in the midst of the movement.

The explosives drifted before me, rendered useless now. Safe, diffused by indescribable distance.

I pulled myself back and collapsed on the floor of Agreement Hall, breathing the sweet taste of oxygen before realizing why my face was sticky. I scrambled up to a seat as all hell broke loose around me. Doors burst open all around, and the hall flooded with delayed safety.

It was over.

# TWENTY-SIX

## CAN WE JUST AGREE THAT EVERYONE SUCKS SO I CAN GO HOME?

**"WE NEED TO GO. NOW," SAID BLAYDE, APPEARING** by my side so suddenly and silently that I almost leapt out of my skin. Why was I trembling? I had gotten rid of the explosives. There was nothing left to fear, but my face … it was cold. Why was it so cold? What was dribbling down my chin?

"We can't," I stammered, staring forward at the throng of soldiers streaming into the hall. "Where's Barshook?"

"Bouncing around on the ceiling," said Blayde. "They'll fish him down eventually."

Zander walked toward us with his hands up. For once, there were no handcuffs. None of the soldiers wanted to risk it. "I'd rather not linger here either, else we get yet another massacre in our names."

"Come, Sally," said Blayde. "You did good today. There's no shame in leaving now."

"No," I stammered. "We stopped this. We saved people. Doesn't that count for anything? We were just going to save one life to gain our pardon. Instead, we saved maybe a hundred times that. Shouldn't we gain more than a pardon? The Alliance needs to start telling the truth."

"A pardon?" said a man, joining our circle, unafraid. Old and wrinkled beyond what age should bring to the table, he stood with his hands clasped behind his back, observing us.

Sekai and Kork had emerged from the shadows, both looking, thankfully, intact, with the woman from the coat check by their side, approaching but stopping just short of us.

"That's why you were here? To beg for a pardon?" the man asked.

"You can stop pretending now," said Zander, shooting me his best '*can you believe this shit*' stare before turning to face him. "Good to see you again, Mister President. I'm sorry about your coat."

"Oh, please. My coat has probably returned to my estate by now, and that is not what you want to talk to me about, is it? How long have you known?"

"Not from the start, but I recognized you eventually." Zander shrugged. "I remembered you from an eternity ago. You were much younger then, though."

"And you haven't changed at all," he said, letting out a heavy breath.

"They killed a decoy?" said the woman who had waved to me from the coat check, scrambling, dumbfounded, away from the soldiers. "They assassinated a decoy?!"

"They did." The president brushed off his sleeves. It was hard to imagine this frail man as anything presidential, much less the head of an empire that spanned hundreds of worlds, but here he was, raising his hand, bringing his soldiers to attention. "My own ministers were plotting against me, and they thought I wouldn't know? Anyway, enough of the chitchat. Arrest them all! Arrest the Iron and the Sand! And the … Sand's consort, I suppose?"

"Oh lordy, we didn't see this coming, did we?" said Blayde, shooing me a glare.

"The *Sand's consort?*" I stammered. "Come on! That's what you're calling me now? There are millions of different nicknames you could have picked, and instead, you define me by a relationship you're only guessing at? So much for being an evolved civilization. I should have let the rebels carry out their evil plan."

"You have thousands of charges against you. Seize them!" he snapped, pointing at Zander and Blayde as they inched their hands closer. "And the girl for being an accomplice!"

"Sir, if I may—" coat check girl said loudly, clearing her throat.

"Not now!"

"Sir, I think you should be aware that I am a journalist."

The emperor-president turned to Kork, reaching for his lapel and dragging him forward. And Kork just let him. "We have a hero here tonight. The great James T. Kork, Captain of the intrepid *Traveler*, our greatest hero, saved the day again."

"That is not *the* truth," said Kork, casting me a quick look of sheer terror.

"It is if you ever want to see *your* ship again," said the president. "And Ambassador No-Oji. How nice to see you again. For your aid in defending our great Alliance against our oldest foes, we shall accept your planet's candidacy and process it much faster than the usual two decades."

"I will take no part in a cover-up of any kind," said Sekai. "And if this is the kind of treatment I can expect from your leadership, then perhaps we shall retract our application forthwith."

"I wonder how sad your planet will be to hear of your passing at the hands of these criminals," the president spat. "By will or by force, this story will not leave this hall."

"It's not going to be as easy as that. You see, I have a lens-cam running right now. Every moment of your cowardice and duplicity is being recorded and made public in real-time."

"What?" The president froze.

"They saved your life. Twice, in public," she said with a smirk. "It'll be fun to see how the public will react to your … response."

The man sighed heavily, glaring at the reporter. He turned to face the three of us, the smirk gone from his face, replaced with an expression of a sore loser.

"You want your pardon?" he spat. "Fine. Beg for it."

Zander blinked. "I beg your pardon?"

"Don't play smart with me, boy," said the president. "If you want your pardon, get on your knees and beg."

"I just saved your life," Zander spat. "And who are you calling boy, boy?"

"It was a team effort," said Blayde.

"All three of you. Come now. This opportunity will not stay on the table forever."

"Me?" I said. "What did I do? I have no charges against me!"

"You are an accomplice to them, are you not?" he said, raising an eyebrow. "If you want your pardon, beg for it. Or so help me gods, I will bury you all so deep you'll forget the meaning of the word retribution."

Zander folded to his knees. "Pardon me, please, forever standing up to your great empire. The Alliance is forever strong. Forever sturdy. Solid as diamond. Please forgive me of my trespasses."

"I don't believe you," said the president. "Try harder."

"You know what? No," said Blayde, dragging her brother up by his shirt collar. "This Alliance would not still be here if it weren't for us. And not just tonight, but all the other moments we've had to step in and stop you from crawling face-first into your own shit. It should be *you* begging at *our* feet."

"The gall," he said. "The gall of—"

"Remember Tijuana?"

Earth Tijuana or was there a planet by the same name? Either way, to say the man was red in the face was an understatement. He was a tomato practically ripe for the picking. The slight green hue was alarming.

"Fine." He sighed heavily. "You are hereby pardoned for your crimes, as you have, in the face of danger, taken it upon yourselves to save the rest of the victims who had no affiliation with you. Normally, that would merit a medal of honor, but I will have to waive that because of the crimes of your past."

He pulled a tablet out of his jacket, quickly entering his proclamation and sealing it with a thumbprint. The tablet played an annoying, jingle-ified version of a victory march, which he handed to the journalist.

"Congratulations," he said gravely.

I turned to Zander, who held the same slack-jawed expression as his sister.

"We're free?" I asked.

He nodded.

"We're free."

He nodded again.

And started to laugh.

I leapt at his neck, hugging him with joy as he swung me around in the room with glee. He put me down, hugging his sister as well, smiling the entire time. Free at last.

"Well," he said to the crowd, "our work here is done."

"And it's time for us to go," Blayde said with a smirk. "Good luck reconstructing your government. Let us know if you need any tips."

# INALIENABLE

· · · · · · · ●● ● ●● · · · · · · ·

**JUMPING HAD BEEN AS EASY AS WALKING**
through a door. No beacons. No Zanders from the past.
Nothing to guide me but instinct alone. I breathed in
deeply, the salty gulf air filling my lungs so completely
that I felt like I was going to float away. The warm
Florida winter air heated our skins, comforting me as I
realized just how free the three of us were.

"Where the frash are we?" asked Blayde, letting out a
massive breath.

"Home," I replied, pointing across the street. There
was my parents' house, all lit up in the setting sun, the
dimmest orange rays lingering on the horizon.

"How …?" Zander's hand held mine even tighter
than I gripped his. "I don't remember this moment.
How did you bring us here?"

"I don't know," I replied. Through the window, I
could see my parents settling down on the couch for
popcorn and a movie. Had they been told about our
escape from the Hill Institute yet? Had Foollegg
managed to cover it up? "It just felt right. Like this is
where we were meant to be next. The right time. The
right place."

"You're going to have to teach me to do this," said
Blayde, and I realize she hadn't let go of my hand
either. "I don't know how you do it, Sally, but it's
impossible."

That was the straw that broke the camel's back. I didn't realize how hard I had been shaking until my feet gave out beneath me and I collapsed on the sidewalk, burying my hands in the bloody drapes of my once-beautiful skirt.

Oh god, the blood.

"Sally!" Zander dropped to my side instantly, clutching both my shoulders and drawing me into his chest. I embraced the warmth, but only for a second. The smell on his chest was no longer the reassuring scent of him, but one of sweat, of blood, of death itself. I flew backwards, jumping a whole ten meters up the street.

"What?" he started.

"Stay away from me," I sputtered, pushing myself to my trembling feet. "You're covered in death."

"We'll go clean up, all right?" he said, reaching for me while keeping his safe distance. Blayde only watched, silent as the grave, staring at us with her arms crossed over her chest.

"We can't … I can't go in there," I spat. "Not like this. Not like … I'm a killer, Zander. I can't go back to my family as killer."

"You're a hero," he said, taking a tentative step toward me. "You saved lives today. So many lives."

"Did I, though?" I couldn't stop my hands from shaking. They were trembling so hard I thought my tendons would snap. I wrapped them around my skirt, but when I touched the gore again, I found myself ripping off the silk entirely. "They killed everyone, Zander. All those guests. Each other. Rebels killing rebels over the same freaking cause. I couldn't save anyone."

"Even if you saved one person, it was worth standing up to them," he insisted, his hand still outstretched. "And you saved everyone in the end. I couldn't have done what you did with Barshook."

"I saved a building," I said, kicking my soiled skirts into a storm drain for the gators to devour. "I saved a president who only pardoned us because there was a camera on him. Instead admitting centuries of fabricated crimes, he pardoned you for things you never did."

"You saved Kork; you saved Sekai. You saved all those people who weren't even grateful enough give us their names."

"And killed how many in the process?" I fell back on my ass and let the tears start flowing. Zander stepped forward, and I flinched again.

"Let me help you," he begged. "Please. I don't want you to be in pain."

"Right. Because painless is what you do," I sputtered. "How many people did *you* kill tonight, hm?"

He didn't answer. I wasn't sure if he was even trying to do the math. If he was even able to.

"You don't even know. You don't even know."

The tears were flowing freely now, running down my face and through the sticky mess I could still feel there.

"You don't get to lecture us," spat Blayde. "This was all your idea! You wanted to save your planet! Well, did you think there wouldn't be a cost? You might sleep better at night thinking the bloodshed is on our hands, not yours, but we were there for you. This was what you wanted, wasn't it?"

"No … not like this."

"I tried warning you," she continued. "But you just kept insisting. You were just dead set on tearing down the Alliance and getting your world back. Well, guess what? People don't like it when you mess with what they think is theirs. You thought the fight for Earth would be bloodless? Well, look at you. You managed to get a seat at the table without a single Terran life lost. Whoop-de-doo. You should be thanking us."

"Blayde," said Zander, "enough."

"We warned you time and time again, Sally. You knew who we are and what we do. You knew who you were throwing your lot in with. We don't topple civilizations as a parlor trick."

I stared at my feet, coated a murky brown from our barefoot run through the carnage. Carnage I had partially been responsible for. Maybe entirely responsible for. But, no, *I* had not brought rebels down upon the Alliance's head.

I wanted freedom for my planet. Was that too much to ask?

"Now you know," she said. "So, you either suck it up or say your goodbyes right now."

# INALIENABLE

The sun had set now, streetlights flickering on to line the street. Waves crashed on the beach behind me, bringing me down to reality, anchoring me here in the now.

I looked up at Zander, his face distorted by viscera. He was a different man than the one who had driven me to the ball. He was a different man who had admitted his love to me on this very beach, just two, three weeks ago. A lifetime ago.

Accepting what he was felt different now. I had seen him take a life before, but never like this. Each time, I could pinpoint the exact reason that person had needed to die: to save more lives. It was a fair trade for peace, continued existence. Wasn't that exactly what we'd just done, back in the hall? Just on a much grander scale?

"I need … I need a philosopher, I think," I stammered. "I don't know what to think about what I just saw."

"It's the very definition of a traumatic experience," said Zander, and I reached for his hand. He breathed out in sweet relief. "You don't have to process it all at once."

"You do need to wash, though," said Blayde. "You smell like death."

"Too soon," Zander hissed. "Come. The beach is right here. Beats spreading the trauma to your family."

We rushed into the waves, divested ourselves of our once-elegant clothes, our underclothes clinging to our skin as we dove into the water. I broke the surface of the ocean, my ocean, water of my world.

I crawled out of the water, clean and sticky with salt, wishing for anything other than my gory dress to put back on. Though I suppose there were worse things than showing up on a parents' porch severely under-stressed after escaping an asylum.

What had they been told about that?

"We need a convincing cover story," I said, staring at the house, all lit up for the night.

"Hey, so long as you don't start advertising off-world products to your parents, anything will work," said Zander. I turned to face him, staring into those beautiful eyes, wondering if I would ever forget what I'd watched him do.

Kissing him felt like coming home, but to a house you no longer recognized. Warm and inviting, but with secret additions you had never noticed before.

I didn't have to accept him all at once. Just bit by bit, step by step, making sense of the lifetime I'd lived in a night.

"I got a new translator," I said, as calmly as I could muster, which ended up being me awkward laughing and sputtering in Zander's arms. "Future Me gave it to me."

"Future You?" he asked, raising an eyebrow.

"Apparently, I look after myself," I replied. "It's called practicing self-care."

He laughed, kissing the top of my forehead, his soft lips turning the skin warm, and I sunk into his arms, letting the sheer relief of being alive rush over me.

"Ready?" he asked, nudging me toward the house.

"Ready," I replied.

I expected my parents to be relieved when they saw me. I expected them to reach for me and tell me everything was all right. They must have heard the news about the institute at the very least. If I was lucky, the Alliance pardon had already reached its way here, and I would be free of Foollegg's threats too.

I didn't expect the tears.

The world was thrown upside down as I was grabbed forcefully around the waist and suddenly wrapped in an intense hug, a hug with tears that fell heavily into my hair.

I didn't realize I was crying, too, until I tried to speak.

"Don't you ever run off like that again, understood?" Mom ordered, grabbing me so tight I probably wouldn't have survived it if I weren't immortal. I hugged her back with enough force to crush a mountain.

My dad came next—my *bearded* dad?—trying to hold back his tears as well, though failing miserably. I sobbed into his shoulder, overwhelmed with the sudden reassurance of a father's embrace. As he pulled away, there were no words. None were needed.

But he pulled away further, staring along with my mother at Zander and Blayde, who were still frozen on the threshold. A silence fell upon the room as both parties looked each other down, unsure of how the other would react. And with a sudden jerk, my father lurched forward, wrapping his arms around Zander and patting him across the back in a kind and reassuring manner. Following in his footsteps, my mother stepped forward to embrace Blayde, who, surprisingly, let it happen, smiling as she returned the hug, though confused all the same.

"I like the beard," I said, staring more intently at my dad. "Have you been taking hair-growth stuff? I mean … that's a magnificent beard to have grown so quickly."

His eyebrow achieved liftoff and was halfway to orbit when he reeled it back in. "Quickly?"

It was only then that I saw the gray in his hair, more than he had had when we'd said our goodbyes outside the courtroom.

It was then that I saw the living room had been changed: a wall repainted blue, the pictures different from when we'd left them, and I was oh so sure the cops hadn't left a dent when they'd arrested me.

"Hold on. What the hell?" I stammered.

"Did you get the date wrong?" asked Blayde. "I retract what I said earlier. Maybe you shouldn't be driving."

Except the date was exactly right; I had been so sure. My head started to spin, counting back, counting forward, connecting the lines of space to time and time to space until it became so clear and evident I would either burst out crying or laughing. Either way, there were going to be tears.

I fished my phone out of my pocket. Of course it didn't have any new messages. I hadn't paid the bill in years.

# INALIENABLE

The only message that mattered was the one that swam into my mind, pulled back from the dregs of memory, from when Future Me confided it to a past Meedian.

*Five. Years. Early.*

"We're back at the right time," I said, my voice so dry it chapped my lips. "The exact moment when we were granted our pardon. But that took place a week after we saved the *Traveler*. Which … was three years after Da-Duhui."

"I think you might need to sit down," said Mom.

"One second, Laurie." Zander gave her hand a tight squeeze, turning back to me. "Da-Duhui, which took place two years after we saved Sekai."

"So, you're saying we didn't miss the mark," said Blayde. "We're just …"

"You escaped the Hill Institute three years ago," said Dad. "You've been missing for three years."

SALLY'S ADVENTURE CONTINUES IN

# DREADKNOT

# ACKNOWLEDGEMENTS

**IT SEEMS IMPOSSIBLE TO THANK EVERYONE**
who needs thanking for this book. Once again, I
couldn't have done it alone, and this year brought so
many new challenges none of us could have anticipated.

First of all, to my brilliant editors, Michelle, Anna,
and Cayleigh. You've turned my drafts into readable
(dare I say utterly enjoyable?) books time and time again
and I couldn't thank you enough. For your council, your
dedication, and especially for believing in me. Thank
you for helping me bring these characters to life.

To Jenny, for letting me pick her brain about how
court procedure is meant to go, so that I could take it
off the rails. You are amazing and the work you do
changes lives.

To my incredible parents who helped me through the
terrible isolation and confusion these lockdowns have
brought. I can always count on you, and that brings me
to much joy. I could not have written this book in the

headspace I was in that lonely month of quarantine, you gave me a sanctuary where I could recharge and create. I also have to thank Penny and Bertie for their constant love and affection. Not that they can read this, being dogs, but I'm sure they know the thanks is there.

Massive, massive, immensely massive thank you to Cora, gave me feedback on the chapters as they went, keeping me sane during the process. I can't wrap my head around how I've made such an incredible friend who I can count on entirely. I truly could not have done this without you.

Thank you to the brilliant Denise Kawaii for her keen eye and precious feedback, without whom I probably would have done far more screaming into the void.

To my writing buddies Madeline, Lisa, Emily, and Heidi, who have helped me grow so much as a writer and keep me in awe of everything that they do. I wanna be like you!

To Hugo, for his endless enthusiasm, tireless support, and perfect partnership. Thank you for responding to every one of my strange, out of context texts, and inspiring me with your lovable humor.

And finally, to you, dear reader. We made it through a strange and terrible year. We're still going. We're still here. I'm still writing these books and you're still reading them. I wouldn't be here without you. Thank you.

# ABOUT THE AUTHOR

**SARAH ANDERSON CAN'T EVER TELL YOU** where she's from. Not because she doesn't want to, but because it inevitably leads to a confusing conversation about where she was born (England) where she grew up (France) and where her family is from (USA) and it tends to make things very complicated.

She's lived her entire life in the South of France, except for a brief stint where she moved to Washington DC, or the eighty years she spent as a queen of Narnia before coming back home five minutes after she had left. Currently, she is working on her PhD in Astrophysics and Planetary sciences in Besançon, France.

When she's not writing—or trying to wrangle comets—she's either reading, designing, crafting, or attempting to speak with various woodland creatures in an attempt to get them to do household chores for her.

She could also be gaming, or pretending she's not watching anything on Netflix.

# CONNECT WITH THE AUTHOR

www.seandersonauthor.com
facebook.com/seandersonauthor
instagram.com/readcommendations
twitter.com/sea_author

Printed in Great Britain
by Amazon